Shelby Hearon

BOOKS BY SHELBY HEARON

A Small Town

A SMALL TOWN

Shelby Hearon

Atheneum 1985 New York

Library of Congress Cataloging-in-Publication Data

Hearon, Shelby. ———
   A small town.

   I. Title.
PS3558.E256S6   1985   813'.54   85-11249
ISBN 0-689-11583-0

TO THE INSEPARABLE FRIENDS OF OUR CHILDHOOD

Patty Babb Travis

Lloyd Alvin Peterson

Robert Lee Riffle

BECAUSE NOBODY WANTS TO BE A KID ALONE

CONTENTS

A Small Town

Prologue

I C O M E in early and sit by the door. In the back a pair of tourists are having lunch. We are at a mom-and-pop-café, which—this being the Show Me State—is called the Mom & Pop Café. (They, the vacationers, are more than likely staying up the road toward Cape Girardeau at the Do Drop In, a Tennessee-owned outfit which got the word that around here a spade is a spade and changed its name from Dew Drop Inn.)

Tourists are a recent phenomenon in our sunken, scalped part of the state. When I was in Venice Public School, anybody who showed up inside the town limits was someone's kin and duly reported by my predecessor in the *Gazette*— "The visiting daughter-in-law of Mrs. Rogers of Main Street hails from Memphis"—in order to let people know who that was roaming General Dry Goods in the middle of a Wednesday wearing bright red slacks.

But now that *National Geographic, Scientific American,* and the AP wire have picked up on the crews of seismologists colonizing our part of the Mississippi like ants to study the rumbling Kentucky Bend fault line, carloads of southerners, heading catty-corner to the Grand Canyon or Yosemite's campsites, detour to see firsthand where old Venice plunged into the roaring river during the gravest quake ever to shake

3

the Western Hemisphere. Especially they like to come at this time of year—skirting danger, riding the old roads like rapids—when the floodwaters are high and the skies are dark with seasonal storms and the big bridges into Tennessee are sandbagged.

Mr. Tourist, wearing a Hawaiian shirt left over from other years, reads aloud an eyewitness account of the disaster as reported in our three-color promotional brochure:

On the 16th of December, 1811, about 2 o'clock A.M., there came a violent shock of earthquake, accompanied by a very awful noise resembling loud but distant thunder, hoarse and vibrating, followed by complete saturation of the atmosphere with sulfurous vapor, causing total darkness.

The screams of the inhabitants, the cries of the fowls and beasts of every species, the falling trees, and the roaring of the Mississippi, the current of which was retrograde for a few minutes, owing as it is supposed to an eruption in its bed, formed a truly horrible scene.

Fissures vomited forth sand and water; the banks overflowed with a current rapid as a torrent, receding with such violence that it took with it whole groves of young cottonwood which edged its borders and settled the site of the town fifteen feet.

"Is that business true?" Mr. Tourist asks Pop.

"You bet," Jimmy, Pop, declares, serving up a duo of the Reubens he has just recently added to his stock menu of burgers, egg salad, and blue plate special.

"They must've thought it was Judgment Day." Mrs. Tourist, in an off-blue hair net, sucks in her breath.

"Tell them, Alma," Maudie, Mom, calls to me, wanting a little audience participation from the front booth.

"Parted like the Red Sea," I declare, as firmly as if I'd been there to see it.

4

"Aren't you folks scared to death?" Mrs. Tourist presses, thrilled. "Right down the street from the levee and all?"

"Nah." Jimmy wipes his hands on his apron. "Lightning never strikes twice. Look at the odds," he says, his face red from the griddle. "It already happened here."

Feeling obliged to give the tourists their money's worth, I offer a dissenting opinion. Wiping egg salad from my face, my eye on the door, I remind them: "History repeats."

One

The Fall

I

———◆———

I W A S nine when I began to spy on my father.

Had anything else occurred to me, I would have tried that, too. Things had reached such a level of misery at home that I'd already checked out all the books from the library (which Audrey, the bucktoothed librarian, would let me have at my age), hunting for some clever way that some kid had dreamed up to leave home. My favorite was *The Prince and the Pauper*, but as far as I was concerned, I was the pauper, and no one came offering me a nice canopied bed, a clean well-candled palace, a country to run, or even a royal seal.

I had two older sisters, but they'd escaped through the cracks in our parents' early marriage, aided by war and rationing, pointed bras, and being named Gloria and Greta for movie stars. (Swanson and Garbo, in case that doesn't ring a bell. All of us born in the forties had sisters named for movie stars.)

We lived, all of us and then only my parents and I, in what was called Marie's house, after my father's mother, long dead. How he felt about going to live in the house where he'd grown up a solitary boy, I have no idea. Sympathy for my father was not on my agenda as a child.

Marie's house, our house, sat smack in the middle of Main,

halfway between my grandfather August van der Linden's house, to the north, and his brother Grady's, to the south. Although the two men had not spoken to one another since the night their own mother passed on, they, the "old doctors," continued to treat the town together, with Dr. Grady making house calls when you were ailing and Dr. August taking over when things took a turn for the worse and you went in the hospital. My father was the "young" Dr. van der L.

Little towns never forget origins. The feud between the two buried brothers continues in the town's eyes fresh as yesterday; my mother, now in her seventies, remains the "middle Jenkins girl" even though no one can recall the others, who once set out for Detroit and then came back; Audrey, the librarian, is still "the principal's wife" even though I've been married to her former husband for twenty years; and "Marie's house," now inhabited by the editor of the paper, will be known by that name until it caves in on its timbers.

Born a full decade after my sisters, I was an afterthought, brought to life, I surmise, either because my daddy wanted to convince my mother once and for all that there was no other woman or because my mother grew tired of having no one to torment.

While Gloria and Greta still lived at home, things were not so bad for me. (Greta is the older by a year and a half, but for some reason my parents always said Gloria and Greta no matter what the situation. Since that pattern started long before I was born, I haven't an idea why.)

I retain some good memories of those years before I started school. Of twilights when all the lightning bugs were out and the trees a new yellow-green with those fuzzy things which float down in the least wind; of evenings when the lilacs had lost their lavender and faded into sachets but the peonies still bloomed comely as Chinese courtesans and the grass looked like low green wheat.

On such spring nights the dusk rang the length of town like a signal, and all the girls and boys my sisters' ages poured forth from houses up and down the old streets into yards like ours for games of blindman's bluff and run sheep run— games with innocent names which made parents recall their own childhoods, with safe names which allowed girls like Gloria and Greta and the boys they necked with to fall into the darkness of snowball bushes and the shadows of grape arbors to kiss and feel until the stars were clearly out. Then my sisters and the rest of the girls would go home, with smeared lips and smudged blouses and scratched legs, to families who tucked them in as if after an evening of hopscotch drawn on sidewalks with chalk.

On such warm nights I used to climb out the upstairs window from my little side bedroom and look down on them. The first-floor roof wrapped around two sides of the house, covering one of those wide, loose-boarded porches that holds a swing at each end of its boomerang shape. A child could sit there for hours unobserved by the old couple across the street or the older boys on the street corner or sisters unfastening their pointed bras in the darkness below. I can remember still the safe feeling of sitting wrapped in a sheet, in my panties, with my feet pulled up, careful not to get splinters from the roof (wood shingles they must have been), listening to the rush of the kids running, the shouts, the laughter, the sudden faces illuminated on the deep lawn as an occasional car went by.

2

LIFE was fine, then, and I recall our parents from those days only as harassments to my sisters.

Gloria and Greta coexisted in the house with our parents by working out their own set of rules. One, the big favorite, was that if you told the truth nine times out of ten, you could get away with murder the tenth time. Gloria had seen that in *Reader's Digest* (she was the one of them who read) and passed it on to Greta. They tried it out and quickly made it Rule Number One.

Probably in the excerpted article it was meant as a general observation on behavior, but my sisters took it as gospel. They kept a little note pad under the mattress of their double bed with marks for the number of times they told Mother something (where they were going; where they'd been; what they had to do after school): 1 1 1 1 and then a cross mark / for five times, then 1 1 1 1 and a *, which meant they could go for it.

"We're staying at Maudie's; she's having a slumber party," they would say. Or, "We're staying at Maudie's; she's giving Toni home permanents."

And they would. They thought Maudie (now Mom of Mom & Pop's) a dull girl, not their kind, but they went to her house every chance they got, checking off the times. Knowing that Mother would call Maudie's mother to confirm their stories until Mrs. Blanchard—a busy woman with a sick husband and a hairdressing business on the side—would shut her up, give her the brush-off, make it clear that she didn't need our mother poking her nose in or distrusting her Maudie, a dependable girl.

Then, when Big Number Ten rolled around, Gloria and Greta would think up the most outrageous thing they could. They would book a room at the motel up the road (ancestor of Do Drop), which meant they'd see half the parents they knew going in or coming out with the other half, things like that. Then they would tell everything they saw, having got themselves enough gossip to last them at school until the next Big Mr. Ten. They were never dumb enough to meet a boy at the motel, as that would have been the kiss of death, but they knew if they were just spending the night to have a hot bath, enjoy the clean sheets, the manager would look the other way. Thinking, as most of the town did, that Gloria and Greta deserved to get away from the crazy Jenkins girl once in a while.

My sisters never had a slumber party or played post office or even held Halloween at our house. Small wonder. The inside of the old brick place—set well back on its fine yard in the middle of Main—looked like the tail end of a rummage sale. Nothing worked. There wasn't even a stopper for the tub; we had to wad a washcloth in the drain. Nothing had a mate; there weren't two cups that matched or two saucers which went with them. We had frayed sheets that would crawl off the bed and end up on the floor every morning, so that you'd be sleeping on a mattress stained from years of somebody's periods.

Every morning, when Gloria and Greta left for school, it was a crisis. There was shouting about where are the socks, are they dry, have they scorched in the oven trying to dry, where is a comb, where is a clean blouse, or, in the winter, why is smoke coming up the furnace and are we going to be covered with soot?

There were other flare-ups between Gloria and Greta and our parents, which should have been a warning to me, but I attributed all discord to their being older and in Venice High; by the time I learned that the rest of the town did not live the way we did, my defenses were already down.

For example, money sometimes disappeared from Daddy's wallet. There were accusations and screams from Mother, blaming the girls. Gloria claimed that Greta took it; Greta said that Gloria took it. Sometimes both of them got a spanking, but more often not. More often Daddy, frustrated at not being able to pin the crime on anyone, furrowed his bushy brows, swung his cane over their heads, then turned and walked off. "Teach those girls some decent ways, can't you, Neva?" he said to Mother, clumping out the door.

One night, when I was pretending to be asleep in my little dormer room, with the covers pulled up over my face in the dark, I heard a big rush of excitement from Gloria and Greta's room and crept out to listen.

"What's ten times ten?" Gloria asked Greta, who was the one who did the math.

"A hundred."

"What happens when we get to a hundred?"

"Let me see that, will you?"

And I knew they were looking at the little 1 1 1 1 and / marks in their notebook.

"Something big this time," Gloria whispered.

"Time to go," Greta told her. "Time for Mr. Century."

By the end of the year Greta had got in trouble with a football player and run away and Gloria had married the son of a banker up in Cape Girardeau.

Mother tore their room apart, looking for evidence to present to our father that their running off was not her fault. When she found the notebook under the mattress, she waved it in his face for weeks: living proof the brazen hussies had been having sex for years and even keeping count of it.

3

THE next fall I started Venice Public, wearing a hand-me-down plaid dress of Gloria's and trying not to make awful Miss Abner mad by the fact that I could already read.

I had imagined that school would immediately have a great fascination for me, something like sitting all day up on the roof watching run sheep run and slinging statues, what with so many new people to watch, the chance to listen in on the big girls in the bathroom and the big boys by the lockers and to recall what I could of tales Gloria and Greta had told about what went on in school. But it didn't; it was more like eating at Grandfather's house on Sundays, with no one saying much, everyone on company manners. It turned out that my favorite part of school was not school at all, but being able to take my time going home, because first grade let out at two-thirty, and Mother, in her fog, still remembered years of Gloria and Greta getting out at half past three.

I was proud of knowing the way home all by myself: along the cracked cement sidewalks going past Methodist and around Baptist, down First by the post office and the barbershop (which was owned by Jimmy's daddy), negotiating the one busy downtown intersection, then turning down Main for the last half a dozen blocks. Starting at Mrs. Rogers's yard next door, I balanced on top of the concrete coping which held back the high yards, teetering slightly to give myself a scare, wishing I had roller skates like the bigger girls or bikes like the boys chasing them.

About two weeks into Lower First I came strolling home as usual and found Daddy there, in the middle of the afternoon. Now he sometimes did that, popped in during the day between seeing patients in his stuffy office over the new drugstore and going on what he called *rounds* at the new county hospital (a huge old house whose owners—a family originally from France before the quake—left it to the town). He would show up to get a cup of his boiled coffee or change his shirt, or his back might be giving him trouble.

But this time he was waiting for me. "Well, miss, it looks as if you're taking after your sisters."

I didn't have the slightest idea what he was talking about because the only way I wanted to take after Gloria and Greta was to have those pointed bras and huddle after dark in the snowball bushes, and I was light-years away from all that.

"She took a five," he was telling Mother, shaking his wallet in the air. "I had it when I dressed; I didn't have it when I got to the hospital."

Mother grabbed me by the shoulders, pinching hard, and shouted in my face. "Meanness in her, just like the others—"

I showed them what was in my hands: the Dick and Jane reader which I hauled back and forth so awful Miss Abner would not think me uppity, and the greasy brown paper sack in which I took my daily peanut butter and grape jelly sandwich and an apple from the bushel of Grandfather's winesaps by the back door. I showed them: no money tucked between the pages of Puff and Spot or in the limp, crumpled bag.

"You hid it," Mother accused.

"Never mind," Daddy told her, sighing. "They copy at that age. They copy what they see." He sat down and put me on his lap, his bad leg feeling like a stick of wood under my skirt. "Don't ever do that again. I'm going to let you off this time, but don't get ideas." He bent his heavy brows close to my face. "Your sisters were handful enough."

The enormity of the false accusation plus his pardon enraged me. "I didn't take your five," I shouted at him.

"I'm going to drop it this time, Alma." He deposited me on the floor, the subject ended.

"But I didn't. I didn't." Why couldn't he get the point? He wasn't believing me, and there didn't seem to be anything I could do. I began to scream. It seemed to me a nightmare worse than any I had ever had. Couldn't he hear what I was telling him? *I didn't take it.*

"Make her stop it, will you, Neva?" Daddy pressed his fingers to the side of his head, the way he did when he was running out of patience.

"I didn't, I didn't, I tell you—"

"Get on upstairs and hush." Mother pulled me after her.

That was the first time she locked me in the closet.

I stayed there all night. Once I heard Daddy in the downstairs hall ask, "Where's Alma?" and it must have been late.

"She fell asleep without her supper," Mother told him.

Frantic from the dark and shamed at the punishment, exhausted and not knowing what to do, I wet the floor and slept in it. The next morning, when Mother slipped up to unlock me, she started to spank me for it, but I pushed her away. "Not all night," I told her in a high voice, startled to hear myself set up the first rule between us.

"All right," she conceded, seeing she was going to have to clean up the smelly mess herself or I would be late for school. "But don't get smart with me."

After that it got to be habit. Whenever Daddy came home early and she didn't want me around, she shoved me into that big upstairs bedroom closet, the one with piles of Gloria and Greta's old shoes, and left me until he had gone to bed. Then she crept up the stairs and let me out, holding her fingers to her lips. She set a bowl of oatmeal on the big bed for me, and usually I fell asleep before I finished it. In this way, gradually, at six years old, I took over the front bedroom which looked down on the street, had window seats full of old flannel blankets, and three wide windows which opened onto the roof. (But I never sat out there again.)

The business with the money was never-ending, and I could not stand it when Daddy accused me. I knew that it must be Mother taking it, and the day after that first time I found a five-dollar bill in her underwear drawer, inside an old stocking with a run in it. I figured she had done it for years and that Gloria and Greta had let themselves be blamed because there were two of them and because it didn't matter so much if you could shift the blame.

I always shouted at Daddy, "I didn't, I didn't," red-faced and stiff with the outrage of being accused of something I hadn't done. I shouted at him even knowing that the cramped, dark closet was waiting for me—because I couldn't help it. I couldn't forgive Daddy for his judgment or for the blindness which kept him from seeing that it was Mother all along.

Later I knew just where in her jumbled closet to spot what she'd bought with the money, the latest silly purchase from the Sears catalogue, accessories with names from another era: snoods, fascinators, peplums. Fancy bits which she hoped would give her style. A waste of time in Venice, where she was what she was and no amount of putting on airs was going to transform her from the middle Jenkins girl into the young doctor's wife.

4

T H E N there was the episode of the rat.

It was winter, and I must have been in High Second, as I was already spending a lot of time with the twins, Reba and Sheba Vickers, who were seated alphabetically with me in the back of deaf Miss Day's class.

Always on my guard now, I'd get home, slip in, hang up my dress (I was expected to wear each one two times before it got washed), and change into the corduroy pants which were the jeans of our day and time. Then, if no one was on me, if Mother had gone to the grocer's or was rooting around in the downstairs closet, I would race outside and play until she hollered for me to come in.

Mother and Daddy had the big bedroom downstairs, which had its own bath, a half bath which had been added when Grandfather let Daddy move his family into Marie's house. The original bath, which opened off the downstairs hall between the living room and the kitchen, was the one I used, which Gloria and Greta used when they were living there, and company, if we ever had any. Originally the parents' bedroom had a nursery off it—a small room which connected the bedroom with the laundry on the back of the house—where Daddy had been kept in a crib as a baby.

Mother used it for whatever didn't go anywhere else. So

in those days the passageway had an old iron crib, as well as all of Mother's clothes, and Daddy's, and out-of-season things packed in mothballs or summer clothes wadded in sacks. Sometimes the crib had Christmas wrapping in it or stacks of *National Geographics*, waiting to be sorted into years or countries.

If I was lucky, Mother would be rummaging around in that little room, searching through Daddy's things, and wouldn't hear me come in and go out again.

Usually, though, she was waiting for me at the door, ready to coax me into something which needed doing. I helped her change the beds or wash out the spreads in the tub because they were too heavy for the washer and might cause it to overflow and break down, and anyway, they wouldn't go through the wringer. Or I scraped carrots for her if she'd decided to fix something, a real meal, for Daddy or helped her pluck a chicken if she was saving money and had bought one from someone's cook instead of the grocer—a stringy, bloody bird with the feathers still on it and the neck barely wrung. Anything she didn't feel up to negotiating on her own.

One day I slipped in and she was in the hall, holding a wet rag to her nose, her eyes red and watering. "I can't stand it," she said. "Something is dead down there." She was pointing to the floor register at our feet.

She was right. A stench came up with every gust of hot air. I took off my hand-me-down coat, which used to be Gloria's, and my leggings and wet shoes and piled them all on the floor in the front closet and came and stood with her.

"I think it's a rat," she said.

(My memory of my mother in those days is of a frazzled woman with no eyebrows, wisps of colorless hair, a mouth turned down at the corners. When I see her today, back at the dilapidated Jenkins house in the country, doddering on the porch, she seems foolish and infinitely harmless. But parents are, in the end, mostly figments of our imagination, and to me, in second grade, she seemed a real live Halloween witch.)

As soon as she said that and poked at the register with her free hand, I knew my job was going to be to fetch it out. In cities now there are outfits which do everything for you—exterminate, remove, service, install—and even here in Venice, Missouri, that's true. But in those days, toward the end of the forties, the rural forties, in flat, rebuilt river towns, you were your own solution to every problem.

"You're little enough to crawl down there." Mother wheedled, sniffling into her wet rag. "Get a stick or something. A coat hanger."

"It's too hot," I pleaded, stalling, overwhelmed with the smell and fear.

"I'll bank it," she promised, peering at the grille on the floor. "I'll have to bank it."

I followed her down the basement steps and watched her fling four shovelfuls of ash on the glowing coals. I hated the basement passionately, as who wouldn't have, with its damp, clammy air and eight-foot pile of dirty coal dumped in a heap? I hated it because it left smears of grime on your hands and legs if you touched it and because it harbored rats and spiders and every other terror of a child's mind. The only time I went down there was when I couldn't help it, when Mother had to stoke the hopper because Daddy had been called out on an emergency and she didn't want to have to go down underground alone.

(I used to thank my lucky stars that Mother never took the notion to lock me down there; compared to that, the closet was the Ritz.)

Back up in the hall Mother pulled up the register, and we stared together down the open chute below us. It was clear that the metal vent widened out to fit exactly the space sawed in the hall floor, and to judge by the distance from us to the bath, which was directly over the furnace, there must be a flat stretch of duct about as long as I was before the pipe took a bend and headed directly down into the banked coals.

"Here," Mother said, handing me the coat hanger.

"You'll have to hold my feet," I told her, and went and got my shoes and put them back on, so she would have something to hang onto.

"They're wet."

"It's just snow."

"They're wet, Alma."

"I'm not going down there unless you hold on," I warned her, making sure the laces were pulled tight. I was leaning over the hole and could feel gusts of warm air on my face; I imagined my bare feet slipping from her grasp, myself plunging into the furnace, and Mother telling Daddy that she didn't have any idea what I'd been up to, messing around in a place where I didn't belong.

"All right," she said, and gingerly took one ankle in her free hand, still holding the wet rag to her nose with the other. "It stinks," she said.

"Both hands." I was making the rules.

"All right." She dropped the strip of frayed washcloth and took the other ankle so that she was behind me, looking over my shoulder.

"Give me that." I grabbed the rag with the hand which wasn't clutching the hanger.

Slowly I edged over the rim of the hole in the hall floor and into the metal tunnel, making sure that it was not going to blister me before letting my weight down on it. It felt like a cookie sheet after the cookies have been pried off, still warm but cool enough to carry to the sink with your bare hands. It was black as ink, and, like ink, everywhere I touched the greasy jet soot came off on my hands and bare knees.

I couldn't see more than a few feet in front of me, but as I inched along, with Mother reaching after me, holding on so tight I could feel every bony finger and thumb, I could smell it right ahead of me, so strong that my main concern became how not to throw up in the duct and add that mess to all the rest.

I held the coat hanger out in front of me—on the level stretch—shoving it along, and then I hit it. I could just make it out: a rat as long as my arm, hairy and looking straight at me, except that it was dead, dead and huge and stinking until I had to lay down the rag and hold my nose. I tried to loop the hanger around it, but that was going to take too long, so I reached out, getting chill bumps on my arms, and grabbed the tail with the rag and dragged the beast back toward me.

Just then Mother let go of one ankle, and I heard her say, "George, you're home early!"

"Mother!" I shouted at her, to remind her what she was supposed to be doing and so he'd be sure to hear I was down there.

"What is that awful stench?" he asked.

"A rat. Alma's gone after it."

"How did it get there, past the furnace?"

"I don't know, George."

"Maybe a side duct?" I heard him clump about, wandering into the living room as if investigating a problem.

"Pull me up," I hollered at them, "pull me up, I got it."

Slowly a bigger hand grabbed my other ankle, and they scooted me along the pitch grimy tin until I was all the way under the hole in the floor, and then they let me crawl out on my own.

"Throw it away," Mother yelled, turning away and bending over.

"Those things carry disease," Daddy said, going to scrub his hands with Borax at the kitchen sink.

I don't remember getting it out of the house or what I did with it or what they did afterward. I do remember Daddy tamping the register down with his good leg, to make sure it was firmly back in the floor, and Mother burning a pan of oatmeal which I couldn't have eaten anyway. And me getting to stay in the tub, with its washcloth-plugged drain, until I fell asleep in the hot water, and then getting myself upstairs and into bed in great relief.

Wondering how I was going to get out of this family alive.

5

I F Mother had spent all her energy lying in wait to get me to do things like that all the time, I would never have survived. But that was not the case. I caught it only when no one else was around for her to pick on; I was a handy scapegoat to mark the time until Daddy got home.

The real preoccupation of her life—the barking dog, the piercing toothache, the mosquito bite that you can't stop scratching—was not me at all or my sisters before me but her raging jealousy of Daddy. Unless you've witnessed a fever like that, it's hard to believe that it can go on day after day, year after year, for a lifetime. A fixation that no amount of denial or testimony will cause to slack off to the smallest extent.

She was jealous of the woman who kept house for Grandfather because she'd been in the family since Daddy was a boy; she was jealous of dark Miss Newcombe, the postmistress, because he liked to stop by the post office to chat on his way to make rounds; she was jealous of the woman who gave manicures in the barbershop to the men packed in hot towels, even though it was never the same woman six weeks in a row. She imagined Daddy with every female patient, making house calls when the husband was away, disrobing her, prolonging treatment. With anyone at all who addressed him with familiarity, called him by his given name.

She went through all the mail that came to the house, misreading every greeting from each old medical colleague, his cousin Wisdom in Chicago, Grandfather's memos on surgery scheduled, uncollected bills from elderly patients.

She held his jackets up to the light looking for loose hairs, searched his shirts for smudges of red. She gave him proof every night of what she'd found: that his tie was knotted in a different way, and how, from when he'd left in the morning; his keys were in a different pocket; he'd said he was going by old Mr. Pickens's to check on his amputated leg, but the Pickenses said he hadn't got by.

"I know there is someone, George, I know it. You aren't the man I married. You've changed. You're secretive."

"Stop it, Neva."

I heard them regularly through the closet floor when they raised their voices in the room below.

"I know there is. I know who she is."

"Don't spy on me, Neva. You make a fool of yourself."

"She's not the first one, is she?"

I could hear Daddy's cane clumping around as he paced. "Stop it, I said."

"You're not fooling me, George."

Gloria and Greta, when they lived with us, fed Mother's flames, just for the sport of it. Telling her they'd seen Daddy on the corner of Methodist talking to some blonde, that they'd seen him go in the post office twice to see Miss Newcombe when they were outside for recess. That everybody in town knew about it but her.

Which taunt was the thing that drove Mother up the wall, to the brink: stories about how she was the only one in Venice who didn't know what was going on. So Gloria and Greta said that, and then denied that they had, and then changed their story—it wasn't the post office, it was the

27

barbershop—and then they would run out the door, fling it open to the dark, off to chase nighttime and lightning bugs and boys all across the yards of town.

Whereas I, who kept my mouth shut, and did as I was told, and helped her out of every pinch, and never told Daddy about the junk she bought with his stolen fives and tens, got it going and coming.

Sometimes I think if it hadn't been for the twins showing up when they did, I'd be under her thumb to this very day.

6

MAKING friends with Reba and Sheba was having a Gloria and Greta my own age, plus being right in the middle of a double life instead of sitting alone on a roof getting splinters in my behind.

Being close to twins is like watching a slow-motion pantomime of a prom queen preening before a looking glass: round white face; rosebud mouth. One beauty pats her hair on the left and the other pats hers on the right; one leans forward and their noses touch; one lifts an eyebrow, the corner of her mouth, so does the image. In the stage lights you can't tell which is real; then one of them turns away and bows— and the other disappears.

From the start I could tell them apart. That was because one of them, Reba, reacted one blink of an eye later than the other. At first I thought her slow, but then I came to see that wasn't it.

The time I figured it out, deaf Miss Day was sending us to the blackboard, which she did all the time for arithmetic and spelling, because she couldn't hear us answer if she asked a question, and though she could get by with little quizzes in grammar or maps in geography, for the rest she had to see the answers. So she sent us to the board twice a day. We were always the last, the twins and I, on the row of *V*s and

*W*s, and by that time the twenty-five kids ahead of us would be bored stiff and writing notes and squirming in their seats to go to the bathroom, or to get outside and play kickball, or, if they were still babies, to go home to their mothers.

I went first on our row, and when I walked back to my seat, Reba and Sheba were leaning down to tie their shoes, getting ready for their turn, their tow heads touching, moving together like dancers playing second graders. Then Miss Day called Reba, and she was gone. Sheba sat there doodling a picture of Reba on her tablet, with a deaf Miss Day looming large as a housetop in the foreground. Then Reba missed whatever it was, the word or the sum, and it was Sheba's turn.

I don't know why I hadn't noticed it before, but that day—with the trees all leafy outside and prissy Patsy Underwood in a blue and white pinafore in front of us—I saw it. When Sheba went to the blackboard, Reba appeared to vanish. As if she simply wasn't in the chair anymore. Sheba was busy writing all over the board in the way that infuriated Miss Day, who couldn't make sense of it and so leafed through the papers on her desk to act busy, and then Sheba patted the back of Miss Day's hair with chalk, which she always did, and the class jumped in their seats and tittered. Miss Day glanced up to catch disorder and wheeled around to see what was going on, but Sheba covered the rest of the board with nonsense and took her seat.

When she came back to our corner, it was like seeing first a head appear in a mirror and then a plaid shoulder and then the crooked corner of a snaggle-toothed smile, and then there was Reba back again, dusting off her hands a split second after Sheba, pushing her tow hair out of her eyes one split second behind her twin.

I used to think about that all the time and wonder how it was with them when I wasn't watching. Did they sleep facing each other? Did they bathe facing each other? Did they sit across the table, watching one another eat, lifting corresponding forks? What did they do when one of them had to go to the bathroom, or maybe it was always both at once.

Reba was left-handed, printing notes to pass to me with her left hand as Sheba drew a little cartoon for me in the corner with her right. (Sheba drew all the time, not just at the board or in her seat when we were supposed to be mapping imports and exports, but all the time. The best way I know to say it is that Sheba always drew and Reba was her sheet of paper.)

What I mostly wondered was this: if you were the one who was the mirror or the piece of paper, then did that mean that anybody could come along and look in you or draw on you? Or did that mean that you were blank as blank all your life except when the edge of your twin's hair scooted into your view or the puff of her sleeve materialized on your page?

Reba and Sheba, for their part, thought it amazing of me to come in a single, and they endowed me with twice what they had—as if single people were equal to two of them or were three-dimensional, maybe, instead of two. Or four, really, because the twins had no sense of time at all except for the present instant. I would ask them about how it was when they were little, when they were in the same crib, and they would stare at each other and wave their hands and laugh. They didn't know; they had no words for earlier and later time. All time had been the same to them, because they arrived in it together.

It was like when you are on an airplane, you have no way to see that you are moving forward except in relation to clouds or glimpses of the ground below. So maybe that is what I did for them. In High Second they began to talk about how I'd been in Low Second, and in this way they had the changes in our fine times together to compare.

What I got from them was the knowledge that if there were two of you, then you always had someone to offer up when you were in a tight spot. "Divide and conquer" is the way I put it.

I hung around them all the time. I went over to their house to play almost every day, and their mother never minded because there is nothing to three if you are used to two. When my mother called, Mrs. Vickers always said, "Yes, Mrs. van der Linden, Alma is here. Yes, we like to have her. She's a sweet girl, and I'm glad to have the twins make friends."

Mrs. Vickers had weak eyes from years of being a seamstress and trying to sew up Easter outfits and formals for everyone in town in bad light and five-and-dime glasses. In spring her bed was always covered with yards and yards of lavender shantung and pink pongee, all spread out on her counterpane in straight-pinned sleeves and plackets and gores and gussets, and then, at the end of the school year, these gave way to mounds of nylon net in greens and blues for recital dresses and Venice High formals.

She squinted and stitched all day and then stopped when the twins got home—to make them a cake mix cake or a batch of roll-out cookies—because her eyes were blinking and watering by that time of day, and she was taking a rest until the girls were in bed for the night.

Because it tired her eyes out, making pleats and darts and buttonholes, Mrs. Vickers had hit on the idea of dressing the twins so she could tell them apart in a wink. Reba would wear red: *r* for *R*. Sheba would wear whatever other color Mrs. Vickers could get in the matching blouse or jumper or dress she'd decided to sew for the twins. Reba, naturally, got sick of always wearing the same color, so Sheba switched clothes with her a lot because red was Sheba's favorite color.

In the course of time Mrs. Vickers passed on her secret to her good customers and to the women in General Dry Goods who sold her all her cloth. So whenever someone on the street leaned down and said, "Hello, Reba," in a smirking voice to whichever twin had the red sweater on, the twins knew where she got her information. "Yes, ma'am," Reba or Sheba answered, quick as a wink. "Aren't you a friend of our mother's?" So that Reba got the reputation among the ladies in town for being the smart twin, just as Sheba had made a name for herself in the classroom.

The twins used that trick for all it was worth on Mrs. Vickers. For example, one of them snatched six still-warm cookies for us off the plate in the kitchen, wearing a yellow blouse, then off came the garment, and both of them put on something red, making sure to appear in their mother's line of vision serially. Naturally she fumed that when she caught Sheba, she was going to get it, but by the end of the day she had forgotten. With her eyes stinging and a night of sewing ahead of her she scolded half-heartedly, and that was the end of it.

After months of my going to the twins' house every day after school, Mother began to get her nose out of joint. She started to nag at me: why didn't my friends ever come over to my house?

So we did. We began to walk home in the afternoons my way, past Methodist and Baptist, balancing on top of the cement retaining walls, running up our front lawn—bright green and ridged with craters from where the plumbing had been torn up by tree roots—straight into our house, Marie's house, with me in the lead shouting, "Here we are, Mom, yoo-hoo, here we are."

With Reba and Sheba beside me I was invincible.

Mother never knew what to do with us or the racket we made. She worried if we were upstairs playing too long (that we were up to something, "experimenting" or something), and she usually stood it for about an hour and then came charging up the stairs, calling out, "Isn't it time you girls went on home now?"

At which interruption Reba and Sheba looked up cool as cool from the bed where we were reading comic books and said, "No, ma'am," and went back to their *Supermans*.

When we got tired of lying around, we raced in and out of the house, pursuing our ongoing mystery stories in which the upstairs was a castle and the backyard with its grape arbor and hedges was the wild moors and the basement was our dungeon, where we were captured and thrown until we figured out our escape.

With Reba and Sheba beside me I tore down the steps into the coal bin without a tremor; the soot, the grime, the presence of rats behind the mountain of black stones which had scared me to death before were now a thrill for me. I threw open the furnace door for the twins and pretended to hurl them into the flames, only to be stopped in the nick of time. Or they pretended to tie me to the clammy wall, where the rodents were going to discover me and eat out my eyes and worse, but then I wiggled loose, and we were back up the stairs and out into the windy, bright yard, having outwitted them all.

"How can you tell them apart? It drives me crazy," Mother asked, tired of my having friends, tired of the duplicate nuisances underfoot, tired of the strain of the change in me, timid Alma, suddenly demanding milk and cookies for us, at least apples, which began to disappear in threes from Grandfather's bushel of winesaps by the back door.

"Reba always wears red," I confided to her. "But she doesn't want anyone to know it."

So then we played all the same old games on my mother.

"Is Alma home?" one of them asked, appearing at Mother's elbow, catching her in the closet rifling through Daddy's things, making her jump a foot.

"I thought she was going to your house." Mother was startled, confused.

"Maybe she went home with Reba."

Then, minutes later, in a red-checked shirt she'd changed into behind the snowball bush, the same twin tugged at Mother's sleeve. "Have you seen Alma? I've been waiting for her at the corner."

34

"But I just told—" And Mother went into a frenzy, trying to decide if they were pulling something over on her, resolving that it would be the closet and no supper for me for sure when I got home, and then there I was, with both twins beside me, at which point she slammed the bedroom door on us and lay down to try to collect her wits.

Leaving us free to race up and down the stairs, hide in the wardrobe, in the closet, under Gloria and Greta's bed, which was now mine; leaving us to undress down to our panties, spy on each other, kidnap and escape from one another—over and over and over.

7

T H E trouble was that gradually, instead of erasing what I had to put up with at home, the twins only highlighted the problem. When the three of us were together, everything was fine. But when they were gone, and all of Mother's accumulated grudges fell on me, it made it twice as bad as before, the contrast. Then I felt like a worm on a hook; the more I struggled against her, the deeper I was caught.

In Low Third, Sheba got deathly sick, in cross Miss Crawley's class. It started when we were all playing outside, in our coats and heavy socks. It must have been November because we had dressed up like three werewolves for Halloween, and that was past.

Mrs. Vickers's bed was piled high with Santa Claus runners for Christmas buffets, and scalloped skirts for Christmas trees, and jumbo felt stockings with individual names—intricate stuff, which meant she spent all day and half the night peering and watering and using a magnifying glass and swearing if she got through this round of felt reindeer and rickrack and gold bugle beads and red sequins and tiny green velvet trees, she would stick to her pink pongee from here on in.

All day in class Sheba had been red in the face and wheezing and sort of choking up and not interested in recess. That had made Reba hysterical with the effort of having half of herself sitting there in the corner shaking with chills and not answering cross Miss Crawley, even when she was sent to the office.

Then Sheba came back and stuck her head in the door and announced, "I'm sick," right in the middle of multiplication. Reba looked at me and I looked at her and we got up and walked out the door, getting our coats off the hooks on the way.

"Come back here," Miss Crawley hollered at me in her gravel voice. "Just who do you think you are?"

"Zeba," I answered, and the class broke up, giving me time to slip out the door.

Sheba was burning up and couldn't breathe except in a wheeze, and the lady in the old principal's office said she had called the doctor and he was headed for the Vickers house to meet her there with Sheba.

So she piled Sheba and Reba and me into her old car, having wrapped Sheba in a blanket first, and the part of me that wasn't worried about the sick twin or the terrified twin took time to realize that meeting the doctor meant my daddy.

When we got to the twins' house, Mrs. Vickers was out of her sewing housecoat into a Sunday dress and had made a cup of black coffee for Daddy, just as if she'd known that was what he wanted. She was half scared to death and asking him would her girl be all right about five times a minute as we all went up the front steps, across the porch, into the snug house.

"Let me see her, Dolly; then I'll tell you," Daddy kept saying.

And it was a shock for me that he knew Mrs. Vickers's name because of all the fights at home. Somehow I always imagined him off somewhere taking old men's temperatures in white sterile rooms, which is how he presented things to Mother.

"You live here, little girl?" he asked me, in an unfamiliar, teasing voice.

"I'm Zeba," I answered, still cashing in on my joke.

Daddy threw open his mouth and lifted his bushy brows and made a noise in his throat; it took me a full minute to realize that I was seeing him laugh.

"Come on in, you two, but stay out of the way." He looked down at the shuddering tow-headed heap whose hand I was holding. "You'll be Sheba then?"

Reba shook her head.

"You wouldn't kid me?"

"This is Reba, Daddy."

"Dolly—" He hollered her to his side.

Then we were all around the bed as he undid Sheba's blouse and listened to her chest. (In all that time it had never occurred to me that he really did stuff like that except in Mother's warped mind. Which made me keep looking over his shoulder, expecting her to charge in, screaming, through the door.) He took her temperature and looked in her ears and down her throat with a tongue depressor and poked around on her stomach, which was bare because he had pulled her skirt and panties down. Then he covered her again with her clothes and the pile of quilts Mrs. Vickers had stitched in her quilting days and pronounced, "You're one sick girl, whoever you are."

Mrs. Vickers started to say, "It's Re—" but then she caught sight of the red jumper, hugging against my chest, and her voice died.

"They say not," Daddy told her. "We'd better check. This is the reason we marked one, remember, to make sure one didn't get the wrong medicine or get it twice."

He pulled the quaking Reba to him and lifted up her tangled corn silk hair and peered behind her left ear.

Then he let her go and gently did the same with Sheba and, finding what he was looking for, rubbed the scar a minute with his finger. "Sheba it is," he said.

She nodded her head yes, but her eyes had closed, and she was panting and still.

"A penicillin shot will fix you up." He got out his bag as Sheba hid her face under the pillow.

Afterward he asked me, "How did you know which was which, Widget?" Uisng a nickname I hadn't heard from him since I was maybe four years old.

"I can tell" was all I said. I was tongue-tied with him because of so much fury being right underneath the surface, along with pride that he was the one who could make Sheba well.

He patted Mrs. Vickers's Sunday dress. "I'll stop back by. I'll send you some liquid aspirin for her and something for her chest. Keep her in that bed. Keep the other one away."

Then he said to me. "See you at home."

But I told him, "I'm staying here."

"I don't know about that." He looked at the twins' mother.

"Let her, George, she's a godsend."

"We'll see. You've got your hands full."

"I'm staying." I didn't budge because I knew that Reba would never make it through the night without crawling into bed with Sheba and breathing all her sickness if I wasn't there to hold her back.

So I did. I stayed two nights, and then by the third Sheba was sweating and whining and drinking canned mushroom soup and begging for vanilla ice cream. Which meant I had to go back home and catch it from Mother.

But the sickroom had opened my eyes to a lot. For one thing that Mother was right about Daddy, about the undressing and all the personal stuff she thought he was up to when he was out of sight. But that she was wrong, too. Because if Daddy never laughed at our house or talked about how many little girls he'd saved from strep throat that day or how many women like Dolly Vickers he'd delivered, marking their babies so they could keep them straight, then it was her fault.

Which made me mad at both of them: him for lying and her for having her screaming fits.

8

THAT summer Reba and Sheba were sent for a month to visit cousins in Eddyville, Kentucky. During Sheba's sickness, Reba, too, had grown puny and pale, had nursed coughs and rashes and sore throats, but then, with warm weather, both had got back their thick calves, their rosy cheeks, and their old ways of dashing around.

We celebrated the end of school by exploring town from top to bottom. We headed north to a borrow pit which had filled with spring rains and caught crawdads in old cling peach cans and toyed with letting them grab us with their pinchers for the thrill of it and then let them go—flopping onto our backs on a stretch of dandelions.

We slipped off south of town to a blue hole, swollen also with rain, and fished with poles made of sticks, lines made of string, and real corks and hooks that Sheba stole from Venice Hardware. Our mutilated garden worms, hauled along in a coffee can, caught us three small, squirming fish, which Sheba pronounced croppie, and we bashed the scales off with sharp rocks and fried them over a twig fire in a small skillet I had taken from the kitchen at home, in half a stick of butter which Mrs. Vickers had left out to soften for cake frosting. Reba had to contribute something, so we'd made her get the matches. The fish were wonderful, and we ate them with our fingers, flaking and separating every bite to watch out for bone and bits of sharp unscraped scale.

Then, when the twins were gone and I was back in trouble again all the time, I dreamed up the idea of interviewing Grandfather as a way to get away from home.

Mother made a big ruckus when I first announced that I'd be going down to his house in the afternoons for a while since I had never set foot there before except for our weekly Sunday suppers. These were rather stiff affairs, with Grandfather in a vest and tie, carving some meat or other; all the adults having a glass of dark wine before the meal (which was the only drinking I saw in those days, as there was never alcohol at our house), to toast the presence of a visitor, a colleague of Grandfather's from up the road in Cape Girardeau, visiting his kin, or even someone from town, a preacher who didn't mind that Grandfather wasn't a believer, or a banker who didn't fret that Grandfather never trusted banks. Or even a long-time patient, on his last legs, who was getting an evening's homage from Grandfather, who hated to see folks die.

"I won't have her down there with him and his hussy." Mother's voice carried up to me through the floorboards.

"You're speaking of my father, Neva."

"I'm telling the plain and simple facts."

"I won't have Elsie White discussed in that tone."

"You won't have, you won't have—I'd like to know what I'm supposed to think about some woman who right out in the open for the whole town to see sleeps in that house with the old goat."

"You're not required to think about the matter at all."

"I don't want Alma going down there."

"Let her be. I've given her permission."

"I don't like it—"

"Let her be, Neva." And there was the usual sound of him clumping from the room and then across the hall into the kitchen. He never left the house once he got home in the evening except for emergencies of the magnitude of car wrecks, but a lot of times, when I sneaked down to the bathroom in the middle of the night, I would see the outline of him at the kitchen table, pouring out the dregs of his pot of boiled coffee into his cup, tapping his hand on his good leg, staring at the back door in the dark.

"Who's that?" Grandfather answered the door.

"Me, Alma."

"How's that?"

"Alma, Granddaddy."

"Come here, Elsie, I can't see a soul," he called, staring through the screen door over my head.

"It's George's child," said a low voice behind him. "Open the door."

Then there I was, alone for the first time in my life with adults who weren't my parents.

"Come over here by the light so I can see you," Grandfather instructed, guiding me gently by the shoulder, steering me into the parlor. "Is that you?"

He was as confused by me in the singular as I was. Perhaps he'd actually never looked at me, only taken in that there we were, his son and the females, lumping me in with the daughter-in-law who stuck in his craw.

"Yes, sir."

"What brings you here?"

"She might like a glass of tea," said the low voice from the cool shadows of the wide front hall.

"Is that right?"

"Yes, sir."

"We'll have it then." He seemed to have no trouble hearing the woman I thought of as his housekeeper, even though

43

Mrs. White didn't raise her voice. He must have trained himself to it.

I'd prepared the speech I was going to give, but he waved me quiet until we had each received giant glasses of minted tea and china plates with slices of marbled cake.

"Now," he said.

"I'm doing a report—" I began.

But he interrupted me again. "For God's sake, come sit, Elsie. I can barely hear the child."

Mrs. White came and sat on the round cushion of a slipper chair and smiled at me. I had never given her much attention before except to note that she was someone else Mother was jealous about because she'd been there to raise Daddy when his mother died and because she still treated him in a familiar way. Whenever we had our Sunday suppers, we were all seated at the table but her, and then Grandfather called out toward the kitchen, "Come on in and sit down, Elsie, the food's getting cold." At which she quickly pulled up a chair as if it were a one-time event, set herself a plate, and lowered her head, out of reflex of saying the blessing at the table, which Grandfather always let company do. She was a broad woman with tiny ankles and a cap of white hair which made me think of nurses and wonder if that's what she'd been in the old days.

I wondered if she really did it with Grandfather—or had when he was young because he was past seventy, I knew. I also knew that she slept upstairs because I'd been up to play in the linen closet on Sundays, inventing games that were part of the mysteries I played with Reba and Sheba, for something to do so as not to get stuck with Mother while the men had their cigars. I had seen Mrs. White's things in the closet of the little bedroom on the back of the house, the one with the tiny writing desk. I'd even opened the closet and seen what looked to be a hundred freshly starched and ironed dresses, some flowered and some striped and some

44

solid with little white eyelet trim, but all blue. More clothes than I'd ever seen in my life in one place, and neat as a pin, the whole closet.

"Maybe Alma doesn't want company," she suggested now, taking off her apron and folding it on her blue-sprigged lap.

"Nonsense," he told her. Then, setting his plate down and unbuttoning the top button of his trousers so he could lean forward without cutting his huge belly in two, he barked at me, "Cat got your tongue?"

"No, sir." I wished I had worn a dress the way I did on Sundays, instead of gym shorts. Maybe he didn't like kids to look messy. "I have to write a report for fourth grade," I began for about the tenth time. "On my family."

"That right?"

"Yes, sir. A biography."

"Fourth. We used the McGuffey Readers in my day." He hauled himself up out of his comfortable chair and took down a thin, stiff book which said *Fourth Reader* from a bookshelf by the window. After thumbing the pages, he finally read aloud in an oratorical voice:

The Wife

1. I have often had occasion to remark the fortitude with which women sustain the most overwhelming reverses of fortune. Those disasters which break down the spirit of a man, and prostrate him in the dust, seem to call forth all the energies of the softer sex, and give such intrepidity and elevation to their character, that at times it approaches to sublimity. . . .

"I don't imagine that's in your curriculum these days," he said.

"No, sir."

"Biography is it?" He tapped his head with two fingers. "Lot of history here." He gestured to his undone trousers. "Here, too."

45

I wondered if Mother had ever heard him talk that way and decided she must have, which would be part of the problem.

I ate a bite of my cake, at a loss for words.

When I didn't answer, Grandfather said, "The Van der Lindens go way back."

I nodded.

"You tried the other branch of your family yet?"

"No, sir."

"You might give them a whirl. Any one of the Jenkinses would sell you anything she's got for two bits and most of them have." He guffawed.

During all this time Mrs. White sat with her hands in her lap, looking amused and not a bit nervous. I folded mine, trying to go along.

"Did your teacher tell you to do this?" he asked.

I didn't know whether to say yes, to give myself credibility, or no, so he wouldn't think the teacher was nosy.

"It's a general assignment, everybody knows that, for Low Fourth." I was proud of my answer.

"Is it now?" He got a cigar out of a big wooden yellow box on the table next to him and began to chew the end of it, with the little paper ring still on it. "Does your daddy know you're down here?"

"Yes, sir."

"How about your mama?"

"She knows."

"Amazing grace." He lit the cigar and then sucked a lot of it and let out the smoke so it rose around his head in a cloud.

"I told them I would be needing to come down here some days."

"You did, did you?" He sat and smoked for a while, and Mrs. White sat there, too.

I studied her out of the corner of my eye; she wasn't nearly as old as Grandfather and must have been really pretty when she was young, in a placid sort of way, with curly hair and that broad face.

When the ash on Grandfather's cigar was an inch long, he stirred, fastened his pants, dumped the ash on the floor, and, rising, gestured to me to follow suit. "The Van der Lindens go way back," he said. "You come again tomorrow, and I'll see what I can rustle up."

9

I TOLD Mother that Grandfather was having trouble with his eyes and that I was going to be reading to him. I knew from library books that this was something children sometimes did as a favor to old people.

"The old fool's eyes have been giving him trouble all his life; that's nothing new," she said, snorting in the way she did the rare times she made a joke.

The next time, Grandfather took me to a small office he'd set up off the back of the house downstairs, directly under Mrs. White's room. It had a big roll-top desk with an Underwood typewriter on it, next to which he'd piled stacks of letters and documents in preparation for my visit. He also had old photographs, in Manila envelopes, and framed family portraits of men with handlebar mustaches and women with high lace collars and thin lips.

"Come in, sit down," he said, and swiveled up a little stool for me, so I could sit at the same height as he. He had his cigar already chewed, soggy on one end, ready to light.

I looked around, getting accustomed to the space, the bare wood floor, the smell of Grandfather everywhere.

"Elsie's canning," he said.

I nodded and got out a thin spiral notebook that I'd bought

at the five-and-dime on my way down, so I would look professional. (It's the same kind I use to this day.)

He reached down and loosened the laces on his run-over shoes, undid his straining trouser button, and let me have it: "My father, christened Grady van der Linden, was the tenth of twelve children, six of whom lived to adulthood. The land that my father's father and his father before him had acquired by grant in eastern Missouri—back before it was Missouri and when what we call Tennessee was still a part of Carolina—was wooded and timbered to the point that it had to be cleared, the stumps cut out, before any cultivation could take place. The first of his family, my father's great-grandfather it would have been, had come as a young man following the fur trade, back when this settlement was known as l'Anse à la Graisse, which means 'cove of grease,' because of the bear fat sold here by trappers to traders going down the river to the port. You following this?"

"Yes, sir." And I strained to make it so.

"His family had been part of the international fur exchange in the eighteenth century, coming down the St. Lawrence Seaway, descended, he claimed, from the Dutchmen who came to this country before it was a country. He, this grandfather I'm talking about, married Pierre Le Clerc's daughter, which is how the French blood first got into the family.

"So trapping and clearing were hard work, but the family prospered, each of the living children of that time having a large issue, until they populated parts of the neighboring counties on both sides of the river. And later they had mills for grinding grain and providing water power more trustworthy than the Mississippi. Eventually this part of the state got surveyed and made into townships and county seats, with the best spots being the ones that afforded a favored river crossing. All that was before they cut down our cypress and oak and sold them, mind; we're talking about the early days.

"My father's mother, now, to get down to a time within

49

my memory or at least what my sisters could pass along, was a famous midwife in these parts, and my father, who was her decided favorite, grew up with that in his background, and so he conceived the idea of being a doctor—all the time helping his father with the timber and the crops, as he was supposed to do. He clung to his idea, even after he married my mother and they had two daughters, born two years apart, as was the way it went in those days, with the mother nursing through the second summer to help with the childhood diseases and avoid a sooner pregnancy.

"Now, then, at that time a man could apprentice himself to a doctor and set up a practice, there wasn't licensing as we know it, but my father wouldn't settle for part way; he was a single-minded man, and he had it in his mind to be a real physician.

"In those days a man didn't have the opportunities today of a scholarship or a bank loan, and so, after they had prayed over it and doubtless had a few family fights over it—but that is not a matter of record, you see—my mother, his wife, Ann Elizabeth, made the decision that she would leave her two young daughters at home with a sister and go with my father to Louisville, where he had got accepted at medical school, and work for the two years it took him to get his degree."

At this point Grandfather tapped his ash on the floor and coughed. He peered across at me, motionless and dressed in Sunday clothes on my stool. "Surely, now"—he spoke right into my face—"you're old enough, Widget, to understand my meaning when I say that one of the provisos of this bargain was that they not instigate any further children during that two-year period. We're talking about 1875, if you get my meaning."

"Yes, sir." I didn't bat an eye.

"So that is precisely what occurred. My mother, Ann Elizabeth Lecoeur she was christened, also a French woman and the finest Christian ever to walk the face of this earth, left her girls with her kin to take a job in a tobacco factory, processing tobacco leaves with a crew that consisted entirely, but for her, of Negro men."

He stopped to let the enormity of that soak in, and my head was reeling. I got only partial notes for all that, although I went back later and filled in what I could remember. Grandfather had talked that first afternoon in his office for three straight hours without drawing a breath. Lots of it I never got right, especially the early parts where the trappers were going down the Hudson and the Seaway and then coming down to Missouri and getting married and having dozens of children, half of whom, at least, always died.

The most fascinating thing that first time was how Grandfather didn't bother with names like De Soto and La Salle, which we had all the time in school, but only with the ones who related directly to him; it was like tracing down to Abraham through the begats in the Bible. I didn't see how he could recall which of them came next and which were kin, but he did. He knew each and every ancestor and at what age which granddaddy had done what, and how many acres of land or how many pelts he'd had, and how many wives, because they died all the time, too, and how many surviving children.

"That's enough for one day," he said, finally, when I was about to fall off the stool and my eyes were drooping. "Your mother will have the sheriff after me. An old man gets carried away on the subject sometimes."

He returned everything to its proper drawer or cubbyhole, pulled the roll-top down until it rested on the Underwood, and helped me down off the stool.

My legs were prickling from being almost gone to sleep when I stood up, and my mind was stuffed as a turkey.

He took me into the kitchen, where Mrs. White was making tomato pickles with something she identified as lime, which I was to be careful of, and she gave me a taste from last year's crop to show me that they got crisp as potato chips after they'd soaked awhile.

She also gave me a biscuit left over from breakfast, which she'd heated up and poured a pool of honey on, as if she could read my mind: that I was worn-out and starving to death. It made me think my daddy had been a lucky little boy, and that made me really mad at him, that he didn't have any idea how it was for me.

"That too big a dose for one day?" Grandfather asked, but he didn't wait for an answer. He walked me to the front screen door and shook hands with me in a formal manner. "That brightened up my afternoon," he said. "You had enough?"

"No, sir."

"I'll be looking for you tomorrow then."

"Thank you," I told him, holding my spiral carefully, like the treasure it had become. As I walked home along the cracked sidewalk, past the blooming lilies and climbing roses, I was already wondering where and how to hide it from Mother.

IO

I T took most of the rest of June to get the whole story, and by then I had forgotten my original reason for coming. Mother and Daddy seemed unimportant minor characters when I was listening to my grandfather, people who had nothing brave in their lives, nothing to qualify them for his genealogy pages—no skinned pelts in the snow to strap to sleds or pile on canoes, no fording rivers in small craft, no cutting down hickory or ploughing up the back forty, or harnessing lazy streams for water power to grind the wheat to make the bread to feed all those dozens of children, most of whom were going to die in your arms with big smallpox scars all over them or turn black on their tongues or big in their bellies from raging epidemics.

Being locked in the upstairs closet didn't seem important when I was at the north end of Main, or Daddy seeing Sheba with her panties down. Or the fights my parents had. All that was baby stuff. I wanted to be a young Christian wife who gave up her daughters and went to work with black men pulling tobacco leaves into strips, staining my hands with nicotine and tar, sleeping across the room from my husband at night on a pallet on the floor, so as not to make the infants which would stop me from helping him become the doctor he wanted to be.

Compared to that, I hadn't done anything, and wished for a chance to be lowered down into the furnace when it was hot as an iron, with the tin ductwork sizzling, in order to drag out the typhus-infected rats by their diseased tails—and never flinch: in order to earn my right to be a descendant in Grandfather's book.

He didn't get around to the rest of the story in a hurry.

One afternoon he read me a long letter from his father to his mother when he was getting started in Louisville, while she was still placing her babies at her sister's house. He had to read it, even though I was looking over his shoulder the whole time, because of the faded ink and the funny way they wrote cursive in those days, with *s* looking like *f*, and endings abbreviated.

My Dear and Beloved Wife,

As I presume you would be glad to hear from me by the time this will reach your sweet hands, for I know that you are always anxious at any and all times to hear from me, I cannot forbear or postpone writing you any longer, and I hope to hear from you soon. I tell you I have a kiss in reservation for you and our dear sweet little babies, and I also have a great deal to tell you when you arrive, for I have seen and learned a great many things that I knew not before. I have learned the most important thing of all, how to be a physician right, or will, I swear it, before I leave here.

I see a great many very interesting cases treated and have done as many myself already as I have wished to at the dispensary outside the College and Hospital, where we have a great many very interesting surgical operations performed, and our regular course of lectures at the College also have shown me a great many new and interesting things, which I will tell you when you are here.

54

I have scarcely time to sleep and am kept busy almost day and night and shall now close these quickly written remarks to go to the dissecting room.

Yours faithfully,
Grady

Then, as I was digesting that, Elsie came in and suggested that we might like to take a break for our tea. But I shook my head; she didn't understand how fascinating it was to be taken back into an earlier, more thrilling time.

"Later then," she said, and left us alone.

Grandfather took his time selecting a new cigar from the yellow wood box on his desk, biting off the end, and then chewing it for a spell while we absorbed his father's letter.

"Some background is needed," he began, after lighting up and drawing a few times to be sure that the end was glowing and the taste was right.

"Yes, sir," I said.

"Religion was a serious matter in those days."

I waited, having learned that it was enough for me to nod and he would go right on where he was headed.

"My father, your great-grandfather, came from a long line of Reformed thinkers, men who lived by the old theology of an eye for an eye and a tooth for a tooth. They kept track of who helped get the ox out of the ditch and who didn't, who brought soup when the babies had diphtheria and who stayed home. Who owed whom what and how much the interest. Naturally they assumed God did the same. The law was their creed, a man's word was the law, and God the same as man was held to His word."

I nodded, my eyes watering at the seriousness of it.

"Whereas my mother, Ann Elizabeth, your great-grandmother, was a member of the Society of Friends, who are also called Quakers, a radical group that put no man above another and woman equal to any man. They held the view, unpopular then as today, that the rain falls on the just and the unjust alike, and were on all issues diametrically opposed to the Reformed Calvinists. For example, on the matter of a man's oath, my mother's sect believed that to swear at all was against the first teachings of Christ because it carried the implication that a person *could* tell a falsehood when that was not possible for the true believer any more than it was for God. You see," he said, tapping his long ash on the floor, "the problem."

"Yes, sir."

"Enough for today then. Elsie thinks I'm wearing you out with all this talk."

"But I like it."

"I imagine what she means is that it's time for my nap."

The next week, when he finally got around to the point he was leading up to, I didn't understand and thought maybe there was something about sex that I hadn't read.

"But *how*?" I asked him. "How could your mother be going to have a baby and him not know it?"

"You don't repeat these conversations, do you, at home?"

"No. I tell them I'm reading aloud to you."

"Do you now? And how do they take that?"

I blushed, recalling Mother's comment.

"Never mind. Don't repeat it." He helped himself to a piece of marble cake which Elsie had left for us on his roll-top desk. "Where were we?"

"The second year, while she was working with the tobacco hands, she got pregnant with you."

"Yes, well, there was a great consternation in my mother's heart over the matter, as she confided it to me later. It seems that twice in the night, in the big double bed they shared, my father had rolled over and, um, availed himself of the sweet pleasure of lovemaking with his wife, but all the while remaining quite asleep. I understand that this is possible to do, and I'm sure that he allowed himself to do so out of his desire for my mother, which, by mutual agreement, he was denying himself.

"The point, however, was that she, being a reticent woman, had not mentioned these nights to her husband, whom, in the style of the times, she called only by his surname. Since she could not bring herself to ask, 'Did you know what transpired between us in the night?' she bit her tongue and got up at dawn to go to the factory and doubtless prayed over her work all day. Then, sure enough, after the second occurrence she found herself in the state she most feared."

"How awful."

"Indeed. My beginning was not a pleasant time for either of my parents." He gazed off awhile at the stacks of portraits. Then he selected one, and we studied the faces of his parents, of whom he had several pictures: when they were bride and groom; when they were old; in middle age. His father had big ears and what I thought of as a cough-drop beard, a drooping mustache, and very bushy eyebrows like my daddy. He was wearing a vest and bow tie and high white collar. Grandfather's mother wore black, with a ruff at the neck, and a locket. Her eyes were set very deep in her face, and her mouth was firm. "He didn't believe her," Grandfather said, putting the photos back.

"Even when she told him what happened?"

"She told him only that the baby was his. She could not bring herself to accuse him of less control than she herself had or than he thought himself to have. She preferred to be wrongly accused and let him keep his good view of himself."

"Oh, no, Granddaddy." I was crying; I couldn't help it. When they didn't believe you, that was the worst thing that could happen.

"He said to her, 'Give me your word. Give me your word that it is mine.' But of course, that was the one compromise she could not make. 'I'll not swear, Grady. Thee knows I'll not swear.' And so he turned her out. She packed up and went to her sister's to wait out her term, and he finished out the year with the assistance of his advising professor.

"At any rate, after my birth, in 1877, at the start of spring, he came home with degree in hand, looked at his wife and son—my hunch is he feared I might not be white—and offered to take her back."

Elsie had come in with tea for us and sat, now, taking off her apron and pulling up a chair, as if this were the part she liked to hear best. It occurred to me then that maybe this story had something to do with them, although I was not sure what.

" 'I forgive you,' he said."

"What did she do?"

"My mother told him: 'God forgives.' "

I clapped my hands at that, and Elsie's broad, gentle face broke into a pleased smile.

Then Grandfather started putting up the day's letters and pictures, slipping them into the little sliding compartments of the desk, turning little keys, as if that were the end of it.

"Did she? Did she take him back?"

"Of course. What else could she do, with three of his children to raise? My brother, Grady, junior, was born the next year. And three more after that who didn't live to adulthood."

"Is that why you and Uncle Grady don't speak?"

He shook his head. "We're foolish old men to be still at it at our age, aren't we? At least your father and his young cousin keep in touch. Perhaps if there had been another generation on that side, we could have got matters mended again." He paused, then added, "No, as a matter of record, my distinguished brother is *persona non grata* to me not because he doubted our mother, although that would have been cause enough, but due to the fact that he received our father's name, while I, the elder, got only the month of the year in which I was so fatefully conceived."

58

At this point Elsie took me on her lap and began to rock me back and forth like a little kid.

Which was the exact moment Mother picked to come bursting through the front door and run, yelling, down the hall.

"Liar," she shrieked at me when she found us. "You little liar," she cried on the front porch as she whipped me for the first time in my life, stinging blows with the flat of her hand on my legs. "Liar, liar."

At home they fought over it half the night. She told Daddy how I'd told her I was reading to Grandfather and how, instead, he was filling my ears with his nasty stories about God knows what filth, and how that woman was sitting right there big as you please, petting me as if it were a Sunday School lesson I was getting, going along with the whole filthy story because she was no better than she should be and was right where she belonged.

I thought Daddy was going to hit her, and I wished he had, but naturally he didn't. He clumped, as usual, into the kitchen and put the pot on to boil, dumping in coffee and then actually taking the time to put in a little eggshell so the grounds would settle. Which was what did it for me: the stupid eggshell. That he could take the trouble to do that when I had been shamed for the rest of my life in front of Grandfather.

If I could have picked up his cane right then and there and clubbed him to death with it, I would have.

I wanted to shout at him with Mother standing there listening that I knew he was doing it with Dolly Vickers and that I knew he was undressing half the little girls in town and that he'd probably done it with the postmistress, too, and Elsie White when he was a kid—anything awful to make him know how I felt.

Instead, I spent half the night huddled on the closet floor

upstairs, so they could devote a few more hours to their fight without little pitchers with big ears in their way.

"I'll get you," I whispered in the dark through the floor-boards, "I'll get you both for this."

II

W E continued to go to Grandfather's for Sunday suppers, and he behaved as if nothing had happened between us, except that on one occasion, when I had worn a too-big blouse and skirt left from Gloria that I was trying to grow into for Low Fourth (it was the kind of pink outfit which you'd expect sisters named for movie stars to have), he slipped me an envelope, which I tucked under my waistband, with the blouse out. When I got home, I saw that it had a copy of the letter his father had written his mother from medical school and a copy of his birth certificate, which said "August van der Linden, 7 pounds 10 ounces, May 22, 1877, Mother: Ann Elizabeth Lecoeur, Father———." And it really touched me that he'd let me have copies of two of his most important documents in the world from the locked compartments of his roll-top desk.

And to learn that his birthday was three days after mine.

But otherwise, we went on with the same routine down at the north end of Main. Grandfather carved the meat; the visitor, now that it was summer, was usually some old chum of his from sixty years back who'd come to town to see what was left of it; Mother sat still as a fence post, not liking the wife of whoever was along or the topics the old men were discussing; and Daddy, as always, sat across from her, eating what was served him, off in some private world that let him not have to pay attention to what was going on. Then, just as it was time for the visitor to say the blessing, Grandfather called out in the direction of the kitchen. "Elsie, come on in and sit down; the food's getting cold." At which she removed the apron from her starched fresh blue dress, set herself a plate and a cloth napkin in its wooden napkin ring, shaped like one of the animals of the Ark, and quickly pulled up a chair. Just as "Oh, Lord, we thank Thee for this daily bread" rolled out across Grandfather's white linen table.

My prying around upstairs was now monitored by Mother, but sometimes I could scoot up to the bathroom (because the downstairs commode was off Grandfather's bedroom, and she wasn't about to let me go in there), and if I was quick enough, and didn't hear feet on the stairs, because I'd left Mother drying dishes in the kitchen or being taken with the company on a tour outside to see what the damson plums were doing, I could pull open the drawers of Elsie's bureau and touch the stacks of silklike camisoles and little boxer underpants which I had never seen before. (Mother wore General Dry Goods cotton panties and the bras with the stitched cups whose metal fasteners were always broken and pinned.) And admire, on the closet floor next to the orderly sets of white shoes for summer and black shoes for winter, a big cardboard box of hats, all wrapped in tissue paper with pearl hatpins holding the paper to the straw summer hats and felt fedoras with tiny upturned brims. Church hats. I knew that's what they were; church hats that Elsie had given up wearing when she came to look after Grandfather, but that she was saving because she wasn't a woman to throw away good clothes or because when he was gone she would some-day be back in her place at Methodist or Baptist, taking the grape juice and cracker bits and asking pardon. It gave me a secret with her and made me want to rush down the stairs and fling myself into her clean blue lap.

The only change, outward change anyway, was that from

that summer on, I never called Grandfather's housekeeper Mrs. White again but called her Elsie. And it didn't matter to me that Mother few into a fit every time she heard me, I did it anyway. To remind me that some gains, at least, had been made.

The twins came back, and August grew steamy hot with gnats and bugs everywhere you went, and tiny red chiggers if you even walked through grass to get to the borrow pit, which had got scummy and slimy on its way to drying up for fall. The twins seemed different to me, and at first I couldn't decide if it was due to the fact of my having grown up a lot during my afternoons at Grandfather's or if they'd been around the cousins in Eddyville too long.

What it turned out to be was that they'd switched. One day, when we were going along and Sheba was deciding that we'd try to buy a pack of cigarettes, pretending that they were for her mom, because everyone in fourth tried cigarettes, and we were going to have mean Miss Matlock so we'd better get used to how to outwit her, and Sheba said all that and clapped her hands in the way she had, and then I noticed something: she was half a beat off, was half a beat behind something. . . . Quick as a wink I leaned over and felt nothing behind her ear, and she turned red, and the real Sheba did, too.

The real Sheba, who had been following along, I could see then, with much too relaxed a "follow," the way a teacher does with a pupil, letting the pupil play the melody or the hard parts and herself falling in smooth as cream with the left hand.

"How come?" I asked them, cross.

"We got in the habit," Sheba said. "The dunces in Eddyville couldn't tell, and I was tired all the time, which I couldn't admit because of Mom having worn herself out nursing me. So Reba promised she would pretend for the dumb cousins if I would do everything she told me to."

Reba looked hurt that I had guessed.

But I got over it. It turned out they may have needed to switch, to toughen them both up, because a sad thing happened to them that summer. Which wasn't a result of their helping me spy on Daddy but more or less coincided with it.

I didn't confide to them everything that had happened at Grandfather's, or my general rage and desire to get even with my parents, but suggested, as if it were just something to do besides look for crawdads or try to buy cigarettes, which they weren't about to sell us, that maybe my father was doing it with their mother, and why didn't we spy on him and find out?

We decided to tell our mothers that we were going to both Vacation Bible Schools, Methodist in the morning and Baptist in the afternoon, since both churches liked to have every kid in town between the ages of six and twelve come make cut-and-paste models of the Ark, or finger-paint slippery, swirling green bulrushes in which to plant Moses, or crayon in stenciled scenes of Jesus riding into Jerusalem on the donkey. Kids didn't mind because the day's artwork was always rewarded with paper cups of Kool-Aid and cookies made by the church ladies, and followed by games called end of the rainbow (Methodist) or yellow brick road (Baptist), where tiny prizes, the kind that look as if they came in Cracker Jack boxes, were wrapped in tissue paper and hidden in the crooks of willow trees or at the edges of drooping sweetheart roses.

We told our folks we were doing both churches, but in fact, we only went to Methodist in the mornings because the head of it, Mrs. Rogers, was my neighbor on Main Street. That way we were free to snoop around in the afternoons, with everyone thinking we were at Baptist. And we even went so far as to sign in at Bapist every day on their attendance sheet and pay our dimes because then who cared? The record would show us as being there, and the frantic Sunday School teachers who did the job of herding all the kids in town would be glad enough to have three less to manage.

At first we hid in the hedges outside Dolly Vickers's house, waiting to see if my daddy would walk up the back drive, which was only two blocks from the hospital, but the big hydrangeas were sticky with something like sap or syrup all over the leaves, and stringy with webs, and full of gnats— because it was August—so we located ourselves in the old neighborhood victory garden, now grown up in okra high as fence posts and squashes and cornstalks, plus a few pumpkins, which the big kids liked to steal for Halloween.

The large lot made a sort of stockade for us, bordered as it was with these stalks and vines, and we sometimes forgot about watching the house and got busy with our mysteries again, or Reba and Sheba did, anyway, since they didn't really have the foggiest idea about what men and women were up to, because they didn't read books, so they didn't understand why it was vital to catch my daddy leaving their mother's house. But they went along with it because they were sharing my excitement at the end of that long, hot summer.

We did see him, finally, and we crept up and peered through the window, and it was just like a movie: she was sitting on the side of the bed, crying, her hands up to her face, and he was standing over her, with his coat jacket off, thrown over a chair back, talking to her in a low voice. You could tell he was giving her the bad news.

It makes me ashamed still to recall the pleasure that washed over me, the lift, the surge of victory I felt. Plus how dumb I was.

When he left, walking out bold as you please, getting into his car, which I hadn't even noticed drive up, we rushed in, hoping to catch her in such a state that she would confess everything.

Which she did. It seemed that she couldn't see to sew at all anymore, hadn't been able to for almost a year. Had been doing it by rote, by feel, measuring waists and remembering, after all those years of doing it, how large a span that would be, gathering the tulles and voiles by touch, catching the threads at just the right point, stitching them by habit, her hands guiding the cloth into the machine and out again in even, finished seams. But anything new, anything she hadn't done before—a gore on the bias, a pattern of intricate checks to be matched, a sleeve that was a dolman instead of a puff— she could only guess at. Now the ladies had begun to complain.

" 'I told you, Dolly,' " she quoted Daddy as warning her a year ago. " 'You have to make provision,' he said."

Then, still dabbing her failing eyes, she showed us, the twins and me, how she would do the fitting, holding me up, the tallest by almost a head, the thinnest, and then how she would do someone else, and she reached for Sheba, cupping her hands around her waist, running them up her chest to her shoulders, measuring down her back by handspans from shoulder to beltline, keeping it all in her head. She placed her hands on the material on the bed: satin for Pastor Yardley's daughter's late-summer wedding; eyelet for another bride, loose through the waist, she wouldn't say who.

Then she got us some milk and cookies and sat down at the kitchen table, laid her head on the red plaid oilcloth, and cried her milky eyes out.

12

———————

I COULDN'T believe that they could just pack up and leave, but they did. It turned out that Mrs. Vickers was only renting the place on Ash, and had been for as long as anyone could remember, at the same cheap price as before the war because Mr. Rogers, her landlord, had a kind heart. So she had nothing to sell, nothing at all to bargain with.

The last week the twins were out of their minds at the idea of having to live with the crazy Eddyville cousins forever and wouldn't come out and play.

That's when I started following Daddy around in earnest, to have something to do and someone to take it out on. I blamed it all on him: that Reba and Sheba were leaving; that Gloria and Greta had run off in such a hurry; that I couldn't go down to Grandfather's anymore; that I was going to be left by myself for nine more years of mean Miss Matlock, nasty Miss Nelson, prudish Miss Pollard, dim Miss Dunlap, silly Miss Simpson, and the rest of them. That I was going to spend all day grinding through multiplication tables and import-exports and then come home after school to Mother, nagging and picking at me all night. Besides, I could already figure out that once I got to the pointed bra stage, she would be on my back like a bad case of sunburn.

Every morning Daddy went to the hospital while most people were still at home having their Rice Krispies. Then he went to his office over the old drugstore. Then, when he'd finished with the steady stream of rheumy, wheezing old folks who went up and down his stairs, which was supposed to be at one o'clock but never was, he walked to the hospital, stopping in to say hello at the barbershop and post office, going past Methodist and Baptist at his slow pace, counting the walk as his exercise. He always ate an apple, one of Grandfather's winesaps, which he put in his pocket in the mornings, and sometimes, if he was ahead of schedule, he stopped at the hospital canteen for a couple of cups of black coffee, which he drank standing up.

Then it was time to go by everyone's rooms and ask about their legs or heads or stomachs and look at their charts and check it all out with the dog-faced old nurse who padded after him. After that he disappeared into the closed-off part of the hospital where everyone wore masks and I couldn't follow. That was where the dying people were, the ones who couldn't afford to go off to the big specialists in St. Louis or Memphis or whose families were too callous to send them.

After rounds Daddy went back to his office one last time, to see folks in the late afternoon. Anybody who had been sent by Uncle Grady, who was still making his house calls at that time, or by Grandfather, who was working mornings with the terminal cases behind the closed doors and who might send a patient to Daddy after she'd been dismissed but still needed looking after. Someone he didn't want to put back in his brother's care.

I followed him like a trained sleuth all day long, dying of boredom as I went through his schedule (they never tell you in library books how dull it really is for spies), sneaking around the corners of downtown buildings, loafing or making up games in my head to pass the dragging time. I learned to say the alphabet backward and then timed it by the bank clock to see how fast I could do it; I made up arithmetic codes—what if 2 was worth 2 the first time you used it, and 3 the second, and 4 the third, and so on, what would 2 plus 2 plus 2 be—and dumb stuff like that. Crunching the numbers on the occasional license plate that went by, which meant adding up the numbers and if the sum was two numbers, like an 11 or a 16, then adding those, too, so the answer was always a single digit. And how fast I could do that. I had about a dozen of those games which I dreamed up to keep myself from going nuts while Reba and Sheba were crossing the river for the last time in the back seat of their old car.

And all the while Mother was thinking that I was out playing with the twins as usual because in her fog she didn't even know they were gone.

In the medical romances it was all exciting—the thrillers about spinal meningitis or brain tumors or leukemia. But when you're waiting around outside in your tennis shoes not wanting to be noticed, in Venice, Missouri, in the middle of August—when the Mississippi looks like a million tons of molasses and everybody in town is sick of kids being out of school, and money is short because people have run out of things to sell each other, and so they're down to returning Coke bottles or coat hangers to the dry cleaner's and serving up a lot of suppers of macaroni and cheese, and they've canned up their garden, and every table has a fan on it—spying is slower than waiting in line for a smallpox vaccine.

I grew tired of hoping Daddy would do something to make all the trouble I was going to worthwhile, was getting discouraged and would have given up, except that I remembered Gloria and Greta's Big Mr. Ten, and I figured that if you were going to cheat in a little town like ours, you'd have to go about your business nine times, dull as dishwater, obvious as measles, so you could do what you wanted to the tenth time. When everyone had forgotten to notice.

So out from under my mattress came my spiral, and I began to make my ı ı ı ı / marks, and sure enough, on the tenth trip, when he'd walked past the churches as usual, Daddy turned north instead of south on Ash and headed straight for Grandfather's house the back way.

Which made me think I was onto him at last. It was him and Elsie after all, and that didn't make me a bit sorry. But the more I thought about that, the more I remembered my thrill at seeing him go into Dolly Vickers's house and then how ashamed I was and how, because of all that, the twins had gone to live with their nutty kin, so I didn't get my hopes up.

I fact, it made me scared to death that maybe something was wrong with Grandfather, that he had had a heart attack, which Mother would never have bothered to pass on to me, or that Elsie had cancer, which was spreading through her whole body, and they were going to tell her today. My legs felt like rubber running down the cracked sidewalks after Daddy, not even bothering to hide myself, with him already blocks ahead down the street, not caring if Mother came charging after me, or anything else except to find out if there was trouble at Grandfather's house.

But there wasn't: either disaster or romance. Daddy went in, as apparently he did every Friday afternoon, to go over the week's cases with his father and settle up what had been done to the patient and what should be done and what there was no point in doing. During most of which I sweated my heart out in the steamy fig bush outside the window of Grandfather's office, listening to the low sound of their voices while Elsie stayed upstairs, changing the sheets on the bed or ironing her blue dresses or whatever she did all day.

After awhile I got tired of that and walked back up the street and sat down on the curb.

When Daddy found me, I asked him straight out about the twins' mother: "Isn't there anything you can do?" I was worn-out with following him and didn't even care at that point whether he had a woman or didn't. I was wishing with all my heart that Dolly Vickers had a twin who would appear and stand in for her and be her eyes.

"Sometimes there isn't," he said, and we trudged back to town in silence.

13

When I actually caught Daddy with someone, it was only by the sheerest accident, except that if I hadn't spent that first boring week snooping in vain, I wouldn't have noticed the change in his routine.

I had given up, reasoning that if you were the town's most able-bodied doctor, and they all had known your family since old Venice fell into the Mississippi, then maybe you had to wait for Mr. Century, had to go through ten times ten. Plus you would have sense enough to wait until every kid was back in school—when the weather was cooler and money was flowing again, and people were taking down their striped awnings and putting out back-to-school clothes and Big Chief tablets and preview Halloween masks, and going back about their business.

I was coming out of the victory garden, dragging along, when I saw Daddy come around the corner in his car at the time he should have been walking back to his office for the late-afternoon mop-up. It wasn't Friday, so he wasn't going to Grandfather's; besides, he was going in the opposite direction, heading down Ash on past the twins' house.

Out of reflex I started trailing him, although I didn't have a lot of confidence anymore. There would turn out to be some obvious explanation: he was getting gas in the car or his shoes needed resoling, or something on that order which I couldn't predict.

Then, as I hightailed it along, I began to get excited because he was all the way down to the end of the street before he turned the corner toward Main. It came to me all at once—in the way that you know things without knowing how you do—that it must be Uncle Grady's house he was going to, which, although I'd never been there, I knew to be as far south of our house as Grandfather's was to the north.

If I hadn't seen him turn the corner with my own eyes, I wouldn't have known Daddy had gone this way. His car had disappeared. Then, after a minute, I saw him limp around the side of an outbuilding at the back of a narrow, deep yard, turn the corner, and head for the house, negotiating the thick-sodded lawn with his cane. I ran down the alley and saw that what looked like a toolshed—on a bigger scale—or an old washhouse from the days of iron tubs in the backyard was really a shed big enough for a car, a converted garage, and there it was: two-door and black and completely invisible from the side street or Ash or Main. Which got my hopes up.

I crept through the backyard and pulled an overturned bushel basket to a low window on the far side of the pink-brick house because the glass ones on the back were a story and a half high. The amazing thing, from what I could squint and see through the sheer curtains, was the carpet on the floor. It looked to me, from my perch, as if all the floors in the whole house had this soft creamy rose-colored carpet on them. Now that doesn't mean anything these days, when no one wants carpeting anymore and spends a lot of money on hardwoods, but in those days all floors were made of wood, and at most you had a few rugs under the furniture and by the beds, so your feet wouldn't get cold in the winter, and people turned their rugs, so that one spot wouldn't get all the wear and tear. But carpeting in Venice in the early fifties meant that you had converted your furnace to natural gas, that you had a maid or at least an Electrolux.

This glimpse of the inside of my uncle's house made me curious, and therefore bold, and I decided on the spot to ring the bell and get myself inside. It might be the only chance of my lifetime to come in and look around. I didn't see how Daddy could get mad; it must be that he came down to check out his patients with Uncle Grady. After all, since the two brothers didn't speak, if there wasn't an intermediary, half the town could die in the gap left between the old doctors.

Around in the front yard, which came right up to the bottom of the front windows, I could see in without any trouble. Pressing my face up close, I looked in to what was obviously a living room—not a parlor like Grandfather's in his big two-story. There, in the middle of the room, Daddy had his arms around a man in a business suit and felt hat. He kept hugging and hugging, which looked weird, and then the man pulled the hat off and threw it across the room, and a lot of brown hair fell out. It was a woman.

At long last.

Big as life I rang the little ivory bell by the front door, remembering what I'd heard about Uncle Grady. That he was a widower, too, the same as Grandfather, but that his wife, Daddy's aunt Nina, had lived a lot longer than Marie and had been a big Methodist churchwoman. That was before my time, but Gloria and Greta could remember her because they said she used to come up to them sometimes, if she saw them on the street, and try to get them to come to Sunday School. It seemed that her main worry was not that the brothers weren't speaking, but that Daddy was raising his kids to be heathens like Grandfather. I got the idea that Aunt Nina didn't have a lot of desire to have our branch of the family anywhere near hers but that she was just doing her missionary work. The carpet must have been her doing, too, and the round flower beds dotting the sloping backyard. Those were not something an uncle would choose.

The woman in the man's suit opened the door. As she was coming toward me, I could hear her ask, "Who could this be?"

A voice that sounded like Grandfather's, only higher, said, "It's all right, Wissie."

She opened and looked down, somewhat relieved to see me, expecting, I imagine, me to go into some speech about Girl Scout cookies or collecting for Sunday missions or something. But I looked right up at her and dispelled that notion. In a loud voice, which I hoped would carry inside, I told her, "I'm Alma van der Linden. Is my daddy here?"

She looked startled. "George." She turned. "George, it's for you."

"May I come in?" I asked when she just stood there.

"Of course." She stepped back to let me through, and then held out her hand. "I'm your cousin Wisdom."

In all those years, I was thinking, how did he keep it from Mother that his cousin was a woman? "My cousin," that's how he referred to her. "My cousin, the economist at Chicago." Naturally Mother thought . . .

"How do you do?" I shook her hand. She was tall, like me, and had the most beautiful face I'd ever seen. It looked a lot like Grandfather's mother, Ann Elizabeth, the one with the high black collar and piled-up hair. The primary resemblance was the very dark, deep-set eyes and the very white skin. In fact, it sort of gave me the creeps, how much she looked like the grandmother who had got pregnant when her husband didn't believe her.

Seeing Daddy's cousin in the man's suit made me wonder suddenly if Ann Elizabeth had gone to the tobacco warehouse dressed like a man, instead of in all those long skirts and bustles and big sleeves (whatever they wore then).

75

Maybe *that* was what made Grandfather's father think less of her—her in pants—and not really a baby coming; maybe he knew all along exactly how that happened.

"What brings you here, Widget?" Daddy stood still as a statue against the back wall of the living room.

"I was messing around, missing Reba and Sheba, and then I saw you come in—" The main thing was for him not to get the idea that Mother had sent me down because then I would have been back out on the street in two seconds, and Cousin Wisdom would disappear in a cloud of smoke.

Then Daddy's uncle walked over, and I really got a look at him, and that was as much of a shock as she was. He was the spitting image of the man in the picture on Grandfather's desk, only a lot older, but the same neat pointed beard, the same starched stiff collar. He was a lot thinner than Grandfather, obviously, but he was also different in his manner. Very much of a dandy (although I didn't have that word at the time). Dapper. Polished. And I realized that the neat pruned beds and the rose carpet soft as a goose-feather mattress under my bare feet was maybe his idea after all, and not the churchgoing aunt's. He looked like someone who had gone off and made a name for himself and then come back and donated a fine new school building to the little hometown where he used to live.

The biggest shock was realizing that I'd seen him on the street dozens of times and that he had spoken to me, but I always thought he was one of those men around the barbershop who spoke to all the kids because they knew our fathers.

"This is an unexpected pleasure," he told me politely, taking my hand in his long, slender fingers. It made me wish I'd cleaned up before I left home, wished I had on my best dress and ankle socks and had brushed my hair so it didn't look like so much tan string.

"How do you do?"

"No need to be formal with us, Alma. We all know you, even if you don't know us. Don't we, Wissie?"

"We do indeed," she said graciously. "Won't you sit down?"

The house was amazingly cool and nonsticky, amazingly clean and soot-free, and I sank like a stone into the lush rose-colored couch, wild with relief. A cousin. What if it was only his cousin?

Daddy was looking at me with that storm cloud look on his face, the brows all knitted up and his mouth pressed together. It had amazed me when he walked over to a chair and sat down—because his cane didn't make a sound on the carpet.

Wissie kept looking over at him, asking him something with her face, but he kept watching me, waiting for me to get it over with and let him know what I was up to. I could see that even as she was asking me about school and all the rest of it that adults do, her eyes were scared. She was like a rabbit that spies a dog.

Having made up my mind what I was going to do, I wasn't thinking too highly of myself at that moment. But I wanted her to remember, after it was over, that I hadn't lied to her.

"We didn't know you were a woman," I said.

"Oh?" She raised her brows, like "Isn't that amazing?"

"Does Grandfather know?"

"Uncle August? But of course."

"And everybody else?"

"What do you mean?"

"In town. Except Mother and me."

She considered carefully and then explained slowly. "Neva was ahead of me in school. We didn't know one another. Her family lived in the country." She looked to Daddy for a sign.

Uncle Grady rose. "Would you care to take a turn outside?" he asked me. "I may not have the opportunity to show you around again." He came over and helped me up from the couch.

Naturally I had to say yes and get up. We went through the dining room, with him pointing out Sheraton chairs, and then into the sun porch on the back of the house, where he showed me several round end tables with plants on them, and brass boxes on legs which held more flowers, masses of them, against the glass in the sun. He said they were all petunias and his favorites and would grow anywhere you put them. That he used to have sweet peas growing up the wall on the outside, but that he didn't bother training them anymore; he was an old man.

He asked me if perhaps I would like to see his garden outside, and as I told him, "Sure," I could hear Daddy and Cousin Wisdom. Not the words, but the sound of their voices, talking together.

"These are my prizes," Uncle Grady told me, in the same cordial voice, when we were down among the round single-flower beds. I wasn't even looking where he was pointing; I was wondering why I'd been so dumb that I'd never come to this end of town before, on my own.

I wanted to ask him if he had ever met my sisters, and if he had liked it that his wife was so interested in the church, and what he really thought about the medical school story about his father and his mother. But he was not the kind of man you would dare ask things like that. He acted more friendly than Grandfather, but at the same time there was a distance you were afraid to cross. He had on a vest and dark blue tie and white shirt, as if he'd recently come from seeing patients, and his black shoes were patent leather, which I'd never seen on a man.

I imagined him holding a hymnbook and singing along in his cultivated voice, putting a five-dollar bill in the collection plate when it came around, but discreetly, taking the big brass bowl in one slender hand and slipping his big bill under a pile of little pledge envelopes. I had seen all that when I tagged along with Gloria and Greta in their church phase, and I could hear the congregation singing "Bringing in the Sheaves" in that loud, off-key church unison that tugs at your heart.

The idea of church services had come to my mind, thinking about Daddy and Cousin Wissie. Because I had an image of the vast exodus of half the town from their old houses up and down Ash and Main and First pouring out into the streets in their hats and gloves and good handbags taken out of tissue paper, and good wing tips polished to a military gloss, the men with handkerchiefs in their breast pockets— all standing with shoulders touching and hymnals shared— while the other half of town had empty houses in which to do whatever it was they weren't able to do all week long.

I decided that was the reason Grandfather was a heathen because as a little boy he had wanted to stick around to see what took place on Sunday morning when his father was off at a meeting of the Reformed Church (which now meets in the funeral home, because they don't have a building), and his mother was with her Society of Friends (who take turns gathering in the parlors of members).

Maybe Grandfather, when he was the boy August, found out that one of them hadn't gone to services after all, which would be enough to make a nonbeliever out of you.

"This is a nice garden," I told Uncle Grady.

But he could see that I was not interested, was not in the mood to tell a rose bush from a radish, so he took my hand again and led me back toward the house.

"I understand my brother sets great store by you."

"Thank you, sir."

"A man sets great store by a daughter," he continued. "Whether his own or his son's." And with that he led me in the back way so that we came again into the sun porch with its bright, cool air. "My late wife used to sit there," he said, being sure his voice carried into the next room, "and watch for birds." He pointed to a wicker couch with creamy chintz cushions.

"I'm sorry," I told him, meaning that she'd died. But I don't know if he got the idea or not; he, too, was listening to the sudden silence from the living room and wondering what to do with me next. "Perhaps a glass of lemonade would be in order after the muggy heat outside," he proposed.

I said that would be nice and charged ahead through the dining room to see what was going on. Daddy and Cousin Wissie were both standing, looking at the plates in the china cabinet, or pretending to. Their backs were to the center of the room, but they cut their eyes in my direction when I came in.

"There she is," Cousin Wisdom said. She had got out of her man's coat, had loosened her shirt to where it looked like a blouse, brushed her hair, and put on deep red lipstick.

"How did you get here?" I asked her straight out, figuring that anything I didn't ask now I would never know.

She looked startled, turned to Daddy, then back to me. "Your uncle met me in St. Louis," she said. But she kept a slight worried line between her deep-set eyes at my asking it.

Daddy kept on looking at the china plates.

He ought to have figured that I was thinking that Uncle Grady's car was nowhere to be seen, that its stall had been cleared so Daddy could slip his black Ford in its place.

"Your father tells me that Dolly Vickers moved her girls to Eddyville."

"She's going blind," I told her, as if it wasn't important.

"That's too bad."

"Her sister's going to put her in the poorhouse." I was not going to let her off with her little crumb of sympathy.

"I doubt that. Bessie was always foolish but never mean." She looked at Daddy, and they smiled—at some shared time long ago, when people named Dolly had sisters named Bessie

80

and when they didn't have this problem of some smart-aleck kid who was going to ruin their lives for them.

It was Daddy's smile that finished him off with me, the same one I'd seen at Mrs. Vickers's—where his eyebrows lifted and his mouth opened and a nice good sound came out—and it reminded me all over again of the fact that I had never seen him do that at Marie's house, our house, not once, not ever. Anywhere else he probably smiled all the time: at the barbershop and the post office, to cheer up all his wheezing, limping, toothless, diseased old patients, and his kid patients with whooping cough and red measles, and all the twins in the county, one of whom had a little scar behind her ear. Probably he smiled all day at all of them. But his daughter Alma, the afterthought, the tag end of the family, who had been darting around corners, peeking across hallways, slipping down side streets, tracking him for more than a week (which felt like most of my life), had got to see only two real smiles face-to-face in nine whole years.

I wondered if he ever went to see Wissie in Chicago or if the times he got away to St. Louis for a medical meeting (with Mother at home carrying on and calling him long distance) this woman had met him there. Both of them had the same name, so there wouldn't be a problem checking into a room—and I was proud of myself for figuring that out. I imagined them in a fancy deep red hotel in a huge city with airports and train stations and bus stations for easy going and coming. Daddy hugging her the way I had seen them through the window, in one of the beautiful scarlet rooms.

For years hadn't he gone with his father to meetings? Maybe Grandfather knew all about his son and Wissie. Maybe the whole town knew about them. Maybe they'd been sweethearts when Wissie was in Venice High, and Dolly and her sister, Bessie, and all their friends knew. Maudie's mom and Jimmy's dad, and Audrey, the bucktoothed librarian, who limited my books, all of them. Every snoop at Methodist and prude at Baptist—everyone except my mother. And me.

We sat around, and I drank a glass of pink lemonade, with a sprig of mint in it and four completely clear ice cubes, which Uncle Grady called a Shirley Temple. The glass was tall and narrow and had green vines etched on it. I remember because I looked at it a lot.

Uncle Grady sat with one knee crossed over the other, and I could see that he had some sort of striped garter thing on his shins, which held his navy socks up.

"Now you'll speak to me when I pass you on the street perhaps," he said affably.

"Yes, sir."

"Did your grandfather, my august brother"—he smiled at his joke—"ever tell you how we got into the business of doctoring the town?"

"No, sir."

"They cut down all our trees. We once owned a sixth of the state's forests, of which not so much as a hickory remains."

I couldn't think of anything to say because I didn't know if he was glad or sorry or only teasing me.

Cousin Wisdom rattled her ice in a relaxed way. "I thought you got into it because there wasn't an animal left on four legs in three states that hadn't been skinned. That's the story I heard." She laughed.

"That, too."

"One day," she told Uncle Grady, "the river will change its course, and then your last excuse for settling in these parts will have disappeared."

"We will have, too, my dear, by that time."

During this conversation Daddy tapped his hand on his good leg, as tongue-tied as I was. I tried to imagine what he would be saying to them if I wasn't there.

"It's my pleasure," Uncle Grady continued, as if I had come just to talk to him, "to get your father down for an occasional sub rosa visit from time to time, all, to be sure, in the line of duty, having to do with certain infirm members of the community whose care we share. It's good for an old man to have company. Perhaps you'll come again yourself?"

"I guess my grandfather wouldn't like that." I didn't want to lie to him either.

"No, doubtless not." He considered his glass. "Best not to tell him perhaps." He looked at me inquiringly.

Which I decided was as near as any of them could come right out to telling me to keep my mouth shut.

"Have you other playmates to replace the Vickers?" Cousin Wissie asked. She was chewing on a stalk of mint, considering. I thought she was probably going to come up with some lie to tell me, that she had a husband and six kids or something or how she and Daddy had grown up like brother and sister.

But she didn't. When I shook my head, she said mildly, "I'm going to change out of my travel clothes." As if every woman went down the highway disguised in a man's suit with a wide-brimmed felt hat. "If you'll excuse me."

After she was gone, the men studied the carpet. Then Uncle Grady asked me where I was in school and said how they'd had McGuffey Readers in his day and how that was what he called learning. Which gave him a chance to get up and escort me over to the glass-front bookcase on the wall next to the china cabinet. He took down the *Fourth Reader*, which I recognized naturally from Grandfather's, and began to flip the pages in the same way. Then, finding something he liked, he began to declaim:

> The boy stood on the burning deck,
> Whence all but he had fled,
> The flame that lit the battle's wreck
> Shone round him o'er the dead.

"Well, rather gloomy for such a nice day. Let me see. Ah, this seems to me in order:

Meddlesome Matty

Oh, how one ugly trick has spoiled
The sweetest and the best!
Matilda, though a pleasant child,
One grievous fault possessed,
Which, like a cloud before the skies,
Hid all her better qualities.

"Well, enough moral lessons for the day."

I told him I knew the Readers, and seeing that this was a better subject than the flower beds, he showed me his complete set of twenty-five Tarzan books, which he said Daddy had come down to his house and read when he was my age.

Daddy perked up at that and came over and pulled out one of them (*Tarzan and the Jewels of Opar*) and read a line from it: "But now that Lady Greystoke had disappeared, though he still looked toward the east for hope, his chances were lessened, and another, subsidiary design completely dashed." He handed the book back to Uncle Grady. "One a week, wasn't it?"

"It took you six months."

That made me happy and sad at the same time, to think of Daddy as a little boy slipping down the street from Marie's house to the forbidden uncle's to read these books, which were bound to be, because all books for children were, the story of how some kid runs away from bad times at home.

I made up my mind then and there to read all the Tarzan books (which had taken Daddy six months) in the week and a half that was left of summer, imagining him a kid like me, running down to Uncle Grady's to hunt the elusive Lady Greystoke.

Then Cousin Wisdom came back in the room in a bright red dress and heels.

Daddy took a step toward her and then remembered me.

"How nice you look, dear," Uncle Grady said.

"Shouldn't you be on your way, George?" she asked Daddy. "Won't your patients be impatient?" And she laughed as the words came out.

"The damage is done," he said lightly, but it was me he was looking at as he said it.

"Not at all." She laid her hand on my shoulder. "It was time Alma got to know the rest of the family. Isn't that right?" She was asking me a question.

"Come on, miss," Daddy said. "Let's go. I'll drop you by home." He moved toward the front door.

Wissie touched him quickly and then stepped away, slipping her hand through her father's arm. "Should you—"

"No," he answered. "Leave well enough alone."

"I'd rather walk," I told him, breaking away from them all. "Thank you for the lemonade. Uncle Grady."

"You're welcome, my dear."

"Alma—"

"Wait—"

But I ran across the soft carpeting and out the door, not listening as they tried to call me back.

I ran all the way up Main without stopping, without climbing up on the low wall to play trapeze or counting the cracks in the broken walk, straight up the street and into our house. I ran as if someone were on my heels because I knew if I didn't do it right then, I never would.

"Mother, Mother." I hollered for her even as I found her where she always was, rummaging in the junky closet.

"Listen to me," she began, having just discovered that the twins had been gone for weeks.

"I saw her." I cut the lecture short.

"What?" She sank down on the side of the bed.

"I saw Daddy's woman. I know who she is."

14

U P the road from here two rivers come together in what is called the confluence. One is the wide and powerful Ohio, which begins its life in the merging of the Allegheny and the Monongahela; the other is the narrower Mississippi, a winding creek swollen by the Missouri, which stretches back to cold, clear Lake Itasca in Minnesota. You can sit cantilevered on the bridge at Cairo, Illinois, and watch their waters converge, the deep gray-blue of the Mississippi swirling into the flat brown conformity of the Ohio.

I used to think, in geography classes in Venice Public, that the Ohio got cheated not being known as the river which continues to New Orleans; now, grown, I imagine the Mississippi bitter that the whole turgid stretch of commerce from their joining to the Gulf has to bear its name. It, which was at the start a clear stream, now a wide and muddy highway plunging headlong to the sea.

That's how I feel about my life: that from the afternoon I ran up Main to our house from Uncle Grady's, the whole of me has gone by a lesser name.

15

THINGS went as could be expected: Mother made Daddy's life hell; he quit speaking to me.

On Sundays, at Grandfather's, when he couldn't get out of it, Daddy would address a comment toward my side of the table. But that was it. At home in the mornings he limped past me without a word, leaving me to my import-exports and math homework, heading for the respite of his office above the old drugstore to winnow out his waiting room.

I didn't care. I'd put in nine years of it with no help from him; he could put in nine with no help from me. By that time I'd be out of Venice High and have figured out how to get along on my own.

(Which I did, jumping from the frying pan to the fire—but I didn't see that at the time.)

By agreement Mother confined her torments to Daddy. For me, no more sleeping half the night cramped among Gloria and Greta's abandoned sandals on the closet floor, or hanging from my heels over the smoldering coals, or all the other torments of my early life. The first time after the trip to Uncle Grady's that she jerked my arm to shove me upstairs so she could get on with her accusations, I pulled loose and told her I was going outside to play run sheep run.

From that time on, whenever things were heating up to a pitch and Mother was screaming at him and he was clumping around on the hardwood floor, I would head out to the library, to battle my old enemy.

Please, I would request, in my best fourth-grade voice, I was doing a report on architecture for mean Miss Matlock, and could I check out *The Fountainhead*? Or I was doing a theme on the Civil War and how about *Gone with the Wind*? Audrey would give me her standard lecture on morals, the saliva oozing out between her buckteeth (because she'd read the good parts herself already), and so I'd shrug and check out the tenth *Nancy Drew* or the fifth *Bobbsey Twins*, and get permission to take down the atlas to copy out the rivers of Brazil for geography. Then, when she was off chewing out the boys who came in the library to look up dirty words in the dictionary or illustrations in anatomy books, I'd slip something big and juicy from the adult fiction rack under my sweater and head home. (*Peyton Place* must have been in that era, and those big, long Samuel Shellabarger novels.)

Back home I'd read until Mother had worn herself out and gone to bed and Daddy was in the kitchen waiting for his bedtime pot to boil.

This state of affairs dragged on through Venice Public with the teachers deciding I was a brain and calling on Alma whenever they wanted to move the class from long division to fractions or from the Lower Volta to the Upper Nile, whatever was the topic of the day.

Then, miraculously, I got to Venice High at last and blossomed like a rose. Everything I had was sticking out and riding up and rotating from side to side, and I played it for all it was worth. (It was exactly like developing overnight into twins: there was the old me, inside, and then this new me that the boys couldn't take their eyes off.)

Venice is laid out on the Mississippi like an open church fan, if you imagine the wide spread of it as the levee, which curves east and then north as the river bends, the downtown as the palm fronds, the residential area as the triumphal procession on donkeys, with Main Street the writing which proclaims JESUS COMES, and, where the fan closes into a fist of splints, the southern tip of the town peters out into blacks and rentals.

By the spring of High Tenth I was walking the entire length of it every day, starting below the borrow pit to the north where Reba and Sheba and I had scaled and fried the croppie, ending at the south end by our best blue hole.

I took my time sashaying in my thin spring skirts, past the men swathed in towels in the barbershop; by the tables of black-haired, waxy bankers and pink porcine accountants having cherry Cokes in the new drugstore. Moseyed all the way east to the Flood Control Building, to smile at the bunch of decrepit old men without teeth, all spitting tobacco juice into tin cans which had held worms when they were young, wanting the sight of me to reach fifty years into their pants and make a stir.

Inevitably one of the teachers, silly Miss Simpson in science, sent me to the principal's office.

This was not for making a disturbance, but for making a spectacle. My crime was that now that everyone was finally into pointed bras, all of them, even the stick-thin ones with no behind at all, I was out of mine. As soon as I got to school in the mornings, in the girls' room I would unhook my Maidenform in the back and go through the contortions of slipping first one strap and then the other out the armholes of my blouse, over one elbow at a time, sticking the whole thing in my purse. Gambling on the fact that nobody was going to let herself deal with the fact that the boys were getting all worked up watching me bounce whenever I went to the board or stood to answer a question.

"Alma." Miss Simpson called me to the front, her face red to the roots of her blue hair. "I'll have to send you to the principal's office."

"Yes, ma'am."

Louis LeCroix was twenty-nine years old and the husband of the cranky librarian I hated. How could I have resisted? How could I have kept from prancing into his office, my bra still in my bag, sitting down with my skirt hiked halfway up my thighs and waiting for something to happen? I couldn't.

(Later I made excuses for myself that it was all Audrey's fault, her and her teeth and her snippy ways. If she'd let me read what I wanted, would I have stolen her hateful husband? Probably I would. Probably by then the whole thing was already in motion and all of us caught in the undertow.)

"Alma?"

"Yes, sir."

"Miss Simpson sent you, I believe."

"Yes, sir."

"Do you know why you're here?"

"No, sir."

"I think you do."

I didn't bother to answer.

"I'm going to give you a warning this time, Alma. Go home and put some clothes on. Next time I won't be as lenient."

He came around the desk and perched on the side of it, and the way he was sitting I knew he was interested. I could no more have kept from egging him on at that point than the river could stop rolling.

I shifted so that I jiggled, and I crossed my legs, and then with both hands I lifted my smooth jelly-roll hair and sort of fanned my neck, making sure my arms stayed raised. (My best Marilyn Monroe imitation.) "Just because everyone else has to wear cheaters—"

"In my school," he said, "we don't put up with trouble-makers."

"Since when is Venice High *your* school?"

"Since I took this job."

"What if I don't?"

"Then you can count on two hours an afternoon in detention hall."

That made me sit up straight and put my arms down. Recess was over. Cooped up inside the old brick building until almost dark every day was not my idea of how to spend the spring. Gone would be my walk, fanning out from one end of town to the other. I had thought detention hall was something which had been invented to scare football players into attending class because they knew they'd be dropped from the team if they missed spring practice. I didn't even know where detention hall was or anybody who'd ever had to stay in.

"Okay," I said promptly, forgetting flirting with the principal.

And that was the end of it as far as I was concerned, not knowing that for Louis it had just begun.

Then, about a week later, there he was, standing in the hall when I went into silly Miss Simpson's class. He nodded as I went by, and I thought he'd come to see for himself if I was strapped in nice and tight so he could decide he'd been a good, firm bully. He and Audrey were made for each other, I thought, two of a kind, birds of a feather. Both snots.

About a couple of days after that—when the *Gazette* was running pictures of Missouri's largest dogwood trees, and I was doing my first story for the school paper, the *Gondola*, entitled "Detention Hall: Does it Deter?"—there came a note from the principal's office to the study hall teacher stating that Alma had been made an aide.

"I like someone who can take advice," Louis told me.

He was very muscled, the kind of man you know works out at home with weights. If you'd seen him then you'd have assumed he was the coach. He wore white shirts and nice ties but no jackets, so that you could see the bulge of his biceps and the cords in his neck. (In that respect, to be fair, I guess we were a couple of exhibitionists from the start.) He had thick, soft lips, and his tongue darted in and out when he talked, as if he were keeping count of the words.

He began to show up everywhere. He hovered at the corner of the schoolyard and nodded as I went by. If I was with Andy and Buddy, which I was all the time, he grilled me about them later. When I really started going with Buddy, necking up a storm every night, coming to class in the morning with glazed eyes and mouth marks, Louis was waiting. During my free period he called me into his office and interrogated me: was I cheapening myself, was I getting a bad reputation, didn't I know that nothing went on in a town like this that wasn't common knowledge?

To torment him, I let Buddy kiss me in the halls, leaning up close to him by the lockers until he squirmed and turned red. I took Buddy's class ring and wore it around my neck, letting it hang between my breasts on a chain, where I could lift it out and drop it back when I was sure Louis was in his doorway watching.

He appeared on the streets when I strolled the length of town (safe because Buddy was at football practice), pretending to be headed for a haircut or to pick up a prescription for his miserable wife.

We stood and talked, very innocent, the high school principal chatting with a student, as I shifted my weight from one foot to the other, to move my hips around.

I stood as close to him as I could decently get and said, "Hello, Mr. LeCroix."

"How are you, Alma?" he always asked, very formal. "Where's your friend?"

"He's at practice."

"I see."

"He has to be in bed weeknights at nine, can you

imagine?" I looked up at him, bent my knees slightly so as not to be too tall, and lifted my jelly-roll hair.

"You ought to take it easy, Alma."

"Jealous?" That was the cue to pull the ring out of its valley and play with it and then drop it out of sight again.

"Don't do that."

Then I turned and sauntered away, slowly, so he could watch the rear action as I headed for the old men with the plug tobacco and the dirty thoughts on the river edge of town.

16

I F I got into the situation with Louis without knowing what I was doing, I got into journalism by an even more accidental route.

Originally, I think, it grew out of feeling bad about Mrs. Vickers, wishing I'd done even one thing nice for her while I had the chance.

What happened was I took up for a teacher. It was dim Miss Dunlap, who had us for junior English, was blind as a bat, should have had a Seeing Eye dog, a tin cup, and pencils, but it was her last year to teach; she was the age of retirement, and none of the kids, not even the scabbiest and most truculent, had any desire to rat on her. For one thing it was a lark, a big game, to tell about the story you'd done a report on for Dunlap and the grade you'd gotten. (Winner to date was Judy, who turned in a paper on "The Telltale Fart" by Eager Alien Foe and got an A on it.)

I was no better than the rest, and it was the middle of spring term and we all had to give her a book review. Mine was on *The Foresight Saga* by Saen Gaelsworthy, but the trouble was that none of the kids knew the original, so it was going to be a waste. I had, in fact, read the whole set of Galsworthy, wept my heart out for Irene, loved/hated

Soames, who I suppose was/is all of our fathers, including the author's, so what's new? Anyway I turned it in, and the standard procedure from Dunlap was this: she had, as the blind do, incredible ears and managed to pick up from other teachers exactly where you stood in school, so she gave you, since she couldn't see but the dimmest outline of what you wrote, exactly the grade you were used to.

Therefore, I, as the brain, should have got my A; but on the other hand, the teachers would also have complained that I wasn't taking my work seriously, was messing around.

What I got back on my paper was this:

B+

Alma, you are capable of better work than this. You might have explored in detail what it signified for women in Galsworthy's time that Soames chose to save his child over his wife and that the author also made credible the thesis of "raping" a wife. Are these conflicting views? Why? Why not?

She must have squinted through a magnifying glass to see what novel I'd picked and known my report would be sloppy at best. Maybe she'd even heard me talking about it. It made me sick at myself that she was actually getting to the heart of the story when I'd handed her a big bunch of Mickey Mouse.

You have to imagine her because she was about four feet tall. Not really, but she was one of those very short, square women who, on Sundays, wear huge floppy hats with flowers and cherries and big-print dresses with white ruffles at the neck, so the effect is of a toad all dressed up. And because of her eyesight, she walked along looking at the ground, so her big, humped shoulders seemed higher than her head, which preceded her like a turtle's, sticking way out and craning around on a short, rubbery neck. Something out of *The Wind in the Willows*.

The exact sort of teacher that students step all over in their haste to get out of school and grow up to be something, anything, besides that teacher.

Buddy had stayed in town after he graduated and was working at Andy's daddy's garage, waiting for me to get out or at least using me as a reason to stay around so he wouldn't have to go to college, which his parents thought he ought to, because Andy's parents didn't see any point in throwing good money after bad, and they were after him to open a Western Auto, which Venice didn't have, and make something of himself.

And Louis was beginning to close in on me, always watching from his doorway, always popping up in the school parking lot or downtown on the street or even at the library to pick up Audrey if I happened to be there midweek.

So at that time I really didn't have anyone. Most of us who had dated seniors were in the same boat; we couldn't go out with anybody else because they were still around, but in fact there was nobody at school to walk you to class or meet by the lockers. A lot of girls began to see someone else, even sometimes a tenth grader on the sly. We could see, Judy and Patsy and the rest of us, that by the time we were seniors ourselves, we'd either be running off, the way Greta had, or feeling like two-year widows by the ripe old age of almost eighteen.

Dim Miss Dunlap gave me something to do with myself, or that was my excuse at the time.

One afternoon after school I followed her home, which turned out to be on Ash, about four blocks past the Vickers place. Which reminded me of all that and made me realize that her blindness had probably gotten to me because of the twins' mother. Maybe I was paying her back for that time we'd done the stupid snooping.

I knocked on Miss Dunlap's door, and she answered, her rubbery neck craning up in the direction of my head, the way an animal locates, by instinct or sound waves. "Yes, dear?" she said.

"It's Alma, Miss Dunlap."

"So I see, dear, won't you come in?" And she turned and led me into a dim room with the Tiffany lamps and lace armrests that you'd expect, but lined with more books than I'd ever seen in my life. Including, on two low shelves plain as day, the complete set of Tarzan books, all of them, in the same exact binding that Uncle Grady had. Plus every other title I'd ever heard of, and many that I hadn't and that I was sure weren't even in the card catalog of Audrey's miserable library. The cases were all old and fit together like parquet puzzles but didn't have glass fronts. (Perhaps they had been removed because they got dusty or cloudy and made seeing the spines harder.)

"May I fix you something, dear?" She settled herself in a rocker, patting the arms to place it precisely.

"No, ma'am. I came to ask a favor."

"I hope you were not too disappointed in your grade. A student of your capabilities."

I wanted to cry right then and there, and a lump the size of a footstool stuck in my throat. "No, that isn't why I came."

"Well, dear, what can I do for you?" She rocked back and forth, her short legs touching the floor with a tap and then sailing up in the air. A midget on a Ferris wheel.

"You see, Miss Dunlap." I launched into my prepared speech. "I need a recommendation for a summer job. I'm trying to get one on the paper, I don't mean the *Gondola* but the *Gazette*, because I want to be a writer when I grow up, and it would be a lot of help if I had some experience on the newspaper. But there isn't anyone to give me a reference because my father is against my taking a summer job, I mean working in the drugstore or something like that, as he thinks that would make him look bad. But I was thinking that if I did something for you, in the way of being a student aide or something, then you could give me a letter. Besides, the editor of the paper, Mr. Rogers, said that the best recommendation I could get would be from an English teacher because lots of people who apply to the paper can't put a decent sentence together."

Miss Dunlap rocked back and forth and listened intently. I'm sure she was trying to figure out what I was up to, if I was going to pull some great big joke on her and make a further fool out of her—because I was convinced by that time that she knew full well what was going on.

"What did you have in mind, Alma?" And the turtle's neck came craning out of the toad's body in my direction. She looked frightened, although she tried to cover it with her matter-of-fact tone.

"I'd like to be your grader. I know it's your last semester, so you might not want to give that up, but on the other hand, you might be tired of it after all these years. . . ."

Her eyes, the whites dense as gristle, got wet, and she stopped rocking. "Describe how you would accomplish this."

So I told her I would read the first two or three papers to her and tell her what I thought and the comments I would put on them and the grade I would give, and then, if she was satisfied, I would do that for the rest of the year. In return, she would write a letter for me to the *Gazette*. She agreed, and I extracted a promise from her that our arrangement was to be a secret, as far as the school was concerned, as it wasn't proper for some teachers to have helpers and not others. Did she understand?

I think she did. Completely.

Which is what I did. Plus checking out her Tarzan books two at a time until I'd read all those Audrey didn't have, and then started on whatever shelf looked the least familiar and the most amazing. I would write the title down on a sheet of paper and leave it on top of the remaining books on that shelf and then check it off when I returned it. We were very businesslike, dim Miss Dunlap and I.

The first thing I did, to warn the kids, was to spread the word that she had a brother in St. Louis who knew a famous doctor who had discovered a cure for glaucoma and that she'd been up there for surgery. Now rumors like that make the rounds in five minutes in little towns, and then they come right back because ten people know that Miss Dunlap doesn't have a brother, and ten others that there isn't such a cure. That if there were, then famous people would have had it first, celebrities, and we'd have already heard about it. (That is one of the main things I remember from those days: the thesis that if it exists, you already know about it, so that if you don't, then it doesn't. A sophistry which precludes the burden ever to learn anything new or worry that there might be knowledge out there somewhere that you were missing out on.)

That was fine with me; I just wanted to plant a suspicion before we turned in our next papers to Miss Dunlap, this time the assignment being to write about our favorite new short story, one by an author we hadn't read before. The premise itself shows how far out of it English teachers were, but we were used to that by High Junior, so the actual words went in one ear and out the other. People began to pass around a library copy of *Great Modern Short Stories* and outdo each other with takeoffs. But it was spring and blanket party time, and no one gave it a lot of energy. There was "The Ransom of Red Meat" and "The Red Phony" and "The Toes of Kilimanjaro," stuff like that, nothing special. None of the originals of which anyone had read, naturally, so it was hard to satirize the unknown.

When Miss Dunlap had collected the papers, I went to her house (a roundabout way) and read her the titles, the real ones, that is, and then I read her manufactured versions of what the kids might have written, if they were typical dumb juniors, posturing and unoriginal, but, naturally, not the slop that was really there. (Such as: "This story is an example of the adventure genre, which attempts to show mankind pitting itself against the forces of nature.") Then I explained that I was going to give the paper a C (nobody failed English in Venice High, student or teacher, who could see light and hold a pencil) and the comment I was going to write: "You could be specific, Judy, as to how the plot demonstrates your thesis." Meaning, of course, that she might have read the story.

Miss Dunlap was clearly relieved and pleased and fixed a tea tray for us, with a sort of rich dark plum pudding drenched in hard liquor, saved from God knows how many decades in little cake tins in her pantry. I hadn't so much as tasted a beer in my life at that time, so here we were, the dumb and the blind, getting tipsy on plum cake in this almost dark room every week when papers were due. With her rocking back and forth and me reading aloud made-up sentences which sounded stupid but credible, leaving out the shit, and then my proposed comments and grades.

When she passed out the first set, the kids nearly fell out of their chairs. Because what I had *really* scrawled in big old-lady writing across their pages was:

Who do you think you're fooling with this drivel?
How have you got this far in school without the ability to read and write?
I'd expect better work than this from fourth-grade students.
I do not think this original work, Patsy; don't make me have to investigate your sources, or you will write the next one at your desk.

The kids were outraged, but whom could they tell? Not their parents because then they'd have to show the papers.

And certainly not the principal or the other teachers because then they'd know the students were smarting off to poor old Dunlap.

So they were stuck with it. And for the remaining month and a half you would see juniors at Venice High reading the prefaces to novels that had never been checked out of the library before, synopses in literature books, and any other material they could find to tell them what a book said—anything they could locate, short of reading the work themselves. And even, for their final report, on themes in contemporary American novels, they would sometimes read two pages of the actual text (first and last, not a bad idea, actually).

I gave them all a B+ on the final paper. Even the drones who had never seen a B in their eleven years; even the grinds who had all As back to conduct in Low First. In my disguise as dim Ida Dunlap I was the great equalizer.

Which didn't make me want to be a teacher—lest you think that what's coming next is Alama, in her voluminous skirts, thick, white, rolled-down socks, penny loafers, and pageboy bleached out with lemon juice, deciding to become vapid Miss van der Linden. Far from it. It did, however, make me think twice about what I'd told her about my aims in life. After all, I'd constructed all the parts in our little play, and it would have been nice to get full credit on the program.

17

T H E editor of the paper, Mr. Rogers, was apparently amazed to receive a letter from his old English teacher, whom he knew to be nearly blind, recommending his neighbor's daughter for a summer job with the *Gazette*. A weekly, it had a three-person staff in those days: him, his managing editor, and the woman who did the features. To his credit, he decided that for the space of three months he could afford to send me out to collect ads, so that I ended up with a job after all. Which is how, rather by the back door, I first got started with the paper. Hydrangea Pickens, the feature writer, my predecessor, liked having me around so she could complain about how much harder she worked than the men and how if the president of the United States of America was shot and she witnessed it herself, it would end up on the society page.

Making the rounds of town with a legitimate purpose was a lot of fun, and I picked up a lot of information besides.

One benefit was that I got to know Maudie, Gloria and Greta's old friend, the one they were always spending the night with to build up their alibis. She had married Jimmy Cox by then, but they weren't yet running the Mom & Pop Café. She was still working for her mom's beauty shop, and he was helping out at his dad's barbershop. When I came in to pressure her mom into running a special back-to-school ad for permanent waves, we visited about the old days.

I liked her from the start; she was one of those Technicolor people, with carrot hair and freckles, bright pink cheeks and chin, cherry lips, and ceramic green eyes, that other girls, my sisters included, always described as mousy.

"I sure envied them," she told me.

"They took advantage of you."

"I got a lot out of it. Some of their clothes for one thing. I never saw anybody dress the way they did."

"I wore Gloria's hand-me-downs until I got out of Venice Public." I laughed at the idea of my sisters dressing the town. "Where did they get all that?"

The topic interested me a lot, because I could remember their closet crammed with clothes, really good stuff, whereas everything I put on my back came from the Sears, Roebuck catalog because that's where Mother ordered hers from. Boxes would arrive, COD, with the jumper or blouse or sweater that she'd let me fill out the order blank and send off for, but it would, naturally, never look the way it did in pictures. Especially as the clothes were made for someone more short-waisted and short-legged than I was. Besides which, the sizing was not consistent; if the top fit, then the bottom was too big, the skirt or pants, or the other way around. Which meant that most of what I ordered Mother kept because she was a smaller woman and didn't mind squeezing into anything or taking it up or pinning over a waistband—because Mother liked anything that came in a box through the mail addressed to her.

From Givens Better Dresses," Maudie said.

"Those clothes cost a mint."

"Your daddy is a rich man."

"Daddy? That's the first I ever heard about it."

"Ask the bank."

"From Givens? Really?"

When I got my first paycheck ($64.50 a month, part-time wages) from Mr. Rogers, I decided to give Maudie's story a try, figuring that I didn't have anything to lose; the atmosphere was so tense between Daddy and me it couldn't get any worse. If they did let me charge, fine; if not, I had my check.

So I sauntered into Givens and looked around at the racks, and then tried on a swirling black poodle skirt and pink Ship 'n Shore shirt which went with it. "May I take these out on approval?" I asked Mrs. Givens. "Charge them to my dad?"

"Looks cute on you, honey," she said.

At first I was cautious, taking only one or two things a month, things that were never going to arrive from Sears, Roebuck. But there was never any trouble. She must have sent Daddy the bills; he must have paid them.

In addition, Mrs. Givens seemed to know exactly what the traffic would bear. I remember a Christmas dress my senior year, in fire engine red with drop shoulders, that I coveted a lot and thought I could wear over the holidays when I'd be with Buddy again, but she steered me away from it. "A mite much," she said. "Let me show you this little number over here."

That summer, when I worked for the paper, I began a diary, a new one that was going to be different from the usual sort, which was primarily about silly stuff. This would be more literary. My first and only entry reads:

It took five men to discover the whole of what we know today as the Mississippi: the Spaniard Alonso de Piñeda in 1519, his countryman Hernando de Soto in 1541, the French explorers Jacques Marquette and Louis Jolliet, and the Sieur de la Salle roughly 150 years later.

I hope there aren't similar long, dry spells between men in my life.

Which was my idea of serious stuff in those days.

I saved that one attempt. I've got it, still, in the same place where I'm keeping this manuscript. That's because Louis reads everything he can get his hands on at home, everything in my desk and purse and every scrap that comes in the mail. All my writing is here at the paper, stuffed in big Manila envelopes in the Old News Stories file, under *D* for "Dunlap"; there is a lot of legitimate copy there, all of which I wrote, back when she died and I saw to it that the County Historical Museum got all her books because I wasn't about to let them end up in Audrey's crummy public library.

I've wished a million times that I'd kept that diary for the same reason that I'm writing this: because what stands out later is not what was important to you at the time. Setting it down is a salvage operation to keep your life from disappearing totally through the blurred vision of hindsight.

One example of what I mean: my senior year, spring, I won the state writing contest with an essay on who should go to college. I won, no doubt, because I was the only student who said not everybody should, which was not the fashion in those days. I've lost my copy of the essay, if I ever had one, but I remember I quoted the man who said he was starting a college for men to learn, not boys to play. (I remember, also, using "he" throughout to refer to student, but that was par, for 1959.) That must have been the big event of my life at the time. Surely it was; I remember a discussion at the *Gazette* as to whether putting my picture on the front page would be a conflict of interest since I'd worked for them the previous summer and Mr. Rogers deciding it was okay.

But now, when I strain to do justice to those years, all I can recall is Louis, everywhere, biding his time.

18

A T the end of that first summer on the paper Grandfather died.

Hydrangea Pickens was the way I heard. "What a shame," she said, catching me on the street. "I'd write the obit, but you know where it would turn up."

I had finished the last ad, and no one had called me.

"Didn't you know? He died in his sleep this morning, they said."

Which was another good thing the job on the *Gazette* had done for me: I'd spent most of the summer heading up Main once a week, getting back in touch with Grandfather again.

That was because when Mr. Rogers called to see if I wanted the job that Miss Dunlap had written him about, he asked me if I could type. A fair question, as every female except me in Venice High had had at least two semesters of business skills. "Sure," I lied, picking a figure I'd heard. "Eighty wpm."

On the theory that anything can be learned from a book, I got myself to the library and amazed Audrey by checking out *Typing for Beginners*. It was one of those books with pictures of which fingers go on which keys, and I practiced all week on the bedspread upstairs, and then took the book with me to Sunday supper, remembering the old Underwood in Grandfather's office.

"I have a job this summer," I told him, "on the paper." I let that amazing fact sink in. "One of the requirements is typing skill. I wonder if I could practice on your typewriter? Until I get good enough?"

Naturally he said yes, and said it when my parents were in the parlor with the visitors.

It had been a lot of years since Mother came screaming down after me, and I hadn't tried to come back on my own when I could have—simply because once I got to Venice High, I'd tried to forget as much of that bad early time as I could.

Now it seemed a natural thing to do, to walk down every afternoon while he took his nap and practice "The quick gray fox jumps over the lazy brown dog."

Then, when I'd got a couple of keys in my head and fingers, I'd quit for the day. The alphabet had twenty-six letters; anyone should be able to type like the wind in thirteen days, was my reasoning. Then I'd thank Elsie, who would be in one of her starched blue dresses, canning away, mostly tomato relish and damson preserves—her plump white hands busy wiping away the thick red juices oozing down the sides of Mason jars topped with crusts of cooling paraffin—and hope that Grandfather would hear me.

Sometimes he'd come out, in a long white nightshirt, and ask me how it was going, forgetting that he should be dressed or exactly who I was in the family, as he would wake up groggy and back in some other generation and mistake me for someone else. "Now, then, you're George's girl, aren't you?" he asked once, which made Elsie turn her face away.

It felt good to get back into his life, even if he wasn't quite there himself, and to remember those early afternoons when he'd told me about his Reformed father and Quaker mother and the circumstances of his birth. If he'd died a year sooner, I know it would have left me with a lot more grief and guilt.

When I left Hydrangea, I went straight down Main to find Mother putting on a heavy black crepe dress that came down to her ankles and had self buttons and some kind of big metal buckle at the waist. She had on a lot of powder and had twisted her hair tight into a bun, skinning it back from her face, and there was a lot of gray around the hairline. She looks old, I thought, and that was a shock. Daddy did, too, when he came limping in the house, passing me without a glance to change into the good suit he wore about twice a year, usually to his patients' funerals. It was black, with a thin stripe, and a shiny look to the knees.

I noticed that he had got deep lines from the corners of his mouth to his chin, which made me wonder if you aged the minute you became the oldest generation. I hoped that if that was true, my parents would live to be ninety. (Which it looked then as if they would, Daddy anyway; the Van der Lindens had all made it at least into their eighties, all the ones I knew about.)

I ran upstairs and put on the dark blue Sears suit, a little wrinkled, which I'd got to wear to Methodist back when I started going with Buddy. By the time I got downstairs, Daddy and Mother were in the car, backing down the driveway on their way to follow the hearse from Pickens Funeral Home down Main to Grandfather's. If I hadn't been watching out my upstairs window while I buttoned up, they would have left without me.

The body was on view in the parlor, and it seemed to me that most of the town came to look at him—knowing this was their only chance, as there was to be no church service, because of his being a heathen. Merrill ("Monk") Pickens, Hydrangea's brother, had laid him out in a new gray suit, three-piece, and propped his big head up on a small blue satin pillow which matched the casket lining.

"Doesn't he look peaceful?" each viewer said in turn. "Just like he's asleep."

He didn't, of course. He looked like a wax dummy with lips too red and face too bronze and a nice slick wave in his thick hair. His big, bulging stomach was now encased under the vest of the new suit, and the baggy lisle socks that always hung in rings around his ankles had been replaced by smooth elastic-topped socks. He looked strange without his cigar, without ashes on his chest or rubber bands around the top of his shirt sleeves to keep them pulled up out of the way.

Most of the crowd had also come to steal a good look at the woman the old doctor had kept down at his house all these years and, those who had never been invited down for supper, to sneak a peek at the inside of the big old four-chimneyed yellow brick.

Elsie wore a white voile dress and white hose and a calla lily pinned to her collar; perhaps intentionally on her part, she was frequently mistaken for a nurse. She put all the food that people brought in the dining room across the big hall from the parlor and stood not by Grandfather but by the table, serving plates and filling cups. The way she always had. I could hear an echo of him saying, "Come on, Elsie, sit down and eat with us."

But he didn't say that anymore and, as it turned out, did not leave her anything.

I overheard her in the kitchen with Daddy, who was asking her about the will.

"But he didn't make one, George."

"He must have."

There was no answer.

Daddy again, "The house is yours, I'll guarantee that."

"He didn't intend me to have it."

"How is that possible?"

"It was important to him to know I wasn't here for what I could gain."

"But surely, Elsie—"

"He had it in his mind that your mother married him solely to have a provider. He did not want that a second time."

There was a long silence, and then Daddy said, "I can't speak to that."

Which was answer enough.

Then he begged her to reconsider, to take it as a life estate, to take it as a gift. That she need not go to her sister's in Memphis; that she had a home here on Main as long as she wanted it.

"He thought you could use it," she said.

"I could," Daddy agreed. And there was a sound from him of sighing or letting out his breath.

Meanwhile, Mother drove herself into a suspicious frenzy every time a woman walked up to Daddy. A dark woman with a shy face touched his arm, and Mother clutched at my shoulder. "That's Newcombe. Look at them, right here in plain sight." And I had to restrain her bodily from tearing across the room. Then a busty blonde walked through, and even though Daddy hardly spoke, Mother hissed that she was the one from the barbershop, the one who liked to hold the men's hands—do their nails indeed. All the while she was darting her eyes all around, asking every few minutes, "Where is she? What does she look like? Do you see her? Alma, are you watching?"

Daddy, for his part, dutifully wrung every offered hand in both of his, but as the day wore on, he began to look more and more the way he did at the kitchen table at home.

The next day we followed the Pickens hearse again, this time to the cemetery three miles out of town—in the palm of the hand which holds the fan splints of Venice.

Most of the graves on the flat, sunken stretch were old and worn down to a bare mound, the monuments broken or leaning to one side. Most of the names were unfamiliar— De Paramo, Mouser, La Forge, Cokenour, Van der Vender— being the Spanish, French, and Dutch who came when the forest was still thick with cypress and hickory and animals abounded to be trapped. Their graves lay untended, all that was left of old Venice, the families who used to mourn them having moved on or been washed away.

A small procession followed us. Keeping a discreet distance, they parked their cars on the damp dirt access road, walked toward the Van der Linden plot, and stood at the back under the mauve tent with the white funeral home message REST EASY WITH PICKENS. Six chairs had been set out, their metal legs poked slightly into the ground to keep them from wobbling, for the three of us, plus Elsie, plus Uncle Grady and Daddy's cousin should they take it in their heads to show. Small towns have it figured every time to the minute and the dime.

Most of the people who made the drive were old-timers, friends of Grandfather's who wanted to put him away properly or patients who considered they owed to him the extra five years or six months of their lives. Others came to see if the feud between the brothers was a feud to the death.

(I found out later, not from Daddy, of course, that Uncle Grady was already in the hospital with failure of the heart and kidney and that he was the one expected to go any minute when Grandfather died, that Daddy had been trying to break away from caring for his uncle to go down and break the news to his father when he heard that Grandfather was gone.)

Elsie talked in a low voice to Daddy, trying to relax him. "In the early days August and I used to make the trip out here Memorial Day to lay flowers on his mother's grave." She nodded to the old stones to one side of us. "Usually there was a service going on in the middle of the cemetery, but we never took notice of it. I picked whatever was out, honeysuckle, iris, peonies. Phlox if they were blooming, which have those giant black and yellow butterflies that none of the other flowers attract. White tea roses and the little climbing reds. We put them in baskets. You don't see that kind anymore, the shellacked ones with the curved handles." She drew in the air. "We would come early in the day, arrange and usually rearrange them, and he would talk about her, tell me the story over again. Then, later in the day, but after we were gone, Grady and Nina would come. I knew they did because whenever I came out to gather the dead blooms, his father's grave would be marked by the same baskets."

Listening to her easy flow of talk about Grandfather and Uncle Grady, I realized that she had one of her hats with her, not on, but held in one gloved hand: a white straw with a small white veil and a few tiny white feathers. A church hat. And I could see that whatever else was going on at the cemetery—Daddy trying not to get his cane stuck in the sodded plot, Mother staring wildly at each new arrival—Elsie had come to give Grandfather to God.

"Isn't that Maudie's boyfriend?" Mother tugged at me, talking in a loud stage whisper. "Look, over there. Isn't that him?"

I felt a brief stab of envy that she could remember that many years later some boy who'd gone with a friend of Gloria and Greta's when I knew she wouldn't know Buddy if he was standing with us right that minute.

I looked in the direction she was pointing, at a man in rolled-up shirt sleeves who was tending the ground around a grave. It gave me a chill to see him, for it was Louis, who stood up, rolling the sleeves down over his muscled arms, his tongue darting in and out of his full lips.

Seeing he had caught our eye, he strolled over, pulling on a jacket. "My apologies, Mrs. van der Linden. With my parents down in Florida, it falls on me to keep our plot out here weeded, and I take whatever opportunity I get. I had no idea I'd be intruding. My condolences." He held out his hand to Mother and then to Daddy, but not to Elsie. "I'm Louis LeCroix"—he pronounced it Lewis—"better known as the school principal, I'm afraid. Hello, Alma." He nodded in my direction.

"I took you for Maudie's boyfriend," Mother said nervously, wrapping her arms around her own shoulders, straitjacketing herself in her confusion.

"A compliment, I'm sure. I'm afraid I was a year or two ahead of your girls, as I recall, but I would have been proud to be thought a member of their crowd."

Mother lit up briefly. "My daughters don't live here now," she said.

"My condolences, Doctor," Louis said again to Daddy, who was looking the other way at the casket suspended on cables over the fresh hole in the ground.

"Fine," Daddy said, not turning his head.

"Should I be on my way?"

Daddy frowned and tried to give his attention. "Not at all. It will be a brief service." A pause, then: "Did you meet Mrs. White?"

"How do you do," Louis said to Elsie, still not offering his hand.

"Thank you, Mr. LeCroix," Elsie replied, as if in response to sympathy. She had prepared herself well for strangers.

"If it's not inappropriate to mention at this time"—Louis went right on—"we have a bumper senior class coming up." He looked again in my direction, and I saw his eyes take in my dark blue suit and my grief and hoard them with the rest of it.

"Fine," Daddy said.

As the service started at last, with no prayers or hymns or pastors from Methodist or Baptist but only a few kind words from old friends, Louis slipped in among the last of the mourners who walked gingerly across the grassy space from their parked cars.

"He knew your name," Mother whispered, nudging me. "Imagine that."

113

I grew cold in the shade of the awning as the old pharmacist eulogized a man I didn't know. Remembering Gloria and Greta's crowd coupling in the dark of the snowball bushes, I wondered if Louis had been watching even then the little girl who sat huddled in panties and bedsheet on the roof.

19

It rained all spring our senior year, forty days and forty nights, the papers claimed. Although the threat of high water always drove Mr. Rogers to hyperbole, him and all the other editors of weeklies up and down both sides of the Mississippi, this was a record. VENICE ALDERMEN FLOAT BOND FOR ARK, the *Gazette* headlined, and the big papers picked it up.

Actually that spring was a lot like most springs. When the rains began, everyone was overjoyed. The lawns and flowers were dry and had to be watered every evening. Both the Methodist ladies planning their Azalea Trail and the Baptists their Dogwood Show were elated. "Let it rain," they said. "Let it rain all week." They calculated bloom, set the dates on their calendars, notified the paper, the printer who did the posters, their circles and Bible classes, and began to refurbish the homes which were to be opened to serve refreshments.

Then the rains didn't stop. Irises (or flags, as they are called in our part of the state) filled with water and snapped on their stems. Azaleas grew sodden and heavy, and shed before they were fully open. Dogwoods—with their tissue-paper stigmata blossoms, palest pink and purest white cruciform—fell to the ground like confetti. Grown women were seen all over town in trousers and head scarves, in mud up to their ankles, staking stems, tying up branches, making drainage ditches around roots, buying sheets of plastic and attempting to guy-wire makeshift greenhouses to fence posts and fruit trees.

And the rains kept on.

The fund-raising tours were postponed to summer and renamed the Rose Festival (Baptist) or held in homes with silver services and hundreds of potted cyclamen and azaleas on glassed-in porches, with garden books and agapanthus lilies for door prizes (Methodist).

(To digress: from my years of covering the churches, I consider their response to the high waters of spring to be typical of their theology, although I wouldn't want to be quoted on it. The Methodists are pragmatists: it's going to rain, let's build the boat and get on with it, pack the oars, the raincoats, Saran wrap, and peanut butter, and wait it out. Whereas the Baptists are salvationists, content to wade neck-deep in the stream with their eyes focused full of hope on the red roses of summer.)

The rains continued, and the truss bridge to the north of us at Cape Girardeau was sandbagged into Illinois, and the cantilever bridge into Tennessee to the south of us at Caruthersville was also. Two little towns up the road across from Kentucky, right above us on the bend, but on the river side of the levee, flooded. People came to Venice to stay with kinfolks and talk about the four feet of water in their living rooms, their furniture floating away, their carpets ruined, car batteries dead as doornails. National newspapers did features on floods, those in the western states from heavy snowmelt and those in the middle states, where ten inches of sudden rain swelled the already high creeks out of their banks and raised the Mississippi to a critical level.

Carloads of people drove to Cairo to look at the confluence and reported back that the Y formed by the two rivers was no longer visible, that the whole resembled a lake, with the V of the land between them completely covered over with lapping brown and gray-blue waters.

Venice refused to panic. Any place that had gone under once was not going to pack up over a few weeks of spring showers. Preachers dusted off the pages of their musty Old Testaments and whipped themselves into seminary zeal over signs of sin and the sightings of doves.

Meanwhile, Venice High got on with the task of preparing for senior week teas and the senior prom (known officially as the Gondoliers Ball). Patsy and Judy and the rest of us got our Lucite heels and rhinestone earrings and garter belts and other essentials. The *Gondola* began to lobby for an all-night party in the gym, getting out a special "Take Home to Parents" issue, promising to provide an abundance of chaperons and a guarantee of no alcohol.

Girls calculated their periods for May and sighed in relief or spent April trying out new products and the result of triple doses of Midol a week in advance.

Givens Better Dresses got in racks of net formals, which made me think of Mrs. Vickers and wonder who had taken over the job of sewing her eyes out so that we who were graduating could show the rounded tops of our breasts to boys who traveled in pairs and dreamed of Western Auto dealerships.

I charged a lemon yellow dress, which had a border of bunched-up net rows that came up to the waist in the front like the opening of a curtain and cascaded down the back almost to a train, with two layers of yellow underskirt to hold it out. Smashing. It came in every color of the rainbow and was slightly finer than the model which had concentric loops of net in bands around the skirt.

Patsy and Judy and I had our senior tea together, but since none of us had mothers in the Woman's Club and so couldn't hold it in their building or daddies who played golf and so couldn't have it at the country club, we decided to have a Coke party instead, with an Ark theme. We held it at Patsy's house, which was the nicest, and made cardboard cutouts of animals, two by two, all around the living room, and got little paper napkins with rabbits and zebras on them, and hung crepe paper in blue and white from the chandelier to the corners of the dining room, sort of like a roof, and wore matching skirts to the floor, to show it was the old days. And there were doves with olive branches in their mouths carrying signs that said DRY LAND AHEAD. Which was supposed to mean life after graduation.

It wasn't the best party, but it was different, and it got us invited to all the afternoon teas that in those days really had spiced tea and iced cakes and salted nuts—to which each mother and grandmother and church lady in the family came. I invited Ida Dunlap to ours (but she probably couldn't read the invitation) and Elsie White (but she had already gone). I told Patsy and Judy that Mother was sick with the flu from all the wet weather; I wasn't up to her standing around embarrassing me in front of every high school girl.

Where was my head at the time? I'm not sure. I didn't think I was going to marry Buddy; college was never mentioned at home. It was as if because Gloria and Greta had simply disappeared when they got to the end of Venice High that I would somehow do the same. Vanish, slip out of town at night, catch a barge down to New Orleans and be heard of only secondhand—a visitor to Mardi Gras who thought she saw Alma in the crowd.

Once or twice I started to ask my parents what was I supposed to do after graduation. Had they thought about it at all? Did they think I would simply stay on in the upstairs front bedroom with the window seats? My old run-over sandals building on top of Gloria and Greta's for some later house buyer-archaeologist to find, six feet of worn-out shoes, owners unknown, to be heaped in trash cans at the curb?

Only Louis had made provision for me.

At the end of April he called me into his office on the pretext of giving out a memorandum concerning the drop in attendance.

"It will be best if you go off a couple of years," he said. "Until things blow over."

I did not know what he was talking about.

"I took the liberty of applying for you to the School of Journalism at Missouri. I sent your transcript, a selection of your stories from the school paper, and, to be sure, a copy of your winning essay. I'm sure that was sufficient without anything further, but to cinch it, I included letters of reference from myself, Rogers, and Pickens. Here is your acceptance letter. Simply tell them at home that you were offered a scholarship. There will be no problem."

I sat down in the chair where I'd first pulled up my skirt to flirt with him, all desire to arouse him gone. I can remember staring at him and feeling like a raccoon in a farmer's trap. Yet at the same time relieved that the future had been decided by someone.

"Thank you," I said.

"It's almost over, Alma," he whispered as he stood over my chair, shoving a sheaf of pink pages into my hands.

By the end of May, Venice was drying out. The bridges had been reopened, lilies were blooming in the ladies' yards, and there was a spectacular rainbow, which brought out all our amateur photographers. Kinfolks went back to Anniston and East Prairie, and the seniors got permission for their all-night party, in reward for the sunny skies.

A week before the prom Louis called me in again, this time ostensibly to hand me the final end-of-year attendance figures.

"I'm renting us a motel room," he said, keeping his voice low and flat, bending over the tallies in case anyone was looking through the open door. "Here is the letter I am sending your mother." He showed me a mimeographed sheet which explained the all-night party and the rules set up and the chaperonage arranged, and instructions where to pick your son or daughter up at 6:00 A.M. if you did not wish him or her to leave the school unattended. In ink, after the "Dear M/M ——" he had filled in "Dr. and Mrs. van der Linden," and then, on the fourth line, where it said "Your son or daughter ——," he had written "Alma." So that it looked for all the world like something that had gone out to everyone.

"To insure that there will be no problem," he said.

What got me was his knowing that Mother in her fog would not compare notes with other mothers. Or even think to show it to my father.

"This is what you are to do," he instructed, speaking in an ordinary low voice, as if on a matter of business. "I will pick you up in a car at the back north corner of the gym at the end of the twelfth dance. Keep track. Tell your young man you got sick and had to lie down in the teachers' lounge. Slip into the lounge on your way out and leave your stole for someone to notice. He'll be drunk by then, your Buddy, and won't recollect correctly. Do you understand? I've timed this exactly, Alma. There won't be any slip-up. I'll have you back in the gym by the time the two o'clock breakfast is served. I'll let you back in the door myself; if anyone sees us come in, I'll say I found you outside vomiting, and that will be the end of it. Do you understand?"

"Yes."

"Repeat it back to me."

In a whisper I did, trembling all over.

I've thought back ten thousand times about what else I could have done that night. Persuaded Buddy to run off with me? Confessed everything to my father and asked him what to do? Gone to Miss Dunlap's and hidden in the pantry?

I didn't do any of those things. In part because I was

flattered that any grown man would take the risk of slipping me out of his own school to make love to me.

In part because I felt myself already beholden to him.

Two days before the prom—when I was putting a final lemon rinse on my hair and laying out my underclothes and trying to decide if I should have other clothes with me for going off with Louis, at least clean panties in my purse, and being so nervous at the prospect of it, especially lying to Buddy, which seemed to me the most treacherous part of it all—Uncle Grady died.

I saw it all over the front of the *Gazette* when I was downtown looking for hose. Here he had hung in there all during the fall, and the bitter, cold blasts of February, and all during the downpours of April, and then had gone one fine, mild morning in May. It said the body had been sent up the road to the crematorium in Cape Girardeau. Which made me wonder if the ground was too wet, still, for a burial. And that made me panic, imagining Grandfather washed up and floating across the flat, muddy ground at Memorial.

I got Buddy to drive me out there, just to be sure that everything was all right, and we put flowers on Grandfather's grave, the first of the day lilies and the last of the irises, which I'd got up at dawn and stolen from Mrs. Rogers's garden next door. I put a few on the Reformed father and the Quaker mother, too, now that Grady and August wouldn't be coming out there ever again to choose up sides between them.

What amazed me was that there was no outburst at home because the paper had his obituary on the front page and even a picture of him the year he received his medical degree, with his wife and small daughter.

It was clear that Cousin Wisdom must be coming to town, if she hadn't already, because the paper said that the ashes would be placed at the gravesite by "the family." But everything was calm at Marie's house in the middle of Main.

It took my mind off everything else, waiting for the other shoe to drop; finally, sure enough, twenty-four hours after the obit in the paper, Mother was back to her old self, screaming invective, her eyes red, her dress buttoned up wrong, her stockings rolled down to her ankles, flopping around in house slippers. "He's done it," she shrieked. "He's done it." All the while brandishing what remained of Daddy's boiled-dry, blackened pot of coffee.

It took me a full thirty minutes to get the story, and Daddy's crime was not what I had guessed; what he had done was move his office into Grandfather's house, holding his consultations in the little room where the old doctor had kept his Underwood and his examinations in Grandfather's bedroom. Apparently his patients had already been well advised of the change in location because the driveway was full of cars when I went down to see for myself. And half a dozen people waited companionably in what had been the parlor, leafing through old stacks of Grandfather's *Country Gentlemen* and *Hollands*, not at all bothered by the new address. Rather, most had the air of being pleased to see the young doctor finally come into his own.

Prom night Mother met Buddy at the door and talked his ear off until I came down in my yards of yellow net.

"Yes, ma'am," he kept saying as I took the stairwell one step at a time. "Yes, ma'am, I see."

In the living room he pinned a white orchid on me, Scotch-taping the top to my bare shoulder, and we left the house by the front door, negotiating my skirt like a wheel chair down the concrete walk.

"Your mom is really upset," he said.

"She'll get over it."

"I guess they hate to see you grow up."

"That's it."

We got into Buddy's car, where Andy and Patsy waited in the back seat. She was in a blue net which matched mine, and her orchid was identical. The boys took a quick look to make sure we were even and gave each other a nod.

In the gym the band was warming up, and all the senior girls who didn't have old boyfriends come back to escort them and who weren't dating juniors on the football team were stuck with senior boys who had never had a date in their life, so were wearing their clusters of split carnations on last year's formals with straps. (Why waste the money for a new dress?)

Judy, who had got tired of sharing Andy, had got herself a tight end on the A team and was wearing a purple orchid big as a pumpkin on her tiered lavender net.

The band was the best we could get, from Cape Girardeau, called Billy and the River Bums. They played big band sound, their specialty being Elvis imitations, which they'd practiced off records for hours.

Buddy and I danced every slow dance because it had been a long time since we'd been together at a real party. And in between slow numbers, he and Andy would slip out through the custodian's entrance, along with about half the boys there, and walk way back in the parking lot, to where they'd left their cache of drinks. They told us, Patsy and me, that it was only beer, but it smelled like whiskey to us, and as the time passed, more and more of the guys were beginning to weave, and the ones who weren't, who didn't know the ritual, were the kind who couldn't dance anyway.

The sixth dance was called Parents Dance and came after the second break. (Billy and the Bums, who had a small repertoire, took a break after every "set," which is what they called two slow songs and then a fast one, so that nobody had to be stuck on the dance floor for more than two numbers.) Every chaperon who had a daughter there danced with her, and the rest of the girls danced with their brothers or uncles or Sunday School teachers or someone like that. It was a drag, but it gave the grownups a chance to get out on the floor.

Louis came up to me and bowed. "May I, Alma?"

Buddy and Andy had already cut out when Parents Dance was announced, thinking they could stay out during the fast song which followed and get a double shot.

I was shaking like a yellow leaf in my miles of crushed swagged net when Louis put his arms around me, and scared to death when I laid the back of my left hand on the shoulder of his suit.

"I'm a very happy man tonight," he whispered, keeping me held away at the distance anyone watching would expect. "I've waited a long time."

Buddy and I danced the twelfth dance together, because it was slow and our favorite, "Love Me Tender," and he was holding me so tight you couldn't see daylight between us. He smelled of alcohol and was hot and horny and ready to leave and go neck but knew that he had hours more of the same ahead of him. My orchid was already turning brown at the edges from being mashed against him, and I shut my eyes and locked both arms around his neck. By that time I truly did feel faint and sick.

"I'm going to throw up," I told him when the music stopped.

"For Pete's sake," I heard him say as I dashed out of the gym in the direction of the teachers' lounge. "*You* haven't had anything to drink, have you?"

At the dark outside corner of the gym, in the parking lot, Louis was waiting. He had exchanged his suit jacket for a tux and had on a white silk scarf like those the boys rented with their tuxedos. He was in a Ford that looked so much like Buddy's to me I almost turned around and ran back in before I saw that it was him.

Very slowly he drove us out of the parking lot, with his lights out, and his hand gripping my leg.

"This is the beginning of a new life, Alma. You'll never be sorry."

Two

The
Churches
of
Venice

20

————

Looking up the Mississippi, almost metallic in the first glint of daylight, you could see toward Cairo and the confluence and, turning south, past a haze of smokestacks, the distant skyline of Memphis. As always it pleased me to contemplate these two towns, which sit in the same relation to each other on our river as did the places of the Pharaohs on the wide and muddy Nile. A reminder of the vision of those settlers at the turn of an earlier century who yearned after a civilization marked even then only by a few stones among the palm trees and an alabaster sphinx or two.

It was the day after Christmas, and we had got up before the birds and by daybreak were in the car, which was tuned up, filled up, the tires rotated, and packed to the limit with suitcases, thermoses, and sacks of fruit so that we wouldn't have to stop before the Memphis airport.

We had drawn places, and Louis's daughter, to her delight, had won the front seat, now neatly filled with extra sweaters, sunglasses, a brush for her still-damp hair, and pink notepaper for writing her best friend.

Louis's son, who had kicked the tires and threatened to hitchhike to Florida if we didn't get off this dumb routine of drawing for seats, had finally climbed in, folded up his long legs, and settled into the back seat beside me.

(I've said *Louis*'s children. That's because he named them. They are, if you are unfamiliar with the Book of Revelation, christened for two of the stones which make up the wall of the New Jerusalem: Jasper and Beryl. Louis had selected the names on the night of his marriage to Audrey, poor Audrey who would still be the principal's wife if she had only provided him with descendants.

(If I had named them, they would be called August and Ann Elizabeth. And sometimes, when I am vexed with them or, more correctly, estranged from them—wondering who these big people are who walk with the authority of the new heaven and the new earth across the floor of Uncle Grady's house, where we live, as if they owned every beast of the field and bird of the sky—I imagine what orderly, felicitous creatures "my" children would have been. Sunnier, franker, more transparent. With different parents perhaps.)

It was my intent to write a great deal about my pregnancies and the births of the children. But the truth is you cannot recapture that Copernican universe.

I do recall that after my son was born, a lot of things became clearer to me about Mother. For one thing, what it meant to her not to have a son; what anger she must have felt toward my older sisters, and especially me, for not being the boy who would add yet another generation of Van der Lindens to the town.

This was behind Mother's jealousy, in part, I'm sure: the fear that another woman would come along and give my father what she hadn't. "You're no king, you know," she used to scream at Daddy. And when we finally packed her up and sent her to the country with her kin, she was screaming in the direction of Grandfather's house, where Daddy had moved, "He's no king, you know." Meaning that only royalty could dismiss a wife for inappropriate heirs.

My having a son first did make it easier on my daughter when she came along, not to be someone's second choice, someone who was getting potty-trained while Mother was all set to try again, that sort of thing.

My only other contribution to Louis's children, besides making one of each gender, was having them as close to simultaneously as I could manage. Wanting to provide them with what I had longed for most as a child, what Gloria and Greta had had, and Reba and Sheba, and Andy and Buddy: the fine cutting edge of duplication.

It isn't easy to summarize children. To say, "Beryl is the one who ——," "Jasper always ——." Although we all do it, all the time. We say Gloria was the one who read; Greta was the mathematician. Reba was the follower; Sheba, the leader. Even though we know our thinking is full of fallacy, that the follower, for example, is often the cart the horse is made to pull.

But to fall into the same trap, I'd have to say that Beryl, like most daughters, underestimates her capacities, whereas Jasper, like most sons, overestimates his.

None of this is news, of course; there have been studies. But it is the particular case you have to rear.

To take an instance in point, let's go to the fourth grade. Each in turn had mean Miss Matlock (by then coasting downhill toward retirement); each was assigned the same map of the world I had had on which to fill in the major rivers and list the primary import-exports. Jasper, when he got home, came in to report, "Any dumb second grader could do that. She's harped on it fifty leven times a day and passed out her stupid lists ahead of time for the retards. Cheez, I got them all right."

The next year Beryl had the same sheet (plus the advantage

of having seen her brother's the year before). She came home in despair. "I didn't know half of them. I wasn't even sure which was the Mississippi, I'm not lying. I was so dumb. I got it all mixed up. I should have studied all night. Don't fix a plate for me, Mom; I don't feel like eating."

Each of them got a 92.

The corollary to this observation about children, which is less frequently mentioned, is that, therefore, a son tends to underestimate his parents and a daughter to overestimate hers.

Take the matter of their dealing with having the high school principal for a father.

Jasper is taller, better-looking, faster on the draw than Louis and wholly impervious to coercion.

Louis wanted him to go to Tulane with an eye to taking over the lucrative medical practice of his maternal grandfather; Beryl wanted him to go to Vanderbilt and pledge Phi Delt so she could follow him and get rushed by Tri Delt; I wanted him to go to Chicago and take a lot of courses from his cousin Wisdom, in the field of economics.

Jasper led us along all fall, some weeks threatening his father with the university which sails the ocean on a ship, some weeks telling me he was going to buy white shoes and go to Ole Miss. Then, just before Christmas, he announced that he'd intended all along to go to Missouri U. Why not? They had professors and classes, and it had been good enough for the two of us, hadn't it?

I see him mosey into the schoolyard in the mornings in his jeans, wallet and comb in his back pocket, strutting like a rooster in a henhouse, and feel an amazing sense of recollection. He arrives, hair slicked back like John Travolta, a white shirt on, his arm around Nadine, his current squeeze, and calls out, "Hi, Dad," to his father, who stands monitoring the students' arrival. Louis, at fifty-four, still in fine shape, his hair cut short in a burr which shows few signs of gray, is eaten with envy at having such a son, filled with anger that he cannot control him.

"Good morning," Louis replies, much in the same voice that he uses to the arriving teachers and other students. "Good morning, good morning." The sound of his son's voice tightening the cords in his neck.

Then close behind comes Beryl, pretty as a picture, in jeans, too, and a nice pink cotton shirt. She has washed and dried her layered brown hair at six in the morning, put new laces in her sneakers, applied two inches of roll-on mascara, and gone over her homework for the fifth time.

Embarrassed, she does not speak to her father but scuffs along until Mandy hollers at her, "Pokey, come on," and then Beryl slips into Venice High with her best friend, a pair of juniors who do not yet have dates for the Valentine Dance.

Louis's children have free rein of the school since naturally they cannot be sent to the principal's office. Which means that whenever there is a problem with one of them, I am the one who is called in for a teacher conference. You might think it would be to answer for Jasper, to deal with his cutting classes or smarting off, but no, it is always for Beryl.

"I don't know what to do with her, Alma," the teacher says. The old ones, who taught me and feel they have a right to speak their minds; the young ones from my class, who remember how we hated all of ours and want to get things off to a better start.

"What is it?" I ask her. Senile Miss Simpson or jolly Judy.

"She tries so hard, you know what I mean?" That would be Judy. Or, "She drives herself, turns in assignments I haven't given yet, then makes a wreck of herself trying to complete them. Do you follow me?" That would be Miss S.

"Yes," I tell them. "I know the pattern."

There were students like my daughter in class with me. Patsy Underwood for one, a priss in the lower grades, though we were friends when she was dating Andy. Always half in tears at the teacher's desk, holding out her six pages of perfect penmanship, wanting sympathy, approval—wanting, and we all knew it, the rest of us, attention. Pretending to worry about failure being a foolproof way to get it from any teacher old or young who is sick of weedy, lazy kids.

Louis's daughter is like that.

She'll get her date to the dance the same way. Every girl in school will be a wreck because no one has asked Beryl yet, and it's only six weeks away. Steadies will put pressure on, and buddies, and within two weeks, give or take, two members of the scrub team plus the runner-up for student council will ask her. And she'll cry a little to each one, and swear him to secrecy, and then confide that she likes him and she'd like to go with him if Jerry Walters doesn't ask her. Naturally, by the third time Jerry hears about this, he'll give in and ask her to go, so as not to be thought a lout by his chums and a crumb by all of hers. Then, by the time of Jasper's graduation in May, Jerry will be in Beryl's pants, and everyone will have her mind on other matters.

(To digress on the subject of loss of virginity, if that can be what it's called these days: the best thing that ever happened to Venice, Missouri, was the arrival of the new pharmacist, who claimed to be the daughter of Miss Newcombe, the old postmistress, although I don't think folks ever had an idea that she'd been married, Miss N. Which, of course, she may not have been. At any rate, when the old pharmacist stepped down, the very next day this lanky, brisk woman about my age showed up, calling herself Bea Newcombe, and saying she'd been waiting for a chance to come back to her mother's hometown. The postmistress was underground and couldn't be consulted, but folks said there was a family resemblance, the old house was standing empty, so Bea began to fill overdue prescriptions that very night.

(After she was settled, she let the word spread that in her view the fact that condoms could be sold over the counter and the pill couldn't was sexual discrimination, and she intended to put a stop to it. If any of us mothers with daughters would care to register our names on file with her, under cover, she would take care of matters when they arose, so to speak. Every woman in town breathed more easily, and Bea was elected to the Woman's Club on the first ballot, ahead of a dozen others, including Maudie Cox, and Methodist and Baptist almost got into a brawl competing for her. The Methodists won; they'd had her mother.)

Louis knows nothing of this. A tendon tightens in his neck at the very sight of Beryl even standing with a boy. Perhaps imagining me in her place, he has become retroactively jealous of Buddy Richmond, whom I have not set eyes on since graduation, and nags and nags me to tell him what Buddy did, what he got to see, to touch. It drives me wild.

In view of how he is, it amazes me that Beryl has not run off with some lout the way my sister Greta did. In the same way I am amazed that Jasper has not flunked out of school to spite his dad. It tugs at your heart: how carefully children do their little dances, prancing to the edge of provocation or disobedience but never going over.

How do I know what goes on at their school? Because I drive by the barbershop and post office and Venice High on my way to work, turning down Ash to pass the Vickers house, which Sheba rents once more, to the site of the victory garden, which figured so prominently in my childhood and is now the location of the *Gazette*'s new concrete-block all-air-conditioned edifice.

My spying irritates them both.

"You going to put it in the paper?" Jasper asks. "What we're up to at Dad's school?"

"You don't think I can even go to class by myself," Beryl complains, sullen at having seen my car go by. "I mean, you have to be watching to see if I've got friends, if I'm doing all right, like I was someone you were ashamed of. Mandy says you wish I was a cheerleader, like Prissy Walters."

As usual, they miss the point.

The truth is I do watch them a lot now that they are reaching the end of Venice High. Wondering if they have any more idea what is really going on in their lives than I did. Wondering, also, how I'm going to survive this marriage once they're gone.

With Jasper only a spring away from graduation, he is sliding into home plate as rapidly as he can. Beryl is only a year behind, and when her time comes, she'll go, too. She'll cry about leaving, act as if she hates it, make us console her for it, but she'll be gone as fast as her brother.

The two of them leaving me back where I started twenty-five years ago: alone with Louis.

21

E a c h time we visited I was amazed anew at the ease with which the children settled into the confines of their grandparents' house. It did not seem to ruffle their feathers that Rhoda and J.D. never left 16505 Mimosa Drive.

I don't mean that my in-laws didn't like to go places or were retired and no longer worked; I mean, they never set foot outside the doors of their fully paid-for home in Jacksonville, Florida. Reputedly J.D. worked in a management-level job in the nearby Blue Cross-Blue Shield sky-rise, and certainly he could talk insurance until the cows came home. But since we never saw him head for the office when we came, it remained a rumor. Rhoda claimed to be employed at the Jaxon Sickroom and Party Equipment Rental in nearby Five Corners, but in all the years we'd been coming down she had yet to budge from the pink asbestos-sided bungalow.

J.D. faithfully followed the dog picks in the paper, jotting down his bets—Telecast in the eleventh, Ardent Break in the twelfth—keeping close track of the time and odds, but he'd never seen a race. The Orange Grove Downs was only minutes from their house, at least according to the map, but they'd never been, not once, to see the effete greyhounds bound muzzled from their stalls after the imitation rabbit. It was too much trouble, J.D. said. Not safe. Bums went. Coloreds. Who knew what showed up at the track? It was better to follow the starts, match yourself against the picks, at home.

J.D. wore mail-order jump suits, size portly, and the only moments of sympathy I regularly had for Louis were when he came into the den where his dad sat watching color TV in his aqua or gold, adjusting the heft of his flabby flesh, slapping his hand on Louis's knee in welcome. It made me understand Louis's preoccupation with fitness, his compulsive weight-lift program.

Rhoda had a thousand wrinkles on her face, so that she looked most like an aging Barbie doll. Obviously if Louis was in his fifties, she was no spring chicken, and my guess was that Rhoda and J.D. had been retired for years, but they never let it out, always saying to us that they took their vacation when we came to visit. In fact, the way they talked about Blue Cross's major medicals and Jaxon Rental's Evactol Bowls reminded me a lot of the way J.D. talked about the dog races—and made me wonder if they'd ever left their house at all.

This year Rhoda was in a froth of excitement on our arrival and ran back and forth like her miniature chihuahuas, so that the three of them, woman and dogs, made a race right there in the aqua and gold plastic-flowered, wall-plaqued house. Rhoda had put a new henna rinse on her hair and donned an aqua jump suit, which matched "Daddy's," and stepped into high-heel sandals, whose gold plastic uppers bowed out over her bunions. Her feet were always hurting, so that she was in heels when we arrived and whenever we ate—even if it was on trays in front of the TV set or for stand-up sweet rolls in the kitchen because eating barefoot was for hicks—but in her stockinged feet for most of the rest of the visit.

The chihuahuas were pushed out the back door twice a day, after breakfast and after supper, to "do their business"; otherwise, the glass door was never opened. Both because the air conditioners ran loud and wet twenty-four hours a day, irrespective of any chill that might be blowing in from the placid river which flowed past their subdivision, and because Rhoda was vigilant about pests. Despite the fact that a fly would have had to be on a reconnaissance mission that would do a British mole proud to get in Rhoda's door, fly strips hung from every corner of the rooms, and Roach Motels and ant traps waylaid all entrances with sweetened glue.

Rhoda told us first thing that dinner was going to be a big surprise. She, Rhoda, had been written up in the paper, and to prove it, she passed out copies of her news for Louis and me and the children to admire and to get our mouths to watering while she fixed the meal. Looking over one another's shoulders at copies of the *Jacksonville Reporter*, we read:

Even though it's called a salad, Rhoda LeCroix (Mrs. J.D.)'s layered creation is sweet enough to serve as a dessert. A resident of Five Corners, Mrs. LeCroix says, "It's always on my table when friends come for dinner. Plus," the career woman-homemaker adds, "you can use it for special events such as showers and club meetings. . . . A whole fresh strawberry makes an attractive garnish," this week's winner tells "Fare Well" columnist, who went back herself for a second helping. Our congratulations, Rhoda, on your prize winning Pretzel Salad.

Pretzel Salad
1½ cups finely crushed pretzels
½ cup melted margarine
1¾ cups sugar, divided
2 pkgs. cream cheese, softened (small)
1 container frozen topping, thawed
2 pkgs. strawberry gelatin (small)
2 cups boiling water
3 pkgs. frozen strawberries (small)

"I said Jell-O, but they don't like you to use brand names. I said Cool Whip, too, and Blue Bonnet, and I don't know if just any kind will do. They added that business about 'small,' not that anybody is going to get mixed up. But I think someone making a recipe wants to know the brands you use, so theirs will taste the same, don't you? But anyhow, they like to write it up so it can be fixed by anybody with whatever she's used to. But you folks are going to get the real thing."

After supper Rhoda settled us down for some girl talk while the men watched a ball game on TV. "I'm going to treat my windows. What do you think, Alma?"

Beryl joined us, this daughter of mine with the clean hair and the nice set of manners. "What are you going to do, Rhoda?" On request Beryl called her grandmother by her first name.

"Swags, don't you think? Swags? I saw an ad for some nice material on sale at Five Corners. New prints. Maybe your mom will get some for me."

"That sounds pretty," Beryl said. She was chipping the clear polish off her nails, preparing to apply a fresh coat.

"You're getting to be real grownup, honey."

"Thank you, Rhoda."

"You might want to try something with your hair maybe. Get yourself a style. You know what I mean, who are you trying to look like? I don't know the young ones today, except what I see on TV, but I see them with lots of curls all strung out, and the new short cuts, you know what I mean. Your shag, I think that's a has-been do, if you don't mind my saying, honey. That ice skater had it, and then everybody did. It's out of date."

"Dorothy Hamill."

"If you say so. I mean, in my day we all had a style you could recognize. Boys don't want plain vanilla, I know that much. You got a boyfriend?"

"I'm dating around."

"You didn't have one last year."

"I was a sophomore."

"You didn't have a boyfriend, and I thought you had got yourself so mousy you wouldn't be getting one. I imagine that's just old Rhoda talking. These days things are different, but the ones I see on TV, the young ones, they look distinctive. You know what I mean."

For reasons not wholly clear to me, the tone of this conversation not only didn't bother Beryl, it in some way comforted her. In part it was a change of pace. Here, where there was no competition, she could take her time, spend an entire evening, for example, on a nail.

"I'm going to enter the Look-Alike Contest." Rhoda changed the subject back to her favorite pastime. "I must be on a lucky streak, with pretzel salad last week, and then Daddy won, or would have if he'd been there, the sweeps at the races. He had them picked to a T. So I figure third time is charm, and I'll go whole hog for the big one. Why not? Look-alikes get their pictures in the paper in color, on the front page of the style section. You and your paper might try an idea like that, Alma."

"We might."

"Last time they had a Superman and a Boy George—they always have a Boy George, and these people tell the paper that they didn't have any idea of looking like a celebrity; who believes that?—and some other I can't recall. Jane Wyman, though who would claim that? You always have a Liz Taylor, and a Linda Evans."

"Who are you going to be?" Beryl leaned toward her grandmother with interest.

"Ida Lupino, what do you think?"

"That's nice." Beryl did not know who Ida Lupino was, I inferred from her tone. I squinted my eyes at Louis's mother in her tight jump suit and tried to get the image. The hair was picked on top into a little bouffant bunch of curls; the brows were arched. I tried to remember Lupino but failed.

"What do you think, Alma? Would I have a chance?"

Who came to mind was my sister's namesake, but that was because I'd seen her in the movies only after she was ancient and had dyed hair. "Gloria Swanson?"

"Too old." Rhoda dismissed her. "They don't like anyone too old."

"What about Joan Collins, Rhoda?" Beryl was making an effort to be a help and had clearly run down the entire list of women over forty on prime time.

"Her hair is dark." Rhoda was delighted and wanted to be encouraged.

"Except for that, you look a lot like her."

"Do I? Well, who knows? Maybe I will. Get a low-cut dress. Wear false eyelashes maybe. Everybody's heard of her, isn't that right?"

Beryl, pleased to have come up with a winning idea, started sliding light pink along the length of her smooth nails. Out of the corner of her eye she watched to see if her grandmother was admiring the way she could do it so fast and slick without a smear.

"You need to get your own style, Beryl, honey, or you'll never get a boyfriend." Rhoda graciously turned the conversation back.

"I'm dating around, Rhoda."

"That's good, that's fine. I'm not stepping on any toes, but take your mother here, take Alma. She's the spit and image of Doris Day, you see. Not like Lou's first one, who was a plain Jane." Rhoda hesitated, going over the history of the matter in her mind, to be sure that Beryl wasn't the first one's kid, then plunging ahead, certain she'd got it right.

I tried to take that in the proper spirit, knowing that Rhoda had looked me over with an appraising eye, gone through the list of blondes with muscular builds in her mind, selected one that nobody could take offense at, one who maybe wasn't twenty-one anymore but had definite staying power.

She'd never got on with her son's first wife and always took the opportunity to let me know that I was a decided improvement. Doris Day, after all, always got her man.

Those conversations continued through the week, with Beryl and Rhoda talking for hours straight about window treatments and hours more about look-alikes, and Rhoda remembering now and then to take notice of the nice way my daughter fixed herself up.

I, as every year, both over Christmas and again in the summer, did their grocery shopping at Winn-Dixie, this time getting the special ingredients for Rhoda's trial recipes, things that Roonie's, which delivered, wouldn't get right: dropped their clothes off at the Quik-Kleen at Five Corners because their usual cleaner, who picked up and delivered, took too long and they might as well take full advantage of our visit; made a drugstore run for shampoo and more nail polish; and got myself a lapful of paperback thrillers from the newsstand.

When the kids were younger, they leaped halfway out of their chairs at the sound of my jiggling car keys, eager as German shepherds promised a ride. Now I made the trips alone, the rest of the household content to stay put.

We had the pretzel salad twice more, once as a dessert, with a fresh strawberry on top, and once as a salad with the new main dish for which we were the guinea pigs. Rhoda being hard at work perfecting a Cheese Bake recipe for a condensed milk contest. It was one of those things where you pour a layer of this and then a layer of that and then a topping of this, and the whole thing bakes into something you can cut with a knife. A lot of hers were like that, and therefore I assumed that a big item in winning recipes was the element of surprise.

This one had a Bisquik bottom (which would be called "prepared biscuit mix"), then a layer of green chilies, a layer of beaten egg and canned milk, slabs of Velveeta cheese, and, on top, a thick dollop of canned tomato sauce. "It needs to be more spicy," Rhoda complained the third night we ate it. "It needs something else."

"Hamburger?" J.D. was missing meat.

"No, I think the sponsors want it to be a milk dish, you know, for if you can't afford chicken or something. But thanks, hon, that was a good suggestion."

"Onions?" I made a stab.

"Chili powder?" Beryl offered.

"Doesn't mix with the green chilies, and I want to call it Green Giant Bake, you see."

Jasper, checking to be sure his wallet and comb were in place, pushed back his chair. "Dump the Bisquik. Use Fritos."

"For a crust?" Rhoda pounced on the idea. "How would I do that? Roll them out, maybe? Lands, that's an inspiration, absolutely."

Beryl looked daggers at her brother—for winning that round and because that meant we'd have to eat it again.

Then, on Saturday morning, J.D. dropped his bomb. "We want to take the boy out to eat."

Out? Did he mean out of the den? Away from the TV? Out? Where?

"Someplace special, that's our idea. We talked it over, Rhoda and me, out to eat, we said, that's the ticket. Eat on the water, have ourselves a first-class seafood dinner. Give the boy a feast he'll remember."

"No need, Dad." Louis flushed, pleased, assuming he was the "boy" in question.

"He's graduating, isn't he?"

"You mean Jasper?" Louis was rebuffed.

"What's the matter with giving the boy a big dinner out on the town? The sky's the limit. You name it, son, and you're halfway there."

The kids used to make jokes, when we were away from the house on Mimosa, that there was an Atlantic Ocean backdrop painted on the east side of Jax for whatever tourists had come to visit kinfolks. That actually Jax was in Kansas, but that nobody was supposed to tell. A seafood dinner? They both looked stunned.

It took J.D. and Rhoda half the day to get ready. First the Joan Collins entry had to be mailed, complete with Polaroid shots, and then the Green Giant Bake with Corn Chips had to be written out by hand, three copies, and these readied to send off. Rhoda liked me to run them directly to the post office; it was one more perk of our visit. She had visions of the postman steaming open her mail and his wife stealing her submissions. You read about such things. . . .

When they were all cleaned up and in matching gold jump suits, and Rhoda had squeezed her bunions into her best high heels, J.D. got out the Yellow Pages and began to read the list of restaurants out loud.

Jasper was strangely (perhaps not so strangely) touched by the gesture on his grandfather's part, this old, fat man with the wavy white hair who was willing to heft himself up out of his chair and rub elbows with every type he was scared to death of because the "boy" deserved a meal out.

"Maybe we should just drive to the water and see what looks good," Rhoda suggested. "There's a big choice."

Jasper, taking his grandfather at his word, was reading out the ads for lobster, shrimp, four-fish platters.

But then Louis, forgotten, began to work on his mother. "Remember, Mom, that place we went when you first moved down here, back in my bachelor days?" He smiled in my direction, to remind me of old times. "Farmer's Basket, wasn't it?"

"Lands, Lou, that must be the bed of a freeway by now."

"No, here it is: Farmer's Basket." He moved Jasper to one side and pointed to the page.

Jasper looked up, confused. Was his dad indicating that

seafood was out of their price range? That his grandfather wasn't serious? Or was his dad trying to hog the show? He leaned down, his dark hair covering his eyes, and I could feel his anger move into all the spaces where his anticipation had been. He looked up and jerked his shoulder away from his father. "Forget it," he said. "Just forget it."

"We appeared to be all ready for an outing here. What seems to be the trouble?" I watched Louis weigh the options. If he cancelled the dinner, he could make his son responsible for ruining what would have been a treat for all of us. On the other hand, J.D. and Rhoda were all dressed up and had started the countdown. If we didn't go now, there might not be a second chance. Louis made his tone conciliatory. "How does the Farmer's Basket sound to everyone? Mom? Biscuits big as saucers. Beryl?"

J.D. shifted his scrubbed bulk. "Shouldn't the boy—"

But Rhoda cut off Daddy. "Lou, that was your favorite, wasn't it?"

"You asked them for their recipe for chicken batter." Louis pressed his advantage.

"Did I?" Rhoda perked up. "Did I get it?"

"You said it had a secret ingredient." He put an arm around her shoulder.

"Mint. Lemon juice and mint. Lands, Lou, what a memory. I should have written it out and saved it."

"How does that sound to everyone? What do you say?"

Jasper turned on the TV.

"Son?"

"It's your party."

"That's settled then."

It was a shock which went all through me to see J.D. and Rhoda actually walk through the door at the back of the house, past the yapping dogs, and step into the yard. I expected the sky to fall on them, Chicken Littles. Expected them to turn and run inside, like gerbils taken out of their home by pudgy fingers, suddenly under a limitless sky they don't understand, dashing back between your feet to be found weeks later behind the sofa or at the back of the construction-paper shelf.

"You better have heat, Lou; this wind is whipping every which way." Rhoda tied a net scarf around her curls.

"It'll be toasty," Louis promised, never as proud of the winter rental car as of his own, in tiptop shape, which he drove down on the longer summer visit.

J.D. shifted the eighty pounds which hung out over his belt and timidly edged across the lawn.

Both got in the front with Louis—Rhoda in the middle, J.D. sort of mashed against the passenger door like a portable water bed. Jasper sat between Beryl and me in the back. Louis's daughter had dressed up, washed her hair, and pulled the left side behind her ear with a silver barrette, giving attention to Rhoda's comments on her style. Jasper wore the same jeans and T-shirt he had on when he got up, plus his jacket as a concession to the mild wind.

Louis drove through downtown across the flat river, which ran like a strip of painted gray toward the ocean. Getting out of the house was monumental enough. That we might actually glimpse the Atlantic, might feel sand underfoot was too much to consider. And I hoped the kids weren't counting on it.

He drove past a dozen seafood short-order drive-ins and come-as-you-are cafés, all crowded already on New Year's Eve afternoon, people feeding their families before the parties began. Proud of his total recall of which road to take to get to the causeway that crossed the shallow inlet which separated town from tourist beach, proud of which feeders to take, which strip of batter-fried restaurants to go past, Louis drove us straight to a boarded-up building adjoining a vacant parking lot.

The Farmer's Basket had moved.

Louis noted the address on a sign tacked to the door, consulted his map, got back in the car, and made three wrong turns. Meanwhile, J.D. was beginning to swell up in his fear and discomfort, confirming that no good ever came of venturing outside, that it was indeed an alien world out here, that he should have made reservations for the boy at some place they could locate. Which misery prompted Rhoda to go on and on about the minty-lemon chicken and what she was going to call the recipe when she tested it out at home.

"You going to write Mandy what a swell time we're having?" Jasper whispered to his sister.

"Shut up."

"Hey, you graduate next year; maybe this'll count for you, too."

"Very unfunny."

I could feel Louis tense up in the front seat, long to slam on the brakes, wheel the car around, drive home in stony silence to prove that the outing had been ruined by his son's going too far this time. But he forced himself to pretend he had not heard, then was further humiliated when, finally, he had to ask directions at a service station.

We got to the Farmer's Basket (now called the Farmer's Daughter) at four o'clock. A bright-eyed, pinafored waitress gave us a number and told us there would be a forty-five-minute wait.

Jasper went outside. Beryl headed for the rest room to freshen up. I sat, like J.D., expelling my breath and trying to relax. Rhoda kept looking around to see who was coming in after us who might be getting a table before us. (Which was every party of two.) Then she had to let the pigtailed waitress know that the LeCroix party of six was here first, had come a long way for this meal, went so far back with the Farmer's Basket that they were practically members of the family and consideration should be given to that fact.

Jasper reappeared at the exact moment we were led to a table for ten, seated with a noisy group who were just mopping up the last of their honey and biscuits. Family style was not what Louis had in mind.

Quickly he read the menu aloud:

Gizzards, 4.75
Half Chicken, 6.95
Chicken and Dumplings, 5.95
All orders with choice of slaw or green beans, black-
    eyed peas or rice and red gravy, plus pan-size biscuit

Everyone got the half chicken, each order served in an individual iron skillet, and we tried all the side dishes.

But only J.D. did justice to the food.

Louis talked about the old days: when his folks first moved to Jax; when there were only the three of them.

Beryl decided she was on a diet and ate only one piece of her chicken, carefully pulling off the crust, and a nibble of slaw. Rhoda announced that they didn't use the same batter anymore, that this was hot and spicy and that was old hat by now. I burst into a senseless giggle, which caused Louis to look up and glare, as if this were all my fault, this hapless meal.

When we were finished, Jasper rooted around in his jeans and produced a round gold pocket watch, which he clicked open. "We ate in half the time we waited," he announced.

The watch looked familiar, and I leaned over to see. Sure enough, on the inside of the case were Grandfather's elegant, engraved initials: *A vd L.*

"Where did you get that?" Louis stared at the watch, his face flushed.

"From Grandpa, for Christmas and graduation." Jasper clicked it shut and returned it to his pocket. "It was his dad's." He said that to me.

"I know."

147

"Is this your idea of the way to repay your grandparents for this festive meal?" Louis half rose from his chair.

"This is your dinner, Dad, not mine. All twenty-two minutes of it."

Sunday I went out to find a national newspaper. Get a breath of fresh air.

"We take the paper, Alma. He puts it inside the screen for us, remember? I showed you the look-alikes?"

"*USA Today*, see what's happening back home on the Mississippi. It's my bread and butter, you know, keeping up."

But Rhoda couldn't give that her full attention. Her interest lagged quickly concerning my job on the *Gazette*, just as, to be fair, it waned at the mention of Louis's position with the public schools. Nine to five, no prizes, no contests? She couldn't get excited.

"I'll go with you." Jasper surprised me.

Five Corners was a two-block stretch of old stores which ran from a public park to a brick post office. We stopped at the newsstand halfway down the first block where I picked up *USA Today*, the *Atlanta Constitution*, and the *Charlotte Observer*. Jasper glanced at, but did not buy, a couple of magazines which would not be welcome on Mimosa Drive.

At the café next door I ordered a cup of coffee. In the back someone had removed letters so that the rest rooms read: MEN, LAD . . s. It was a changing neighborhood.

"You going to let me have a cigarette?" Jasper joined me at the counter.

I looked at him, this tall, thin son, dark like my daddy, with the straight hair and curved nose of the Dutch, wearing the new high-top tennis shoes which were old to me. It had stung me that he got the watch.

I took out a pack of Winstons and handed him one. He pulled a book of matches out of the top of his sock, put one foot on the rung of the stool, and lit up. "When I was little," he said "some guy shot his son. Remember? It was all over the magazines. Shot him and cut off his hair, cut off his hair so he'd look nice in the casket."

"I remember."

"Dad could get away with that."

I didn't answer. It wasn't true.

"Last year we saw on *Sixty Minutes* this kid who'd shotgunned his old man. With his sister's help. They threw the book at him, didn't touch his sister. His mom got a perm and testified against him. Remember?"

"Jasper—" He had a mental catalog of all crimes committed within the family.

"I could do the same, and there wouldn't be a trial. Dad could do it and get a traffic ticket."

I finished my coffee and lit another cigarette. Wondering how old they had to get before you quit being the go-between.

Perhaps he was reminding me that before long he was going to walk across the stage like anyone else, take his rolled-up sheet of paper, clasp his dad's hand for everyone to see, flip his tassel, and stroll out of my life.

Or maybe he was sulking because both grandfathers had already given him a present, but not his father. Were all his buddies getting cars? Trips? But he knew how Louis felt about that, his official position as principal being that the diploma should be its own reward.

"I always wanted Grandfather's watch," I told him.

"You did?" He flicked it open. "One o'clock." He put it back out of sight. "You're a girl."

"I guess Daddy was saving it for you."

"Yeah."

Leaving a dollar under my saucer, I got up. Recess was over.

. . .

149

After lunch Louis sat on the side of the bed, his shoulders heaving in dry sobs. "I ruined it for him, didn't I?" he whispered, aware the walls had ears.

"He'll get over it."

"All my life I've tried to make a family. When she couldn't have kids—" He turned and pressed his face against my arm. "Then, when you could—"

I went after a glass of warm milk, maybe with a little honey in it. Something soothing.

"What's wrong with Lou?" Rhoda asked.

"A touch of indigestion," I reported.

She and Beryl were spreading a double layer of newspapers on the kitchen floor. Rhoda had offered to trim the ends of Beryl's hair, give it a blunt cut. "Did you see that girl at the table next to ours at Farmer's? That was a new style, that straight look to the ends, with the big wave in front. Before your day, honey, but it reminds me of the swirls we used to set with those big silver clips. I'll show you."

"Thanks, Rhoda." Beryl tucked her pink shirt into her painter's pants and wrapped a towel around her shoulders.

When I had the hot milk ready, Rhoda lowered her voice and gave me woman-to-woman advice. "He needs to watch his weight. I told him yesterday, 'Get Doris Day to buy the Weight Watchers program for you,' I said. I do that for Daddy, but then I spoil it with my cooking." She chuckled.

Jasper was back in good spirits, glued to the bowl game with J.D.

"That was a swell meal," he said to his grandfather. "Thanks."

"We thought you deserved a treat. A meal out, that's the ticket, we said."

"How did you figure out what to do with yourself when you graduated?"

"Wasn't a contest," J.D. told him. "I was drawn to my work like a horse to water. A field where a man bets his life on himself, you can't beat that for making sense." He shifted his bulk in order to lean closer. "You got to go with your temperament."

"Yeah?"

Louis stretched out on the orange and green guest bed of his parents' house and let me rub the shoulder muscles, locked in mortal combat.

"I don't count," he complained. "They talk to the kids. The kids talk to them. I'm left out."

"Maybe we should get the recipe," I said.

22

At home spring got under way as usual: the rains came, the churches set their garden dates, the Woman's Club prepared to vote on new members, and the senior class began to lobby for its all-night party, promising absolutely no drugs and only minimal vandalism.

But not everything was the same, and the town knew it. Methodist was in deep trouble.

To understand what that meant, you have to grasp the main fact about the churches of Venice: they operate like two service stations on facing corners, presenting a show of fierce competition, in order to keep all the business in the area coming to their common intersection.

In other words, as long as there is a race to see who gets the most kids in Vacation Bible School or the most attendance at the flower shows, then no one is going to be looking around to see what other options there might be, through what other doors the faithful might be enticed to enter the house of the Lord. Therefore, it is to the advantage of both Methodist and Baptist to keep the balance equal, for if one goes down in attendance or support, then there is the danger that the other will follow suit.

For example, in the twenties, in my parents' day, each

church resurrected itself a new building, on the present lots between Venice Public and the post office: Methodist on the southwest corner of Ash and First; Baptist on the northwest. Methodist is housed in one of those great square red-brick buildings which spell Methodism to any visitor or traveler in any area of the country, with the stained glass windows in brilliant blues and reds, showing Jesus as a boy in the temple, with the sheep of his flock, in the desert, praying with the Marys, on the cross. Whereas Baptist is the yellow brick with the flaring flame-shaped window over the entrance in teal blue, taking those who enter straight to a contemplation of heaven. And the three fully paid-for yellow buses in the church lot for bringing the country folks and shut-ins and anyone from neighboring small towns who wants to assemble in the Kroger parking lot and be transported to the words of Brother Lucas.

Then, two years ago, each congregation accepted the transfer of a black family. It was something of a race (no pun intended) to see which family went to which church.

There was Willie Pettus, whose daddy was the school janitor when I was growing up (before they said custodian). Willie was the mater dee, as we say, at the country club, and although he knew only the citizens who liked to buy their drinks in genteel surroundings, he knew them well, and several had reason to trust his discretion. So Willie and his wife were welcome because the family had been around since the last river water was inside the city limits in 1927. Then there was Junior T. Taggart, whose daddy had cleaned the barbershop when all our daddies were little boys and who went off to barber college, and Jimmy's daddy hired him. He was a favorite around town because he knew how to pack those hot towels on and ease the whiskers off and because he was thought to have some amazing success with baldness. So he was welcome also; the Taggart clan was part of Venice.

Testing the waters, the two men had let negotiations drag

on for about three years before their "decisions," but then, last year on Palm Sunday, there was Junior T. and his wife dressed to the nines in front of Baptist because the Baptists still take a hard line against the evils of drink, and there came Willie in the front door of Methodist with his wife on one arm and his old white-haired mother crying, "Hallelujah, Lord," on the other.

Who is it that is the churches' common enemy? Who causes them to turn to one another in mercy? Not who you might think.

Not Jews certainly. They are hardly mentioned. Take the editor of the *Gazette*, Hydrangea Pickens, and her brother, Monk, the undertaker, for instance. She bought our old house, and he bought the Rogers place next door. Their mother, Rose Green, was a charter member of the Woman's Club, and nobody thinks about it. Because you don't see Hydrangea and Monk trying to seduce small children from the faith of their fathers.

Proselyte is the key word: are they trying to take our children from us, brothers and sisters, are they trying to take our little ones away?

The papists would be at the top of the list, if they were around, but they're not. And although every family has a story about a distant relation who married into the RC Church and gave up the next generation, it's a distant menace, and God nowhere promised to make this an easy world.

No, who the churches fear in the recesses of their hearts are, of course, the Lutherans. Missouri Synod being a term akin to blasphemy in the minds of most of Venice's faithful; the Lutherans seen as hard-hearted, witch-burning, idol-worshiping imitators of Rome. And, above all, as extremely successful at stealing away the remnants of the dwindling rural Protestant denominations in Missouri.

(I know four people in this town who still hold membership in the Lutheran Church, and if Louis finds this manuscript and makes a public example of me, you'll not find me listing their names here, that's how strong the bias is.)

Maudie's mother, old Mrs. Blanchard, bedridden and so having to fall back on minding the town's business for it, was the first to say it out loud: in seven months Methodist's new pastor had not preached one single sermon from the New Testament.

I'm sure every member of the congregation had put this fact together, but it had not been spread around town. The connection hadn't been generally made.

How Mrs. Blanchard came to know this, laid up flat on her back and dependent on a bedpan, was this way. It was my job, as feature editor, to cover the church services. So the shut-ins could keep up, and so the participants could be listed in the *Gazette*. Thus, I reported, in a few lines each week, that Brother Lucas presented us a sermon on ——, using as his text ——. That flowers were arranged in baskets by —— in honor of her late mother. Hymns sung were numbers —— and ——. $—— was collected in the offering. Plus if there was a church supper or a special number by the choir or a special overseas offering, those got a mention. I did the same for Methodist, along with any splinter groups that wished to send in the information (Reformed, Friends, Church of Christ, and the like). No one paid it much mind, except to comment over the leftover chicken and dumplings that Brother Lucas had the Road to Emmaus stuck in his mind or Pastor Yardley did the women and their talents twice for every other topic, things such as that, to show that the speaker was keeping up.

In this way, once it had been said aloud, everyone could consult her papers and see that sure enough, the new pastor was still back parting the Red Sea. There was "The Stain of Sin," Genesis 6:5; "Away from God's Ordinances," Malachi 3:7; "Is Thine Heart Right?," 2 Kings 10:15. There were the Children in the Wilderness and the Abraham Sacrificing Isaac, and all the other standard divinity school sermons which congregations expect to hear again with each new preacher, but no New Testament.

Last fall, when Methodist was sent a new young divinity school graduate to take old Pastor Yardley's place, there was consternation at Baptist that Brother Lucas might not be able to compete. Understanding this delicate matter, Methodist, in a conciliatory move, rescheduled its Vacation Bible for the less popular afternoon slot and even promised Baptist the first choice of weekends for the spring flower show. Now the shoe was on the other foot.

But the congregation refused to lose heart. They liked Pastor Little because he visited their sick mothers, and his wife put on a nice church supper and got on with the circles. And, mostly, because he was young and handsome and had been to divinity instead of seminary and so was an educated man, as Pastor Yardley before him had been. That was what they liked and felt they were accustomed to, not like the revival spirit across the street, which disappeared on the wings of the cold light of Monday morning.

Advent, the four Sundays in Christmas, came, and Pastor Little did the first from Exodus, the second from Judges, the third from Psalms. Still his congregation waited, hymnals wide open, voices raised in song, hands digging deep when the collection plate went around. The fourth Sunday, they consoled themselves, he would have to deal with the birth of the Saviour and the star of Bethlehem. Any member of the congregation down to primary class could have written that sermon for him, word for word.

His Christmas message for the last Sunday of Advent, however, took as its text the Book of Job, ending: "The babe is lying in the manger, but the wolf is still descending on the fold."

With the first cold frost of the new year the elders and their wives and members of the circles and their husbands and even the most occasional communicants were plunged into gloom. They began to have small meetings at members' houses, disguised as dinner parties or coffees for the ladies.

The Baptists, led by Brother Lucas, who had enjoyed the consternation in the fall and risen to a pitch of glee at seeing the swelling pews and visitors in their place of worship on Sundays, also fell into despair. If one church folded, there would be a vacuum left, would be a whole segment of the town foundering and ready for the picking.

There were interdenominational meetings of fathers in the old drugstore and sons in the new one and of all of them in twos and threes in the barbershop. Women congregated in the post office, suddenly interested in the new commemorative stamps, to the amazement of Miss Newcombe's successor, and in General Dry Goods, where the obese clerk knew to let them alone, let them pretend to happen to run into one another over a new wash-and-wear print perfect for the guest room windows.

It was decided among the men that someone should call on Pastor Little and put it to him. It might be that all this was leading up to such a revelation at Easter that four dozen people would walk down the aisles and come to Jesus right there in front of all their loved ones Easter Sunday. It might be Pastor Little had a plan, just as God had, for making the contrast between the bad news and the Resurrection too glorious to bear. (In any town of 2,000, churches such as Methodist and Baptist can count on a core of dedicated members numbering about 80, give or take, with 200 sure to show for Advent, if the tree is up and there are special gifts for the children and special choral numbers and solo offerings. But 350 will crowd each sanctuary for the risen Christ on Easter. For Easter is the testimony on which the church rests its case, the Rock on which it builds its Foundation.)

It might be that Pastor Little had such a plan, but they

157

doubted it. And in case that wasn't how things were headed, a word to the wise, plus a discreet letter fired off to the district office, ought to do the trick.

Pastor Little responded, so they said, with complete understanding. He planned to do his Easter sermon on the Second Coming. How could they doubt him?

The women, deciding that they could take some pressure off the competition over the Azalea Trail and the Dogwood Show, put it to their friends in the Woman's Club that this was the time for a disinterested third party to step in and provide a distraction: an aerial show at the two-ring circus.

Thus the Woman's Club instigated its first Annual Judge and Jury Flower Show, with each entrant submitting in two categories and fifty winners in all.

With these precautions taken, and the paschal full moon having designated Easter as being late this year, the churches waited. Listlessly they fidgeted through the spring rains, listening to sermons at Baptist on the Road to Damascus and the Ride into Jerusalem, waiting for the good news at Methodist.

If there were a hundred more worshipers walking through the doors of Methodist in their new hats and crisp suits than through the doors of Baptist, even Brother Lucas didn't take offense. In fact, it was whispered about he'd spent the last forty days in the wilderness of the spirit, developing nervous stomach and a tic under his left eye, waiting for the outcome which affected not only his future but the Lord's.

Just as promised, while Brother Lucas was rolling back the stone across the street, Pastor Little stood in the pulpit, tall and blond, his young eyes blinking with seriousness behind his glasses, arms raised above his head as he conjured up the vision of what awaited us all on the final day:

If anyone worships the beast and his image, he shall be tortured with fire and sulphur before the holy angels and before the Lamb, and the smoke of their torture shall go up forever and ever, and they shall not rest, day and night, they who worship the beast and his image. . . .

And another angel came from the altar, he who has charge of the fire, and spoke in a great voice to the holder of the sharp sickle, saying, "Put forth your sharp sickle and cut the clusters on the vine of earth, because the grapes are ripe." And the angel put forth his sickle on the earth, and gathered from the vine of the earth and put the grapes in the great press of the anger of God. And the press was trampled outside the city, and the blood from the press came up to the bridles of the horses, for sixteen hundred furlongs.

"Amen."

It is said that when I reported in the paper that Pastor Little delivered his Easter sermon using Revelation 14:7–20 as his text, all the shut-ins checking their King James and Revised Standard had a relapse of symptoms that kept Daddy and his new assistant up half the night.

It was an omen, and I should have known then that it would not be an ordinary spring for any of us.

23

T H E Tuesday after the Judge and Jury Show I was sitting at Mom & Pop's in the front booth, where I usually showed up earlier in the afternoon, to get away from the paper and have a few cups of decent coffee and the sandwich which is my late lunch.

I'd already got the names of all the winners but still had to write up the story.

When the Woman's Club first scheduled the event, to help the churches out of their quandary, they'd promised fifty winners, thinking that there were fifty members of the WC and that if they each submitted in two categories, there would at least be a contest. But they'd reckoned without a boost from the weather.

It rained the way it hadn't since high school, the wettest spring in two dozen years, the paper said, with all the towns on the river side of the levee up from us, all the way past Cape G., having to be evacuated, and the bridges sand-bagged, and our bend of the Mississippi making the front page of the *Chicago Tribune*. With even the coast guard called out to do rescue work because of the intensive "flooding."

The rest of the country does not understand that *flood* is a touchy word around here. It does not, ever, flood in

Venice. That hasn't happened since we built the levee in 1918. Flood means the river overflows its banks; rain is not a flood. Rain is high water in your basement or stalled cars in the streets; flood means river water inside the city limits, and although that did happen once in 1927, that wasn't our fault. Part of the levee to the north of us broke. But that's since been restructured along the successful lines we used to begin with and cannot happen again. The Mississippi has risen forty-eight feet within its banks in the worst rains of this century—can you imagine how many tons of water it takes to raise a river forty-eight feet?—and there was no flood. A matter that national newscasters and weather forecasters cannot get through their heads.

At any rate, we at the *Gazette* did not report it was flooding, but only the cumulative inches. There'd been days and days of rain and then weeks and weeks, with the spring flowers beat to a pulp and both Baptist and Methodist (the latter because of their current problem) moving their garden tours to the middle of June, hoping for late, great rose shows.

It was perfect timing for the Judge and Jury, which was held in the Venice High gym, with a maximum entry of two flowers per contestant, one each in two classes or two in one, which meant that all anyone had to do was to rescue one fat pink Bowl of Beauty peony plus one bitone bearded purple iris—by putting a tent over her entire bed and hoping that one bloom in each patch made it uncrumpled or moving what she thought she could salvage into the house in pots— to be a contestant.

Consequently there were more than six hundred entries in all classes, and everyone was overjoyed. The Woman's Club had heard about judge and jury shows; they'd got the idea from art galleries, and they liked the tone of the name. They thought it sounded different and professional, not sloppy or amateur, but they didn't know exactly why anyone would have both judges and a jury except in cases at law. So what they did was select a "jury" of Woman's Club members to make the first cut and thus, because certain confidences were made, see to it that no one's feelings were hurt who should have been included. Then the "judges" were the garden club presidents from all around the county, and they were free to pick the winners. An additional impartiality was achieved because they were all men, as is usual in these parts, our retired pharmacist being the head of the Wednesday Morning Garden Club.

There was some slippage in the system. Friends who passed on to the jury that their entrant was the *Iris xiphium*, "Gipsy Girl," a bronze yellow, were crushed when the jury members got confused and picked a look-alike and someone no one had ever heard of was elevated to the finals. But those mishaps were the exception.

At any rate, after a full ten-hour day of these fussy old men padding about the gym with their garden books in hand and magnifying glasses and little note pads, they had their fifty winners. (Whose names I was to arrange in alphabetical order, so people could spot themselves quickly; the gentlemen, being purists, arranged the selections in order by botanical name.)

The two runners-up for Best of Show were a *Dianthus sinensis*, "Heddewiggi Gaiety," in other words a pink, and a *Digitalis purpurea*, "Gloxiniiflora," a creamy-pink foxglove. The grand winner, by unanimous ballot, was a *Digitalis purpurea*, "Big Shirley." A huge, dazzling foxglove the likes of which no one had seen in these parts, causing the judges to go into consultation, check their glossy plates against the trembling fragile bells of the real specimen before them, and give it the ribbon.

The winning entry, it turned out, was submitted by none other than Maudie Cox née Blanchard. Who had also taken the second-place prize with her ecru-pink foxglove.

The Woman's Club was stunned. "I didn't know you'd ever grown a flower in your life, Maudie. When on earth did you find the time?" This from the WC president-elect, Patsy Underwood Walters, the other second-prize winner.

"It's my hobby," Maudie told her coolly.

To me, late that afternoon, in a fit of giggles, Maudie confessed what happened. It seems that for years she had been paying the old pharmacist through the nose for medicine for her mama and that one of the prescriptions was for digitalis. She'd asked him did it grow on trees, and he had told her that actually we knew the plant as a variety of the common garden flower called the foxglove. Whereupon Maudie had been growing the big dangling bells all over hell's half acre ever since, she said—in pans in her mother's kitchen, then set outside, then brought back in to grow under more lights, set back out—hoping to learn the secret. But she had never yet figured out how to get the many-flowered, many-hued blooms to duplicate what she was now paying the new pharmacist for.

The Woman's Club prize had a side benefit as well, which was to give Hydrangea just the ammunition she'd been waiting for to vote Maudie into membership. A project she'd been working on for eight years. The story was that in the old days the WC did not take kindly to merchants in their midst. Not merchants' wives, that was fine, but women who ran a place of business; the idea had a certain taint to it. For example, they argued, Mrs. Givens of Better Dresses had never been invited to join, even though every ready-made garment that the WC wore came from her shop. So how could an exception be made for Maudie of Mom & Pop's? Especially since her mother, Mrs. Blanchard, who had that beauty shop in her home and did such a delicate job on gray hair, had never been a member?

But then Sheba had come back, and Givens became Vickers, and, well, the WC was treading on thin ice because Sheba was taken in on the first ballot, everyone being glad to have Dolly's girl back and feeling sad and guilty because of all the time Dolly had sewed for them and they never knew what a hardship it was, the extra darts and tucks, the extra beading on their Christmas runners. . . . But if Sheba, why not Maudie?

(Fortunately I had been exempt from this process. The official word was that since Hydrangea was already a member, it would look like biased reporting if both of us were there. The real reason was that they had Audrey and felt that one principal's wife per town was enough. Which decision is the only time to my knowledge that my stealing the librarian's husband ever got me a public reprimand.)

Hydrangea reported that voting had been set for after the Judge and Jury, when everyone's mind was back on business. My job was to write up a swell front-page feature on Maudie, as winner, in which, as the *Gazette* came out on Thursday, we had ample time to identify Maudie as a new member of the WC.

It was to be on hand when the membership committee arrived to "tap" Maudie that I had delayed my lunch and was compiling my facts in the front booth instead of my office.

But all of a sudden the notes on *Digitalis purpurea* and *Dianthus sinensis* looked like so much Greek to me. Because I glanced up to see the best-looking man I'd ever seen in my life sitting at the counter, talking to Jimmy as if he'd lived here all his life. How could he have been in town five minutes and me not know about it?

I ran my fingers through my hair and cursed myself for wearing an old skirt and blouse that looked as if they'd been slept in (only rained on actually) and smiled every tooth in my head in his direction, to compensate.

"Alma," Jimmy called to me, "this is Dyer Tanner. He's the fellow checking out our tremors."

"Pleased to know you."

The stranger pivoted on his stool and looked right at me,

breaking into a big grin. "She's the one I asked you about, Jim."

"Alma? Well, how about that?"

"I swore I saw the prettiest woman in town walk past my window yesterday and then disappear from sight."

"I told him," Jimmy said, "that to the best of my knowledge Maudie hadn't left the kitchen." He sent a big, sweet glance in the direction of the griddle. "You want the usual?" he asked me.

"Don't mind if I do."

"It's not that Maudie and I don't like resting." Jimmy picked up on their previous conversation as he got out the bowl of egg salad, doubled the tomatoes, and balanced my cup of coffee on his left wrist in the hash-slinging style he had perfected. "We like it fine. This is a nice little place here. But you have to look ahead. We bought ourselves a piece of land west of town and made a good profit, selling the dirt off. Making her into a b'ar pit."

"B'ar?" The visitor squinted as if to imagine it.

"B'ar," Jimmy repeated, thinking he hadn't said it loud enough. "B'ar."

"B-o-r-r-o-w," I spelled out from the front. "They sell off the topsoil. Borrow it. It leaves a big hole."

"I get you." Dyer smiled in my direction.

"Then we bought two hundred and forty more acres with the proceeds of our dirt, and we aim to plant our own maple and cottonwood. These parts used to be solid timber around here. Cypress so big at the butt you could park a pickup behind it. When we get through, our spread'll look like the Skip Kincaid Forest. You been there?"

"Matter of fact, I have."

"Big Oak State Park?"

"No, not that one." Dyer followed Jimmy and the sandwich to the booth and slid in across from me. "Mind if I join you?"

"Not a bit."

165

"Alma, is it?"

"That's right." My voice cracked slightly with the effort of appearing nonchalant. You could tell he didn't come from around here that he would even think about walking right over and sitting down in a booth with a married woman, besides which he had on a ring himself.

Venice, Mo., is a two-mile strip of total chaperonage. If I were to have my egg salad here at Mom & Pop's two days in a row when Maudie was home trying to get her old mama into medical diapers, there wouldn't be a soul from either congregation who wouldn't be putting two and two together about Jimmy and me, good, red-faced Jimmy Cox, who was going with Maudie Blanchard when I was learning multiplication tables.

I understand, now, why Wissie had to come back to her own hometown dressed as a man, riding in her father's car. "Who's that woman I saw you with last night?" "That's no woman; that's my wife," is a small-town joke, old as the cemetery. Based on the assumption that nobody is ever with a member of the opposite sex for any good reason. Thirty-three years ago, if Wissie had come to town as herself—beautiful, fresh from the biggest city in our part of the world—word would have spread like a forest fire. "Old Dr. Grady's girl, is she? How long since she's been in these parts?" . . . "Does she have any friends left? Wasn't Dolly Vickers in her class? Does she know about Dolly?" . . . "Old Dr. Grady keeping her all to himself, is he?" And within the hour an informal watch would have been set up on my uncle's house, and no one could have gone in or come out unnoticed or uncommented on.

Whereas, bringing her to town in his car, dressed as a man, Uncle Grady had to mention only once, to one con-valescing patient, that some whippersnapper intern from Cairo was nosing about, wanting some guideposts for setting up his practice, and the town would immediately move on

166

to other matters, not having the slightest wish to waste gossip on outsiders from up the road and across the river.

"I was telling Jim that I thought maybe you folks called your town VeNEECE. What with CAYro up the road and New MADrid at the bend, and my old daddy used to tell me if I ever wanted to unload a used car, that LeBANon, Mo., was the odometer rollback capital of the world."

"Actually my grandfather called it VEENis," I told him, making that up on the spot, my mind running ahead with fantasies. I couldn't take my eyes off him. It wasn't that he was slick handsome, like a movie star; he was just so full of looking as if he got up every morning tickled to see the sun arrive, as if he leaped out of bed to see what the new day would bring. A man whose smiles didn't occur at ten-year intervals and who didn't dole out his words like federal grants was something to latch onto around here. And how I wished I could.

My hopes fluttered up like doves sighting land, but I chased them away. Reminding myself that eyes never close on behavior here. That the membership committee of the WC was going to walk through the door in about two minutes, and this man and I were going to be sitting here face-to-face all cozy and beginning to moon at each other in this front booth at Mom & Pop's. It would be across town and back in ten minutes.

I didn't know what to do. Tell him quick to get out of here, that we were going to be in big trouble, before he'd even said two words to me, or get up and leave myself, remember a deadline, leave my thick helping of grated egg with homemade mayo, and scoot out, run for my life. Or perhaps pass him a note which said I'd fallen like a ton of bricks, and would he meet me in St. Louis in two years and three weeks when everyone had forgotten about today.

"What do you do around here?" he asked, digging into the remains of a Reuben which he'd carried over with him.

"I'm on the paper."

"You do your stories here?" He gestured to my list of fifty winners.

"This one I am. Maudie—" I started to tell him about the "Big Shirley" but thought I'd save the plug until she appeared out front. "Jimmy's wife is the big winner in the local flower show."

"Is that right?" He was looking at me and liking what he saw, and I noticed him look at my ring and the blush and the fact that I wasn't eating my sandwich. "What were you doing at my end of the street?" he asked.

"It's an old walk I used to take. What makes it *your* end of the street?"

"Memphis State sent a crew of us around to forecast the rate of recurrence of the major earthquakes in the Venice zone. My office is there, in that old building. We're going to monitor the tremors twenty-four hours a day and feed the information into the Earthquake Center."

"Why the sudden interest? It's been a hundred and seventy-five years since the river ran backward in these parts."

"The money comes from the Nuclear Regulatory Agency. That's the big interest. They're just using our outfit at State. Too many plants have been planned in this five-state area for them to rest easy. They figure that even a middle-size rumble on the Richter could make a hell of a devastation." He was giving me all the words, but he was also letting me know that he knew something else was going on right here.

I couldn't take a bite.

Jimmy wandered back over, in part to set the visiting scientist straight, in part to keep eye on me. "You can save yourself the time and trouble," he told Dyer.

"How's that?"

"It's a simple progression, that's what it is. I've got it computed. See, look." He began to draw numbers on the paper napkin. "These are the bad years, the real ground rolls, okay? Now 1843 was *thirty-two* years after the original in 1811; then 1895 was *fifty-two* years after that; and, in 1967, *seventy-two* years later. Get the idea? So, if you take *ninety-two* years, you get the next one, bad one, in the year two-oh-five-nine." He looked up, proud. On account of the tourists' beginning to show up, Jimmy had taken his pencil out the way he did to figure the profit per cubic foot of dirt from his pit, and covered a few dozen napkins with figures, and come up with a theory.

"That's not far from our predictions." Dyer looked impressed and a bit amused.

"Yours must be a tad off."

"Must be."

"More coffee, Alma?" Jimmy remembered his manners.

"I let this get cold." I handed him my cup and was in a total nervous state as he walked off. "Dyer?"

"You got it."

"Would you . . ." I hesitated and then plunged right in, repeating myself in a firmer voice. "Would you go back to the counter?"

"You got a deadline?"

"I'm waiting on some people."

"Your husband?" He was getting the idea.

"Might as well be."

"I don't see any harm in my sitting here, telling the local paper what we're up to."

"I'll come interview you."

"Now that's a real good idea."

I calculated as best I could. Next week's deadline was Tuesday; deadlines were always Tuesday. I would tell Hydrangea about the crew from Memphis today, take my time, bring it back up, as if I'd run out of other things to feature. Folks were tired of the old quake stories by now, almost as tired of them as of the rain, but I could slant it toward the nuclear angle. Remind them of movies they'd seen. Plus the threat of the feds sending money in to mind our business always had an audience. "Tuesday morning," I said.

"You've got to be kidding. *This* is Tuesday. Is this a brush-off?"

"No." I hesitated. "No, it's not."

"Excuse me if I sized up the situation wrong."

"You didn't," I told him right out, and could feel the color rise in my face. "I'm afraid you sized it up just about right."

He took one finger and drew lightly on the back of my hand. "I thought I did." He took a good long look. "You come here a lot?"

"Not at this time."

"Too bad."

Jimmy brought my fresh cup and again lingered at our booth, not quite thinking he should leave us alone. He cast about for another topic to bring up with the stranger. "Where you from?"

"Memphis."

"Thought maybe it was Dyersburg."

"Everybody asks that. I wish I could claim it. Maybe my old man got my name off a road map. He served a big territory in his day, selling Havanas."

That's a good feature angle, I thought. How does someone get interested in studying what goes on underground, coming from a cigar salesman? That would perk up the interest of the men in the barbershop. Would be something they could toss around under the hot towels, while Junior T. massaged the follicles of their thinning hair. My old man sold —— (pharmaceuticals, or fertilizer, or bait and tackle), and look at me now. A lot of men could identify.

You could tell that Jimmy was about to get electrocuted by the sparks going on between me and the new man and didn't know what to do about it. He didn't want to be involved in complicity because he and Maudie had eyes only for each other, but on the other hand I think he liked it that he could see what was going on. It would be a story that Mom and Pop could whisper to each other under the covers: how Alma nearly fell out of her booth at her first look at the man from Memphis, and him already asking about her the first peep out of the box. How you could have set up one of those Geiger counters between them from the word go.

I couldn't stop looking at him. I'd like to think it was love at first sight, but I don't have illusions about that. It was plain and simple, cut and dried: he was the best-looking man in town, and I was the neediest woman.

He got up, taking his coffee with him, to let me know he'd got the message. "I'll be ready for that interview," he said. "Look for you tomorrow."

"Friday." The words jammed as I tried to think. "It will have to be Friday, after Maudie's issue comes out."

"Friday it is."

Back at the counter he and Jimmy picked right up with their earlier conversation. "How did those holes get the name b'ar pit anyway?"

I wondered if women and men in cities knew how lucky they were. In a middle-size town of forty thousand, say, you could mention, "I had lunch with an editor on the paper," or, "I ran into my old friend Sheba and her brother." But not here, not those stories. Here there is only one editor, and everyone knows who she is, and there is no one over the age of ten within the town limits who doesn't know that Sheba Vickers never had a brother. And in a really big city you could just slip each other phone numbers or agree on a big red velvet hotel room, and that would be it. It made me want to cry with envy at all those happy, lucky people out there living in bigger places.

I made do with a cigarette.

Suddenly Maudie appeared, dressed as if she were going to a coronation. Her red hair had been teased up like Lucille

Ball's, and she had round pink rouged cheeks and deep green eye liner, and her short frame was engulfed in a hot pink striped dress with gathers at the waist and a nice big bow. She'd got on nail polish in a corresponding shade, her good silver ear clips, and a heavy silver ID bracelet. Not bad for the mousy type.

"You still here, Alma?" she asked.

"You look prettier than your Big Shirleys," I told her.

"Wasn't that a sketch, though?" she asked. "Me, winning the prize."

It came to me then, looking at her made up as if she were trying out for the lead in *Carmen*, that naturally Hydrangea had called her and let her in on what was about to follow. Hydrangea, protective, would not want the WC to find Maudie in her old wraparound skirt and greasy apron.

"I was just going over the books," she said to me, to show there was more to running a café than serving up the blue plate special. Getting in practice.

"Why don't you come here and let me inspect your finery?"

There was something familiar about the bracelet. Even before she got to the booth, I remembered where I'd seen it. It was her mother's; it was Mrs. Blanchard's medical identification bracelet, engraved with the warning that the wearer was allergic to Valium and penicillin. I burst out laughing. She'd literally plucked it off her old mama's arm to doll up for the ceremony.

She laughed, too, when she saw I was looking at it. "It's good-grade silver," she said. "Solid sterling."

We were in stitches when the door swung open, and there they were at last, with Patsy Walters in the lead— catching me and Maudie making hen talk and Jimmy giving details on diversifying your crops to the newcomer sitting at the counter.

Amazing grace, as Grandfather used to say.

172

24

I WENT to Hydrangea's Thursday night to plan out the next week's edition of the *Gazette*.

She liked her papers to have a "plot," a "theme," which was rather a challenge for a weekly which had to cover all the churches, Scouts, graduates, weddings, crime, and federal interventions likely to go on in a township of two thousand people in any given week. Nevertheless, that was the way she ran her show. For example, if our pimply-faced court reporter, Estes Cox, a nephew of Jimmy's, reported a record number of items under his weekly heading DE-FENDANTS BOUND OVER, then Hydrangea might do a whole issue on the rise of lawlessness among the young today. When, in fact, the actual incidents of kids charged with breaking windows (2), transients passing hot checks (3), or neighbors stealing each other's TV sets (4) might be exactly one more than during any given week in the last five years. But it gave her the kickoff idea.

(*Bound over* was Estes's cover-all phrase for *indictment, incarceration, arraignment*, and all other longer terms the meanings of which he was not quite sure and which took up a lot more type and were not as satisfactory an umbrella for every snitch and sneak in town as well as those nastier types who stumbled at the wrong moment of their lives into the wet streets of Venice.)

This week my problem was to figure out how to convince Hydrangea that an interview with Dyer Tanner was a natural part of the upcoming issue, an essential thread in whatever weekly tapestry she was planning to weave.

We were sitting in her living room having a glass of wine, warming up, needing to get our business done before Monk wandered over to have a big supper of chicken fricassee with us—Hydrangea's only recipe, served with a sidecar of Crowder peas, lifted from the Woman's Club cookbook, circa 1938, compiled and edited by Rose Green, a rare gesture to her mama.

I like to come to Marie's house, our old house, Hydrangea Pickens's house; am homesick from the moment I walk through the door. Sad at the absence of floor registers and the telltale line of soot that used to edge the high rooms like a molding. She had fixed it up to match herself: the walls, covered in a brown Victorian print, were hung with bad turn-of-the-century oils depicting umber cows and sepia countrysides; the floors were stained and polished and strewn with dark Orientals; the big, square living room was dressed with pots of dried pussy willow and touches of black cloisonné. In the midst of which Hydrangea sat, all in brown, her black hair pulled tight in a sleek bun.

(Hydrangea tells a story about her naming. Her mother had always enjoyed being named for a flower and so called her first daughter Iris and her second Myrtle. But when her third came along, she'd run out of inspiration and named her for the first thing she saw blooming when she got out of bed and into her clothes. Hydrangea says she's glad it wasn't a rhododendron. It seems that when her brother came along, there was such elation that he received the names of all four grandfathers. Something like Merrill Olle Nathan Kizer Pickens. Oliver? Kaiser? Something like that because the initials spell *Monk*, which is what everyone calls him; only the funeral home signs say Merrill.)

We did a feature on her "at home," when Mr. Rogers moved to Florida and she got the post of acting editor, a title she will hold to her grave, as the publisher in Cape G. is never going to put a woman in officially as editor. Still, to give him credit, he had sense enough to know it was Hydrangea's paper and not ring in a stringer from *Time*.

One of the reasons I love this weekly tossing about of ideas which precedes the next week's paper—and is simultaneously a celebration that this week's is out (with Maudie and her Big Shirleys)—is that Hydrangea's is a safe house for me. Once I am inside her familiar walls, Louis leaves me alone. Here there is no prying or eavesdropping or hectoring of any sort. It is the way I imagine Daddy to have felt when he put on his scrub suit: savoring the privacy and freedom of a tonsillectomy or gall bladder, scrubbing up with all due deliberation, doing his job as leisurely as a cook boning a chicken on a hot July Sunday, in no rush to leave the white antiseptic arena off-limits to Mother. That's how I feel.

I always hope Monk will get delayed with some nasty last-minute problem, such as someone not wanting to finance a wormproof metal casket for her loved one, wanting instead to settle for "shod," someone from the country, who was in Monk's mauve premises only because the law says you can't plant your mama among the pole beans the way you'd like to. When that happens, he rushes in late, about the time Hydrangea has decided to serve us anyway, his sallow face in a scowl, an Alka-Seltzer ready to drop in water, and asks for a big glass of pineapple juice: his single addiction.

We took our wineglasses, and Hydrangea laid her materials out on the dining table, a pedestal affair paste-waxed to a shine like a pair of shoes. She was incensed, she explained, because the *Post-Dispatch* in St. Louis had sent a reporter to Venice pretending to have a big interest in our

Historical Museum, who went back and wrote up a piece headed FATALISTIC FOLK OF VENICE ARE NOT QUAKING, about how we were a bunch of hicks without sense enough to know we were sitting on a time bomb. *Newsweek* had picked it up, and there she was, misquoted in both accounts: "Acting editor H. G. Pickens professes indifference. 'These predictions are far-fetched. Most folks in these parts don't give it a thought.'"

"It's not that what they're saying doesn't have a grain of truth, but they don't take certain factors into account. Such as reportorial integrity, for starts." She showed me a copy of her reply, in pencil draft. "Here's next week's editorial, what do you think?"

The attitude of the *Gazette* editor in regard to a possible repeat of the devastating earthquake of 1811–12 in Venice in the near future has been misinterpreted.

It is not that we do not believe in geological scientists when they predict such a catastrophe; it is the futility of worrying about and attempting to prepare for an event which some of those same scientists say may occur before the turn of the century and some say may be in six hundred years.

Certainly there is danger of a quake here; in fact, one strong enough to be noticed by laypersons occurs every year or so, and smaller ones affecting seismographs are noted almost daily.

Yet we remind national readers that Venice has a very small percentage of structures of more than one story and similarly a small number of masonry structures, so the danger of injury from a collapsing building is minimal. The few double-story buildings are mostly public and so are occupied for less than a third of the day. Lastly, architects can doubtless plan and contractors build "earthquakeproof" buildings, but nobody but the federal government can afford to construct them.

"That's smashing," I told her.

"I got my idea when Versie LaValle from the museum sent me this." She handed me a copy of a letter handwritten on heavy lavender vellum.

Joseph Pulitzer, Jr., Editor and Publisher
St. Louis Post-Dispatch
Dear Mr. Pulitzer:

I am writing this letter in response to the article which appeared in your paper on May 4 about our small community of Venice. The article was written by someone calling himself a reporter who came into my office requesting a tour of the museum, in order, he claimed, to show our town as a place travelers along the expressway to the World's Fair in New Orleans might want to visit.

I feel in fairness to our community you should send another reporter (sic) who would not spend quite so much of his time in our local bars and who might see our lovely town as it really is. We are not some hillbilly little town sleeping away until we are dumped into the river by your earthquake. We are a very progressive town with beauty and history in our location.

Also, the individuals interviewed are personally known to this writer, and their use of the language most certainly does not resemble that used by members of the *Hee Haw* cast as your reporter's (sic) snide remarks suggest.

Sincerely,
Versie LaValle

"How about that?"

"Maybe we should offer her a job."

"I'm considering it. She's the one, you recall, who offered to cover the delicate matter of Pastor Little's Easter sermon for the church page. Isn't she kin of yours? I think so."

"That side of the family is harder to divide than iris bulbs. She's some relation to Uncle Grady's wife."

Hydrangea then made a big show of rifling through her notes. "Now, then," she said, looking very efficient, "it seems to me the next order of business is for you to get an interview with this visiting fireman, the doomsday expert, the one checking out our quakes. In which he says that Venice is a swell place and right to do exactly what it's doing, that quakes aren't like volcanoes and you don't have a lot of warning for Johnny Weissmuller to swing into town and rescue the natives.

"Volcanoes you can run from, but ask him how the hell are we supposed to run out of a five-state area when it cracks like the bottom of a borrow pit in August?"

I looked at her, and it all seemed too easy. "I've already met him."

"Where's that?"

"At Maudie's, the day she got tapped."

"You didn't say."

"Her ID bracelet took it right out of my mind."

"What does he look like?"

"Don't ask." I smiled, to keep to my usual tone of finding any man but Louis too attractive to contemplate. The old air of wishful thinking.

"That good?"

"You should see."

"Take a picture then. We'll give the ladies at Methodist someone else to think about."

"He may break the camera."

Our plot for the next issue decided, Hydrangea settled us back in the living room.

"You ever wish you'd made a bad marriage like the rest of us?" I asked her, over a second glass of wine.

"Sure. Two divorces. I'd like to have had two divorces. The first a tragic misfit type, say he was a queer or already married to an invalid. The second purely fiduciary. A nice settlement, held in trust. People could say, 'Pickens has the damnedest luck.' That would be a lift. Give a rich texture to the years gone by. Keep the pimply-faced court reporter and the newsboys from calling me Deranga behind my back."

I contemplated that.

"But, no," she finished, "there was no flesh-and-blood opportunity I wish I'd taken."

"Not even the pharmaceutical salesman?" I mentioned an occasional visitor to town she'd been known to admire.

"He was a change-of-life fantasy." She checked her watch. "Monk must be tied up with country people."

"I'm in no hurry."

"The fricassee will be shoe leather." She put a cigarette in a tortoise holder with fingers that wore no polish: surely a single woman's combination. "Not like Monk," she continued.

"What?" I'd got lost.

"He had someone special, and I wouldn't let him have her."

"Monk?" I didn't believe that.

"He burned the torch for Janet Givens for half a dozen years. Givens Better Dresses. I put my foot down. Told him mother would rotate in her coffin. Taking on a bumpkin with no education."

"I didn't know that."

"Everyone has some guilt stored in her attic; Janet Givens is mine. I think it was spite on my part, envy. If I couldn't have a family, why should he? Why shouldn't he have to live the kind of life I did?"

"He could have married her anyway. Her husband was long gone, wasn't he?"

"He couldn't; he needed permission. He believed me that Merrill Otto Nathan Kizer Pickens could disappoint his mother."

"Don't brood about it. We all were rotters when we were young," I told her.

She got back to work. "So have your seismologist come up with a couple of concrete ideas that will make folks feel they're coping. Storm cellars or rope ladders or hip boots or rowboats, you know what I mean."

"If we put his picture in the paper, Louis will hire a detective."

"Tell your husband he has a boyfriend."

"You would have made a fine divorcée."

"Tell me."

Monk arrived, mopping his brow, which looked beaded and ashen. "I've seen everything now," he moaned. "Everything. Black. They wanted one lined in black. I tried to tell them their old daddy would look like Count Dracula, but they wouldn't take no. Black satin lining. Black suit. The old man must have been a tyrant."

"Black casket?"

"That, too." He dropped his wafer in the water Hydrangea had ready. "Give me time for a glass of pineapple," he said. "My midsection is burning like a brush pile." He took a detour to kiss the top of my head. "I like you sitting." He sighed. "That way I can lean over you like a proper uncle."

"I'll bend at the knees next time." It doesn't bother me that Monk and his sister come up to my shoulder, but I forget it bothers him.

That made me wonder if Dyer was going to be shorter than I was. I'd been sitting down after all. I didn't care; he could come up to my armpits. He could use stilts. He could climb on a box and I would stand in a sand trap, the way movie stars did in the old love scenes.

In my excitement at that train of thought I reached over and gave Monk a squeeze—sorry that he'd been cheated out of the love of his life, but suspecting that he preferred it this way after all. Would he actually have wanted the former Janet Givens armed with inventories and racks of sale blouses and ads for the paper, climbing over display cases to give him a peck and ask him could he get his own supper? I doubted it. I tried to imagine Hydrangea and her brother as kids, sitting on someone's roof watching teenagers groping in the dark below or themselves with steadies in the back seat of someone's daddy's car. But it was impossible. They both had come just as they were straight from the womb.

It was the middle of the night before it dawned on me that, of course, the interview with Dyer was a setup job. Maudie, returning the favor for the WC invitation, must have called Hydrangea and told her that Alma had tumbled like a ton of bricks, and what could they do to help?

25

I HAD rehearsed every eventuality that came to mind, had notes for any and all occasions and any and all interruptions. But despite the scenes that played in my head—in which she walks toward him with the wind blowing her hair and they (a) climb in the car and ride away, (b) hold hands across the candle in the dim café, (c) lock the door behind them as he says, "I've waited all my life for this moment"— I knew one thing for a fact: this being Venice, and not any of the above Casablanca-type settings, Big Mr. Ten was going to have to be the operative rule. I didn't have older sisters named for movie stars for nothing.

The problem was how on earth to explain to this beautiful married man, who probably wasn't asking for anything more than a good time, that it was going to take nine times of us "happening" into Jimmy's at the same time, him carrying a cup from the counter to my front booth, us talking about ground swells and where the fault lay, so to speak, before we could slip off for one time alone.

It had a totally hopeless feel to it.

The worst of it was that school was going to be out in a couple of weeks, and then that many more eyes would be roaming the streets. ("Who's that guy I saw Beryl's mom with yesterday?" Prissy Walters would be asking at home.)

Besides which, Louis was expecting us to make the usual trek back to Jacksonville, to check up on what Rhoda and J.D. were up to, later in the summer. And that was just my side of the picture. Maybe Dyer had three end-of-school picnics to go to, plus maybe he took the wife for half the month of June to the Ozarks to commune with the great outdoors.

Sometimes it seemed to me the best thing to do was to get it over with: have him come right down to our house, Uncle Grady's house, while Louis was at school and the kids were, too, throw my arms around him in that carpeted room with its row of Tarzan books, and then just wait to see what snip rang the doorbell and tattled all over town.

The one thing I did know was that there was no point in asking the nice friends who had cooked up this interview to give me a hand with getting him to bed. Flirting with sin was one thing; committing it, another kettle of fish. Maudie would say, "I have to tell you, Alma, that we don't like it, Jimmy and me, we don't, and I can't help that. That's just the way we are. So don't count on us, and don't come around making it look like we're going along with it because we're not. We're not that kind, Jimmy and me." Hydrangea would cloak her feelings in a different, professional mode: "Consider the paper—will you?—before you go off half-cocked and get yourself killed by that husband of yours. Think about the *Gazette* if you can't think about yourself." In other words, you can look but you better not touch, as they say in the song.

The whole town would be the same. They'd get a kick out of watching Alma and her earthquake man run into each other now and again and send out a few sparks that a blind man could see to light his cigar by, and say that was no more than she deserved, having got her own self in that predicament by marrying the principal in the first place. Besides, Venice likes unrequited love. It's a heart warmer to watch the old lawyer's secretary pad along after him without so much as a shoulder pat for thirty years, some say since she was nineteen if you can believe it, and never take her eyes off his face. It's fuel for sympathy when someone has a crippled wife, say, or one locked up, and he takes to going to church, which he's never done in his life, and sitting behind the widow Smith and looking at the way the little curls of hair grow on the back of her neck. Such longing can take an entire congregation's mind off the best of sermons. And no one, absolutely no one, thinks a spiteful thing about it or tries to put an end to it. It is vicarious living that young and old relish alike. It's human nature: getting yourself in a fine pickle; wanting that green grass on the other side of the fence. But the real business is definitely beyond the pale.

So why was I prancing down First Street toward the levee, then, with my arms full of note pads and papers, anything to lend credibility and give me something to hand him if the troops were out in full force? Because I had thought of nothing else but him since I'd seen him Tuesday and because this wouldn't be the first mistake of my life if it turned out wrong, but it would sure be the first break if it turned out right.

Just whom did I expect to show up this morning? All the folks in town not actively engaged in pursuing their livelihoods at that moment. For instance, Versie LaValle, who had begun to creep along after me on First Street and who would come huffing and puffing half a block behind me into the old Flood Control Building.

26

I MADE it into his office at as fast a clip as I could manage. He was waiting, standing looking out the window, where he must have been the day I strolled down here not so long ago. I smiled at the old men chewing their brown-leafed cud and called a fond greeting to their deaf ears but didn't slow my pace.

"This may be more trouble than it's worth," I told him, letting him take my hands and hold them while we stood like foolish teen-agers in his doorway. He had that good build and big grin that nearly put my eyes out.

"Don't talk the customer out of buying," he said. He was looking me over, and I could feel my face get hot and imagine the look I was sending back, big as life and as willing as I knew how.

"I'm staying at the Do Drop In," he said, "on per diem till I get settled. Let's take advantage of it. Wear a scarf and pretend to be my wife."

"It's all I can do around here to pretend I'm talking to you."

"I'm beginning to believe you." He sighted Versie out the window. "This place is a goldfish bowl."

"I know."

He was my height, had a caramel tan, the sort of crooked

white teeth which let you know his father couldn't spring for an orthodontist, a few lines around the eyes. A red plaid shirt, no jacket or tie—and that's all I had time to take in.

By the time the museum curator got her busy little body through the door, he had moved behind his desk and begun to shuffle papers. The room was vast and worn. He had a drafting table with a light in its glass top, a lot of equipment against the wall, and several topographical maps taped to the cracked plaster.

"Do you mind, Alma?" Versie puffed and wheezed. "I heard you were interviewing and thought I'd kill me two birds with one stone."

I had to laugh at that one.

"Copy down my own notes, you know, for us at the museum. There's a lot of questions when summer comes, people wanting to ask how we feel, sitting on the hot spot here. The ones who come to stand on the levee and look at the river like they're going to see the earth open up and the barges sink right out of sight."

"Dyer, this is our museum director, Mrs. LaValle. Who is sort of a cousin of mine, isn't that right, Versie?"

"Your great-aunt Nina was my plain aunt. Now that makes us once-removed, doesn't it? Except you're not blood kin."

"Well, ladies, what can I do for you?"

"Before we start—Versie, why don't you go down the hall and get Hershell? No point in hogging all this good information for ourselves. You can bet the Port Authority has a bigger interest in this than either of us. Ask him would he like to sit in on Mr. Tanner's answers."

Versie toddled out as she was told, not quite sure how this turn of events came about. I was operating on my primary rule: divide and conquer.

Hershell Cox was Jimmy's older brother. There had been three of them: Boy, the youngest, father of Estes Cox, our court reporter, who was killed, fell off a tractor in his prime, he was the one with the looks; Hershell, who had the brains; and Jimmy, everybody's favorite.

"Hidey," he said to Dyer. "Believe you met my brother."

I got them settled, making sure Hershell and Versie sat next to each other, knowing that neither would want to be bested as to who was the most conversant about the county and its dangers or the most knowledgeable about such terms as *fissure* and *Richter*.

"Didn't you speak up at SE MO?" Hershell asked Dyer, to get the ball rolling.

"See Mo?"

"Southeast Missouri. The quake conference at Cape Girardeau?"

"No, they're your professors doing that. I'm just the man who gives them their information."

"That right?"

"I have a list of questions you might look over," I told Dyer, staring into his tanned face to try to read his reaction as I handed him my scheme for Mr. Ten, typed and numbered to fool any prying eyes.

1. Go to Mom & Pop's every day after 1:30.
2. Some days I'll go at the same time.
3. Nine times we'll "happen" in together.
4. The tenth we'll meet somewhere alone.
5. Trust me, please.
6. Mr. Ten is the only way.

Sure enough, quick as a wink, Versie leaned over, saying, "Let me just jot down a couple if you don't mind."

"I made copies," I told her smoothly, passing out a legitimate list of inquiries based on having skimmed the material we got from the conference Hershell was talking about. (Potential hazards, suggestions for further precautions, and the like. Including a tiny scale map with a bunch of little circles on it, each representing a "seismic event" since 1974, which looked like nothing so much as a close-up photo of a bowl of popcorn.)

What followed in the Geological Survey office was very much like a quartet, with everyone singing her or his part, all aimed at the audience, arms waving and chest heaving, the whole showing off the range and tone of the singer's vocal cords.

My part of it, which consisted of passing messages to Dyer before their eyes, reminded me of the old days at the Methodist Youth Fellowship when you stood, shoulders touching, singing the Lord's praises, and running an eager finger along the double-meaning messages on the hymnal pages.

I handed him a copy of the *Gazette* ostensibly so he could get an idea of our feature stories. In fact, I had underlined key sentences from alderman's ads, general news stories, club items, ag reports, anything to get my meaning across.

. . . I would like your support. . . .

. . . We will be able to pit ourselves against the complexities of the society in which we live. . . .

. . . I believe that these measures make a great deal of sense. . . .

. . . In order to allow sufficient time to comply with the new policy presented, each member was provided with an outline which covered every phase of . . .

. . . the warmer weather usually triggers increased activity. . . .

I thought Dyer might not get the point or, if he did, that he'd be totally disgusted at being transported back somewhere in the vicinity of seventh grade, but he was a sport about it, skimming the paper quickly while making encouraging noises to Hershell and Versie, as if he were following what they were saying.

Hershell, naturally, was trying to explain to the visitor

why it was that making a lot out of nothing, a disaster fore-cast out of a deep bleep in the earth to be exact, was not going to do Venice's economy any good. Did the visitor know that following the Civil War our town was the busiest harbor on the Mississippi? Yes, it was. And today we were fortunate enough to be in the middle of a reawakening with regard to the economic value of that harbor. Did Mr. Tanner, Dyer, that's right, did he know that? "We've got two big companies—I'm not at liberty to name names at this point, I'm sure you can appreciate my position—that are very interested in settling here. In fact, I can tell you they are more than interested. You follow me?"

"I'm right with you, Mr. Cox."

"Hershell."

"Right."

"We don't want this industry scared off, do you get my meaning? We're unequivocally the best harbor in a natural stage along the river. Now you see the problem with you forecasters?"

Dyer nodded. "Would it help if I told you that our best guess is a good six hundred years for a recurrence of the magnitude of the 1811 quake?"

"That it would. Did you write that down, Alma?"

"I wrote it down."

Versie, who had taken about all she could stomach of her own silence, tuned up. "Now see here, Hershell Cox, you're looking at this matter with your usual tunnel vision if you don't mind my saying so."

The long and short of her side of the story was that for most of her memory the only folks who set foot in the museum were the sixth-grade classes on their spring local history tour and a few quarrelsome kin who came in regular as clockwork to check that Grandfather's portrait or Uncle Ed's triple gourd or the old aerial photo of the house they once owned next to the PO was still where it had been the last time. Now, she was glad to report, the influx of tourists had already financed half a dozen renovations and two new display cases. "People hear how the earth rose and fell like ocean waves that day, they want to contemplate the idea that it'll happen again, when they're back home, comfortable. They want to read about it in their local paper and be able to say, 'I stood right there, my own self, on that spot, and I could feel trouble in my bones.'"

Dyer leaned across in her direction. "Mrs. LaValle, I think you can tell your visitors that we're overdue for another midsize quake, one that will rattle the dishes and maybe break out a few windows."

"My goodness." Versie sucked in her breath in delight.

"Mr. Cox's brother, Jim, on the other hand, has a theory about recurrence which bears looking into."

Hershell didn't warm to a mention of the town favorite. "Jimmy always has his pencil out figuring the odds; I tell him take it to Las Vegas if he's so good."

Versie went right on. "I don't mind saying that's a comfort. That self-styled reporter from St. Louis—I hope you're not from St. Louis, Mr. Tanner—"

"Memphis."

"—didn't help with his saying our county came in all shades of flat. He was showing off his writing if you ask me, and I told him so. If you'd be interested in a copy of my letter—"

"Versie," Hershell interrupted, "I'm sure you can be proud of your correspondence, but I bet Dyer, here, has other things on his mind—"

Keeping my voice at the even pitch of a newspaper reporter, I talked under the rising din. "Readers appreciate a little personal history," I told him.

"I'm thirty-nine."

"It could be worse."

"I'm old for my age."

I laughed at the line we all used at thirteen.

"My wife is named Maydelle."

"That's nice." I wrote that down. That would help. People would be comfortable if she was named. They could say to each other: Did you see the eyes Alma and that quake fellow were making? Maydelle better get herself across the bridge if you ask me, and that would be putting a name to it. "Children?"

"Two of each."

"I have half that."

"His name?"

"Louis. He's the high school principal."

"Oh, great."

"My daddy's the doctor."

"I get the idea."

"My family always makes a trip to see my husband's parents when school is out."

"Where's that?"

"Jacksonville, Florida."

"We like to visit Maydelle's folks in Knoxville. They've got a nice place, lot of pine trees."

"Are they young?"

"The oldest, Kathy, is thirteen."

Versie cut in. "Are you getting this down, Alma?"

"I'm getting it down. I hope you don't mind if I quote you, Versie. Your being the curator will balance out with Hershell and the Port Authority. I think I can see a story here, with Mr. Tanner commenting on the two views."

"I don't mind being quoted, and you can quote me on that."

We could probably have said even more than we did, but I was trying to play it safe. "Will you be staying here for some time?" I asked him.

"I wouldn't mind if I did. Things in Memphis have seen better days."

"You're under the sponsorship of the USGS?"

"I'll give you a few pamphlets to copy from." He rose and motioned me over to inspect the seismograph humming away against the back wall. It was a round drum in a glass case, and I could see a small wired stylus draw a continual wavy line on a roll of white paper. Every sixty seconds it made a tiny jiggle, to mark the time. Big tremors, I could see, would make large leaps.

In the corner were stacked long, smooth sheets of the same paper, which looked exactly like electrocardiograms, and I was thrilled. I looked at him and then at the paper, and it was clear to me that he was monitoring the heart murmurs of the earth. I got a chill thinking of it, that our bend in the river was the chest; this piddling, meddlesome town the very bone over the thoracic cavity of the whole U.S.A. I imagined the aorta struggling with every swell of the Mississippi, the surrounding tissue suffering the edema of spring rains. I saw that bowls falling off shelves and streets rolling like the deck of a ship had only been an occasional touch of fibrillation. Anxiety in an aging patient.

Imagine, here was a man who knew how to hook up suction cups and wires to the pulse spots of our sickly old world. What a leap beyond the doctors in my family who could hardly predict a heart attack ten minutes before it happened. I gazed into his tanned face and fell in love with the earthy cardiologist.

"It never floods in these parts, does it?" he asked.

"A lot of folks take their chances outside the levee."

"Don't they wash away?"

"That's better than being left high and dry."

But our time was up. Versie and Hershell, sensing their common duty, crowded around us, ready to sandbag our bridges.

Dyer helped us all to the door. "I'd appreciate it, Alma, if you could check the facts with me before you run your story."

"All right." The idea filled me with happiness. "I can give you a call."

"I'd be obliged."

"Thank you for your time."

"My pleasure." He gave me back my list as he saw us out. "You might want to consult your notes," he told me.

Walking back up First alone—Hershell and Versie still going at it on the steps—I read what Dyer had written:

7. You're paranoid.
8. You're beautiful.
9. I must be crazy.
10. I'll give your Mr. Ten a try.

27

T H E R E is no sadder widow in the world than half of twins. Sheba broke my heart whenever I saw her, which was almost every day with the class reunion coming up. Not that it was anything other people noticed, but then they hadn't been with her night and day as a kid.

I imagine that if she'd lived somewhere besides Venice, Mo., she would have climbed into bed with woman after woman for warmth, for the familiarity of someone who reminded her of Reba—and gone crazy with the difference.

Here she didn't do much of anything except clothe the women in town the way her mother before her had done. Only where Mrs. Vickers spanned a waist, made a few tucks here, eased out a seam there, Sheba did the flattering and camouflaging with her ready-mades. So good was she that even the oldest, most finicky ladies soon forgot about Givens, that's how much better they looked when they walked out of Vickers.

The only concession Sheba made to old times: there was not one red garment in the shop. Women understood, and when they simply had to have a splash of crimson, they slipped up the road to Cape G., pretending, when someone noticed, that it was a leftover from Givens's days. Preferring to present themselves as wearing old clothes to being disloyal to Vickers.

Sheba swore she didn't know why Reba ran off. What happened was this. The dreadful cousins in Eddyville had read a book about twins and informed the school that the girls should be placed in separate classes, to develop their individuality. That was the start of it. Sheba worried herself sick, trying to catch glimpses of Reba on the playground, to send her notes at lunch period. Reba, who didn't make such a fuss about it, simply stopped attending school. It was a couple of weeks before Sheba found out about it, and the school never did. There were three fifth-grade teachers, and each of the two teachers without a twin assumed the girls to be in the other classes.

The cousins didn't catch on either because at grade card time Sheba presented them twice with her report, including her high marks in deportment, a maneuver which made the adults conclude they'd been right to separate them.

That might have continued all the way through Eddyville Public except that Mrs. Vickers got sick, and then sicker, and then she died. The very next day Reba ran away.

For ten days Sheba managed to cover up even that. "She doesn't feel like coming down for supper. I'll just take her up some food if you don't mind." She counted on the fact that the kin were busy first with the funeral and then with wondering what to do with two foster children left permanently in their care.

Finally, one night, a grown-up cousin came upstairs, feeling a slight twinge of guilt, to see what was the matter with the missing child and found a heap of pillows under the covers on that side of the bed.

They never believed Sheba that she didn't know where Reba went, or why, or how long she'd had leaving on her mind.

. . .

I stopped in just about every day to say hello, on my way to have my sandwich. To see what she had out, what idea she was promoting for Easter or the midsummer doldrums, or back-to-school and back-to-meetings, depending on the time of year. We ran her ads in the right-hand top of the page, always next to news about an upcoming event that clearly called for a new dress.

She couldn't stand Louis and said, whenever it came to her mind, that if she and Reba had stayed in Venice, I'd never have married him. That I only did it because the twins weren't there to keep me from making a mess of things.

Which I couldn't argue.

Louis's attitude to her was even cooler. At first I thought it didn't have anything to do with her personally; it was only that he was crazy-jealous of anything to do with my past. The way he went into a fit if a photo of anyone whom I'd known at all in the old days appeared in the *Gazette*. For example, if we ran a story on some boy who'd played football on the team with Andy and Buddy, back in town peddling personal computers. Or some girl who'd been alphabetized with Patsy Underwood and the twins and me in grade school, a Ussery or a Vine, long forgotten by everyone, now back working as a cashier in the bank.

But it was more than that. Sheba was singled out with a special antipathy. "She has a bad effect on you. Don't think I've forgotten that except for the two years of their major influence on you, that pair, you were an all-A student, an honors student. They led you into bad ways, and now that this one is back, she'll do it again if she has half the chance. I wish you wouldn't have anymore to do with her than is necessary."

The reunion had made half a dozen such fights already, as, naturally, I was handling it for the paper. Just as I had done the last Fiftieth Reunion, for Jimmy's daddy in 1981. (It was never a given that there was a fiftieth or a twenty-

196

fifth. It depended on who was around and wanted to get sentimental. For instance, Mother's year, which was also Mrs. Blanchard's year, there were only the two of them around, and Maudie and I walked on tiptoe, hoping neither of them would remember. And Hydrangea was already saying that when 1988 rolled around, there wasn't going to be any mention of who was what age and that certainly she was not about to have her picture made in the same class as Versie LaValle. Which was probably the key to when reunions were held and when they weren't: if there were enough men egging it along, then it happened; otherwise, not. As the women were not too keen on having their ages spread around in newsprint.)

Andy and Buddy had cooked up our reunion, delighted that they had me and Judy and Patsy Underwood still around. And that Sheba, who after all counted because she would have graduated with us if she'd stayed, was back. And a couple of others they'd tracked down who were living on the other side of the river.

Sheba offered to contact everybody, to give herself something to do and to keep Louis from making my life miserable. But it didn't help; she just got blamed as the one stirring up the waters.

"She's doing it for you, isn't she? Using her dress shop as a cover to bring back your young man for you. Don't think it's escaped my notice that she has no regard for me. I know that woman's type, making trouble in marriages because she doesn't have one herself, nor is she likely to in this town. She's sly, Sheba Vickers, sly to the bone and without a scruple."

"Louis, it's my paper and my reunion."

"Let your editor do it if it's so important."

"It's my assignment."

Which brought the fight to a standstill, with me worn-out defending things that didn't need a defense. Wondering what it was that Louis feared most from the past. Usually what I ended up thinking was: Damn Audrey and her stupidity for not getting pregnant.

Now, with Dyer in the picture, I was changing my tune. Was not going to minimize my time with Sheba but advertise it. Use her as a decoy. Divide and conquer.

I began to run around with her all the time. To talk about the reunion, about meetings at Vickers Better Dresses to plan stories. Talk about how we might do a series, with pictures of the class then and now, the ones we could locate. Might even give a nod to the teachers, the mean and fat and silly and dumb, to show that we had grown up and knew they had first names and real lives and should be thanked for putting up with us, those who were still alive.

My feature with Dyer had come out, plus enough seismic material and information on the fault line on our bend of the river to bore even the shut-ins, plus a reprint of the article in the *Post-Dispatch* and Versie's rebuttal. The whole to show that we were giving serious space to the matter, were not as hick and unconcerned as the national press had suggested.

Louis barely commented. "Haven't you and your editor done this matter to death?"

His mind was focused elsewhere—as I intended it should be. "Is it necessary, Alma, to have lunch with Sheba Vickers every day of the week in order to copy down the ten names who're going to show up for your touted class reunion? I would hope you didn't get into the habit of associating with her to such an extent."

"You've got your hands full with graduation."

"That is a function of my job, as you, above all, should remember."

"Sheba's an old friend; I'm glad of the chance to see more of her."

That took him by surprise, and I was afraid that it might

have set off a small warning in his head, as any change in my behavior, any deviation to the slightest degree, did. It was obviously something I would never have said earlier, was not my style intentionally to heighten his anger. Seeing him suddenly silent, considering, I drew back, not wanting to overplay my hand. "We're on the home stretch, Louis."

"I certainly hope so; you've relegated the rest of us to the back burner if you don't mind my saying so."

Sheba and I had coffee at her shop after lunch, the Tuesday of graduation week, as I gathered together the feature on our class. We looked at all the old *Gondola*s, particularly the years with her and Reba, side by side. Trying to decide, for one thing, if the photos were correctly labeled, because one of their tricks had been to sit for each other's class pictures and bring home the wrong packet of those little one-inch by two- snapshots which we all traded around.

But Sheba swore she could tell. "She always looked out the sides of her eyes that way. I never did." She peered up close at second-grade shots.

"You read about twins who meet after thirty years and look just alike."

"I don't."

But I knew Sheba hadn't given up hope that Reba would appear at the reunion, looking just the same as her twin, as if she'd continued to be the mirror of her sister all these long years.

Sheba seemed older to me than the rest of us. It was because she looked the spitting image of her mother, the same wire-rim glasses, same Dolly Vickers Sunday dresses, same plump frame, the tired eye-rubbing way of looking after others. That, and because she was gone so long. People who die or disappear stay exactly the same in your mind. Gloria and Greta still have that Rita Hayworth hair and pointed bras and crimson mouths—don't they? and Mother, out there in the country, is still in her snoods and fascinators—isn't she?—whereas the ones you see all the time age with you into the present moment.

Being with her made me feel like Alma's mother, a nicer one than foggy Neva Jenkins, but a mother nonetheless. As if Dolly and I were fretting about our girls, silly Alma and the silly twins. It felt like playing grownup.

We were sitting on the green silk settees, behind a nice pair of screens that Sheba kept so mothers could rest their feet while their daughters shopped or where husbands could sit when they wearied of watching their wives check the price tags on the better dresses.

She'd found us matching outfits for the prom and brought them out on hangers for me to hold up and admire: pink blouses with jet buttons and waltz-length skirts, each with a two-foot border showing a black silhouetted skyline on a deep pink which faded to tan at the waist. Very classy and reminiscent of the old poodle skirts.

An idea took shape in my mind. "Why don't you pick me up?" I asked her. "Be my date."

"Louis will shoot me at the curb."

"He has to be at the gym two hours early."

"You wouldn't be in that mess if we'd stayed—"

"I'd be Mrs. Buddy Richmond instead."

"Wish you were?"

"It'll be strange to see him. I know from the grapevine that he runs that Buick dealership in Tiptonville and that Andy, naturally, is partners with him. And that they married cousins. So I guess that worked out fine. Sometimes I think about the two of them: planning great big surprise birthday parties for each other, or switching wives, or looking at old Venice High football movies, whatever they're into these days."

"He had his good points."

"You don't remember him at all."

"He couldn't spell *niece* in High Third." She laughed.

"It seems to me that one day you showed up here again and the very next you were putting up the green Vickers sign."

"Seems that way to you. I must have tried to call twenty times when I first moved back. Why do you think I joined the WC except as a last resort?"

"Sorry."

"You had your hands full." She rubbed her eyes and then studied me. "Want to tell me how he got you?"

"I was in J school, and thought I'd gone to heaven because there was a public library that I could trudge up the hill to every free afternoon, without Audrey breathing down my neck, and take out a stack of old novels in those wonderful heavy, transparent covers.

"The other kids were heading out to the bluffs along the Missouri for blanket parties, but I never went along. For one thing, I didn't like that river, which muddied our waters here; for another, I was afraid if I went out with those bad-skinned, adenoidal, glasses-wearing journalists, I might end up in bed with one.

"Louis, back home here, had got his divorce. The first time he came to the door—after my sophomore year—to take me out, Mother almost came apart at the seams. At first, when she saw him at the door, she was delighted. 'Why, look who's here. Remember? He knew your name. Now what in the world? Help me get my belt on, will you? Where are my slippers?' I think she thought, in her fog, that he was coming to call on her.

"But when I came prissing down the stairs in my high heels and a white linen dress I'd charged at Givens, she began to holler. You remember how she was. 'What's the meaning of this? You've got a wife, young man, whether you choose to remember it or not. I'll not have my daughter making a spectacle of herself.'

"To which Louis patiently explained that alas, his first marriage had unfortunately come to an end. Whereupon the very next day Mother took up with Audrey. By the tail end of that summer, it was Audrey and Neva everywhere you looked. They were inseparable. Mother went to the library and hung around the desk, confiding in a stage whisper about the hussies who come along, those you trust the most, and take away what's lawfully yours. That her own daughter was no better, a tramp cavorting around plain as day and not a bit ashamed of it.

"Anyhow, Louis took advantage of the fact I was as good as kicked out. The next fall he called to say he had a house for us. 'A house?' I could never deal with what he was saying and always jumped a mile when I heard his voice in my ear. 'A house?'

" 'I thought you might like the idea of living in a Van der Linden home.' The long and the short of it being that he'd talked my dad into selling him Uncle Grady's place."

"That's all it took?"

"I loved the house in those days because, I guess, it had been forbidden to me as a kid."

"Well," she said, "we all sell out."

"Not you."

"Didn't you ever wonder where I got the money?"

"Should I have? Where?"

"Monk."

"Monk?" Amazing.

"He used to be sweet on Givens, you know. I think it wasn't her but the clothes. He used to drop by our house, too, in the old days. Mom thought he wanted to play dress-up and chased him away. But I think it was to look at all the stuff on her bed, those junky chest-high piles of net. Then, when Givens folded, he called me up in Eddyville. Offered to stake me out. In return I'd help him dress his stiffs. His clients, as he calls them. Get the men's stuff up the road if something fancy was needed, provide the ladies' things myself. We have a nice partnership; I drop by whenever he's ready and bring a rack of clothes so he can take his time selecting."

"Does Hydrangea know?"

"In her way. I think she doesn't want to imagine that baby brother has anything you'd call a bad habit, but she's real nice to me, buys all her clothes here, and never brings the matter up."

"You're still playing tricks the same as always—" I smiled, hesitating. "Even by yourself."

"Sure enough." Sheba stared off toward the screens that hid us from the door. "You know, I wrote every name in the book about the reunion. I wonder who all will show up?"

28

A LOT of the old class of '59 did come back, but not the one Sheba was hoping for. Andy and Buddy were there, with big, fat beer-drinking bellies and double chins and big, pink, slick shirts, like old times. Buddy gave me a hug right in the middle of the dance floor, and I knew that Louis would bring it up the rest of my life, but I hugged him back with a lot of warmth. Andy, too.

Their wives looked a lot alike, having good bodies and lots of hair and giving the impression they'd just spit out their chewing gum and stuck on their rhinestones ten minutes before. (I admit that way back when I heard they'd married cousins, I'd constructed this little fantasy that the wives would turn out to be Reba and one of the awful Eddyville crew, but naturally, they weren't—)

Louis danced the Parents Dance with a shy, radiant, embarrassed Beryl, and the next slow one with me, and then spent the rest of his time watching sheep-faced Jerry Walters paw his daughter with obvious familiarity.

Things couldn't have gone better.

Patsy Walters née Underwood had squeezed into the blue net she'd worn at our prom, the one which had matched my yellow, and a couple of other women had, too. Judy,

Andy's other girl and Beryl's favorite teacher, was in her lavender tiered. A few people, seeing Sheba and me in our matching black and pink outfits, came up to us and said, "But I thought you two were identicals."

After about a dozen dances, mostly hard rock provided by the Gears from Cape G., when most of the senior boys were stoned out of their minds and the girls were woozy on the wine they'd smuggled in their purses in "perfume" bottles, I said to Sheba very casually, "This is giving me a splitting head. Louis is watching me like a bloodhound after a convict. I'm going to the teachers' lounge and have a cigarette."

"Suits me. That guy with your old boyfriend—Andy— has danced with me twice with no sign of daylight between us, and his wife is about to stiletto my instep with her Day-Glo pumps."

We ducked into the hall, while Louis sat in the line of official chaperons, talking with his teachers and the parents of his students, fuming over the repeated absences of his son from the dance.

My plan was that if Sheba wanted to linger, I'd pretend to go, and if she was in a hurry, I'd decide to stay. I smoked my cigarette and then told her, "I'm heading back."

"Not me. I'll take a little snooze, pretend I'm mean Miss Matlock with the cramps. How'd you get up your nerve to come in here anyway? I still think this is off-limits to us."

I slipped out the back door of the gym, skirt tucked up in my hand, knees bent, head ducked so that I might be mistaken for Sheba if some student looked up. I headed straight for her car, which was parked under a streetlight, where no student was about to venture.

Dyer was sitting at the curb, and I scooted across the front seat of Sheba's car, out the door, and into his. It was something out of a Marx Brothers' movie, actually, but worked just the way we'd planned.

Once safely inside, I laid my head on the seat so I couldn't be seen, and he drove us straight to the old Flood Control Building and his office.

I won't say it was great. We were skittish, feeling scared and stupid and looking over our shoulders half the time. Dyer didn't think I got a lot out of it, and then I cried, of course, and clung to him and told him that I loved him and his heart-monitoring machine and didn't want ever to go back.

He didn't have an idea in the world what it was like for me finally, at the age of forty-two, to have real, enthusiastic, wholehearted, uncomplicated sex.

I was back in the lounge, dragging Sheba out with me, in exactly thirty minutes—and I guess you could have lit the Venice High gym with the light I was putting out.

29

WHEN the opportunity presented itself for us to use Daddy's house, it was Louis who unknowingly urged me to take it.

"It's time to put your animosity behind you, Alma; your talent for grudge bearing does your family no good."

"Apparently he's going to be all right."

"A stroke at his age is hardly a case of the measles. You might as well take a good look at your future. Your father is a man of considerable means. You owe it to your children to mend your fences."

Maudie used to tell me that: Daddy was a rich man. The words conveyed nothing. And still didn't to anyone but Patsy née Underwood's husband, harboring stacks of deposit slips. What had money ever done for Daddy? When had we ever had even a moment of ease or harmony from it? I thought about all those bowls of oatmeal, Mother's closet of junk. You could have stacked the kitchen waist-high with hundred-dollar bills and it wouldn't have changed a thing: the bathtub would still have been without a stopper; the beds, with frayed sheets which crawled off every night of the world onto the floor. Money might be a shovel which enabled you to dig a hole to plant a future, but it was never Daddy who hefted that hoe.

. . .

What had happened was he sprung a leak.

He was operating when it occurred, trying to put what was left of Mrs. Blanchard together again, "patch up the old inner tube" was how he used to say it when I was young, or "retread the tire," if he was talking about an old man. Daddy was standing up, reaching for clamps, the wound pulled together, the worst of it over, when he felt the hammer blow on the back of his head. Not saying a word, he took slow, shallow breaths and let his young assistant, Dr. Baker, mop up. (Maudie says her mother ended up with a pleat in her midsection, but then she's had the pleasure of recounting the adventure to a hundred friends from church.)

Calm as a pond, Daddy told them what was happening, who to call in St. Louis, what to do for him, and went and stretched himself out on a hospital cart and waited to die.

Except that he didn't. He got a blind spot in his left eye and couldn't see, and then he began to have trouble with his words, which came out garbled and then only as croaks and then not at all. Dr. Baker, who'd done his reading, kept scraping the bottom of Daddy's foot with a tuning fork and sticking pins in his right hand and watching the blood pressure, but apparently the hose wasn't going to burst.

By the time the specialist got to town, in an old private plane, the aneurysm had sealed itself over, clotted like any kid's barefooted tear on a tree stump. Leaving some dysfunction, a lot of discomfort from the pressure of the blood in the spinal column, and a few erasures of memory. Nothing permanent.

They decided not to operate. The specialist flew Daddy back with him, and they stuck needles in his neck and looked at the movies made by the dye—an interesting procedure, the assistant reported, awed, that felt like turning on a low oven inside your head and let you see, as if on a screen, all the tiny capillaries within your own brain. Had Daddy been younger, they might have cut a piece out of his skull and sutured up the balloon with a nondissolvable clip. Past seventy, well . . . the neurosurgeon made the call. The odds were better to let it be.

Word had it that Daddy called the man a weak-wristed coward and, disgusted with their "pussyfooting," insisted on coming home.

The young assistant—who was the type to be embarrassed by any part of the body south of the adenoids—broke into a cold sweat of relief. A Michigan graduate with good credentials, he was scared to death of responsibility and terrified of being left in charge of an ailing town.

"Give me two weeks, Charlie," Daddy was reported to have said. "Things that are going to work will be working again; things that aren't, won't."

"I'll go see him," I told Louis. "Old people like to be read to."

"We can postpone the trip to Jacksonville if you think that necessary."

"No, he'll be up by then."

My husband assumed that my estrangement from Daddy was my own idea, which had some truth to it. I hadn't argued, anyway, all those years, partly out of not wanting to turn over to him any scrap of information to use against me about what had gone on between Daddy and me and partly out of a sense of relief that the two men need never be in the same room.

I'd half a notion that if I showed up at the other end of Main the door might be barred to me, but I could always try.

Having a sudden motivation.

The first few times I took the kids with me every night after supper, to establish a pattern. They, like the young Alma before them, had made their own trips down to this house. Jasper starting when he was in elementary school and fed up with things at home; Beryl now that she was in Venice

High and hearing talk about this grandfather whom the town held in such high regard.

"Hello, Grandad," she said, and bent to kiss his mottled face.

"Widget," he mouthed, brightening up. "Look who's here."

That stung me to the bone, the old nickname given away so lightly while I wasn't looking.

"Hey," Jasper said, "you look like shit."

"They wouldn't retread me," Daddy whispered to him, trying to pull his face into a scowl but able only to move random muscles, making a grimace on one side and a blank plane on the other. "Too old."

"I'm sorry, Grandpa," Jasper said, staring at the feeble face.

Actually Daddy's words were much harder than that to understand; we all had to lean over and fill in some of the consonants. Which we did under the skittish gaze of the assistant and the silent presence of a white-faced vocational nurse, hired to bring Daddy bowls of tepid oatmeal and keep nuisances like us from tiring him out.

Her I thought of as a chaperon to be eluded and could never get her name right. I called her Mrs. Bosoms (Beasom? Beeson?), the white-breasted tyrant who had a propensity for not leaving when her shift was up or for darting back in when I was sure she'd gone—for one last peek at the patient, one last admonition. The truth was she thought she should have been paid to live in, and as it wasn't that the doctor couldn't afford it, it must be that his kin, we, were tightwads and didn't care a fig about the old gentleman.

A local woman, she was from the country and asked me that first evening, "You want I should notify your mother?"

"Let's see how it goes—" I stalled.

She never brought the matter up again.

. . .

I continued to go down after supper, alone, when Jasper and Beryl tired of this trip or rather grew embarrassed at not being able to understand their grandfather, lying flat on his back.

I read aloud to him every night. Usually warming up with the McGuffeys, which I carried from home, beginning, as every schoolboy did in the old days, with the *First Reader*:

What makes the lamb love Ma-ry so? / The eager
  children cry;
Oh, Ma-ry loves the lamb, you know / The teacher
  did re-ply.
And you each gentle an-i-mal / To you, for life,
  may bind,
And make them fol-low at your call / If you are
  al-ways kind.

When I tired of the little moral lessons, I read him from *Tarzan and the Jewels of Opar*, the pages of Uncle Grady's book now yellowed and brittle.

For a time in sheer exuberance of animal spirit he raced swiftly through the middle terrace, swinging perilously across wide spans from one jungle giant to the next, and then he clambered upward to the swaying, lesser boughs of the upper terrace where the moon shone full upon him. . . . And then he went more slowly and with greater stealth and caution, for now Tarzan of the Apes was seeking a kill.

He never made a sign that he heard, yet I knew he did because the assistant had worked out a scheme whereby he called Daddy every night at nine and each morning at six, and Daddy was simply to lift the receiver, then hang it back up, a signal that he was fine.

When I had finished what seemed to me a decent page or two, enough to get Tarzan out of one adventure and into the next, I put the book aside and looked at my watch. Calculating carefully when it got dark—after eight, before nine—and then straightened the covers on his bed.

Downstairs I boiled him a pot of coffee, black as tar, and set it and a mug on his bedside table, near the phone, but not so close that in his effort to lift the receiver he'd knock it over. (Complete, even, to the ritual eggshell in the bottom.)

I spared him some indignities. For instance, I never looked in the closet off the small bedroom to see what had replaced Elsie's rows of starched blue dresses. Or went into his consultation room below, where the old Underwood still sat. Now, when he didn't need it from me, couldn't use it anymore, I scrupulously respected his privacy.

"Good night, Daddy," I said, counting the time it took me to gather my things together.

But he made no answer.

I never knew if Daddy touched his coffee, and didn't want to. If Mrs. Bosoms found it and dumped it out, thinking I'd made it for myself (and I always rinsed a little in the cup, so it would look used), that was fine; she could think me uppity for expecting her to clean out the pot. If he did, then there was at least one thing he got out of my visits that he was helpless to get on his own.

30

D Y E R, meanwhile, had been working out his own schedule with the town, his own Big Mr. Ten, not that he put it in those words. He began to hang out at the Last Chance bar, running into Hershell and some of his cronies midweek for a few short beers. Letting it be known that weekends were spent with the wife and kids, the first part of the week given over to burning the midnight oil over his charts and graphs at his desk in the old Flood Control Building.

Before long people got used to thinking of Dyer hitting town on Mondays, working like a man preparing his income tax returns, then slowing down, tapering off, as was natural, showing up along about Thursday to swap stories, have a couple of Millers, be agreeable and accessible. People got used to knowing that you could drive by Last Chance and see his car, with the bumper sticker saying OUT OF WORK? EAT YOUR TOYOTA, and know he'd be inside, glad if you were in the mood to detour before the supper hour, chew the fat with the scientist who'd come to our town to take its pulse.

Our plan was that we'd meet every other Wednesday night, when folks at Last Chance would think he was still in his office, and anybody happening to look for a light through the blinds at Flood Control would guess he'd closed down his night work for the week.

It meant a lot to me the way he fit in, better than either Daddy or Louis, born and bred in Venice, ever would. People liked him and told him all their stories, and he asked a lot of the right questions to draw out their confidences.

When we "ran into" each other at Mom & Pop's, he had already heard by the grapevine about Daddy.

"Understand your father's been sick," he said, carrying his Reuben to my booth and sitting down.

"Ask her," Maudie called, "to tell you about the pleat in Mama's stomach. She's selling tickets."

"We have a right to refuse service," Jimmy said, leaning his head out from the griddle, "to anyone who fraternizes with my brother Hershell."

"Fraternize? I have to office with him. I'm trying to train him to save his favorite long-winded tales for after hours."

"I've been down reading to Daddy," I told Maudie, wanting it to be public knowledge.

"I never knew him," she said, coming up and wiping her hands on her apron.

"I thought he'd kept your mama alive for twenty years."

"As a doctor, sure. I meant, when Gloria and Greta and I were running around, I never knew him."

"Me, too."

"That's good news, then, you seeing him."

"It makes me sad; he looks the spitting image of my grandfather when he was old and showing up in his BVDs."

"It's when I look in the mirror and see my mother staring back at me that I lose sleep."

"She never looked so good."

"She never had Jimmy."

Which was an occasion for going back and giving him a hug.

It went like that when Dyer and I met, with the four of

us talking back and forth, none of it private. But at least we had a chance to sit across from each other and look. Plus, if they didn't have anyone else to wait on, after a spell Maudie and Jimmy usually got real busy cleaning the grill or arguing between themselves about expenses. They were kind people, as long as we stayed in the wishful-thinking category.

Big Mr. Ten was out the window, I told him, it was time to escalate, and passed him a note about where and how we were going to take advantage of Daddy's stroke.

"Ask your dad how he got that bum leg," he said, folding the note and slipping it in his pocket.

"It's an effort for him to talk still."

"How's the new assistant doing?"

"Nervous."

"Small wonder. Nursing your chief would be like doing a nose job on a plastic surgeon."

"Mrs. Bosoms does the actual nursing."

"Around the clock?" He was getting information.

"Day shift."

He took that in and then told a story about his daddy, the cigar salesman, what a con man he'd been, what territory he'd covered, how he'd been run out of town across all the bridges from Cairo to Caruthersville in his day. It was conversation for public consumption and probably much of the same stuff he told at Last Chance, but I liked to listen.

Wednesday night we went to Daddy's.

I arrived as usual, pulling my car around the back driveway by the office window, just as Mrs. Bosoms and the assistant were due to take their leave, thereby insuring that they did so, as how could they linger when the doctor's daughter was there? How could they graciously not call it a day?

Then I read my selections, being up to the *Second Reader*.

The Greedy Girl

6. Did you ever see a squirrel with a nut in his paws? how bright and lively he looks as he eats it!

7. If he lived in a house made of acorns, he would never need a doctor. He would not eat an acorn too much.

8. I do not love little girls who eat too much. Do you, my little readers?

9. I do not think they have such rosy cheeks, or such bright eyes, or such sweet, happy tempers as those who eat less.

Then, when we'd taken Tarzan for another swing or two on his quest, I laid the books face down in the chair (did I do that to bother him? bending the spines? or because I had done it as a child?) and slipped down to make his coffee.

As I was leaving, I heard him laboriously drag himself to the bathroom and made sure to let the back door slam.

Dyer was waiting for me in the shadows halfway between his office and Last Chance, north of the intersection where Main and First meet, where two ruffled mimosa trees hung out over the sidewalk in front of a vacant house. He got into the car, put on a white wig as near to Mrs. Bosoms's hair as he'd been able to match from my description, purchased at a costume shop in Memphis, and I drove at normal speed along Second to the side of Grandfather's house.

I parked exactly where I had before, the whole trip taking ten minutes on the outside, more like six. During that time I left the kitchen light on, for anyone who was looking toward the big house from Main. From Second all you could see was the parlor and a clump of fig bushes behind a stand of hickory trees.

We went in the back door, straight into Grandfather's old bedroom, now Daddy's examining room. I longed for us to go into the parlor, to make love by the stand which once held

Grandfather's wooden cigar box, but the risk was greater. Daddy could have got it in his head to lumber down the stairs; after all, it was his house, and he could break his neck if he took the notion. Or Mrs. Bosoms or Charlie Baker could come back to check on things. Whereas now, all I had to do was cross the back hall from the examining room to the kitchen and be heating water if they came. It seemed foolproof.

Once in the old bedroom I pushed the door almost shut and set a pillow against it, not wanting to provide the noise of a door's clicking. Then, where we would be hidden even if the door was opened, near Grandfather's old bath around the corner, we lay down on a pallet of starched sheets, at last, and, almost beneath my father, made love.

I couldn't get enough. The marvel of the ease and speed with which he touched me, his excitement and pleasure, his wish to do it in all the ordinary ways that a million men had made love to a million women thrilled me. He worried that he was not doing enough for me, and then I cried onto his shoulder, at how I loved him and how I could not bear to be apart.

We talked in whispers, stopping very minute or two to listen for the sound of footsteps or cars, relieved when the phone rang exactly at nine, only once, and then the silence fell again. Pinning the patient in our minds precisely a room away, overhead.

Once I imagined Daddy creeping out from under the covers, groping his way across the upstairs hall, and putting his ear to the floor of the closet in the big bedroom over us, listening just as I had done among the broken sandals three dozen years ago at Marie's house. Turnabout, I thought—surprised to find, still, such a residue of anger.

Dyer cradled my head on his shoulder, my feet hanging down below his, our legs and chests bare, a sheet pulled over us.

217

We talked about our current families. Careful to touch on nothing that would be disloyal, giving no violations of confidence. For example, I never told him what is recorded here about Louis, just as he never told me what had made things turn bad with Maydelle. Rather, we talked for the pleasure of being able to do so without an audience.

"Do you worry what's going to happen to your kids?"

"Sometimes," I admitted.

"I mean, they're getting out, yours, and what will they do? Kids get out these days, that doesn't mean there's a job waiting or one to be had. They don't have a concept of work; then they get bitter when they don't land on their feet. Kathy, my oldest, she'll be fourteen. She doesn't give it a thought. I've tried all the gimmicks, allowances, chores, rules, but they grow up how they're going to, and it doesn't make much difference what you do. That twig is bent when the head crowns if you ask me. Nothing you can do makes a dime's worth of difference."

"You made it."

"My old daddy taught me to work the territory."

"So teach them."

"The days of learning at home are over. That's past tense."

"I'm not sure we learned anything at home in my day."

"Sure you did; else you wouldn't be here reading to your dad."

"It's only to see you."

"You're fooling yourself if you think that."

We agreed we'd risk twice a week, for the two weeks Daddy was supposed to be in bed. Other than that we agreed not to talk about the future. But, of course, we did.

"Will you be here in the fall?"

"It looks that way, that I'll be around at least twelve months, until we can begin to see what the new equipment turns up. The nuclear folks want definite figures, which are not easy to come by. Everyone wants it to be cut and dried like the San Andreas in California, but out there they've got surface scars and measurable offsets; here the faults are buried under river sediment, which makes it tough."

" 'What's it doing, this corner of the world?—Falling apart or reshaping itself?' "

"Is that a question?"

I shook my head, smiling at him.

"I get it." He rocked me back and forth, proud that he could tell it was from a book. "You still want to go to all this trouble?"

"You know I do."

"This place is all eyes."

"I told you."

"This, here, makes it harder for me to go home."

"I know."

"I'm short-tempered with them when I should be the opposite. I leave feeling great, telling myself I'll make it up, that I'm going to take them out to someplace special. Then, when I get to the house, all I can think about is how you're here."

"Me, too."

"Some men can compartmentalize. My old man, for one. But I've trained myself on the job not to do that, to keep an eye peeled for what's in all directions, because you never know when you'll pick up a clue that'll give a different meaning to the wiggles on the paper."

"Make love to me once more before we have to go."

"Do we have time?"

"I wish we never had to leave."

Then, as swiftly, quietly, and carefully as we'd come, we left. Dyer back in his wig (Who was that woman I saw you with last night? That was no woman . . .) for the casual eye of whatever stray citizen was walking around in the evening shadows, thinking she saw Alma take the nurse home.

Back we went slowly down Second, then under the

branches of the mimosa tree, from which tryst I set out down Main for home and Dyer walked down First and in the back door of the Last Chance to end the evening with his boon companions over a bottle of beer.

31

AUGUST steamed in like the first slow day of Creation.

Maudie and Jimmy put out a new red and white sign, which proclaimed EIGHT BIG POTATOES COMING SOON, that made me laugh whenever I saw it. Never mind that apparently every other living soul in town understood that microwave spuds with fancy toppings were the new culinary treat, I couldn't read the sign without imagining an old stage pulling into Dodge and eight tough potatoes getting out. (It reminded me of all the jokes the twins and I used to pull as kids. Calling the drugstore to ask, "Do you have Prince Albert in a can? Better let him out." Calling the grocer: "Do you have loose crackers? Better catch them." Ha-ha.)

Bea Newcombe, the lanky new pharmacist, and Junior T. Taggart, of the barbershop, had got together on a new scientific find, which Junior T. had read about in *Time* the same week that Bea had seen it in the *Harvard Medical Newsletter* to which she subscribed: a substance called minoxidol which was a miracle cure for baldness. It seems that the pharmaceutical company which issued it had originally taken a patent on the medicine as a new breakthrough for hypertension, but it had had the unpleasant side effect of causing hair growth all over the body (the Wolfman syndrome, Bea called it); not deterred, the drug company had reissued it as a salve to combat baldness. Because, as Junior T. told his eager clients, of its ability to increase the supply of blood to the hair follicles. It was tested, he explained, on a few hundred bald monkeys before it was made available to barbers such as him. Bea did up some pretty tubes, which she sold Junior T. at cost and which he then marketed as his own Preparation J for a hefty profit to all the balding of Venice whose domes were dripping sweat in the motionless, humid tail end of summer.

As every August, everyone was waiting for something: for the kids to get back in school; for your big, fat mother-in-law to go home to Kentucky, where she belonged; for the electric bill to settle down to a size you could think about paying; for the Democrats to quit invoking our Harry Truman, whom they never gave a nod to while he was alive, and the Republicans to quit claiming Abraham Lincoln from the front seats of their Cadillacs, and for both of them to get off our television sets so we could see what our favorite teams were up to.

Shut-ins were waiting for Dr. George to regain his strength, so they wouldn't have to discuss their personal problems with new Dr. Charlie Baker, who was embarrassed at the mention of anything "below the equator"; Methodist was waiting to be relieved of Pastor Little; Baptist was waiting for its Good Hope tent revival to pick up steam; Versie and Hershell were waiting for the last swell of tourists heading home from Yellowstone; and I was waiting for Big Mr. Ten.

Being with Dyer had transformed my life. You read, I've read in all those years of getting my romance from library books, about how taking a lover sickens you, makes you turn on your old life with discontent, pulls you toward the tracks of trains (toward the dark night of the moon on the levee, I guess, in our part of the world). But that wasn't how it was at all.

After a couple of decades of not getting even the warmth that the gum-chewing cousins got from Andy and Buddy, it was like new blood from head to toe to be desired like any pretty woman in any small town.

I grew incandescent, and anybody could see it.

"You get a face-lift down there in Jax?" Hydrangea asked after I returned from our two weeks with Rhoda and J.D. on Mimosa Drive.

"It's the light at the end of the tunnel."

"What is?"

"Getting the kids gone," I told her, feeling weightless as a balloon, needing to smile all the time.

"I thought that was giving you depression."

"Having them gone? Why would it?" I laughed. She was talking about some time I couldn't even recall.

After years of falling asleep before the evening news because I could not stand to be awake another hour in the time of day when Louis was home, willing myself to fade out until it was another day and I was safely back in my office at the *Gazette*, where he couldn't reach me, I was now lying lightly on my side of the bed, head whirling too much to sleep, waiting for Louis to doze off into his fitful slumber, so I could go over the last time with Dyer in my memory, savor it, and dream about the next time, anticipate the look and touch of him again.

Instead of letting Louis get up before me, to work out with his weights before walking to school for his summer hours of seven to four, I got up before him, letting my first cup drip through while everyone else was quiet, even Jasper, who was working a seven to three shift on the digging crew at Jimmy's borrow pit.

Some mornings I took a walk all the way down Water Street to the levee to watch the sun rise across the river, where it lived, to watch it hit the slow-flowing glacier of water as it glided past our doors in the half dark, returning home by the time the birds began to splash in their bath by the sundial and peck in the lush grass while Uncle Grady's painted daisies opened at the touch of daylight. These were retrospective strolls, designed to stir old memories of a blossoming Alma. Reminding me of the days of flat shoes, thick socks, jelly-roll hair, of moving my stuff all the way from the borrow pit, swollen out of bounds by rains, through the center of town, to the Flood Control Building, where the old men, who looked a lot like my father now, chewed Redman and watched my skirts swing by.

I was writing all the time. In my mind, under the sheets at night; in the morning as I watered the boxes of snow-white petunias on the sun porch; in actuality in my office, hard at work two hours before the rest of the staff arrived at nine.

I was working on a novel about twins, consumed to tell the fictional tale of the urge to repeat, the desire to be two. I'd named my twins Ann and Elizabeth, dividing the great-grandmother, herself divided: one of them the Quaker who would not speak out in her own defense; the other a soldier stripping tobacco leaves shoulder to shoulder with a battalion of men. I had set it back in time, speaking first in the voice of the woman who went forth and then as the one who held her peace, being, in turn, as we all are, the activist and the pacifist. I had dozens of drafts of half a dozen chapters and began afresh each day.

Working on the story made me think of the thousands of library books which had filled my early life, imagining each of them beginning this same way. Conjecturing Tolstoy touching thighs and breasts and writing of war and peace, Undset admiring a farmer's flanks and filling volumes on a changing Norway. I reread each much-loved book in my mind, wondering what moment of lust and love had brought forth the story of the stolen candlesticks, of the girl with the secret garden, of the boy mislaying his royal seal. Wondering what hired woman caught beneath a blanket, what stablehand pulling up a yard of skirt had seized heart and pen and demanded the creation of a universe to explain it.

I told Dyer about my story. "I'm working on a novel," I said.

"Not about us?"

"About twins."

"Your old friends?"

"Made-up people."

"How come?"

But I didn't have the words to explain that if you wanted to tell about the joy of love in a trailer park, the last thing you could write about would be love in a trailer park. Just as, if I had really wanted to write a story of twinning, I would have had to pick a different way to say it.

Dyer had rented what was called a recreational vehicle, in an RV camp southwest of town, a park which had apparently existed for years, but outside the town's interest. The site provided water and sewage connections for mobile homes and campers crossing the country, plus offered six trailers for rent, identical aluminum units in rows of three on each side of a gravel drive in the back of the site.

There were two ways of reaching Ed's RV Camp from Venice. One was to go directly south down Main, through the rentals and blacks, until you came to the Memphis highway, then turn right; the other was to take First Street due west, out past the cemetery, to the interstate, and turn left.

Dyer's idea was that he'd pick me up in the service alley behind Uncle Grady's house, his car blocked by the shed where Louis worked out with his weights and by the neighbor's wall of bamboo, and I'd duck down and we'd head south through the part of town least likely to recognize his car.

I amended that for the two weeks when Beryl would be home and not at the lake with Jerry Walters's family or in the Ozarks with Mandy's. Those times I'd leave my car at the cemetery, so I could say, in case Louis got wind of it, that I'd been gathering dates on old settlers for a piece the *Gazette* planned for its bicentennial issue.

Dyer and I worked out a simple schedule which didn't require Gloria and Greta's complicated counting: we would meet at Mom & Pop's on all the days which ended in five, and we'd go to the trailer park, late in the morning, on all the days which ended in zero. Taking the nearest weekday when a date fell on a weekend. Which meant that some weeks we would see each other twice: August sixth, a Monday, and then again the tenth, a Friday; the twentieth, a Monday, and the twenty-fourth, a Friday. It seemed a wealth of access to me after the weeks without him in Jacksonville.

Most of my time not with him which wasn't spent in writing was given over to daydreaming. To imagining how it might be to be a public twosome. "Alma and Dyer" rolling off people's lips the way they said "Maudie and Jimmy"; Alma and Dyer in a cozy house all their own, not Marie's, not Uncle Grady's, but a new one, all ours; us having friends over for smoked ribs in the backyard, churning peach ice cream for all my children and his to celebrate the end of summer. Alma and Dyer sitting on their sofa, arms lightly around one another, plying Hydrangea with wine and Monk with pineapple juice; coaxing anecdotes from Sheba about the old, funny days when Reba was here; piling a second helping of cake on the eager pharmacist's plate, finding out if the old postmistress was *really* her mother and if she knew but wasn't telling who her daddy might be. Nice, long gossipy evenings in Alma and Dyer's new living room: the town at home with the couple, the new couple at home in the town.

Having Methodist's new pastor over, when he arrived, for a big plate of fried chicken and buttermilk biscuits, giving him the chance to meet Brother Lucas on neutral ground without a lot of parishioners looking on. Having a Christmas party for all the *Gazette* staff, the typesetters and mailroom clerk, the bookkeeper, poor, pimply-faced Estes Cox, the court reporter, even the publisher from Cape G. himself, all getting high as kites on eggnog at Alma and Dyer's—not in the press room in the concrete-block building on the site of the forgotten victory garden.

Alma and Dyer eager to climb into bed each night, reluctant to let each other go in the morning, slipping away from their jobs sometimes to make love in the bright light of midday in their own big, wide bed—laughing and hugging at memories of the crazy, sweet times in the trailer park and the old, foolish, passionate times on the floor beneath Alma's speechless Daddy.

I was happy in the present, willing myself to ignore all the danger signs. Blaming my uneasiness on the sticky slump of August.

32

D Y E R talked a good bit about his father, lying on his back with his arm under my head, staring at the smooth curved ceiling above our trailer bed. Usually right after we made love, his dad would come up. I think it was Dyer's way of handling his guilt about what we were doing. Bringing his dad into consciousness, mulling over how it had seemed to him as a boy, how it seemed to him now. Forgiving them both.

"I caught my old man once talking to one of his women on the phone. Mom was out. It was pretty plain what he was up to, and he didn't hide it. I told him. 'I'm going to tell Mom on you.' He said, 'Do that, son. Save me a lot of money, that would. She don't want it, and I don't aim to do without, but I can't make her pack. You make a stink, she'll have to walk out. Get me off the hook.' "

"What did you do?"

"I was a kid. Later I understood what he was talking about."

"But what did you do then?"

"Let him be. Went off to school and did some growing up."

It was the fifth, a Monday, and we were on the pulled-down RV bunk, in the compact, chilled space which was like a Pullman car, with a living room which became the place to sleep, a tiny stainless steel cooking area, a closet bath with a pull-down chain. Outside, over the hum of the air conditioner, trucks wheeled down the highway toward Tennessee.

Listening to Dyer talk about his father drove home to me every time what different worlds we came from. The idea of my saying anything to Daddy directly ("I'm going to tell on you") was preposterous, but trying to picture him in the kitchen at Marie's house, drinking his boiled coffee and tapping his bad leg, answering, "Do that, she doesn't want any, and I'll not do without," was inconceivable.

I tried to imagine what being a kid would have been like if you'd had the Havana salesman for a father—saying all those things which parents in my world never said.

Dyer liked to hear about my growing up, about the years before I married. I told him about how Reba and Sheba used to switch clothes, the three of us running in and out, playing tricks on my mother and theirs.

He laughed, having daughters himself. "I can see you in that house," he said, thinking of Grandfather's.

"No," I told him, "we lived where my editor lives now."

"I thought, when we were there, that was your old place."

"No. That was Grandfather's."

"But he lived there, didn't he? Your dad?"

"Yes, since I was grown."

"After your mother died?" He was trying to get it straight.

"She's still living."

"Is that right?" He frowned, confused. "But she wasn't around when we went down—"

"She's in the country, out in the county, with her sister."

"I guess it never occurred to me. I mean, their generation, you don't think of those folks as living separate. Being separated."

What a strange word. No, I wanted to respond, but they're not. No more than Uncle Grady and Grandfather, who never spoke, were separated.

"So you never lived there?"

"I'd like to have. I live now, we live, in my daddy's uncle's house."

He got off the subject. "Homes tend to stay in families around here, I guess. It's different in big cities. I don't even know the man we bought our place from; never saw him before and never saw him since."

It was hard to have any conversation that didn't lead to touchy ground. You could see he was sorry he'd brought up the trouble between my folks when I had never mentioned it. It was the same way we seldom talked about Louis or Maydelle.

I imagined him in Memphis, lying awake on his side of the bed until almost daylight, wishing himself free, unable to see a way out—because of the kids, or fear, or not knowing how to go about it. But not letting himself tell me any more than that they took their vacation to see her folks in Knoxville or that it was her birthday and he had to get back.

"Make love to me again," I said.

"Do we have time?"

"I can be late."

"I'm not objecting," he said, pulling me tight against him. Glad to be making a woman happy, glad to have her do the asking, he was always ready to go again in our cozy, private space.

It was hard to leave him, as always. We clung and kissed before I brushed my hair and slipped on my dress. I touched the bed, his face, his outstretched hand, filled with joy at what we had.

Outside he walked me to the car, both of us moving slowly in the bright, damp, shimmery, sticky air.

It took me a minute to see the photos stuck under the

230

windshield wiper. A moment more to take them in. I looked at each of them twice before handing him the three smudged Polaroid shots: one of Dyer in a white wig, standing behind Grandfather's house; one of me ducking into his car in my pink and black skirt on prom night; one of my car parked at Ed's RV Camp.

"Jasper!" I couldn't believe my eyes. I could feel my face get red. I wanted to tear the incriminating pictures into bits. "Spying on me—"

"He could have showed them to his old man. He didn't."

"How do you know?"

"Polaroid. No copies." He took them from me. "He's just mad. You think at his age it's all right for you to have a grudge against your dad, but your mom isn't supposed to."

He was thinking of his own daddy, I could see.

"What should I do?"

"Let him cool off. Let it blow over. He's made his point. He's leaving soon, isn't he?"

Nowhere on his face could I see the fear I was feeling. Slowly I caught my breath and let him put me in the car.

33

IF you asked anyone in Venice when the dreaded quake had taken place, she would doubtless have said, "Back there in August." It hadn't; it was a cold December. But the attitude of the town remained that August was the crevice of the year into which all trouble naturally fell. More miscreants were "bound over," more traffic tickets issued, more divorces threatened, more kids in deep trouble, more shut-ins gave up the ghost, glad to escape the last dog days of summer.

It came as no surprise, then, that Methodist got what it considered the final plague of locusts the week the preview of back-to-school supplies appeared in the five-and-dime window.

What happened was this. The district superintendent had given reassurances from the start: if the flock was slipping away, if decreased attendance and pledges could be demonstrated, then by all means Pastor Little should go. A personable young man, he would be welcome at a dozen churches in a dozen fine communities, was perhaps—did they agree?—slightly too well educated for a small-town congregation. (A dig which, in all fairness, he was entitled to.) Therefore, a new minister would be sent, had already been called, as a matter of fact. The only hitch, rather, the only pledge that the district office would require, and certainly only fair under the circumstances considering its generous response and quick action, was that the new pastor be assured that she would get a full four years at Methodist.

She.

Versie heard it from a kissing cousin on the other side of the family, whose husband had been one of the elders making the trip up the road for the selection committee. She called Mrs. Blanchard and the members of her circle. Within thirty-seven minutes, give or take, it was all over town. "Did you hear?" "I heard. And did *you* know—"

She was not a married woman. Not a mother.

Not a— Surely not. Surely not.

The only person instantly delighted was Hydrangea. "The women's coalition must sit in the front row Sunday."

"The women's what? You've been watching TV."

"Make a statement. You and I, Sheba, Bea. The women who run this town."

"Maudie?"

"She's married."

"Thanks a lot."

"You're newspaper. Louis doesn't count."

"Don't remind me."

The elders met in private session, up and down the street, in the barbershop, the old drugstore and the new, and more than one was tempted to stop in for a couple of quick ones at the Last Chance but fought the temptation—not wanting to give the enemy anything more to crow about.

Brother Lucas, it was reported, could not give the Wednesday message at the tent revival but sent a lay brother in his place, the tic under his eyes having made him incapacitated, his stomach having put him to bed. Mrs. Lucas was seen making two trips to the pharmacy within the hour after the news was out.

Pastor Little, already notified and highly offended both by his own reception and by the gender of his replacement,

233

gave notice that he didn't intend to hang around, unwanted, and preach on Sunday. That *she* could fill in if that was what they wanted.

Three of the senior men were sent to greet her on her arrival Saturday; she had sent word, through the district office, that she would meet with them in the sanctuary and then, if they had no objection, would like to confer with her colleague at First Baptist across the street.

About forty old-timers were seen walking their dogs, checking their mailboxes at the post office, calling on old aunties, long neglected, and running other sudden errands of necessity and mercy in the vicinity of Methodist's red-brick building.

But no one saw her go in. A strange car was in the church lot, although nothing could be told from the license plates or from staring at the stack of garment bags in the back seat, even though half a dozen people circled it like cops checking for evidence.

Word came out toward the end of the afternoon that she was already in conference with Brother Lucas and that it might be all right after all. She was a local woman.

A rumor which started the buzzing all over again.

Everyone had a theory, but mine was that it would turn out to be a long-lost "daughter" of dim Miss Dunlap's. The way Bea Newcombe had presented herself as the old post-mistress's girl. Someone, say, who'd had enough sense to check the death records or had a cousin who could provide a name. Briefly I considered a returned Wissie, who would stand in the pulpit with her lovely deep-set eyes and say (in words I recalled from long ago), "We know you even if you don't know Us. You who have been often foolish but never mean."

Actually I was the first to see her, when I was leaving the paper where I'd been gathering my church news, getting ready to head home.

First, walking down Ash toward my car, which I, too, had

"happened" to leave parked near Methodist, I saw Brother Lucas strolling along on the side of Baptist with his arm around the shoulders of a dumpy little woman who was rubbing her cheek against his. He wasn't strolling, actually; he was bounding, bouncing, walking them along at a bustling clip toward the cluster of elders waiting at the curb.

She looked across the intersection at me and waved.

It was Reba Vickers.

Before I could react, amazed at how much she still looked like Sheba, yet at how instantly I knew it was not, she put her finger to her lips and moved into the cluster of men, who walked her to her car like a Secret Service cordon on television.

Did Sheba know? Should I tell her?

I went home, and about eight, when Louis was working out to calm his nerves and both kids were gone on dates, and I was pacing around the carpeted living room, thinking that Monday I would see him at the trailer and Friday at Mom & Pop's and that in exactly two weeks to the day Jasper would be gone, the phone rang.

"She's here." It was Sheba.

"With you?"

"Here. At the house."

"Did you know?"

"She called from Baptist. Rather, she got Brother Lucas to call, locate me. Get me prepared."

"That's why she went over there?"

"So she says."

"How are you doing?"

"Alternating between feeling like I could cry or that I'm going to throw up and wanting to break her neck."

"I didn't tell."

"She wanted me to call."

"How are you doing?" I wasn't sure what would keep you from falling totally apart in that situation.

"No better than the last time you asked."

"Is she going to stay with you?"

"We haven't got that far."

"What made her—"

"Don't start with the questions. I'm still working on them."

"Sure. You must be, it must be—" I gave up.

"I'm still going with you and your boss in the morning."

"All right."

"Alma, my God, do you know how long it's been?"

It turned out Sunday that I was not the only one at our house heading to hear the new pastor's sermon.

Louis came in from stringing up an electronic bug zapper on the tree by the shed to find us all dressed.

"What, might I ask, is going on that no one has seen fit to advise me of?"

"I'm going to church with Jerry," Beryl said, speaking up first, to claim it as her idea. She had on a deep wine cotton dress with big shoulders and a bow at the waist. Charged, to be sure, at Vickers. She seldom attended the morning service, but was, with Mandy, a faithful member of the Methodist Youth Fellowship, where the girls and their boyfriends went every Sunday night to see the other kids.

"May I ask what is the occasion?" Louis had grown short of breath lately and was taking shallow breaths after his exertion outside.

"Don't you ever listen, Daddy? I told you last night that Methodist had a woman preacher. The Walters want to hear her."

"Is that right? And have they invited your mother as well?"

"I'm going for the paper, Louis. She's big news."

"I suppose your friend Sheba is also attending?"

"That's right."

"And that you two plan a long afternoon at the cemetery

afterward? That seems to be your new interest outside the home."

"No. Hydrangea is picking me up here. I'll be back to fix lunch."

"Would you like to inform me as to why you also are suddenly curious about the advent of the female clergy?" Louis focused on Jasper, who was tying his tie and straightening his shirt collar.

"Nadine's folks wanted to go."

"It was my understanding, correct me if I'm wrong, that on previous Sundays this Nadine of yours was a member of First Baptist. Has she perhaps switched her membership?"

"Get off it, Dad, everybody's curious."

"Perhaps if I had been notified that this conspiracy was taking place, I might have joined the moral majority of the town in gawking at the newcomer. As it is, since I was not, I'll content myself with watching a more edifying service on TV."

Louis never went to church. He wasn't a heathen like Grandfather; it was rubbing shoulders with a coughing, crowding, whispering congregation that he didn't like.

"Louis, they say the new pastor is from here." I considered that I should prepare him somewhat, given his bias against Sheba, for the news that the other twin had returned.

"I should think there was a policy against sending someone from the hometown in. It would seem to me common sense."

"Dad, can I have the keys?"

"There's Jerry's daddy in the driveway. Does my hair look all right in the back, Mom?"

My car pool had also arrived.

I was as undone as if I'd been going to give a recitation in front of the entire fourth-grade class. By the time Hydrangea and I picked up Sheba at her house and Bea in front of the drugstore, I'd sweated through my dress in the back and down the top of my legs. Three times I'd taken off my earrings and put them back on.

What must it have been like for Sheba?

"It's weird," she said. "Completely weird. I went into total shock when she showed up, and then, by midnight, it was like she'd never been gone. We were eating the way we'd always done and talking about those old red skirts and the tricks we'd played on Mom. All that stuff. It was like she'd never left. Do you remember the victory garden, Alma? And Mom's bed, with all those half-cut formals? Remember how your mom would always be in that closet?" She was talking a mile a minute, on a bad dose of speed—the speed to erase thirty years.

"I do."

"Yeah, okay, I'm wired. I know it."

"How does she look?" Hydrangea, by necessity, having been let in on the secret.

"The same," Sheba said. "You'll see."

"Like Sheba," I explained. "That's what she means, Exactly like Sheba."

But not, of course, exactly. Which had always been the point.

In the church there were more women than men, a good two to one. All the Easter-only crowd was there, some of the curious from across the street (like the long-haired Nadine, who was a cousin of the Blanchards), all the faithful, and a very edgy bunch of elders.

The news had cut both ways, of course, and a number of families, who agreed with the Baptists that women didn't belong in the pulpit, had switched over to the yellow-brick building with its teal blue flaring window, to enter the door of Brother Lucas's church.

Bea and Hydrangea and I did not sit on the front row— we weren't up to that—but halfway back, with Bea on the aisle, Sheba surrounded. All of us had dressed in red. It seemed an accident but must, of course, have been subconscious. I know I'd thought I was just reaching for something cool, without much sleeve, when I'd settled on an old red checked cotton which I hadn't worn for years. It must have been the same for them.

Reba, too, had a thin red collar showing at the neck of her black robe.

Dr. Yardley had always worn the robe, appearing at the pulpit from the wings, past the choir, like a fussy teacher about to give a commencement address, adjusting his horn-rimmed glasses, the skirt of his gown, missing only the cowl of school colors. Pastor Little, on the other hand, had worn his suit and I'd thought the long black robe a vestige of the past. But Reba had made a good decision; it gave her a needed air of authority, of being literally "of the cloth."

The two steps below the wooden pulpit were banked in a dozen pots of white chrysanthemums, so that it looked like the start of a new season rather than only the Thirty-first Sunday.

The choir came in, voices slightly tremulous, Versie in the lead, and we joined them on the last stanza of the opening hymn:

> For Thy church that ever more
> Lifteth holy hands above,
> Offering up on every shore
> Her pure sacrifice of love,
> Lord of all to Thee we raise
> This our hymn of grateful praise.

In a sure voice the new pastor led us in the prayer of confession:

Almighty and most merciful Father, we have erred and strayed from Thy ways like lost sheep. We have followed too much the devices and desires of our own hearts. We have offended against Thy holy laws. We have left undone those things which we ought to have done; and we have done those things which we ought not to have done. And there is no health in us. But Thou, O Lord, have mercy upon us. . . .

She read the Old Testament lesson from 2 Kings 2:11: "And it came to pass, as they all went on, and talked, that behold there appeared a chariot of fire, and horses of fire, and parted them both asunder, and Elijah went up by whirlwind to heaven."

And the New Testament lesson from 2 Peter 1:10: "Wherefore, brethren, give diligence to make your calling and election sure; for if ye do these things, ye shall never fail."

No one heard all the words, for watching and comparing. Those who knew Sheba from the dress shop but not from before stared in amazement, first at the small, plump woman at the podium and then at her double halfway back in the church. Those who had known them as indistinguishable children could be heard to whisper, "But they *still do.*"

Then Reba started talking.

"Friends, members of First Methodist, it is with some trembling that I return to you, more than a little hesitation that I accept this call.

"I told the Lord when he came to me, 'Lord,' I said, 'Your Son may have walked on the water, but You're asking me to skate on thin ice.' "

There was a collective gasp and then a ripple of laughter.

"But He wouldn't let me beg off, brothers and sisters. He said, 'Why do you think I've come to you, Reba Vickers?' He said, 'Why do you think we're having this conversation? Do you think this is happy hour talk? Do you think I'm just passing the time of day? No, I'm calling you to come to Me and My house.' 'Wait, Lord,' I told Him, 'no offense, but I think you've got me mixed up with my sister.' "

240

Then we all laughed aloud and let out our breaths.

Her sermon would have made everyone nervous if anyone else had preached it: someone old and lumbering like Dr. Yardley, or someone with razor-cut hair, a pretty face, like Pastor Little. But coming from Reba's lips, the words seemed to build and belong to the bright sanctuary with its red and blue stained-glass Jesuses, and we opened ourselves to an evangelical message that Methodist had never before received.

It was the old Reba talking, shining herself back from a reflected image, watching out of the corner of her eyes for cues, speaking just a beat behind a louder, clearer voice. Only this time it was no longer Sheba she was following.

"First I want to say that the flowers on the altar were placed there in memory of our mother, Dolly Vickers, who has been with God more than a quarter of a century.

"Now I know that, and those who knew her know that, but the question is, the question today is: can we be sure of our *own* salvation?

"When this earthly house, this tabernacle of flesh is dissolved, can we be sure we have a house not made with hands awaiting us?

"Can you be sure?

"Tomorrow's too late and today's too long to be uncertain of your salvation, friends. Now I know that many churches have committees, a committee on every way a soul can get lost, but I say to you that these works are no guarantee.

"There is only one way, there are not two ways or three ways, but only one way to ensure your salvation, and that is through Jesus Christ.

"He who was and is and ever shall be:

"Abraham's Ram,

"Jacob's Ladder,

"Joseph's Dream,

"Jonah's Whale,

"Noah's Ark,

"Ezekiel's Wheel in the Middle of the Wheel,

"Daniel's Stone Cut Out without Hands,

"In Matthew, Mark, Luke, John, He is the King, the Saviour, the Man, the Holy Ghost, the New Covenant. In Revelation He's the Vision, the Churches, the Seven Seals, the Seven Trumpets, the New Jerusalem, the King of Kings, and the Lord of Lords.

"Here, today, in this sanctuary He is your salvation—if you will let Him into your hearts.

"From the hot anointing of my soul I beseech you to ask yourself, when you rise in the morning and when you lay down your head at night, are you sure? Can you look at the blind-healing, leper-cleansing Son of God and say, 'I'm sure'?

"Brothers and sisters, can you be *sure* you're *sure*?

"Let us pray."

Shutting our eyes with her, we wanted, each and every one of us, to believe, at least for that one morning, in the promise of salvation.

Three

In the
Last
Days
of My
Father

34

THE general euphoria, the sense that we'd weathered another summer and that matters were under control, turned out to be misleading. In fact, something worse than we could have imagined befell the town.

Not the act of God we'd braced ourselves for, or pretended in order to titillate the tourist, but, far harder to comprehend, an act of our own hands.

It started when Prissy Walters didn't come home from the Methodist Youth Fellowship. It was her mother who discovered it, and how it happened was like this.

There was an unexpected storm, not the deep-watering kind, but the sort of light show which fills the west sky with sheet lightning, then the jagged bolts which leap from cloud to cloud, following by rolling claps of thunder. Patsy, who was terrified of "electric storms," as she called them, always wandered around the house with a candle in her hand, in her gown, unable to sleep if it was late, or read a love story in her new bifocals, if it was early and Hadley, her banker, was watching TV.

It was on such a wandering, looking in on the children, whom she assumed to be safe in their wing of the house, teen-agers so model that their curfews were never checked, that she saw Prissy was not in her room, blowing her hair.

Jerry, who was smearing Clearasil on like shaving cream, didn't have any idea. He'd left her, he said, in the car with Fred. Maybe she was making out, he suggested. Patsy told him to hush himself; it was his sister he was talking about.

She peered out front. But nobody was there. Her car and Hadley's behind it were in the drive. The street was empty. If there had been trouble, a wreck or anything of that nature, she'd have heard already. No news traveled faster in Venice than a teen-ager doing damage to his father's car. Unless it was the same teen-ager running into a lamppost with the banker's daughter in the front seat.

The sky turned bright as day, she told it later, light enough to read by, and then there was a soak that stopped almost as fast as it began, and then a crash that sounded like dynamite right in the hibiscus. Patsy screamed and blew out her candle.

Hadley came out to see, knowing her nerves fell apart during storms.

Later he couldn't tell what had made him look in the car. Most of us guessed it was the memory of having necked in the back seat of his own father's car, parked in the drive, but after what he found no one was about to say that aloud. Prescience, we called it, a sixth sense where his baby girl was concerned.

Because there she was, lying on her back on the seat, her legs hanging down, with all her clothes on.

(That news almost made the rounds before the worst part: "She had all her clothes on when they found her." . . . "She was fully dressed, they said, in the back seat." The worry was, naturally, that it was—although no one quite said the word aloud, asking one another only if she was "all right," had she been "hurt," the dead girl—rape. And for a time it looked as if we weren't going to find out. Daddy's assistant was in charge, if you could call it that, because Daddy was up the road in St. Louis, having tests. Dr. Baker said he hadn't thought to check—why should he?—his job was to help, or in this case, to break the news to her family that it was, in fact, what they'd seen with their own eyes—certainly not to tamper with a young girl's body at a time like that. Hadley Walters was half-crazy and would have run the new doctor out of town on the spot if Monk hadn't come to the rescue. No, he said, categorically not. He'd called the coroner, matter of routine. No. Put that out of your mind. She'd died from having pressure put on her windpipe. Period. Other details, Hydrangea related in private to me, he'd deleted out of consideration. Such as his hunch that someone had maybe tried but not got the job done, had maybe put some of her clothes back on her, and not too neatly, that she had bruises elsewhere besides her neck.)

What bothered the town the most about the death was that it had happened beneath its nose. Impossible, everyone said, to imagine that some stranger, a vagrant from up the road at Cape G., a transient crossing the river at Caruthersville, had been able to get into town and out without being seen. By anyone. The phone lines were busy starting at midnight, continuing until the crack of dawn.

Then everybody stopped talking about it.

Because the fact was that no stranger *could* have come into Venice and loitered in the bushes, stalked a teen-age girl, got out of town again unseen. Certainly not on a night when you could see a face on the street for two city blocks in the flashes of white light.

Therefore, no one had.

Therefore, it wasn't a stranger.

Everyone went back about her business, and his. People sold one another haircuts, over-the-counter appetite suppressants and analgesics, yards of wash-and-wear plaid, specials on detergents and fresh shoe peg corn, end-of-the summer sleeveless dresses. People suddenly had a lot to do.

Everyone had thought, first, naturally, that it was Fred. The boyfriend. The son of the owner of the picture show. They might have gone on thinking that for a long enough time to have him "bound over" or at least checked up on if he had gone into a state of grief or remorse at letting her out at the curb or general guilt at not having seen to it that she was inside her door before he gunned his motor.

Or cried and said how much in love they'd been or anything along those lines. But he didn't. When Hadley and Jerry came together to tell him, themselves numb, but not wanting to trust the news to the son of a bitch sissy doctor or the new preacher, who'd just got herself back to town, Fred had punched them both in the face, giving Hadley a split lip and Jerry a bloody nose. When Monk came later, to set Fred's mind at ease about certain delicate matters, Fred had hit him so hard he fell flat on his back and spent the rest of the night in Hydrangea's living room on the sofa under a blanket, alternating pineapple juice and Alka-Seltzer.

Jasper went by Fred's and they rolled around in the grass until both of them had dirt head to toe, and then Fred got drunk, really drunk, and Jasper stayed with him, and Nadine came over, and so Fred made it through the first night, and nobody ever raised the question of did he do it. His wasn't the behavior of a sneak or a pervert; he was crazed like a stuck bristleback hog. Which everyone could understand.

Her brother's rescue mission made Beryl furious because the victim was her boyfriend's sister, and that made her right in the thick of it. Jasper could think he was smart, going over to Fred's and getting in on the act, but it was Jerry who needed consoling; he'd been closer to Prissy than anybody, and Beryl was the only one he wanted to be with.

A new facet of human nature, that competition, which, fortunately, I hadn't run into before: whose bruise is bigger when tragedy strikes.

It made me hesitate to go by and see Patsy in case she thought I was more of the same, crashing the party. But not to call on her would have been unthinkable.

I took a pot of yellow mums, and wore a subdued dress, and hoped that she wasn't going to shut the door in my face. Thinking that it was her business and she had a right, at that point, to be as rude as she liked, or as prissy. After all, she'd lost a child, and there isn't anything worse than that; on the Richter scale of normal lives, that's the big one, the grand slam, the one you never get over.

"Alma, is that you?" She stepped back in the dim doorway, all made up and dressed in a church dress. Awkward. Uncertain as a little girl playing dress-up. Grief, it seemed, changed us all.

"Hello, Patsy."

"I'm so glad to see you." She threw her arms around me and cried wet tears in my V neck and on the front of my dark dress.

"I'm sorry," I told her.

"Everybody treats us like a disease. Hadley says they do that when it's ugly. He can hardly stand to have to go to work."

She led me back into the bedroom, which was also a sitting room with a window on the backyard. Hadley was tying a striped tie and looking as if he had a stage seven hangover. Which he may have, or that may have been his upright, upstanding way of falling apart. (The actual drinking, or looking the way he did, either.)

"Hi, Alma." His voice was groggy and slightly unclear.

"You've got on brown socks, hon," she told him.

"What the hell." Hadley Walters, president of Venice National, did indeed have on brown socks with his navy blue pin stripe.

He sat down and deliberately took off his shoes and socks and started over, with Patsy holding out a navy pair.

"You ever lose anybody?" he asked me.

"No," I answered, not wanting to detract from his visible collapse, thinking that yes, there had been a few back there, in the old days, but that I would be too polite to say so, with him in such shape. And then unable myself to remember ever losing anyone. It was a sort of amnesia of the kind where you forget what it was that was worrying you when you see real trouble.

"Don't. See that you don't. It stops the clock, you know what I mean. Stops the clock. Are these navy, you sure?" He squinted down at his feet, but his stomach was in the way.

"Don't worry. You look nice. Honest." She patted him like a kid reassuring mommy who has just got a third-degree grease burn and is taking three Empirin and calling the doctor. There, there, Patsy kiss it and make it well, don't cry.

As if she had decided she was tired of grownup; it wasn't any fun after all.

When Hadley was gone, we had a Coke and a couple of cigarettes. The Coke seemed strange, and then I realized we were more or less back in high school. Sneaking a smoke in her bedroom. Had I been there in the old days? I must have been; we had our senior tea in her house. Then I could see it, a lot of pink pillows, stuffed animals, and dried corsages.

"Nobody's come to see me." She sniffled.

"Beryl said you had a houseful or I'd have come sooner."

"Oh, you know, all the bank people, they don't care, and the old snoops from Methodist wanting to see inside the house. But nobody from the old days. Friends, *my* friends."

"People hate to intrude."

"That's not so. They love to poke their noses in where they don't belong. Can you believe that some of them, even before I roped off the back, wanted to go look in her room. Can you *believe* that?"

"How awful."

"Buttinskies. They don't like me." She blotted the tears which were rolling down her face again with a Kleenex. "Hadley's family came from Memphis in chartered buses. To see how I'd let it happen. Clucking around because they'd always said I'd ruin the family." She wiped off the front of her navy dress, which was sopping wet.

I had no idea what to do. Or what I'd have done differently in her shoes.

"You never liked me either," she said. "None of you did. You were always running around with those twins—and what do you think about that one coming back, there's a shock, or maybe you knew all about it, you probobly did—and even in V High when we were double-dating all the time, you never wanted to be with me."

"You and Judy ran around. . . ." What could I say?

"Judy couldn't stand me. We were not ever friends. She just wanted to get Andy away from me, fat chance, and then when I got him, she never spoke to me again. Did you know she stuffed her bra with Kleenex?" She giggled. "Weren't they a sight at reunion, Andy and Buddy? Old men with those tacky wives. Can you believe Andy danced three times with Vickers and twice with Judy, no telling what his wife thought, and not once with me. And me back in the very dress I'd worn then, not one single pound heavier. Not that I cared; he looked like some kind of garage mechanic, he really did. He wasn't the type to ever amount to anything, was he? I mean you knew Buddy wasn't either. Didn't you?"

"His family wanted him to go to college."

"But then you were always one to shock people. You could have blown me over with a feather when you went out with Louis, I mean it. My teeth fell right out of my mouth." Then thinking of high school reminded her all over again, and she began to bawl. "Prissy wasn't like me. She was popular from the minute she was born. I mean it. Church nursery the other kids were fighting to have juice and graham crackers by Prissy. Priscilla we were still calling her, but little kids couldn't say that. Jerry had come along by then, and I thought the Walters would make over a boy, little Hadley Jerrold the third, but they were all wrapped around her finger by then, honestly, the way she could play up to folks. You know she was class favorite in tenth and junior year and was going—"

"She was a lovely girl, Patsy."

"It was like she could be as pretty as she wanted to and get all the attention I had from the boys and nobody held it against her. Nobody was jealous. Every girl in V High has come by, every single one, and all of them brought a rose, one rose, that was somebody's idea, so I could see how much they loved her, and by the end of the day—" By this time she was crying so hard she could hardly get the words out. "By the end of the day there were twelve dozen roses in her room. Twelve dozen. Every single girl all the way down to the little ones brought one." She hugged herself and rocked back and forth. "They loved her. Can you imagine that, all of them coming, one at a time? They really did? Isn't that something? If—it—had—been—me, there wouldn't have been half—a—dozen."

I tucked her down on the bed and threw a comforter over her. Wondering where the hell that wimp of a doctor was with a dose of horse tranquilizers. I thought of pouring her a glass of whiskey, but then, if she was on something, I'd mess it up for sure. I looked around in the medicine cabinet ("Can you believe Alma went right in my bathroom and spied on what I was taking?") and finally gave up and sat on the side of the bed until she cried herself to sleep. She was right; nobody came. I fretted about what I would do if the doorbell rang, but it didn't. And the phone didn't ring, although I checked it twice to see if it was disconnected. Where was everybody? How could Hadley have trotted off to service installment loans at a time like this? That wasn't fair; he was as wrecked as she. Finally, I called Bea at the pharmacy and gave her a rundown. She sent a boy with something that she found still listed in Patsy's name, ordered for her by my daddy ten years ago, when she'd had a D and C, to steady her nerves. Pharmaceutical license. It seemed that Dr. Baker had suddenly got a lot of pressing patients in the hospital.

(It reminded me of what Maudie had said about him. That he was like her old grandmother who used to give her a bath as a kid and who would say, "I'll wash down as far as possible and up as far as possible, and you wash possible." Anything real was something he didn't want to touch.)

I thought of how Daddy had been with Sheba the time she'd been burning up with fever, laying his hands on her and making it better even before the penicillin. And wished I could call him. As if he'd appear in Patsy's bedroom the same as he was then, the young doctor, but I guess that was because Patsy was back in those times, and so I was, too. We were little, and I was trying to be her friend—about a zillion years too late.

I called Hydrangea and gave her the situation and stayed at Patsy's until Hadley came home at three, having put in as much of a day as he could tolerate. He was having a second highball when I made my exit. "Where the hell," he cursed, "are all the busybodies who were supposed to stop by? They show when you'd like to wring their necks, and then they crawl into the woodwork. Thanks, Alma, I mean it. This has knocked the wind out of us, you know what I mean: knocked our sails flat." He offered me a drink. "You'd think kids at least . . ."

"I believe they're having a memorial service this afternoon." Louis's orchestration.

"That's right. I forgot." He refreshed his drink. "How's Jerry doing? You probably see more of him than I do; that girl of yours has been a big help. He'll come in, and then he's right out the door again. Can't stand to be in the same house. Well, that figures, but sooner or later he's got to; it's the nature of things."

"He's fine. He's a fine boy."

"She was the strength in this house. We all leaned on her."

253

He wiped his red eyes. "God might be trying to teach us a lesson, get us to stand on our own two legs, if you believe there's a reason to these things." He sat on the side of the bed and took off his shoes, straining to reach his feet, while Patsy slept curled behind him like a kitten.

"You think it was somebody did it?" he asked.

"I don't know." That didn't seem something to explore, that it was someone we knew.

"They thought it was Fred." He made an attempt to chuckle. "See this?" He pointed to his puffy lip. "He busted it wide open." He shook his head. "He's the one torn up."

"They all are."

"Thanks, Alma, I mean it. Those big church ladies didn't knock themselves out, did they? You think your daddy would know a nurse?"

"I'm sure he would. Call when he gets back."

"Keep this to yourself, will you? Patsy's proud. She's got a yard of pride up her back like a broom handle. No need for them to see her down."

"She's just worn herself out."

"That's it, that's right. We could all use a good night's sleep around here."

35

BUT, at least at my house, not all of us got it.

Louis couldn't close his eyes.

He sat on the side of the bed, miserable.

I kneaded his knotted shoulders, rubbing them with a little alcohol, trying to relax him enough that he could stretch out and fall asleep.

I got out a pair of new pajamas, thinking the freshness and unfamiliarity would be soothing. They were in a drawer of Christmas pajamas from J.D. and Rhoda, unworn, old men's drawers, he'd called them, the maroon and white striped kind with the string-tied waist and the collar and cuffs piped in white.

"I'm hungry," he said.

In the kitchen, with only the night light on the stove, I made him a fried egg sandwich, a soporific from the days before Rhoda took up recipes.

"Louis—" I handed it to him, the egg coated in catsup, lettuce on both sides, bread toasted, just the way he liked. He sat up, still in his shorts, letting the red and yellow dribble on his bare chest.

"They know," he said. "I can feel it, like a solid object. Downtown on the way home I literally walked through it. I'm telling you, they know. They didn't take their eyes off me and some of them were snickering and some of them were scared, but there wasn't a one of them who didn't know."

"What, Louis?"

"Who did it."

I took the napkin and wiped the spills, trying not to give in to a great longing to lie down and sleep the clock around.

I drew him a hot bath, the only other thing I could think of to calm him down.

"She was special," he went on, lowering himself into the hot water. "Not like your rest. She'd come right up and talk. She'd pop in the office, to say something nice about Beryl: 'Jerry's really lucky to have found her.' If I ran into her on the street, she'd come right up and talk to me. Not turn the corner like the rest of them or laugh and wave and pretend to see someone they have to catch up with."

"Poor Fred," I said, settling myself on top of the commode, seeing that Louis's chest hair was gray which I'd never noticed before.

"That boy's cashing in on this. She didn't hang around with his type. She was clean. She was a clean, decent girl."

"Louis—"

"They know, they all know."

I brought him a mug of hot milk with a tablespoon of honey in it and fixed the same for myself.

He looked up, red as a lobster, with the steam rising around his face, while his wife of twenty years served him like a baby, and began to cry. "You can feel it in the air."

I didn't know what to say.

"Why would they do it? Protect a killer? Why would they side with him?"

"Let it sift through the grief. Give them some time. It may be too much to deal with at once, the death and then turning someone in. . . ." I handed him a towel and then a robe, ready to call it a night.

"It's my school." He whipped his skin dry. "I've given

my life to that school. I've worked for thirty years, you know that, to make it amount to something. How could it happen at *my school?*"

Once again I was on the wrong track with him, thinking him somewhere he was not, attributing to him a set of feelings he did not have.

"It's like a dye which seeps into the whole fabric, I tell you. The papers pick it up, you're branded as the high school where they found the girl. Then it starts to stain everything. You'll see, attendance at games will fall off, and then inter-mural invitations. We'll get dropped across the board."

"You're not responsible." I got him into the pajamas, the creases still in the sleeves and legs.

He was beet red, and the flush gave him a look of fury. "I've wasted my life," he declared, and pulled the covers to his chest and folded his hands on top of the sheet in resignation. As if to say the matter was closed.

The next morning he slept through the alarm, and I had to bring him three cups of coffee to rout him out.

36

To my surprise Daddy showed up at the funeral.

He looked gray and feeble, and I had to glance away. Not like Grandfather had, wandering about in his BVDs, the same old body with a slightly absent brain. This was the body going; his mind was still in the driver's seat, but the vehicle was running on empty. With slick tires.

I'd been standing with the kids, or rather in the same vicinity but by myself, watching Louis and getting knots in my stomach. It made me sick the way he was standing on the front row, by the casket which was covered in a blanket of pink carnations, his shoulders quivering, his tongue darting in and out as he looked around, letting everyone see him suffering because tragedy had ripped into the well-stitched fabric of his school.

All at once it was clear to me that if I left him, he'd turn it into a full-scale production, with him as the injured party, and that the limelight of betrayal would be far sweeter to him than anything I could ever do as his wife.

In college I'd read about a famous man in England who'd gone bicycling about the countryside one day, admiring the heath, and suddenly come to see that he no longer loved his wife. He hadn't known it, and then he did, and that had been that. All of which seemed stupid and British to me when I was twenty.

But something on that order took place inside me at Prissy's funeral. Not that I'd ever been in love with Louis, but I'd been tied to him, bound to him, and then, in the bright and steamy sunshine of late summer, I saw that the cords were threadbare, hadn't been strong enough to hold anyone in years.

It was at that moment that Daddy limped over and spoke to the kids.

"Sorry, Widget," he said to Beryl, who was holding Jerry's hand.

"Sorry, son," he said to Jerry.

He gave Jasper's shoulder a squeeze, and I saw that my son was the taller now, because of Daddy's stoop, but still resembled him, his dark hair falling over his forehead as Daddy's still-dark hair did also. "Heard you've been a help with the boyfriend."

"Fred's okay."

"It makes it easier, having friends."

He turned in my direction as I was wondering how we were going to handle this, with the kids there and perhaps half the town looking on to catch the latest development in the Van der Linden feud. Should I nod as if we were speaking? Wander off as if we'd already said hello? I could feel my chest tighten as I held my breath.

Then an amazing thing happened: he spoke to me.

"Thought you were the young lady who always read to grandfathers when their eyesight began to fail?" He said it lightly, a teasing tone to his voice.

It was then I knew he was dying.

"I've been derelict," I answered, smiling at him but not quite meeting his eyes. Smiling more for the onlookers than for him.

"You have indeed. Perhaps you'll spare some Sunday afternoon for an old man one of these days."

"I'll do that."

"Don't forget your McGuffey Readers." And he made a cackling sound in his throat. Then, lowering his voice, he said, "Understand they don't like my new assistant."

"He's not very likable."

"My intention was to stall a few years, then stampede my grandson into taking the job. But it looks as if I'll need an interim replacement."

Jasper looked pleased.

"You could come around, too, you know," Daddy told him.

"Yes, sir, I will."

"Before you get off to school."

"Right."

"Don't wait too long."

"No, sir."

"Get on down front, then, you kids. Let's get this over with. I see they've got Brother Lucas as well as Dolly's girl to do the honors."

"Granddaddy, did you know she was *murdered*?" Beryl whispered, still holding tight to Jerry, her proof that she was on the inside track.

"So I heard," he said, as we walked through the freshly cut grass to our ringside seats in the old Walters plot.

37

T H E Y found Prissy on Sunday night; the funeral was Wednesday. Monday had been the twentieth, but naturally Dyer and I did not try to meet. At least I didn't wait for him at the cemetery but spent the day with Hydrangea trying to work out how to deal with the death in the paper. I assumed that Dyer, hearing the news when he got to town, had stayed as close as possible to his desk all day, watching the stylus wiggle itself along in geologic EKGs on smooth strips of white paper.

We met at Mom & Pop's on Friday the twenty-fourth (the twenty-fifth being on the weekend) and made our plans. The thirtieth was a Thursday, which was good; from mid-morning on, with the paper out, I'd be free. Skittish about getting Dyer in trouble, with the whole town watchful, I suggested I go see Mother, then drive myself to the trailer park along the interstate.

We didn't have much to say, but that was the general mood.

Jimmy came over, and we talked about what a mess the new doctor was, as if his timid behavior had somehow caused the crime.

Nobody mentioned Prissy directly. There wasn't anything to say. The sheriff's office was busying about, going through a lot of motions, but no one, probably least of all Patsy and Hadley, believed that the law was going to come up with anything. In a small town anybody can have an alibi for any hour, friends who are willing to stick by you or your folks. Or it was a time when no one had one, so why pick on you? How it would work, which we all knew, was something akin to the way the body operates when you get a splinter deep under the fingernail: after a while the fester pushes it out. There wasn't much to do but wait.

Sunday the pews were swelled as if for Easter but without the celebration. The town feeling the need to huddle close, stand shoulder to shoulder with friends and enemies, and hear the Word.

Patsy and Hadley slipped stiffly into Methodist and sat in their gray suits in the middle of the third row, center and front. Timid and stiff, sticking together, they made an aisle wherever they walked, as people drew back, nodded, smiled, squeezed each other's hands at the sight of them, pulled out hankies, men and women, so that there was a lot of wheezing and blowing in the groups they passed, and craning, as if a parade had just gone by and was now nearly out of sight.

They sat in front of their son and my daughter and me, so that we were a fivesome, a little square of people blocked out on two rows, the three of us there to lean over and touch their shoulders, murmur in their ears, defend their backs. Beryl was bursting with pride and never let go of Jerry's hand. He seemed barely present in his new, unfamiliar suit and was probably off somewhere in his mind a zillion miles from or days before the church service that Sunday a week after his sister's death.

Behind us Maudie and Jimmy came in, and hearing their voices, I turned around, glad to see them, old faithfuls, wanting them to see that even I was here, come for the sight of familiar faces, the warmth of assembly.

Maudie was in her Woman's Club dress and Jimmy in a neat dark blue. Behind him Hershell, in the same suit, a cut or two larger, a forty portly maybe, instead of a forty slim. And over Hershell's shoulder, but with him, Dyer. All dressed up in stiff white collar and pin stripe with even a handkerchief in his pocket.

My heart almost burst at the sight of him, and I hoped that they would sit where I could see him, and not behind us, where I would feel his eyes on me but not be able to look at him.

With one part of my mind I knew he'd probably been urged to stay over, to make church, to be sure the town thought of him as one of their own and not an outsider, to quell any possible worry that maybe he was not all he presented himself to be. Certainly he could be counted on at the Last Chance, but that was not the best place to be seen at a time like this. But with another part of me I wanted to believe that he'd come for the sight of me, to make up for our missed rendezvous, to let me know that he was being with me, in whatever way he could, in full view of Venice, Mo.

As if Maudie and Jimmy could read my mind, and probably they could, they proceeded down the center aisle and took their seats to our left, one row behind us, because directly across from us were the remnants of the Rogers clan, rowdy grandchildren and in-laws, ten strong.

I could hear a faint swell of voices, with people placing Dyer, getting him straight. Husbands explaining to wives.

"Who's that with Hershell Cox? Not Boy; he's dead. Wasn't another, was there? Were there just the three? Can't be the nephew, can it? Estes? . . . No, he's still a boy. Wait, wasn't there a younger one? I'm thinking of Boy, the age he passed, aren't I?"

"The new man, honey. I told you it's the new man works with Hershell, down at Flood Control."

Dyer looked right at me but then past, as if he were placing Patsy and Hadley, who must have been pointed out to him. Everyone was taking covert glances at them anyway, so his added along with the rest wasn't going to be noticed. Plus a lot of necks were craning to see Jerry and how he was taking it, if he was angry or bothered or maybe just wishing that all the fuss would go away.

(It might be that a few necks were craning in my direction also. Saying there's Alma come to church again; every cloud has its silver lining. Saying that maybe even the old doctor himself would be here if he were still alive. But time flies. Young Dr. George is an old man himself now. You forget. Dr. August was older than my daddy, older than yours, too. He'd be, I don't know, a hundred now at least.)

The choir came in to one side of Pastor Vickers in their black robes. Versie was there with her hair freshly done. Beside her were Hershell's wife and, standing where Mrs. Blanchard used to, Willie Pettus's wife, and in the first seat on the front row, which once belonged to Uncle Grady's wife, Bea Newcombe added alto harmony.

> We gather together to ask the Lord's blessing;
> He chastens and hastens His will to make known;
> The wicked oppressing now cease from distressing;
> Sing praises to His Name; He forgets not His own.

Reba gave a brief call to worship, "The Lord is in His holy temple; let all the earth keep silence before Him," and the congregation saw, posted on the board to one side of the choir, that the New Testament text for the day was Matthew 5:4. Which even the backsliding could guess at once was the Sermon on the Mount, and most of us could recognize as "Blessed are they that mourn, for they shall be comforted."

We stood and read the responsive reading, with Reba giving her lines and us answering her back in unison, and the words seemed to fit us like our own skins, as if they'd

264

been selected, instead of just being the reading for the Thirty-third Sunday and automatic. But maybe, folks whispered, that was the secret of the message: that it always found the words for where you were.

> *God is our refuge and strength, a very present help in trouble.*
>
> Therefore we will not fear, though the earth be moved, and though the mountains be carried into the midst of the sea;
>
> *Though the waters thereof roar and be troubled, though the mountains shake with the swelling thereof;*
>
> There is a river, the streams whereof shall make glad the city of God.
>
> *God is in the midst of her; she shall not be moved.*

The sun poured through the stained glass, casting rays of blood red and royal blue on the fresh dresses and dry-cleaned suits of the congregation. Here on our right Jesus held safe in his arms a snow-white lamb, the fine lines of the metal that contained the panes making an outline, like in a coloring book, within which the deep primary colors lay flat and rich. To the left was Jesus with the Marys, one kneeling, the other embracing him, thorns on his head, his eyes gentle, his forehead bloody, his robe in tatters, the green grass of Golgotha behind him, the brown weight of the cross pressing down on his shoulders.

Dyer looked up to see me looking at him, and we smiled, each past the other, me at the brilliant windows, him at Patsy and Hadley—because of whose suffering he was there, with me.

I tried to recall which was the window that Daddy's aunt Nina and Versie gave in memory of their common grandmother and decided it was the young Jesus in the temple, robed in purple, talking to the bearded Pharisees.

As we sang the last hymn together, "O, Thou who changes not, abide with me," I could hear Dyer's voice, loud and deep, buoying up the thin chorus of the choir:

> Hold Thou Thy cross before my closing eyes;
> Shine through the gloom and point me to the skies;
> Heaven's morning breaks, and earth's vain shadows
>   flee;
> In life, in death, O Lord, abide with me.

Then we all stood together for the pastor's benediction: "The Lord bless you and keep you; the Lord make His face to shine upon you and be gracious unto you; the Lord lift up His countenance upon you and give you peace; both now and evermore."

"Amen," we replied.

Patsy and Hadley turned toward one another and then, over their shoulders, leaned toward Jerry and Beryl. "Let's wait a minute," Hadley said, "for things to clear." He was hoping that folks would go on out, shake Reba's hand at the door, step into the dazzling sunlight and frazzling heat, and go home to their oven-fried chicken.

But they didn't. They lingered, chatted, waited, made again a double row for Hadley and Patsy to walk down, straight as if roped off, touching them quickly as they went by, saying, "Good morning. God bless. Take care."

"You look nice," Patsy said, gesturing to my silk dress.

"Sheba picked this out."

"I don't see her." She seemed distracted as she glanced all about.

I realized I hadn't either. But surely she always came; had to, nowadays.

"In the hat," Hadley said, as if that made it clear.

And in fact, it did, because we weren't looking for her to be dressed that way. Sheba was toward the back, in a green hat with a black veil, vintage 1940, and a nipped-waist shoulder-padded suit. Without realizing it, we must have, still, been looking for Reba's twin to look like Reba. It made me wonder if, in part, the preacher had answered her call in order to guarantee there'd be no more dress-the-same garments.

I moved slowly, so Patsy and Hadley could walk ahead with the children, letting the crowd go past me, until Maudie and Jimmy were at the door, and Hershell was down front waiting for his wife to get out of her choir robe, and only Dyer was there, standing with one hand on the back of a pew.

"Hello," he said. "How are you?"

"Good to see you," I said.

And then there were a dozen people come between us, a sea of faces as we all spilled out as one body into the sunlight.

On the steps Reba shook every hand; across the street Brother Lucas did the same. At the intersection Baptists mingled with Methodists, communicants heading for their respective homes.

38

On the way to the country I realized that I must have picked today, knowing the thirtieth was Mother's birthday; you don't forget your parents' birthdays, dates surely etched on the large wrinkles of your childhood brain. I counted up: seventy-five. A big one. Mother, the grim harridan of my youth. Imagine. Time does make harmless biddies of us all.

Remembering, I turned around and wheeled back to Vickers, one eye on the time, and picked out a short, bunchy housecoat, in the lavender that such drip-dries always come in. Pretty awful, but a present.

I didn't like going to see her. Not just her, but going out into the flat, grungy bits of half-farmed land; old tires tied from trees, rusted-out cars up on blocks, remnants of outhouses overgrown with vines, every other farmhouse half fallen down. Signs that claimed TIMBER, BLACKBERRIES, PECANS, FRYERS, QUILTS—but with not a vestige of any such riches in evidence. The brightest garden a single stand of bee-stung hollyhocks; the fanciest house a cracker box with asbestos siding. Even the occasional horses looked sway-backed and dull-coated. Load animals put out to pasture. Fence tops hung with FOR SALE signs, split and rained unreadable.

It reminded me of Monopoly. How it is when you have to sell your hotels; then you mortgage the yellow properties and the plum ones, and there is no way to get your money back. You finally go out of the game not because they have hotels but because you don't. When the land got scalped of its trees and, therefore, its pelts, it might as well have thrown in the dice and quit.

It made me think of Grandfather and what a different world he knew.

"Glory," Mother said when she saw me. "Glory be."

She was a chameleon. When she was still in town and I'd come by, she'd say, "Look who's here." . . . "Look at that, Miss High and Mighty herself." Now, picking up country ways, she said, "Glory."

Her face was a puffy mass of dumplings pocked with dents. She was thicker in the middle than last time, her arms and legs even skinnier. A sausage with toothpicks. A sausage in a new polyester dress with acrylic ruffles at the neck. Someone else's gift, a beige wash-and-wear.

She introduced me to a gaggle of women, some without teeth, some with tufts of hair, some with cantilevered fronts and spike heels holding up fat legs and big behinds. There was Mee Maw and Mama Dee, old as the hills, Effie, who looked like Mother, a couple of women she called "my girls," one with hennaed hair, one a champagne blonde, both on the far side of fifty.

"This is my baby," she said to everyone. "Glory, can you imagine. I barely know her these days." She grabbed one of my arms in both of hers and squeezed until I thought my bones were snapping. "You're my baby, aren't you? Sure you are."

It was always like that; the instant I got to the country was the instant I wished I hadn't come.

A folding aluminum table was set up under a scrawny tree, a young cottonwood, and flies were beating us to the food. It was covered-dish, maybe, or maybe all the women lived there and had rustled it up for the occasion. I knew

Effie was her sister; the rest—I had no idea. There was potato salad and a squashed orange pulp salad with coconut which must be ambrosia, and slaw, of course. Lots of salads. And lots of desserts: birthday cakes, of the thick-icing type, two made with coconut. If there was meat, I didn't see it. Fried chicken might be cooling in the kitchen, but I doubted it.

"There's pimento; we decided nothing fancy," Mother said, pointing to a stack of crustless sandwiches which I'd missed. "Well, now, thank you, ma'am. Thank *you*." She took my package from Vickers. "Where did you get this? Doesn't she shop at Givens any more for her mother?"

I explained, but her mind was off the subject. She had put the housecoat on over her dress and was pirouetting around, showing it off. With the two garments on, both way too big, too bunchy and too long, she looked like a pincushion.

"You've got thinner, Mom," said the woman with the bright red hair.

"You're little they allow for growth and we wear things down to our gazoo, and now we're doing the same, making sure it won't be too small if it shrinks." The uplifted, wrinkled blonde poked Mother.

Then she poked the redhead. "Don't think she knows us," she said.

"Why should she? We don't know her."

The two of them waddled over and began to give me half jabs and half hugs, look at my skin, look up at how tall I was, look down to see what I had on my feet.

Probably I knew the minute I drove up and saw them with her but didn't feel up to dealing with it all at once. Which would be Gloria? But it must be the champagne hair. Greta was dark. So . . .

"Hello, Gloria," I said tentatively. "Long time no see."

"Close but no cigar."

"Greta."

"Right."

"But you had—"

"You telling me yours isn't coming out of a bottle?"

"I guess that's true." I was struggling, struggling to find in these hourglass old Jenkins girls the sisters named for movie stars. The sisters whose discarded shoes once filled my closets, now duplicate Mae Wests.

Gloria: I studied the thin, teased, red hair. Greta: the older, in the pale Spray-netted helmet.

"Glory," Mother said. "Take a picture. Effie, take a picture of my girls. This may be the last time unless you count my funeral."

She came and stood between Gloria and Greta, both birthday garments still on, and put her arms around their waists. "Take us," she ordered. "Take us, Effie. It's my birthday." She smiled and stepped toward the snapping shutter. "Get the baby," she squealed. "Get her."

We helped ourselves and took our plates onto the porch, all the women but Mother wolfing down the salads to get to the wedges of layered cake. I looked around for coffee, but there wasn't any, or tea either. They didn't seem to be drinking anything. I hesitated even to ask for a glass of water, not quite sure who was in charge, if anyone was. Mostly they were all, even the doddering old ladies, smoking and eating at the same time, with a lot of wiping off crumbs and smacking lips and blowing out smoke rings.

Were all these people kin to me?

"Do you get here often?" I asked my long-lost sisters.

They answered at the same time, then started over.

"When we have to put her in or take her out," Greta said.

"She wanted to come home for her birthday; they didn't want to let her. But when she sets her mind to it, they generally do. They have to. So we got her out." Gloria was explaining. "I'm still in Cape G., working as a teller—not in my ex's bank, I can tell you that."

"I do the same, in St. Loo. Trying to learn how to use all that money if we ever get it. That's a joke. How's the old man doing? We'd rather have him alive, to tell the truth;

some executor might not get the picture why he pays us what he does."

"We keep up with the hometown," Gloria said. "Through your husband's ex. She reports you're patching things up with the doctor. He must be on his last legs. That right?"

"I think he is." I looked around to see if Mother was listening. But she was edging toward the screen door of the dilapidated farmhouse.

"*You* patching things up, that's one thing," Greta said. "You got a right."

"She means we hear his other girl is trying to suck up. Get her share."

"Get a share she hasn't got coming, you mean, Glo. I say born on the wrong side of the blanket means you don't get to crawl under the covers just because you take a mind to."

"Look—there she goes." Greta tugged at Gloria's sleeve.

"Anybody want a drink of water?" Mother said as she slipped inside.

"Get her," Greta whispered to the old ladies in the tan hair nets.

"Won't do any good."

"You girls come down with her, you go."

Greta and Gloria followed each other swiftly through the door, small staccato heels clicking in unison.

"Girl got herself killed, Audrey said. Nasty thing." This from the oldest woman, who was rapidly gumming white cake.

"Yes, it is."

"Any ideas?" She leaned toward me.

"No, not yet."

Gloria and Greta reappeared with Mother in tow and RC colas for everyone.

"Talking about the killing?" Greta settled back in the chair next to mine. "Try the undertaker. Maybe he wanted to play dress-up."

"He had ideas way back then, didn't he, Gret?"

"We're used to it up my way. St. Loo is one of the most dangerous cities in America."

"You made that up."

"I live there, I should know."

"Crime is universal."

"I'm not comparing it with L.A. or New York, but your average place, it is."

"There she goes again." Gloria looked at Mother's sister. "Effie, you go."

Mother had indeed scooted through the screen door, still dressed in her ruffled polyester topped by the lavender housecoat, dressed like an Eskimo in the sweltering, sticky, flat heat.

"I don't know why it has to be me every single time."

"What did he bring you back from Detroit for?"

"He don't pay *that* much."

"You don't *do* that much, or we wouldn't have to carry her off every week and put her up there."

"Audrey brings it. She says not, but it has to be." Effie, a huge woman in a dimity dress, with Mother's eyebrowless face stuck on top, shoved open the screen and hollered, "Neva. Come on out, Neva."

Gloria and Greta looked over at me.

"You were out of it back when we lived at home. A baby," Greta said.

"She must've caught the brunt later." Gloria took up for me.

"Remember Mom in that closet?" Greta laughed.

"Always digging around in the mothballs for where she put the gin."

"She'd forget where she hid it."

"Dad never bothered to root all the bottles out."

"No way you can do that. They want to hide one, they'll find a place."

"He'd get the liquor store to promise."

"But how're you going to refuse somebody with the money? Other customers standing around."

"The man did. He always called Dad."

"Remember how she used to steal money out of his bill-fold? He took to carrying nothing bigger than a one."

I drank about half my RC to wet my throat. "She took money after you left," I told them. "Daddy thought it was me."

"No, he didn't, honey. He knew better."

"He was putting on, that's all. Saving her face. We took the rap in our day. Did we ever!"

I felt like some kind of dunce. Wake up and smell the coffee, Alma. "I didn't know she drank," I told them.

"You're kidding?" Gloria raised caramel eyebrows to her hairline.

"I didn't."

"Where've you been? You been running around with Maudie Blanchard? See no evil, hear no evil."

"Mom thought she'd have a big time when he moved out, down to the old place."

"You decided that, Glo. I said then nobody likes to drink in an empty house, remember? I said that. Part of the point is pulling one over on somebody."

"You did, that's right. And sure enough she took up with Audrey the minute he was gone, worrying her toward an early grave." She made a gesture like it was good riddance.

"Audrey carries it up here if you ask me."

"You been listening to Effie."

"She's the one would know."

"Maybe so, maybe not." Gloria lit a fresh cigarette and offered me one.

"My first ex, his brother, his sister, even the doctor he could get to slip it to him. They can charm the paper off the wall." Greta showed all her teeth in an imitation of ingratiation.

"That's your ex."

"I must have been blind," I said.

"Little kids got their own problems." Gloria gave me a friendly poke.

"*Your* ex, Glo, wasn't exactly a teetotaler."

"That wasn't his problem. His problem was skirt fever."

"He was bragging."

"That's what I told him."

Mother had got herself behind Effie's chair and was cracking the screen door silent as a mouse, sticking one toe through, and then a shoulder.

"I'll go," I told them as the women all looked at each other and sighed. "It's my turn."

Inside I caught her in a junky room which must have once been a pantry for the old farmhouse. Caught her turning away her shoulder, one hand appearing to grope in a sack of trash, the other wiping her mouth with a furtive swipe. That was all I saw, but seeing that, the whole of her gestures, I knew I'd seen it in Marie's house one thousand times.

"It's my baby," she crowed. "Aren't you my baby?"

"I never did get even with you," I told her. "All that work, and I never did."

"I need a glass of water," she whined, smiling up at me.

"It was right under my nose, and I couldn't figure it out." I'd have gone without lunch at school, saved my money, saved my first summer's salary, never mind the poodle skirt, if I'd known; taken all the money I could earn and steal and bought her a whole case of gin. A whole case.

"See the pretties my girls gave me?" She began to stroke the layers of gathers and ruffles.

"I'm going to get you something else, Mother," I told her. "Something you've been wanting for thirty-five years."

"It's my birthday," she said. "They forgot to sing."

39

I WAS kicking myself all the way to the trailer park. Driving down the highway so fast, I almost whizzed by the entrance. I got there early, what with speeding and having allowed considerably more than enough time to disengage myself from Mother. Having imagined a long scene in which I had to break it to her about Daddy and maybe the old sister who was caretaking her. Not knowing he'd been keeping half the county for twenty years, plus my sisters, plus the drying-out center, wherever that was. That he'd probably fixed up his will to take care of her into perpetuity.

Between kicks I tried to rewrite history. It was easy enough to see, now, all those times I'd come home and caught her rummaging in the crib closet; all those times that burned oatmeal had been the most she could get on the table by suppertime. Me pulling the feathers from barely dead chickens so she could save the dollar it cost to buy it plucked from the grocer. The bushel basket of winesaps from Grandfather so that Daddy and I would get at least our apple a day. The fact that we could charge anything, but there was never cash to spend. That the only drinking I saw was the weekly wine at Grandfather's—with Daddy sitting watchful and silent. What wasn't so clear was what difference it would have made to me, not me but that Alma, that kid, who wasn't, then, me, of course. Would she have said, "Take your dead rat and shove it"? Would she really have given her mother half a dozen bottles? Or would such a demise seem fast enough to a child, the stages of incapacitation? It was a fruitless pursuit of what-if. Like those sci-fi stories from my sixth-grade days, where the hero steps off the path back in time and mashes one fern and then, when she gets back to the twentieth century, there are ten-foot-tall red ants called humans.

What I wanted from Dyer as I floorboarded the car was to escape all that. Lie along the beautiful length of him, scoot my head down to his shoulder, be held, cradled, loved. Have him do all those things to me that ten million lovers were doing all across America this very afternoon; whisper those things, those passionate promises and pledges which ten million others were whispering. As if we were all safe, safe in the litany of repetition; all alike, normal, undistinguished, in the very sameness of our avowals of never-before, never-again, only-you, only-now, only-here.

I wanted him to make love to me until I forgot what time it was, what day it was, why we were jammed on a fold-down ledge of bed, why we couldn't be together every day all day. Amnesia was what I wanted: the amnesia of love. Before your touch I was empty. Before your voice I had no replies. Before your eyes I was unseen.

I would leave Louis. We would open a Mom & Pop of our own. Dyer's Donuts, to capitalize on the familiarity of his name along the river. Alma's Automat. Tanner's Truck-stop. Van der Linden's Vegeteria. We would go somewhere and settle in, safe; safe, and forgetful of all those dumb long years before we met. The six children would . . . would . . .

But that was when I noticed I was almost past the park.

I went in, turned the air conditioning on in the dim, hot box, and put on the coffee. Sorely needing a cup, after the pile of potato salad and heavy slab of cake. I'd brought Dyer a piece of the coconut, the best of the lot. It was twenty minutes before he got there, which gave me time to freshen up, loosen up, pull down the bed, and be terrified he wasn't going to show.

When he did, dusty and damp from having driven with the windows open, he seemed distracted, depressed. Not where I was at all; not wanting to lull the world, but to scold it.

Primarily he was thoroughly fed up with the town.

"Jim said they hadn't even called the boyfriend in for questioning."

"But he would have told them if he'd known anything."

"Don't you start that, too. You can't tell me that any other place on earth would sit on its hands waiting for the killer to give himself up. Why, I'd have that kid in all night, going over the evening fifty times in a row, to catch a slip or get him to falter."

"But Fred didn't do it."

"After a few nights like that, he'd put his mind to giving me a few clues about who did. You can't tell me that he doesn't know something. She would have told him if there was somebody bugging her, somebody hanging around. Grill him. Grill the brother."

"Jerry? Dumb Jerry?"

"Jesus, you, too." He was down to his shorts, cooling off. But pacing around the tiny space or, to be exact, taking two steps, taking two more in the other direction. Jabbing the wall with his fist. "Jim said—do you know what Jim said?"

"What did he say?"

"He said it would take a couple of weeks."

"His guesses are pretty good."

"We're not talking about rainfall, you know."

"People are easier to predict than weather."

"If I was the sheriff's office, I'd have every kid in that high school through my holding cell, one at a time, until somebody let loose a clue."

278

"Maybe it was a vagrant." Which I didn't believe for a minute.

He sat down on the side of the bed. "They've got me doing it now. This hick town decides it can't be an outsider, so I go right along with it. It must be catching. Makes all the sense in the world it was some nut taking a detour off the highway. Jim says Monk at the funeral home told him they didn't even do fingerprints."

That's only on television, I wanted to tell him but didn't. Why would the parents need to find out where, exactly, Fred's fingerprints were on Prissy's body? What earthly good would come of that? Or her own, for that matter. Or some kid at MYF who'd been horsing around. In fact, I couldn't recall ever having seen fingerprints lifted off a body even in the thrillers; maybe it had to be off glasses and door handles. So they got Hadley's off the car. And put him through the third degree. What grief. I didn't see why Dyer didn't understand, but more than that, I was sick of talking about the tragedy, wanting to talk instead about what a dunce I'd been, what a stupid kid blind in both eyes climbing from the frying pan to the fire.

But I'd told him nothing about what a sneak of a child I'd been, having some pride, so there didn't seem a reason to get him off Prissy's sad case onto my own undramatic muddle.

"If it had been Kathy—" he said, settling back against the two pillows we shared. "If it had been her, I'd have dragged in every guy on two legs in the county."

Kathy. The one who came to mind first, whose loss would be the most evil. His oldest daughter.

Then I said what, in retrospect, must have turned him away from me. With my fine-honed propensity for false moves.

"I can't get it out of my mind that it could be Louis."

"Who?" He drew away. "You're kidding. You don't mean the principal?"

279

"Not really. But something about how he was, in my day anyway, how he was with high school girls. Calling you into his office, leaning over you, following you around. I can see that if he got a fix on you and you didn't go along . . . if you told, or threatened to tell, your daddy. I don't actually think it, but let's put it this way, he could have. He could have and then gone right on the way he is, acting as if it's his play and he's the director and star."

Dyer didn't say a word.

I turned toward him and took off the rest of my clothes.

"I don't feel like it," he said, looking at his feet. "Not right this minute. Shit, Alma, I got myself worked up on the way out, thinking about that girl. What I'd do. I read in the paper—I don't mean yours, the *real* paper—about some father who'd hunted down his daughter's killer for eleven years and finally found him and brought him to justice. Then here's that banker going on about his business, and the boyfriend, too, so I hear. Like nothing had happened."

"I read that, too," I told him. "But the daddy didn't find him; it took eleven years before some ex-wife got free from him and told the police, to get the reward."

"You sound hard when you talk like that."

"But that's what happened."

I slipped my dress on over my head and got us both another cup, which emptied the tiny percolator. What had he wanted from me, then, when he drove out here in the heat, sweating in the car, taking off from work, running a risk? Something. Something he wasn't getting.

"You know her mom, don't you? Aren't you friends?"

"We go back to first grade."

"I mean now, don't you know her?"

"Her son goes with my daughter."

"So you must see a lot of them, right? Don't you want to do something? Doesn't it make you want to hunt him down? What if it had been your girl? I mean wouldn't you have gone nuts? Wouldn't they? The boy's family?"

"You expected me not to want it, didn't you?"

"Not expected." He looked away.

"Wanted me not to." I couldn't help it, I turned my face to the damn ugly trailer wall and could feel tears squeezing out of the corners of my eyes. Of anger mostly, at all of it, everything for not being the way you thought it was, everybody for not having the first foggiest idea where anybody else was, not even a glimpse. Dyer, then, driving out south into the haze, turning west into the glare of the sun, had imagined the woman he was coming to meet dealing with her old mother about her dying father and all the while the burden of a young girl's death weighing her down. Had anticipated finding her disheveled, distraught, weeping perhaps, saying, "I can't, Dyer, not now. Not so soon. It was so awful."

Laying her head against him, or, no, perhaps they don't even unfold the bed—gross—but sit, instead, out in his car. She hasn't been able to make herself go inside, feeling tawdry. They have a cigarette (he doesn't smoke, shouldn't have the smell of cigarettes in his car; well, then, they sit in hers). This is a crummy movie, start again. He is already there. Has made their coffee. Sees her unglued, trembling, uncertain, grief-stricken. Suggests they take a walk across the field behind the trailers; there is a slight line of straggly trees, some soggy ground which would be a creek if it were April. Yes, they take a stroll. She has her cigarette—I'm not giving that up—crushes it out on the ground with her heel, sighs, links her arm through his. He feels protective. She doesn't get chiggers. He doesn't get burrs on his socks. She doesn't need to go to the bathroom or blow her nose from all those tears. It turns cool under the limp branches; they look down at their reflections in the caked mud. Maybe they get one kiss. On the forehead. She bends her knees unobtrusively so he can bestow it by the hairline.

At least he got some of it. I did cry. If not the way I should have. Digging my fists in my eyes like a little kid. Alma at nine having just done a dumb, rotten thing and then finding out that there wasn't any point to it at all.

I wanted to be loved all afternoon. Until it hurt to walk, speaking of the movies; until the final scene in the late dusk when he throws back the sheet and says, I want to remember you like this always.

Fighting with someone you see only on days which end in five and zero is a total crushing mess. Because you can't. Anything said today can't be rebutted until another day which ends in five or zero. September fifth, two days after Labor Day, I could say, sotto voce over my egg salad, that about the time in the trailer park, I was wrong. I should have been more upset. Less greedy.

But if I'd been any more upset for any more reasons, I'd have had to be two people.

I'd tell him I was sorry, should have sensed his feelings for his own child. Of course, any father would be upset. "You worry about Kathy," I said, to get back on the right track.

"Don't condescend to me."

I dried my eyes on the hem of my dress and dug out my cigarette. It was my habit not to have one until we were getting ready to leave, being always too eager to bother before then.

If he noticed, he didn't comment.

He was still in his shorts, but he eyed his clothes.

"It isn't that the town doesn't care."

"Funny way of showing it."

"If you talked to Hadley—"

"Who's Hadley?"

"Walters. Prissy's daddy."

"What I hear he hasn't missed a day of work."

"It helps some people to go through the motions."

"The man in the paper worked eight hours a day to find the killer."

Eight hours a day for eleven years, and then it took some

282

ex-wife who ratted. That isn't what I'd call mourning. I'd call that . . . Which reminded me of Louis. Because that's what he would do. If it had been Beryl, he would have started out to hunt the killer and spent the rest of his life in pursuit, hoping maybe that the guy had long ago driven on to Oklahoma, so as not to interfere with the drama of his vendetta. Which the town would make into a legend: the father who never let it go.

That was what had turned Dyer off, not the rest of it, but what I'd said about Louis. I tested it out. "Louis would behave that way."

"A minute ago he was the one who did it." He stood up, with his back to me, as far away as he could get in the doll-house space.

"Awhile ago he was a fanatic. He is a fanatic. He could have done it; he could crossbow the guy who did it; he could hunt for the killer for twenty years. It's all the same."

"Don't talk like that. That's defaming the character of someone you don't even know."

"Louis?"

"The man in the newspaper."

"Screw the man in the newspaper." I could feel the tears come back, total frustration.

He turned and looked at me. "How could you suspect someone in your own house?" He paced back and forth, back and forth, then came and sat down on the bunk bed with me. He took my cigarette and threw it in the sink. "I didn't get it," he said.

"What?"

"I couldn't figure out you being callous that way; it didn't fit with you." He kissed the top of my head, pulling me against him. "It must have been thinking about Kathy. I don't see her much, being gone all week like this. I didn't mean to get on you."

"It's okay." I wasn't sure what had brought on this big change.

"You must be half-crazy, what with the close call, it being somebody in your kid's crowd. What if the guy is still loose? What if he's right under your nose? I get it now. It's not the principal you mean. Just the idea. Somebody right there, and nothing you can do about it."

Oh, shit. The same scene again. Now if I could only let the tears fall without any noise, without the sniffle, and not say anything else. No, say, I'm sick with worry. Or, We loved her like a daughter. Or, Louis won't help with finding the killer. Anything.

But I never was very good at picking the right response and so didn't see any reason to change midstream.

"I don't think my husband did it," I said, in what I'm sure was a stiff voice; maybe resigned was more like it. "I only said he was the sort who could have."

"You shouldn't live with someone that you can say that about."

"A thought which has occurred to me more than once."

I got up and started over, pulling off the dress and putting back on my panties and bra, skipping the hose I'd worn in a fit of gentility for the country. Pulling my hair off my neck and letting a little breeze float around it. My eyes must be red, no doubt, and I went into the bathroom to see, forgetting it was a closet with a pull-down chain and no mirror. But I stood there, facing the back wall, until I got myself back together.

When I came out, I sat on the side of the bed and put my shoes on.

"Where're you going?"

"We're not going to do it, are we?"

"You don't have to go off in a huff. You shouldn't drive like that anyway. You'll have an accident."

"You said you wanted a woman who wants it, but you don't."

"Don't say something you'll be sorry for."

284

"Why should I change my ways at this late date?" I got up and brushed my hair.

"Calm down, will you?"

"You don't really think it's normal for a woman to want it all the time, do you? I mean even when girls have been strangled or she's got her period or it's hot as steaming hell or she's crazy with worry about what's going on or any number of events such as occur with regularity every day."

He put his trousers on, but not his shirt. He looked angry. At least you knew with Dyer where you were. And beautiful; he was beautiful, and nothing could take that away. He looked like the bare-chested men in movies who always knock the dishes off the table before they lunge at you.

Only maybe they didn't lunge when you were panting and ready.

In vain I hunted mentally through all the great love stories of my growing up, stack upon stack of library books, covertly devoured treasures, committed to my heart. There wasn't a single one that came to mind in which the woman wanted it with all her soul and got away with it alive. All right, alive maybe, but ruined. Ruined, finished, off to the nunnery, the nursery, the null and void of folly.

"It might have been best not to meet today," I said. As if this were nothing more than a missed connection, a grounded plane.

"I waited at the cemetery last time for an hour."

Why hadn't he said that when I'd seen him at Mom & Pop's? "It was the day after." My God, I'd assumed he'd understand.

"You could have let me know. You never said a word about not showing, like you didn't give it a thought."

"I was at the paper. We were trying to figure how to make it easy on Patsy."

"Patsy?"

"Prissy's mother."

"Oh, sure, your old friend. The one you're so torn up about all of a sudden."

"I was afraid for you. To get in your car."

"For me?"

"I didn't want anyone—"

"Maybe you think I did it? All that carrying on about your principal was just a way of testing me, is that it?"

I couldn't even get myself together enough to move. This was worse and more of it. Was he still angry that I hadn't come out to meet him the morning after they found her? Surely he understood. He didn't. He thought I was lying. I felt like I was a kid again, nine, ten, shouting at my daddy that I didn't take the money, I didn't, I didn't. . . .

I looked down at myself almost surprised to see an adult woman. How composed she seemed, in her thin summer dress. Not even shouting. History repeats—but it plays a different tune for an encore.

"I love you," I told him. "I wanted to make love."

"You run hot and cold. I don't get it."

"Let's call it an afternoon. You can't fight with someone you don't live with."

"Suit yourself."

"Walk me out to the car."

"Is this quits or something? Is that what you're getting at?"

"I don't know. Let's meet after Labor Day. Things will have cooled down, or we will. I'll be at Maudie's."

He hesitated. "I asked for a replacement."

"When?"

"Starting as soon as they can find one."

"I mean, when did you *ask?*"

"Last week."

"When I didn't show up?"

"When the girl got killed. It didn't make sense for me to be hanging around here all week. I got kids at home. It started me thinking."

286

"You picked a fight today because you knew you were leaving."

"Could be." He wouldn't look at me.

"Please make love to me."

"Thought you were walking out."

"Please."

"Come here, then, will you? Get down off your high horse and come here."

"Why didn't you tell me?"

"I guess I couldn't."

"I can't stand it here without you."

"Seems to me you're doing fine."

"Don't go, Dyer."

"Get out of that dress, will you?"

It was late when I left, almost dusk. I'd have hell's own hard time making an all-day trip to the country out of my story, but if I'd left the paper late . . . Maybe we hassled a long time about what to put in and what to leave out for next week, about Prissy, or maybe we were reading it over for errors a day early. Hydrangea was not about to give Louis a time clock report; at least I could count on that.

Dyer led me to my car, and we weren't saying anything. What was there to say? I was numb with wanting to cling to him and numb with the idea of his going away.

He saw it first, tucked under the windshield wiper.

A Polaroid shot of me letting myself in the door of the trailer.

You could have heard him holler into the next county. "God damn it," he yelled, "that does it. That's the last goddamn straw. Tell your kid to get off my back, or I'll break his neck with these two hands. If you've got to blame someone under the same roof, there's a good start. Ask that snooping son of yours where *he* was the night she got it. Maybe he's got a boxful of pictures of her he's going to offer around. If I ever see that kid face-to-face—"

287

I tore the photo into small pieces and handed them to him to throw away.

Maybe my life fell apart in cycles. I'd have to ask Jimmy about that; he had a way with figures.

What's the point in writing down that I cried all the way back into town?

40

SUPPER was endless. I felt like a zombie. Jasper chattered away to his father in the manner which made Louis imagine he was being made a fool of. (It reminded me of Sheba at the blackboard in deaf Miss Day's class, powdering the teacher's hair with chalk while the class snickered.)

I carried our plates to the kitchen. Roast beef. I'd made a nice rosemary-coated roast beef, which tasted to me like the uppers on an old pair of pumps.

I brought out pears and cheese and a glass of wine for myself. My mind was pegged on the past in these rooms and wouldn't come back to the present. I kept seeing Daddy and Wissie and Uncle Grady, and then this snot-nosed kid, the serpent in the garden, allowed to run all over the lot of them.

"Am I to assume," Louis's voice rose, "that the reason no mention has been made as to why one member of our family is not present at this evening meal is that our daughter is once again at the Walters'?"

"I assume so," I told him. Not having heard from Beryl, who had all but carried her belongings—hair dryer, jeans, mascara, and all—up the street to Patsy and Hadley's. It was a mutual clinging. She had filled part of the gap left by Prissy, had literally filled the fourth chair at meals, had provided the sound of a girl's voice, the daughterly touches such as helping with the dishes, which Prissy had probably never done, but it was the gesture. In return, she was getting good, trustworthy Hadley—and a very lonesome Patsy—in the bargain.

"You did not check on her whereabouts? Is that what I'm to understand?"

"Louis, they need her up there. I told her to do whatever helped."

"If you don't mind, I'd prefer that these unilateral decisions involving our younger child . . ." He sliced himself a piece of pear. He never ate desserts, which accounted for the fruit. It occurred to me that it might have done him good, done all of us good, to have a thick slice of chocolate devil's food with chocolate icing, but that wasn't how we "ran our ship." In lieu of that I put on a pot of decaffeinated coffee for him and got myself a second glass of wine.

"I believe you skirted my earlier query about your day. Perhaps you were collecting nostalgia sketches around the county?" Louis's face was slipping and sliding around, like rapid sequential images of the same person flashed on a screen. It happened when he was holding on with both hands and noticed that he'd grabbed nothing.

Tonight I was too frayed to watch myself. "No," I said. "I took off from the paper and went to see Mother. My sisters were there, if you want to know."

"Sisters?" Jasper looked up, amazed. "Did we know you had sisters?"

"I'm not sure I remembered it myself," I told him.

"This was some sort of celebration you hadn't seen fit to share?"

"It was her seventy-fifth birthday."

Louis frowned. He still thought of my parents, as he did his, in their fifties, even though he was there himself. Reminders of aging made him anxious. "May I inquire why this wasn't mentioned, an event of such importance that you had to leave your place of employment in the middle of the day?"

"Please, Louis. It was a mess. She was sneaking into the house for a drink the whole time. Has apparently been a drunk for years."

"You're exaggerating for effect." He folded his napkin and rose. "If you'll excuse me, I missed my workout twice this week already."

Jasper followed me into the kitchen. "Want to have a smoke out front?"

We seldom did that, sat on the front steps. It was in public view of the street. But with Louis gone to the shed, the backyard was out.

"I thought your mom was a vegetable or something," he said, digging the matches out of the top of his sock and accepting a cigarette.

"Me, too."

On each side of the front steps bloomed remnants of Uncle Grady's planting: a mass of white football mums, slightly browned at the edges; three rosy clumps of phlox.

"Something bothering you?" He busied himself with lighting up.

I looked at my son, the narrow nose, dark hair, thin shoulders, good looks. But beneath that? "You tell me," I said.

"Come again?"

"You want to tell me what's going on?"

"Give me a clue, will you?"

I let my breath out. Wanting to take the offensive. "You're blackmailing me."

"That's what I call a world-class idea, but it beats me what my grounds are. My hunch is I could follow you and Dad for ten years and end up with even more boring lives than I can imagine."

"Don't do it again, Jasper."

"How can I quit when I don't know what you're talking about?"

"I don't want it to happen again."

"Believe me, I'm with you. Stamp it out. Once and for all."

I flung my cup into Uncle Grady's chrysanthemums. "Damn it." I was suddenly uncertain. Was it possible he hadn't taken the pictures? Louis could have followed me. Maybe that was behind the interrogation about my afternoon; maybe he knew exactly how far, and where, I'd been. Jesus, what if it was him?

"Look at me," I said to my son.

" 'Here's looking at you.' " He gave it his old-movie voice.

"Tell me the truth—" I began, but then there came Beryl and Jerry, cruising right up to the curb in Hadley's brand-new Olds.

"Hi," they said, getting out, coming up to where we sat.

"How's your mother?" I asked Jerry, putting on a smile.

"Doing all right," Jerry said, which certainly wasn't true but was all the polite, sheep-faced boy knew to say. "All right," he repeated without conviction. "How's Fred?" he asked Jasper.

"Not okay, okay?"

I laughed.

"I don't think that's funny," Beryl complained, offended. In these solemn, tragic times, to laugh about Prissy's boyfriend made her want to put her hands over her ears and shut her eyes and pretend she didn't know either her mother or her brother.

Jerry made a shy grin which reminded me of Hadley. "You know he gave me a bloody nose?" He seemed proud, as if it proved he was man enough to have a real fight, and someone had cared a lot about his sister.

"Nobody goes to see him," Jasper said.

"It's hard on Mom and Dad."

"So what's that got to do with you?"

"I guess so. Yeah, you're right."

"Bet you don't know where Nadine is," Beryl said, getting even with her brother.

"I gave Fred a choice: my sister or my girl." Jasper flicked an ash on her shoe.

"Very unfunny."

Jerry took Beryl's hand, which was about all he knew to do in her defense. From the set of his shoulders I surmised that maybe at night he practiced in front of a mirror and that perhaps in about a dozen years Jasper was going to be walking down the street and Hadley Jerrold Walters, III, the new vice-president of the bank, was going to rush through the revolving door in this three-piece pin-striped suit and knock his block off. Having just the night before mastered the technique.

"They want me to ask you, Mom, could I go to the lake with them again this weekend? Mr. Walters thinks it would be good, you know, to get out of town."

"Sure." But then I hesitated. "You might check with your father," I amended. "He's working out."

"We don't need to bother him," Jerry said, terrified of Louis.

"Not at all. He was disappointed that Beryl wasn't here when he got home."

"If you're sure—"

"Come on. Daddy won't mind." Beryl blinked and ran her tongue over her lips. "He was asking about me," she said, pleased, walking past us and around the house with dignity.

"Everybody asks about old Fred, don't they? He's a total mess if they want to know, which they don't. Nadine goes by. I guess he'll take up with her when I'm gone."

"Do you mind?"

"Sure, but I'm not coming back to this place. I figure I don't have a right to mind."

"I went with a boy like that in Venice High. I think I knew even then it wasn't going anywhere, but it's a help at the time."

"What happened to him?"

"He's selling cars in Tennessee."

"You ever wish you were selling cars in Tennessee?"

"Sometimes." I tried to gauge where he was.

"How come you're not?"

"It's a long story."

"So what's going on now?"

I studied his face. "Swear to me you don't know what I'm talking about."

He placed his hand on his heart. " 'I'll not swear, my Lord forbids it.' "

"Where did you hear that?"

"You don't think you're the only one who got a full dose of faithful Ann Elizabeth rousting about with the tobacco hands, do you?"

"Daddy told you about that?"

"And the one about his dad's feud with his uncle. Let's see. And his mom and dad falling out over his lame leg. And—"

"He told you?" When even I had no idea how Daddy got his limp. I saw red. Before I could stop myself, I stood up and shouted down at him, "Maybe I ought to ask you where you were on a certain Sunday night."

He looked as if he'd been hit. He made a short laugh. "You must have some big thing going, is all I can say." He pinched his cigarette out. "Save your breath. Nobody would believe you. Everyone knows who did it."

"Even your father?"

"Jesus, Mom, you've gone nuts."

I turned from him, kicked the steps in frustration.

"What the fuck," he said, and slammed the door into the house.

Louis came around the side yard. "Apparently our daughter is packing her things in order to move in with the Walters for an indefinite stay. I had hoped we could have at least one evening with the whole family present before our son sets off for college. Or had you forgotten?"

"I'm going for a walk," I said, "it's been a bad day," and turned and headed up Main before Louis could collect himself to stop me.

41

THE next day I dragged around at the paper like a dog with three legs. Went down into the sterile room below-ground, where the unused rolls of newsprint waited for us like six-foot-high rolls of toilet paper under the heat ducts, by the fuse boxes and the closet of cleaning supplies. Ostensibly I'd gone down to check on something, but when I got down in the basement, I forgot what and wandered around, suddenly interested in the layout of the room, the platform for the paper, the carts, the whitewash on the walls, the bins heading for the compactor.

Upstairs again, I read over, as we did on Fridays, the whole issue for errors, circling them in red. Estes Cox was messing up his "bound overs" something dreadful, with burglaries at the wrong addresses and the sheriff's and victim's names switched. We'd let a lot slip through, but probably folks would understand. The whole town was operating on half power.

It was clear, what with Labor Day, we weren't going to get much done. I'd checked over the schedule of ads for the next issue, making the usual phone calls. Vickers Better Dresses wanted a First Fall Shipment spread; the five-and-dime, to post a sale on tablets and pencils, or whatever kids used these days, spirals and Bics.

Usually Hydrangea and I sat around with our doors open, reading all the big-city papers, getting story ideas. Seeing what was going on in the Middle and Far East (meaning the mid-Atlantic states and New York City) now that those places had returned to the news after the conventions and competitions. (Sometimes it gave me the idea that everyone held acts of crime and violence back for prime time, much as was done with gold medal events. Imagine trying to kidnap the wife of a consul or the child of a movie star and getting even a flash of your picture on the screen when Carl Lewis was finishing his third big heat or Mary Lou Retton was hanging in the air, hoping for a ten. In fact, in a couple of papers, poor, handsome Richard Burton had to have his stroke on the back pages, a mistake he would never have made in his prime.)

Tuesday afternoon Hydrangea left me a note which read: "At Monk's." My guess: they were up to a little off-the-record detective work, comparing notes on their public and private sources.

Wednesday morning I gave up and called in "with a bad cold," which was right up there in office excuses along with "My grandmother died." I could as well have told her my grandmother had; she got the idea. I was not coming in until after lunch.

Louis had scheduled a Curriculum Day at school right smack in the middle of the first week of classes. A command performance for all teachers and staff; a holiday for the students most unwelcome to their parents, who had already gone about their fall business. It was his way of protesting Labor Day. He could not stand to give the students the annual Monday off, could not stand to be relegated to that work force known as labor.

Beryl and Jerry were at the Walters's, helping Patsy sort through Prissy's things—the hardest task of all.

Jasper, unforgiving and unforgiven, had left for college without a word.

. . .

I headed south, toward Memphis, which was careless, to drive right out of town in the bright light of day. But there was no one to see me, or rather whoever had been trailing me was busy, or gone, and whoever hadn't didn't matter. (It reminded me of a story about Maudie and her mother. With Maudie telling Mrs. Blanchard to pull down her shades if she was going to get into her nightgown, and her mother snapping, "The good ones won't look, and the bad ones will enjoy it.")

More or less my thinking that September morning.

For a few miles I paralleled the levee, moved as always at the sight of the wide brown tonnage on which a line of flat-bottom barges crawled toward New Orleans.

Almost, but not quite, through the haze, I could see distant smokestacks on the skyline. Somewhere across that river, in Tennessee, Dyer was back again with the wife named Maydelle and the quartet of children, of which I knew only the name of one special daughter.

Circling with the sun to my back, I went on the county road past the trailer park: another car was parked at the dingy mobile home in the back. It was stupid to spend the morning driving, as if I had to prove to myself that he was no longer there, anywhere he'd ever been. I didn't bring it to consciousness, but on some level I knew I'd end up at Mom & Pop's, having my egg salad, as if starting the reel all over again—without him.

I stopped at the cemetery on the road back to town. Fresh flowers were on Prissy's grave; I could see across the dirt road, which divided the plots, but didn't go over.

I tried to remember the story that Grandfather's woman, Elsie White, had told at someone's funeral. Uncle Grady's, it must have been; no, Grandfather's, of course. About how they used to gather flowers in the old lacquered baskets, whatever was in bloom on Memorial Day, and carry them to the cemetery, to put on the parents' graves. One son placing his on the mother's plot; the other, on the father's. It seemed so foolish, all the years of bitterness. When Daddy and Wissie were gone, who would even remember it?

(Who but us who repeated it?)

Assiduously I pulled a bloom here and a bloom there from overburdened bouquets, until I had a small handful, which I tied into a bundle with a slick green iris stalk, planted to border someone's French aunt. I laid the bunch on Grandfather's grave. For old times' sake.

A car drove in the gate and wheeled slowly around the road. I could see that it was Hadley, in his banker's gray, come to mourn alone, and, quickly bending down, spread out the loose flowers in the grass and climbed in my car. I waved out the window but didn't stop to speak. Let him think I was preparing a place for my father. Why not? And what if I was?

Back in town I stopped at Sheba's, to see what she had on special. Back-to-school clothes. A pink shirt and black poodle skirt maybe. Some of those soft, flat shoes we wore, flatter than bedroom slippers, with our bulky white socks.

"Hey," she said, pleased to see me, coming from behind the green silk screens at the sound of the door.

I hadn't seen her much since Reba showed up. They were an instant twosome again, and it was strange to see them around town, ducking in and out of stores, talking their private language: two Dolly Vickers, doubling up and down the street. Reba, certain of her unseen cues; Sheba, hesitant lest once again her twin decide to vanish.

"Something devastating," I told her.

"Charge it to your dad, miss?"

"That takes me back."

"What did Givens say the first time you came in?"

" 'Looks nice on you, honey.' "

"What else?"

" 'Maybe that's a trifle out of your range?' "

She gave me a hug which went around my arms in the vicinity of my elbows. "Haven't seen you," she said. "That awful business."

"Jasper left for school."

"I heard."

"Something devastating."

"How about a red jumper?" She showed me a very long skirt gathered on a tight bodice, with deep pockets almost to the hem. Not a fourth-grade jumper. Plus a red blouse of the same material with shoulder pads that looked like a World War II poster. Swanky. It took me a minute to register. Then I saw that there were at least two dozen red garments hanging in plain sight.

"Old times," I said.

"They simply appeared." She was grinning, and then she stopped and frowned. "I've got bad news. Maybe you heard?"

"No more. Cease."

She waited.

"Do they wear earrings anymore?"

"It's about that damned crumb of a helper your daddy hired."

"I've heard that one." I sat down on one of the green silk settees.

"It's Junior T."

"Can customers smoke?"

"You can."

"Tell me."

"Seems Dr. Baker couldn't bring himself, you know, to stick his finger up a black ass, and so last year and this year, when Junior drew the assistant for his physical, it was just a lick-and-promise exam. By the time he figured out the trouble—"

"Prostate?"

She nodded. "He and Bea, you know, they've been working together on this foolproof miracle cure for baldness, Junior T.'s been rubbing in the salve and wisps have been growing on heads all over town like a crop of spring grass, and so the two of them are thick as thieves. Finally, he gets up his nerve to confess to Bea that things have got bad 'down there,' that he has to strain and what not, and she asks a few pointed questions—after all, they've been dealing with the failures of the body for over a year, you might say—and she sends him quick as a wink to somebody she knows up at Cape G. Who relays back the word that the word is bad."

"Jesus. What was Daddy doing all that time?"

"Monitoring himself, I guess."

"Looks like it."

"We need to get ourselves a doctor." She rubbed her eyes.

"How does a town do that?"

"Beats me. But Bea is putting her mind to it, and Reba is praying over it."

"Well, then."

"Your kids interested in the job?"

"Not today."

"Thought we ought to keep it in the family; everything else around here is."

"I'm going to get lunch."

"You might stop by the barbershop."

"Does Junior T. want people to know?"

"Does he have a choice?"

"I'll do that. Want to join me?"

"I need to mind the store."

"You're looking good."

"It's like old times. Those years in between, they might as well not have happened."

"That's great."

"She says twelve foster homes, the last one in a parsonage."

She shoved the clothes at me. "You want the jumper? It's a Norma Kamali."

"Not now. I was touching base."

"Don't make it so long."

42

Jɪᴍᴍʏ waved from behind the counter. "Coming up," he said. "Be a minute. My boss is gone."

"Where is she?"

"When news of Junior T. made the rounds, she took off for Cape G. I expect that doctor has a waiting room of home folks this afternoon."

"Is she all right?"

"Scared us all, Junior did."

"I just heard."

"Maybe your dad will get back on his feet."

"Charlie Baker said it was just a 'little stroke.'"

He made a face to show what he thought of certain unreliable sources.

He was setting my egg salad on the plate when Dyer walked in.

"Hi," he said.

"Hi."

"Hello, Jim."

"You back?"

"Just for the day. Getting the new guy set up in place. I'll have my Reuben here with Alma. Leak a little news to the paper."

He slid into the front booth across from me.

"Today's a five," he said, real low but with a sweet grin.

Sure enough it was, September fifth. I could see the wall calendar in my mind's eye. That must be why I'd taken off the morning. "I thought you'd gone." I was so happy at the sight of him.

"Have."

"I drove to the Memphis highway this morning. Quite a haze."

"I might have passed you."

We were gazing all over each other, talking more with our eyes than our words. He was still the best-looking man I'd ever seen, and always would be.

"I wanted to say good-bye proper," he said. "I felt bad doing you that way."

I shrugged. He was here.

"I was of two minds, if you understand, and I took it out on you. I felt bad, doing that."

"Where's your car parked?" I could see that he didn't know about Louis's Curriculum Day. Students would be pouring in for afternoon Cokes. Already there were two stray tourists at the table in the back, taking an Indian summer sojourn to see the land of the rumbles, plus two boys at the counter who looked about ninth grade and as if their mother went to church. I placed them as Rogers grandkids; Versie would know for sure.

"At the Flood Control."

"Let's walk down there."

"That's pretty public."

"It doesn't matter. Today's a school holiday."

"How's that? Monday was Labor Day."

"Never mind."

"I promised to bring the new guy a sandwich. He's getting set up."

"We'll take it down there. That's an old walk of mine, remember?"

"I can still see how you looked, out that window."

"I could use the exercise."

"Make me another to go when you get the time, Jim. For my partner."

"Thought you might stick around awhile." Jimmy looked up from making the Reubens. "I'm short-handed today."

"Maybe I'll look in on you before I shove off."

"I got a new set of figures for you."

"He's not as smart as me, the new man." Dyer laughed. "He might not see the wisdom."

Jimmy brought us the sandwiches and hung around while we wrapped them in paper napkins. He didn't know how he was supposed to take us heading out together in broad daylight and Maudie not there to tell him.

It did feel really strange to be out on the sidewalk, walking along like any two normal people. I could imagine that making the rounds, on the heels of the sad news of Junior T., meeting itself coming back again before I got to the office. Never mind. I was going to have my stroll, just once more.

"This was a good idea. It's hard talking, with Jim keeping his ear on us."

"Why did you come back?"

"We were in the wrong, don't you see? We were thinking of ourselves and our personal interests when there were all the rest of them. I got home, and there was Kathy waiting, and Maydelle had wrecked her car, and all the little ones, they were clamoring around, waiting for me to get home, having to do with a weekend father. I was ashamed. I was."

I dropped my egg salad in the mailbox at the corner of Main and First, but he didn't notice, caught up as he was in his confession of guilt.

"I'd fallen away from church, and Sunday I went and got myself in the right mind again. Alma, we were in the wrong; that's the short and the long of it. I told Maydelle, not naming names, that I'd got interested in a lady and that it was over now, she had my word. That it was over and we were going to start again, the way we used to be; she could count on that. And she cried and called the kids in, and then we prayed. We all did that, held hands in a big circle, the way we used to. It was seeing myself getting like my old man. He two-timed my mother and lied to her and never thought twice about it. I swore I wouldn't be that way if I had kids. If I ever had kids, I swore I'd be the kind of daddy I never had. Then there I was, you might say, selling Havanas myself."

"We do that," I told him, not even bothering to wipe the tears away.

"You were the prettiest thing I'd ever seen, going by that window. It turned my head."

I took his hand. What the hell. Let them take pictures. Two blocks, I had two blocks left, and I was going to claim them.

"There's a car behind us," he said, pulling away.

"I'll crunch its license plate." I wiped my cheeks with the back of my hand. Maybe I should have bought the jumper and the big-shouldered blouse. Not stopped in Mom & Pop's, just sashayed down this way, blinded his eyes again. Maydelle doesn't have to know, I'd tell him, I'll move out to the country—who cares what goes on out there in that tangle of falling-down shacks and pecan shuckers and pig farmers?—be one of the Jenkins girls.

"It's some kids," he said, clearly nervous.

I turned in time to see Beryl duck down in the front seat of Hadley's car, while Jerry, behind the wheel, sped up, looking out the window the other way, as if he hadn't seen us.

Beryl?

"It's okay," I told him. "Nobody we know."

He was so full of trying to do right, to say his say, to face up to it like a man, that he didn't even hear me. As if there could be anyone in this town I didn't know.

"You understand, don't you, Alma?"

"No, I can't say that I do."

"I'm not going to put myself in a position of temptation again."

"Is that what it was?"

"I thought I should come back and say it straight out, not leave it the way we did."

"Let me walk on by myself, to the levee. Take your sandwiches and eat them with your friend by the lovely seismograph."

"I'm sorry to hurt you, Alma."

"Me, too. I'm sorry, too."

I pulled ahead of him, going by the old men with their plug tobacco and yellow eyes and half-buttoned shirts, sitting with their knees spread, nothing to hide anymore. "Hello," I said to them, in passing.

From Cairo to Memphis, I scolded the Mississippi, you big brown bastards just keep rolling along, while we on the banks fool ourselves that we can now and then make the river run upstream.

43

"You!"

Beryl sat cornered in her room, trying to keep a smirk off her face. "You went through my things," she said.

"Damn right." In her top desk drawer I'd found a shot of me talking to Dyer in the phone booth in Jax, two others of my car outside the trailer, one of Dyer with only the white wig showing in the dark, two of me holding hands with him on First Street.

"You never even thought of me, did you?"

It all fit. That was what had been missing when I confronted my son: the abscess of revenge. It takes one to spawn one, and there she was, seventeen years of psychic toothache, beginning to throb. "No, I didn't."

"Jasper said you'd gone off the deep end; he didn't even know what you were talking about."

"You let me accuse him." Do to him the rotten thing Dad did to me.

"Not even once. I could have walked right up to you in Mom and Pop's and given you a poke, and you still wouldn't have thought it was me. Carrying on with him in church like I wasn't sitting right beside you. It was always Jasper, from the start. He got all of it. If he made a fuss, then everybody had to turn upside down till he got over it. All that business about his chicken dinner at Rhoda's; he ruined the whole visit for us. Nobody cared that I was getting along with them and helping Rhoda out with her recipes. Nobody cared that I'm the only one in this entire family she can talk to."

Oh, Christ.

"When Prissy died, it was the same thing. He got the big attention for getting Fred out of the dumps when Fred didn't even care. He'd just as soon be making out with that Nadine as Prissy; he wasn't even anything special to her; she never once brought him around, I know that. But me helping Jerry out, that doesn't count, me cleaning up for Mrs. Walters and listening to Mr. Walters and being the one they want to have in the house, that doesn't count, does it? Granddaddy at the cemetery, coming up and asking Jasper to come see him sometime when I was the one who went down there the most last time he was sick and always sent him a card every day, which I bet nobody else in the family did. But I don't count. You don't even know I exist. I could be sitting in the booth right beside you and you wouldn't even see me."

"I saw you."

"With that man in broad daylight, like you didn't even care it would get right back to Daddy."

I located the camera, which had been stuffed in her crocodile pajama bag, and threw it in the wastebasket.

"Leave my things alone."

"You let me accuse your brother." I was still ashamed.

"I thought you'd think it was Daddy—" She looked up from under the thick layer of gummed lashes.

"Wanted me to?"

"You deserved it."

Wanted me to accuse Louis, or be afraid of Louis, or confess to Louis? Which? All of the above? Wanted to make trouble between us. To what end? "Why didn't you tell *him?*"

"He'd think I was a sneak."

So Mom needed to get in trouble, but daughter had to be blameless. Daughter wanted to get revenge for . . . what?

"When I was a kid, I spied on my father—"

"I'm not interested in your big life story. I don't want your true confessions. I saw you. I got pictures of you. You cheated on Daddy."

Which served him right for . . . what? But of course. "This didn't seem the time to tell him, don't you see? He was all broken up about Prissy. She was a very special student of his. I didn't have the heart."

"She hung around him all the time." Beryl leaped up, her face out of control. "She was after him. I don't care what she said, she was. She was after my daddy."

My shot had hit home. "Maybe she was trying it out on someone safe."

"You don't know. You don't know a thing about it."

"How long had this been going on?"

"My whole life." Beryl covered her face with the crocodile bag. "My whole life. Why do you think"—her voice was muffled, and her body shaking—"I started going with Jerry? That dope. He doesn't know, he thought she was this perfect person, his precious sister, that's all he could talk about. I thought she'd quit if I was practically in the family."

"But she didn't."

"I think she wanted him to—do it—with her." Her voice was almost inaudible.

Beryl. Who would have thought it?

"I was going to drop a button of your boyfriend's in the Walters' yard—" She looked at me, and then her eyes slid away.

"How could you have?"

"He always left his jacket on the chair down there in that old place. I was going to drop it by the driveway—"

My God. "Why didn't you?"

"It wasn't him I wanted to get." She started crying, black

goo streaking her cheeks, her face wet and the ends of her hair.

"Why not leave something of your daddy's then? If he's the one you're mad at."

"I did." It was a whisper, and then she flung herself into my arms. "Help me, Mom, help me find it. What if they find it? I can't tell anybody I put it there, but I don't want them to t-take him away." She was sobbing into the front of my office shirt.

I called Hydrangea and told her my grandmother had died and I wouldn't be in that afternoon.

44

PATSY looked puffy and pale; I'd caught her without her make-up. "Prissy had all these notes in her room," she said, staring at me in the doorway. "Boxes full of notes kids had written her in school. I didn't read them, I wasn't prying, but you could see, with all the exclamation points and hearts and little faces . . . They really liked her, didn't they?"

"Beryl thinks she lost a contact in your yard." I gestured behind me. My job being to keep Patsy occupied while my daughter searched for the button cut from her daddy's seer-sucker suit.

"Contact lens? She'll never—Come on in."

We had a Coke, and Patsy smeared on some foundation and dabbed on bright red lipstick. "I look a mess. Being up at the lake helps Hadley, so I can't say no. It drives me crazy. Look, I've got hives all over me. Don't tell. I don't miss her around here because I was here all day long by myself any-way, but up there we never went without her. I can see her, in her shorts, kids around, and I nearly crawl out of my skin."

"Beryl said you packed away her things. That must have been hard." I sipped the Coke, to be polite, wishing for a black coffee. Trying, still, to sort out Beryl's anger, or smolder, perhaps, was a more apt word.

"Prissy wore contacts," Patsy said.

"I guess they all do now."

"I mean, I wonder what, you know, if Monk—" She dissolved again and began to scratch on her arms. Finally, she got up and brought us a plate of homemade butterscotch cookies. "These still show up, plates of them. I never know who to return the dishes to. Last week I had three casseroles and couldn't remember who brought them. All made with mushroom soup." She giggled. "And almonds."

"Can't you throw them out?"

"I guess so." She giggled again. "Maybe." She pulled her sleeves down so she'd leave herself alone. "Beryl's been the sweetest thing, I can't tell you. I know you know that we couldn't have got along without her. She's been sweeter to me than my own. I don't mean that the wrong way, but that's how it goes, isn't it?"

"She likes you a lot."

"Is that right? Did she say that? That's sweet, that really is. You're lucky, you know it? Some people have kids they can't stand."

"We all feel that way sometimes."

"Oh, not you, not with yours. Jerry says Jasper saved Fred's life. I guess we're not good about the boy, but I don't like to ask him around because Hadley can't stand to look at him, like it was his fault, which he knows it isn't."

"Fred understands."

Patsy brushed the air with her hand, willing herself to get off the subject. "I looked in the mirror yesterday, and I thought, who is that matronly person? I still have a cute young person inside me, not this dowdy thing walking around in her housecoat."

"You look fine."

At that instant Beryl rushed in, out of breath, near to tears but clearly successful.

"Well, Mom, I found it. Mrs. Walters, can I just wash my hands, put it back in? Would you mind?" She held out a lens, neatly plucked from her eye. I assumed the button was in her shoe, which is what we'd decided upon. She looked crazy with relief and gave us each a hug in turn.

"Of course, sweetie," Patsy said, watching her scoot out of the room. "She's got such nice manners."

I sipped in silence until my daughter came back. She'd brushed her hair and got herself together. Looking at her composure, I decided that we might as well go all the way. She owed me one, a big one, and this seemed the time to collect.

"Patsy, I think Beryl has something to tell you."

"Mom!" She sent me a stricken look.

"Apparently," I continued, as if she weren't half out of her chair with anxiety, "the kids all have an idea who did it."

"Mom, we don't know."

"Have an idea."

Patsy shook her head. "Jerry swore to me they didn't have a hunch." She peered at Beryl. "Sweetie, she's not right, is she?"

"Nobody knows for sure, Mrs. Walters, I mean there's no evidence, you know, it's just a feeling. Somebody who was always—pestering Prissy."

"Should I call Hadley?"

"Why don't you tell us who it is?"

Beryl looked all around, as if reinforcements might arrive any minute to rescue her. She stared at me but then ducked her head, seeing that I was getting my pound of flesh. "It's Estes, Mrs. Walters. We think it's Estes Cox."

I called Hydrangea and suggested she might like to attend my grandmother's funeral.

"Where are you?"

"Patsy's."

"I'll be right there."

We worked it out one step at a time. I called Hadley and

314

told him to come on home. Hydrangea called Monk and said he might like to meet us at the paper in half an hour.

We found Estes writing up his column, and as soon as he saw us, he went to pieces. "I didn't mean to." He groaned, "I didn't mean to. Honest. If she'd have held still." Monk talked with him about the fact that he knew she hadn't been raped, and that would count for him, and just to go over it in his mind and then write it out for us.

Then we made a list of who to tell. The uncles first: to call the old pickled attorney; to post bail; to figure out how to present it to the town. ("A word to the wise, boy," Monk said, "I'd delete that 'hold still' business.")

They said Jimmy closed up Mom & Pop's for the day, the way he'd been told, and Hershell closed the door on the Port Authority. That they met at the corner of First and Main, sighting each other with some relief, glad it wasn't to see the other put away that they'd been called.

Louis next. It would be up to him to present it in a proper light to the school. Let them know that their secret had been lifted off their backs, and they could return to work. Beryl, we agreed, was not to be mentioned. Our story was we'd found him writing out a confession at the paper.

But nobody wanted to tell Louis. Least of all me.

"Why not?" Hydrangea asked. "He'll be relieved, won't he?"

"He'll be livid."

"How's that?"

"Because he was right. He said they all knew, and he'll know he was right. That they protected Estes at his expense. Monk, you go."

"Louis and I don't get on."

"You were in the same class."

"Like I said."

Hydrangea stuck her pencil through her sleek black hair. She considered. We could hear the uncles in the next room, saying a lot of stupid stuff to Estes, which is all anyone could have done in their shoes.

She shoved her brother. "Go together. If you come in together, he'll have so many bad thoughts running through his mind—who is it this time? another one? his own kid?—that by the time you tell him, it'll be a relief."

Monk and I looked at one another. Mutt and Jeff. I placed my arm across his shoulder and pecked the top of his thinning head. "Have some pineapple juice, and let's go."

We went up Ash to the school, a strange pair in the middle of the day: mortician and reporter. We must have scared half the town to repentance. "Why don't you like Louis?"

Monk hemmed and hawed. Finally, he admitted, "He thought a lot of himself in those days."

And not much of you, I finished for him.

Louis reacted as Hydrangea had predicted. He blanched on seeing us, panicked when we pushed past the secretary and came into his office, shooing out the teacher who was clutching a sheaf of papers. "What is it?" he demanded.

"Good news, bad news, depending on how you look at it."

"Not another?"

"No."

"Ours are fine?" He looked at me.

Monk told him, not having a good time with the cross-examination. "We got the boy did it," he said.

"Who? Who is it?"

"Estes Cox."

"Why, that filthy, perverted—" There was a lot more of that. Then he began to look around the office, the veins in his temples standing out. "They protected him, all of them. Who told? Who told you?"

Monk and I, in our mutual haste to protect Beryl, blurted out at the same time, "He confessed."

"Where is he?"

"In custody." Monk headed off that idea, mopping his

damp forehead. He looked seriously in need of an Alka-Seltzer.

"Custody? Where?"

"I couldn't say."

"I want to see him."

"Louis." I touched his arm. "I didn't want you to hear it from someone else."

"But I have, don't you see?" he screamed. "I *have*."

We got it in the Thursday paper, and the wags around town said it read as if Estes had written his own "bound over." Which he had; we gave him that.

Everyone knew it was true. It felt right. The pimply-faced son of Boy Cox, a real looker, it figured. How could you live up to it: your daddy killed the age you are now, and not a dry eye in town?

Hydrangea followed me around as if she'd just discovered Bob Woodward on her staff. "I should have known when you took the day off. I should have known that something big was going to break."

"Win a few, lose a few," I reported factually.

45

M A U D I E came back with a bad scare.

Hydrangea called a meeting of the powers-that-be at her house for supper, to solve once and for all the medical problem of Venice: how to dump Daddy's assistant. Included were Pastor Vickers, the proprietor of Vickers Better Dresses, Newcombe the pharmacist, and we members of the press.

"Women have taken over," Hydrangea said. "They're taking over the small towns of America."

I added a couple of names of my own.

"Patsy Walters."

"You're kidding."

"No." I was tired of Patsy's being on the outside all the way back to the row of *U*s and *V*s in deaf Miss Day's class. It was time she got invited in.

"It's the sympathy vote."

"Think of her as our banker."

"Secondhand status."

"A banker banks. We'll need one."

"If you say so."

"Plus my daughter."

That was too much. "No offense to your sudden motherhood, but let's keep this to consenting adults. Besides, a set of six is all the good plates I've got left."

"The woman who stands to inherit the town's medical practice should have a say in its disposition."

"Now who? Your cousin? I thought you hadn't heard from her in years—oh."

I'd caught her. She lifted her jaw and glared at me, not liking to have her slip show.

"She won't be interested," she said, "at that age."

"We'll let her decide."

It wasn't quite how it appeared: that we'd gotten riled up only when Maudie came back with news of a malignancy and hadn't moved ourselves to act when it was Junior T. Those were the facts, but what was behind it was that women didn't know that much about prostate, how you could tell, at what stage you could save a man, at what stage you couldn't. But there wasn't a woman up and down both banks of the Mississippi who didn't know each and every detail about lumps in the breast, starting with self-examination, which always caused wild confusion, and ending with removal, and whether that ever constituted total escape.

That Maudie had been too hesitant to prod Dr. Baker to check her out, intent as she was on getting help for her old, declining mama and timid as Baker was about fondling anything below the ear lobe, was a scandal. That she had let almost a year go by without bringing attention to herself, an outrage.

Enough, they said over the phone, in General Dry Goods, at Methodist and Baptist, on the street corners. Enough.

It was a disparate group that sat in Hydrangea's stylish brown-and-black living room hung with umber cows and sepia countrysides; we started half a dozen times to make small talk out of years of common ground, then hesitated, not certain what propriety permitted. Could you talk about the glue-sticky weather at such a time?

Patsy had asked me what to wear, and I'd said a skirt and blouse, having found the red pocketed jumper on my desk, boxed and delivered by Sheba the day after the news broke about Estes Cox. Patsy had overdressed, though, in her excitement at being included, had dressed for the Woman's Club, in a designer dress with its own jacket, and a lot of good jewelry. Seeing she'd made a mistake, she took the jacket off and downed two quick glasses of wine. "You know this is the very first time in my life that I've left Hadley to see about supper. He nearly dropped dead." Then, seeing this was the wrong thing to say, in about a dozen different ways, she began to run her fingers along her arms, then caught herself and stopped. "Can you believe," she hurried on in the silence, "I've never been in this house before? Alma and I had our high school tea together, but it was at my house. I used to be so curious to see what the inside looked like."

"Not like this," I told her, trying to put her at ease. "I wish."

"Remember how we used to run up and down the steps and drive your mom nuts?" Sheba was back in childhood.

"Is the cellar still here?" Reba asked. "I mean whatever happened to the furnaces and coalbins around town? By the time I got back, everybody had gone to nice clean gas."

She and Sheba sat facing each other, looking like an actress and her understudy working out the part of a gentle middle-aged seamstress.

"I'm not giving a tour," Hydrangea declared, not wholly pleased that her house of many years was still Alma's to these women who had been girls together. "I checked some figures on the going salaries for starting physicians in mid-size border state towns," she said, and proceeded to lay out on the high wax of the coffee table six pages of figures.

"Who's going to pay this salary?" I asked.

"That's why we're here."

"But if he's the only doctor in town, he won't need it, will he?" Patsy was thinking like a banker.

"My plan is if we could subsidize him for a year, two, guarantee it, then we would be in a position to check him out and get top quality."

Bea Newcombe sat by Beryl on a deep brown love seat. The narrow face, dark hair, and thick eyebrows were familiar to me. I could shut my eyes and see Daddy talking to Miss Newcombe, but it wasn't the postmistress she resembled. Gloria and Greta's words about his other girl came back to me. "*Him?*" she asked mildly, looking around at the roomful of women.

Hydrangea took out a black cigarette holder. "A manner of speaking. But you're right. It might be a *her* these days; after all, look at us."

Beryl was in her prettiest purple shirt and a long cotton skirt. She'd come by herself, my doing. I said I was going to come straight from my office. That she could tell her daddy where she was off to. Leaving it up to her if she could stand up to him. She had on half a pound of mascara, which, somehow, the extra layers, made her look about twelve years old. Or maybe it was the contrast with the rest of us. Her hair was pulled back on one side, in the way she'd devised for Rhoda; her countenance was the one used for teachers, of wanting very much to please. "Can I say something?" she asked. "I mean, since I was invited . . ."

"Go right ahead," Hydrangea replied, in a tone which would have caused any adult to bite her sentence off in midstream.

"I mean, we're the ones who're going to be around to need this doctor someday, you know what I mean, all of you—"

Great, all of us will be six feet under, just what the assembled crowd wanted to hear, especially with Maudie Cox née Blanchard on the risky list. I fretted over her lack of tact but swallowed my wine and tried to remember that her presence was my idea. Let her be, I told myself. Let her be.

"Don't rush us, kid," Hydrangea said dryly. "This is a double feature, and it's still our show."

"So what I was thinking was: who really takes care of us around here now?" Beryl went right on, little spots of color on her cheeks but with no pause in her speech.

"And?"

"What I mean is, if Miss Newcombe is like the doctor anyway, and I don't mean that Granddaddy wasn't a really fine one, back then, but if Miss Newcombe is the one who prescribes, you might say, for all of us—Mom, Mrs. Walters, you know what I mean." She was blushing now but still holding her own.

At first the others in turn looked at the pharmacist and then away, as if afraid certain confidences were about to be breached. It occurred to me that we weren't talking only about Beryl (and Prissy's) birth control, or Junior T.'s salves, or Mrs. Blanchard's medications, but an arsenal of ministration. Hormones to ward off hot flashes, remedies to loose the viselike grip of headaches, ease for stiffened joints, diuretics for swollen ankles, all sold quietly under the counter.

I studied Bea, admitting the family resemblance, wondering how long I'd been aware of it.

The postmistress's daughter wrapped her arms around her shoulders and looked at us. "I always wanted to go to med school," she announced. "Why don't you send me?"

The rest of the evening was spent with everyone talking at once. What a medical specialty cost, how old Bea was (forty), how long it took, what we could do in the meantime—for pharmacist as well as doctor—and mostly, how we could sell the town the idea.

At one point Bea reminded us, "Dr. George will have to agree to it, of course."

I don't know whether she met my eyes on purpose as she said it or I only imagined it. I remember thinking that she knew as well as I that he wouldn't mind: our father, hers and mine.

Finally, after our good dinner, Hydrangea served us pecan pie and thimble glasses of brandy, back in the living room.

"What a story this is!" she declared, proud of what she'd wrought. "I hope we can do justice to it."

46

I WALKED down to present Daddy with the plan for his successor but ended up, as always, hurling accusations.

"How could you not have told me what was going on?"

That was concerning Neva Jenkins and her drinking.

He located a smile on the half of his face that moved. "You've been back to your detective work, I see."

(His words didn't always come out in tidy rows, but to give him some last measure of dignity, I present them as if they did.)

That wasn't my greatest anger, Mother's deception, but by the time I was sitting by his bedside again, it seemed one I could throw my energies into.

As it says in the McGuffey Reader: "I will have revenge on him, that I will and make him heartily repent it, said Philip to himself, with a countenance quite red. . . ."

"It's a long story," Daddy said. "Maybe you'd do best to come back tomorrow?"

"I'm too late as it is."

"Well, then—" He made a signal, and I left to boil him a pot of coffee while he dragged himself into the bathroom.

Mrs. Bosoms was downstairs shooing out the patients, those who hadn't yet heard about the second "little stroke"

and were arriving at the back door with their hiatal hernias
and clogged sinuses and aching joints, wanting the good
doctor to do a little laying on of hands, effect some healing
in their bones.

"Who're you?" she asked me, distracted by the troops
arriving in all directions.

"His daughter."

"That's right, I've seen you. I can't keep all his women
straight." She scowled a moment and then waved me back to
the stairs. "Don't tire him out. I can't be running up and
down to look in. Some folks can't read the sign that says
he's not in today."

As I passed the waiting room, I saw it looked like the tail
end of a rummage sale.

Daddy didn't let me help him with the coffee, so I was
silent until he had negotiated it alone.

"Those two," he began, "your sisters, her first two, didn't
amount to anything from the start. Not their fault, bright
girls they were, always cutting up. But they saw right
through their mother. She didn't pull one thing over on
them. 'At it again,' I could hear them whisper when they
didn't know I was listening. 'Nipping while we're napping.'
Then they'd be off into gales of laughter and run right out
the door, any hour of the night. She had no control." He
half raised his head. "Are you following me?"

"Yes."

He lifted up on one elbow then. "You try to do your best.
Remembering what was done you, you set about to do the
other. Are you with me?"

I nodded.

"I let them run wild. Let those little tykes poke fun at their
mother. What could I do? It was no secret. All the Jenkinses
drank, but I thought she knew better. I went into it with my
eyes open, you might say, but what I was looking at was
where I was coming from, not where I was headed.

325

"No harm done, I thought. They weren't troubled; they had good spirits, were fed and looked after. When they're grown, I reasoned, we'll have ourselves a talk.

"When you came along, by then I'd come to see it a different way. You don't amount to a hill of beans if you have disrespect for your parents.

"I did it hind part before with you. Made sure you minded her. One of you at least was going to amount to something."

Two of us, I might have said but didn't. "I could have been consulted."

"That would have spoiled it."

"You gave Jasper Grandfather's watch."

"Good kids, your two."

There was a commotion downstairs. Dr. Charlie Baker had arrived to tend Daddy's flock, get back in good graces with his chief, but the ailing would have none of it. When I went down to check, Mrs. Bosoms was trying to restrain a pair of old men who were punching Dr. Baker in the chest with their canes, hollering at him about Junior T. and how he wasn't going to get to put so much as one pinky on them. Did he know half the town was up the road at the Cape? They'd be gone themselves, but their old cars, like their old tickers, had dead batteries.

Daddy got the gist of the ruckus, if not the particulars.

"Hear we're going to have a new doctor," he said.

"She wants permission."

"She came, Bea. Found me crawling down there." He gestured to the floor. "Couldn't get to the phone. Lucky thing."

I hadn't known that.

"I aim to give her the money to send herself through."

"I don't care about the money."

"Hear me out, Widget."

"When I could have used it—" I turned my face away. Don't jump on a dying man, I instructed myself. But then

326

the obvious answer came shouting back: you sure can't jump on a dead one.

"I waited for you to say you wanted to go off. I'd been disappointed in the others."

"Forget it."

"Hear me out." He shifted around, trying to see my face. "You going to take it wrong?"

A flood of anger came over me, which was clearly stupid; I didn't want to go off and become a chest thumper and never had. What difference did it make now? A lot. "No," I said, and then "Yes," and began to cry. "It wasn't Louis having to send me to school; that isn't it. Or Mom's drinking either." I was going to get it all said, this being my last chance.

"What then?"

"It's *her*. That all that time she was there, someone of my own, someone to have the way my sisters had each other, and the twins. It's knowing that for all those years the sister I longed for was there, so close, in age, in disposition, and I never knew it. That's what I can't bear: that I did it all alone, and *there was no need to*."

He didn't say anything for a long time, then: "We don't always call it right."

Which took the wind out of my sails. "So we don't." I glanced around the small bedroom, with its rented hospital bed, suddenly worn-out. I wondered if Elsie's dresses still hung by the dozens in the closet.

At that moment Mrs. Bosoms barged in, to shoo me away. "Time for his rest," she said. "You've overstayed."

Beyond her shoulder I could see Dr. Baker come to report to Daddy on how he was looking after the infirm and impaired and get his pat on the back.

"Get out," I told them. "Get out. Visiting hours are not over." And closed the door in their disapproving faces.

One time, one time in this town I was going to have my say without a steady stream of snoopers.

327

"Tell me about your leg," I commanded, thumbing through the McGuffey.

> With books, or work, or healthful play,
> Let your first years be passed;
> That you may give, for every day,
> Some good account at last.

"Your boy asked me."

"I heard."

He indicated the pot, and I poured him out the dregs.

"The year I was nine. Fourth grade. It was the flu epidemic, 1918. My baby brothers had died; half the town. Dad was working around the clock, and Uncle Grady. Burying the hatchet with the corpses, at least for the time being. Armistice was signed, and nobody noticed. Men came home, those who did, to worse dying than they'd seen overseas.

"I'd got a bad scratch on the cistern, fell into a rotten board, splinters and a nail, but then it healed over. I didn't mention it. Mother had come out of herself again. It looked as if the worst was over. Folks got around to remembering appendectomies again, allowing themselves the luxury of diabetes and gout. Mother shortened her mourning, started giving parties, serving port. They got themselves a fine piano. She was of French descent, Marie Cokenour; she didn't like the grimness of my father's practice.

"Uncle Grady spotted it. I was down at his end of Main. I used to sneak down." Daddy made half his face into a small grin. "It goes with the territory at that age." He was talking almost in a whisper. "He saw me wince. He told me later it looked like I'd hit a red-hot coal when my leg brushed the chair. I jumped a foot. He took a look: red streaks into my groin and down to my toe. It had gone into blood poisoning.

"Wasn't much to do in those days but cut the leg off; that was how my father read it. Mad at me for traipsing down to where I didn't belong, for its being Uncle Grady who found it. Nevertheless, he took that on himself and made the decision. Amputate. Uncle Grady sent word he concurred. Mother wouldn't have it. She'd lost the little boys; she wasn't going to be left with only a cripple. 'You saved the Rogers's son,' she told my father. 'Had that blood poisoning in his arm. You saved that good-for-nothing in the country that had the accident in the field. Save him or let him go. I won't let you cut off the boy's leg.'

"I heard the whole debate upstairs, in the front bedroom, through the floor."

"He could have gone against her, couldn't he?"

"I expect not. In those days the decision was the woman's most of the time, who to take, who to save. Figuring that having nursed them, she knew their strengths, their chances, knew better than the doctors about such things. Later, later they presented it that she'd had a mother's second sense, was holding out for me to have a normal life.

"But my father never bought that; she'd risked his only remaining son's life. He moved out of the bedroom. They never reconciled. I'd become a bone in the throat of their marriage, and they never got over it.

"Still later she got ill herself, after the worst of the epidemic was over. She got sick and died, tended by Uncle Grady."

"You made it."

"I was lucky. There's a reminder." He tugged with his good hand until he uncovered his left leg. Above the knee I could see what looked like a small pox vaccine—but about the size of a silver dollar and slightly sunken in.

"How did you feel?"

"Pretty sick."

"That they didn't amputate?"

"Hindsight, I was grateful to her. But by then she was gone."

"At the time?"

"That I should have watched myself, have called it to

Dad's attention. Have had sense enough to know what it meant when it started streaking up my leg."

I covered him. Enough exposure, more than enough.

My eyes were dry, and my mouth, and even my hands felt dry as I rubbed them together.

> Matilda, smarting with the pain
> And tingling still, and sore,
> Made many a promise to refrain
> From meddling evermore.

"The house," Daddy said, worn-out from the effort of his long story. "You didn't let me finish. I'm going to leave your mother with enough; what I mean is leave enough so they can look after her." He tried to arrange his face in a questioning look. "The house is yours."

When I didn't answer, he asked, "You hear me?"

"Yes."

"Thought you could use it."

"I can."

"Seems to me it's time you had yourself a life."

"It is."

When Mrs. Bosoms and the assistant banged on the door, having given me all the leeway they could stand, Daddy was asleep.

That was the last time I saw him alive.

47

I LEFT the paper late, heading down to Grandfather's the back way, wanting to look around the old yellow-brick place while my ownership was still a secret.

Dragging my fingers in age-old reflex along the iron fence posts, pointed like arrows, I wished again for that feeling I had, as Alma the child, of hastening to sit with Grandfather in his back room to hear his story of settling old scores. Of having left behind my own world, in which, on warm summer nights when dusk rang the length of town, we children hid in snowball bushes, until—the sight of faces glimpsed and run from, a game of tag suddenly illuminated on the deep lawns—we hurried home to waiting kin.

Being formal with my soon-to-be residence, I walked around to the front, wanting to get my possession off to a proper start. At the door I hesitated, half hoping, in my present frame of mind, to be let in by Elsie White in her sprigged, starched blue. Half hoping that Wissie, again the woman in the doorway, would invite me in and hear me out.

For a moment I saw someone move, but it was only me, reflected in the leaded glass. I put the key into the old brass lock and entered.

The long hall which split the house in two was dark, its

floor waxed to a high gloss. The umbrella stand stood just inside the door, as it had in Grandfather's day.

With relief I saw that the parlor was empty of patients and pulled the heavy draperies back to let in the soft, slanting, amber daylight of Indian summer. Two issues of *Hollands* magazine protruded from under a slipper chair, as if the stage had not quite been cleared of its waiting-room set.

I took off my jacket—it was stuffy in the old rooms—and wandered about. Dr. Baker had made off with most of the evidences of medicine; Mrs. Bosoms, I presumed, had tidied away the rest.

Grandfather's bedroom, for a time an examining room with stacks of white sheets, had, again, only its marble-top chest of drawers, hall tree, and standing mirror. Things I had only glimpsed as a child, barred from entering by my mother or the fact of Grandfather's napping in the afternoon.

The consulting room still contained, beneath the framed portraits of Ann Elizabeth and her husband, as a young couple and at the end of their lives, evidences of the young doctor's stay. On the desk where Grandfather kept his Underwood, the departing assistant and the woman from the country had left a small pile of mail, addressed to Daddy. Not even Mrs. Bosoms having the nerve to throw letters away, to tamper with the U.S. mail.

On the bottom of the stack, already opened (before he retired for the last time to the upstairs bed?) was a book by Wissie, *Prices, Population and Prime Rate*. The inscription said "TO GEORGE" and was signed "W VD L."

A box inside the front cover asked: IS ZERO INTEREST RATE THE ONLY ANSWER?

Beneath that a quote from the author summarized the thesis of the book:

We hold conferences on the necessity for population control and conservation of fossil fuels, at the same time that we make extraordinary efforts to resist a cessation of *monetary* growth. Yet the maintenance of a constant price level in a nongrowing industrial system implies either an interest rate of zero or continued inflation. The tenets of an exponential-growth culture, such as non-zero interest rates, are incompatible with a stable economy.

A box on the back cover contained a graph charting the relation between physical growth, interest rate, and price inflation (p equals m over q). Further text correlated the ratio of sum of money to what that money would buy, factoring in generalized output of the industrial system and its rate of growth. The conclusion being that in order not to have continued inflation, the rate of money growth and that of industrial production had to remain constant.

Inside the back flap was a small photo of the noted economist, a woman of seventy, still striking, still compelling, her gaze staring levelly out at me from the slick paper.

I longed for her to appear, in a black suit of the forties style, with the broad shoulders now back in fashion, and a scarlet silk shirt. Reading glasses, perhaps, clipped to her lapel, and a locket.

I wanted her to ask, "You know it wasn't me?" So that I could tell her, "Yes, perhaps I knew that all along."

Instead, the book served as a stand-in for her presence.

Turning the pages of the text with a sense of familiarity, I understood at once the story she was telling. The story, of course, of the Reformed grandfather and the Quaker grandmother, of the brothers August and Grady, of the young doctor and his recalcitrant daughter, of the cost of escalating family feuds and the high interest which accrues from one generation to the next. (The story of a steep price that perhaps she, Wissie, remained childless rather than pay.)

. . .

Suddenly, I grew eager to see what remained of Daddy's little bed and the nightstand where I'd last seen him with his boiled coffee. Perhaps that, too, had again traces of an earlier era.

I had been afraid that the years when I used to visit Grandfather on Sundays were lost to me forever, but instead, as on such warm evenings long ago, my steps quickened on the stairs of the house at the north end of Main.

Postscript

———◆———

I TAKE my time in Mom & Pop's while Maudie is up the road, getting her treatment. Giving Jimmy a little moral support.

Some days when the tag-end of the tourists have come and gone, and he's cleaned up the Eight Big Potato orders, he brings a cup of coffee to my booth, and we play numbers.

He shows me how he's calculating the cubic yards of fill his new land will yield, and how many seedlings a good acre will support.

I refine how to crunch license plates, now that we've got such a flux of tourists. Compute how to add letters in, whether to go straight alphabet ($A = 1$) or alphabet backwards ($Z = 1$).

We agree that it is a comfort to add things up. See where you stand.

"He'll come back," Jimmy tells me.

"No, he won't."

"Your boy."

"Jasper. Yes, some day." I think that over. "He'll find a bushel of winesaps when he does."

Then, as Jimmy starts to get us a refill, the floor rolls under us like a ferry crossing the river, and six china cups rattle off the shelf onto the floor.

THE author of nine novels, Shelby Hearon has been awarded a Guggenheim Fellowship for fiction and a National Endowment for the Arts Fellowship for creative writing. Her previous novels, which include *Group Therapy*, *Afternoon of a Faun*, and *Painted Dresses*, have twice won the Texas Institute of Letters Jesse Jones award; her short stories have appeared in literary magazines and anthologies and have received two NEA/PEN syndication prizes.

A native of Kentucky and long-time resident of Texas, she now lives in Westchester County, New York, with her husband, philosopher Billy Joe Lucas. She has taught at the Universities of Texas and Houston, and, recently, as writer-in-residence at Clark, and has served on the literature panel of both the Texas Commission on the Arts and the New York State Council on the Arts.